Promise

Me

Once

PAIGE WEAVER

Promise Me Once
Copyright © 2015 by Paige Weaver

Published by Paige Weaver LLC
P.O. Box 80016
Keller, Texas 76244

ISBN 978-1-5117068-3-4

Cover design © Sarah Hansen
okaycreations.com

Promise Me Once

A Novel

To my late grandfather ~

For those moments in the early dawn, with the sounds of squeaking saddle leather and horses' hooves clomping on the ground. You rode beside me then and I know you're still riding beside me now.

Chapter One

-Cash-

Before

Some say we are invincible. That we will continue to live as we always have or better. We will never know hunger or thirst. We will never know war or bloodshed. It will never touch us here. On our own soil. In our own land. We are safe.

But we were wrong.

Our perfect, little world was about to crumble. Who survived and who died was a mystery. A game of life or death. One that I was determined to win.

~~~~

"Lord, I ain't complaining but we sure could use some help today. Got fields to plow and cattle to vaccinate. Please be with us today. Keep my son and me safe and keep us focused. In Jesus name, Amen."

"Amen," my mother and I said at the same time, my own lips twitching in a smile. My dad was as religious as they came but he was a farmer. Prayers were about plowing and rain amounts and crops growing. They were about the health of animals and the price of grain. That's all he had ever known and what his livelihood depended on. Now it was my life. My heritage. My land to share with him.

Farming was in my blood. A part of me I couldn't escape. My dad was a farmer. My grandfather had been a

1

farmer. Hell, my great-grandfather survived the dust bowl as a farmer. We lived off the land. We ate what we raised and traded or sold everything else. We got our hands dirty and we worked them to the bone.

And we were damned proud of it.

I ate my breakfast in silence. There wasn't any time for talking. Work was waiting. The sound of silverware hitting ancient plates was the only noise in the kitchen. Somewhere outside, a cow bawled and another answered. They were the sounds of home, as familiar to me as my own name.

I stabbed a piece of bacon and stuck it in my mouth, chewing quickly. My dad would be itching to get outside and get to work. Losing daylight meant losing dollars. And losing dollars couldn't happen when we were barely scraping by.

"You hear on the news that they think we're heading for another war?" my mother said, breaking the quietness of the morning with her gentle voice.

My dad didn't look up from his farm report. "They're always saying that, hon. War. Fighting. We need to keep our noses out of other people's business and focus on our own."

"But that's not going to happen. You know that. They're going to send soldiers over there and I hate to think…" My mother's eyes filled with worry. "Ruth's son is stationed somewhere in that area and she's beside herself with fear."

My dad grunted a response, too focused on the price of cattle to comment. Without taking his eyes off the paper, he stabbed his last bite of scrambled egg and stuck it in his mouth, staring at the numbers in front of him.

There had been talk of war lately in the news. Every damned time I turned on the TV, there it was – pictures of soldiers training or journalists in bulletproof jackets reporting from some dusty, foreign country. They always sounded nervous, almost scared. I wasn't much on keeping up with the news – I was usually outside working – but even I knew something was going on. I saw it in the deep lines edged on the President's face when he held news conferences. I heard it in his voice. War was imminent; it was only a matter of when and how.

I scarfed down the rest of my eggs and bacon in record time and jumped up when my dad rose from the table. War could wait. There was work to do. Grabbing my cowboy hat, I slapped it on my head and pulled the brim low. My worn boots made shuffling sounds on the old wooden floor of the kitchen as I followed my dad to the back door.

I grabbed the thermos of hot coffee my mother offered and let the old screen door slam behind me on the way out. The sun was just rising over the horizon. Pinks and purples mixed with the blue of the sky. Green pastures met the colors' edge, making our place look like a postcard instead of a farm in the middle of nowhere, Texas.

We lived quite a distance from town. Close enough to head in when we needed something, far enough away to not see a soul for days.

My dad said he would never sell out to the big companies that nosed around every so often, buying up farms and ranches. Can't say that I blamed him. There was just something about being surrounded by peace and quiet that called to me. Soothed me on a rough day.

Life on the farm was perfect for me. I was the loner. The quiet boy who sat in the back of the room in school. The one who didn't have many friends to call his own. But here under the sun, with nature all around me, I was home.

But soon that would change.

~~~~

I sat high on the old tractor, plowing the pasture in the late afternoon heat. Sweat rolled down my temples and made my worn shirt and jeans stick to me like a second skin.

I pulled my cowboy hat further down on my forehead, shielding my eyes against the sun. It sat high in the sky, blazing down on me like a ball of fire, barreling straight toward earth.

I could see my dad up ahead. He was on his own tractor. The metal blades gleamed as they dug into the clay dirt, turning the rich soil. The sun reflected off them, almost blinding me. I squinted and focused on what I was doing. The tractor rumbled under me as I shifted it into a different gear.

We finished the row and stopped at the end. My dad climbed down, sweat rolling down his rail-thin body.

"Break," he said simply.

I threw the tractor into neutral and cut the engine. The old 1950s motor sputtered then gave out, sounding like it was on its last leg.

Puffs of dirt rose around my boots and legs as I jumped to the ground. It only added to the dust already on them.

It was damned dry even for summer. We needed rain badly. But needing it and getting it were two separate things when it came to Mother Nature.

I took the canteen my dad offered and unscrewed the top. Bringing it to my lips, I let the lukewarm water fill my mouth and slide down my parched throat. Once I had my fill, I took another drink, swished it around in my mouth and then spit it out, tired of the taste of dirt. A few drops of water lingered behind on my upper lip. I wiped them away with the back of my hand then handed the canteen to my dad. Sweat trickled down past my hat brim and into my eyes as I watched him take a long drink.

When he was done, he lowered the canteen and ran a rough hand over his chin.

"Hot today," he said in his usual gravelly voice, squinting against the sunlight to gaze across the land. "Ain't a drop of moisture anywhere…no, sir." Deep wrinkles fanned out from the corners of his eyes, his skin tanned and leathery from years spent under the sun.

"Yep," I said, staring across the field also. "It's dry."

We were men of few words. We didn't waste time on small talk or useless conversations. He said anyone could spout a bunch of horseshit, but it was a man's action that really counted.

I took that to heart at a tender age, talking less and watching more. Like now. I watched my dad and saw more than he could ever tell me. He was a man worn, tired, weathered by nature and the elements. A man that worked from sunup till sundown just to put food on the table for his family and clothes on their backs. A man with pride but humility. A man that would die for his wife and fight tooth and nail for his children. If I could be half of the man he was, I would be lucky.

"Well, we better git back to it." He pushed his sweat-stained ball cap further back on his head. "Work ain't going do itself."

"Yes, sir." I turned back to my tractor. Minutes later I was driving it down a new row. The grinding, nerve-rattling engine filled my ears as the big blades of the old John Deere turned the soil.

A bead of sweat ran down my back, soaked up immediately by my cotton shirt. Another ran down my forehead. I wiped it away, keeping one hand on the wheel.

We had only twenty more rows to go then we could call it a day. I could head into town and spend my Friday night on a barstool.

Don't get me wrong. I loved the land. I loved the quiet. But every once in a while a man had needs that couldn't be found on a dusty, old farm. I could find what I needed at one place – Cooper's Bar.

I just didn't realize what I needed wasn't what I wanted.

Chapter Two

-Cat-

So I told him, 'What the fuck is your problem? I don't have time for you or your shit,'" my friend Tessa said from one of the stalls. "I mean, who the fuck does he think he is?"

I didn't bother answering as I pushed open the stall door and let it slam shut behind me. My heels were loud on the dirty tile floor as I headed to the sink to wash my hands.

"Are you listening to me, Catarina?" Tessa called out from behind a closed stall door. "This is some important shit."

"Uh-huh," I mumbled absently, turning my head one way then the other to check out my makeup and hair in the mirror.

"Hello? Earth to Cat?"

"What?" I bit out, leaning closer to the mirror to wipe a smidge of lipstick off the corner of my mouth.

One of the stall doors flung open, hitting the metal frame. I gave Tessa a quick glance as she walked out of the stall then refocused my attention back on my reflection.

Long, dark hair cascaded down over my shoulders, brushing the tops of my full breasts. Each curl was perfect, each wave photo-ready. My skin was spotless, not one blemish or pimple anywhere. I had a delicately angled nose and high cheekbones, both to die for according to most. My green eyes were enhanced with thick mascara and the eyebrows above them were dark and arched professionally.

I was beautiful. Everyone said so. Someone had even described my face as being Photoshopped in real time. But I knew the truth. The ugly truth.

Inside I was flawed. A mess.

"I just don't know what Junior's problem is. I mean, god, I love the jerk but he can be a real asshole sometimes. You know what I mean?" Tessa's words flowed as fast as the water she was washing her hands under.

I gave her another one of my 'uh-huh' answers as I tucked a wayward curl back in its place, my mind on my looks and nothing else.

"Stop it, Cat. You're gorgeous," Tessa scolded, grabbing a paper towel from the dispenser and drying her hands with jerky, fast movements. "I should hate you. Half the men in here can't stop staring."

I sighed and turned to face her, giving up on my hair. "Half the men are so drunk they can't see straight, Tessa."

She snorted, a very unladylike sound coming from the mayor's daughter. "Half the men in here could be my dad, they're so damn old."

I smiled, my lips turning up in what one man had described as the smile of an angel on the lips of a vixen.

"That ever stopped you before?" I asked, leaning a hip against the counter. "I thought you liked older men."

Tessa stuck her tongue out at me, tossing the paper towel in the trash. "Bitch," she grumbled, her eyes lighting up with mischief. "Not *that* old."

I linked my arm through hers, laughing. "Come on. Let's raise some hell."

I pulled her around a couple of girls and headed for the bathroom exit. The music grew louder the closer we got to the door. The sound of country music was almost more than I could bear.

I was a city girl with roots in the country. Like my dad said – I had dirt under my nails and stilettoes on my heels. Of course, my dad didn't know the first thing about dirt under his nails. The man had never worked a day of manual labor in his life.

The sound of a steel guitar greeted us as Tessa and I stepped out of the bathroom. Smoke filled the air and sawdust covered the floor. Yellowed pictures of country western singers from the '80s and '90s were stapled to the walls along with an assortment of beer labels.

Cooper's was a rundown country bar set in a rundown town. The place smelled like stale beer and piss, a combination that could either make you sick or make you feel at home. A small stage was set up in one corner, occupied now by a girl belting out a Miranda Lambert song at the top of her lungs. Cowboys and cowgirls milled around, most of them hanging out at the bar. A few couples were dancing on the slick dance floor, their arms around each other and their feet moving double time to the fast song.

I had been hanging out at Cooper's since I was seventeen. My friends and I called it 'slumming' but I liked the place. They didn't ask questions and didn't give a damn who we were. Most nights that's just what I wanted.

I scanned the crowd. Tessa was right – the majority of the men were old enough to be our dads. But there were a few…

Two men standing at the end of the bar caught my attention. They were older than us, maybe twenty-five or so. The straw cowboy hats on their heads looked new and so did their boots. I could spot a fake cowboy from a mile away, having lived among the real ones my entire life. The two standing at the bar had money, that much I could tell.

They each had a longneck in their hands and were staring at Tessa and me with obvious interest. The look on their faces let me know that they had only one reason for being in this backwoods bar tonight and it wasn't for the cheap beer.

It was to get lucky.

"God, I love cowboys," Tessa said, checking out the men.

I smiled, more for their sake than for what Tessa had said. I wasn't normally attracted to cowboys, either real or fake, but I was back home and that meant I had the overwhelming urge to be wild. One of those men could help me with that.

"Come on," I said, pulling Tessa's arm.

We headed across the bar, bypassing the dance floor and maneuvering through the crowd. Out of the corner of my eye, I saw the men watching us, ogling our bodies, sizing us up as potential one night stands. I should know. It's what I did. Party. Flirt. Use.

And then walk away.

I was going to hell, my grandmother said. I was rotten to the core, my stepmother claimed. I was perfect, my dad insisted.

I was all of the above and more.

I lengthened my stride, letting my hips sway just right, knowing my thigh-length sundress teased the men in the room. The cowboy boots I wore cost more than most of the men in this place made in a month. But they were scuffed and scarred, just the way I liked them. Just like the way I felt sometimes.

I pulled Tessa to an empty table in the center of the room, finding the perfect place to see and be seen.

"I'm so glad you're home," Tessa yelled over the music as we sat down. "I missed dancing and drinking with you. Just like old times, baby."

I nodded, half listening to her as I checked out the people at the bar. A cute guy tipped his hat at me, grinning as his eyes dropped down to my chest.

I smiled back at him, giving him my best smile. The one that felt empty but looked perfect. The one that told the world all was okay.

"So, tell me about college," Tessa shouted over the music, oblivious to the guy at the bar making eyes at me. "I want to hear all about the crazy parties and hot guys at UT."

I tore my gaze away from the man and glanced at Tessa. I might be a bitch but I was always a good friend and she was one of my best. I wasn't going to ignore her just to flirt with some stranger.

At least not right now.

"School's okay," I said, flipping my long hair over my shoulder. "I'm just glad I'm home. No more early mornings. No more studying for a few months."

"Yeah. School sucks balls," she declared with a frown.

I nudged her arm. "No, that would be you."

Tessa smiled with mischief. "So you've been talking to Junior?"

"No, but ewww." Tessa's mind was almost as dirty as mine. Almost.

We both just finished our first year of college. She was going to the local community college and I was attending my dad's alma mater – the University of Texas. So far I loved it. It got me away from home and that's all that mattered. In fact, this was the first time I had been home since I left for college. Nothing had changed. The town and the people were still the same.

And so was I.

"How's school going for you?" I asked Tessa, crossing my legs under the table, aware of the men watching me.

She shrugged then sighed. "My parents are driving me crazy and Junior is being an ass. What else is new?"

Before I could respond, a waitress appeared at our table.

"Excuse me. Those men over there bought you these." She nodded at some guys at the bar then placed two drinks in front of us. "I'm not going to ask how old y'all are because, frankly I don't care. Enjoy, girls."

"Hell yeah," Tessa mumbled as the waitress walked away. She grabbed the straw and started sucking, not caring who had bought the alcohol for us. A drink was a drink, no matter who it came from.

I took a sip of my own drink, catching the eye of one of the men at the bar. He had lust in his eyes and sinfulness on his lips when he smiled at me. It was just what I needed but he wasn't the only man in the room.

Frozen, sweet margarita filled my mouth as I glanced around. The place was small and crowded. Most of the people were men. A few were women. Tessa and I were probably the youngest, prime meat for the male patrons of Cooper's. I wondered how many of them knew my dad or maybe Tessa's father, the mayor. How many of them would run away as fast as they could if they found out who we were and what our dads would do if one of them touched us?

But the reality was it didn't matter much. My dad was never home and Tessa's father didn't give a damn what she did or who she did it with. In their eyes we could do no wrong.

Thank goodness they didn't know just how bad we could be.

I took another long drink of margarita. What I needed was another drink after this one and a man that only wanted one thing, in that order. A man could always make me forget and a drink could always make me give in.

I glanced back at the bar. The two men who had bought us drinks were leaning casually against the bar counter and smiling smugly as they watched Tessa and I chug down the alcohol. I skipped over them and kept going.

There was a couple arguing. The woman got in the man's face, shouting at him. There was an old man talking to the bartender, clacking about something funny. There were three women that looked to be about my mother's age, checking out the men in the room. Just cougars out to play.

Further down was a heavyset guy staring into his beer. A lone cowboy, his hat pulled down low, sat near him. He was nursing a longneck, keeping his back to the crowd. His long legs straddled the barstool beneath him. His body was lithe and well defined under his crisp shirt and worn jeans. I could tell by the way he sat, the way he didn't move a muscle, that he was dangerous, someone who wanted to be left alone.

I looked further down the bar, searching for someone that might interest me. That's when Tessa appeared in my line of vision. She was watching me warily, squirming in her seat. There was only one reason Tessa squirmed.

"Spill it," I said, giving her my full attention.

She faltered but then gave in. "I know we're here to have fun but…well…I put some flowers on his grave last week, Cat."

All the air left my lungs. Her words slammed into me. Oxygen, so sweet and plentiful, disappeared. I struggled to breathe. My heart stopped beating. The music, the people around me, faded. There were only those two words, ringing in my ear.

His grave.

Tessa started stammering. "I…I know you don't like to talk about it but…maybe…maybe if you go see him…" The words tumbled from her mouth as if she was afraid I would stop her. Interrupt her. Scream at her to stop.

I wanted to do all of the above and more.

"You haven't been to his grave since they buried him. I…I think he would want you to go," she continued, forcing a smile on her face. "He loved you, Cat."

I snapped my head up, fire burning in my eyes and rage boiling in me. "Love? He stopped loving me the moment they put him in the ground, Tessa."

I saw her flinch. In that moment I hated her more than anything. I hated everyone that talked about him. Everyone that reminded me that the one man I had loved was gone.

And I was the one who had killed him.

I shot to my feet, unable to sit there any longer. *Screw her. Screw him. Screw everyone!*

I was two steps away from the table when Tessa grabbed my arm.

"Cat, wait! You've got to stop doing this to yourself!" she exclaimed above the music, knowing full well what I was about to do. Find a man. Fuck him in a bathroom.

Go to his truck for a quickie. Feed my problem and screw my guilt away.

I yanked my arm from Tessa's grasp, angry. "What am I doing, Tessa? Living? Having a good time?" I threw my hands up in aggravation. Anything to stop them from trembling. "Tell me. What the hell am I doing that's so wrong?"

Tessa looked up at me, sadness in her eyes. "Hiding, Cat. You're hiding."

Pain almost shredded what was left of my heart but I hid it well. I smiled at Tessa with wickedness.

"I'm not hiding, Tessa. I'm not hiding at all."

Without another word, I headed for the bar. I needed another drink and a distraction. My eyes zeroed in on the man that had bought us the margaritas.

I needed him.

Chapter Three

-*Cash*-

"Another round?" the bartender asked, glancing down at my empty beer.

"One more."

"I've heard that before," she said with a grin, grabbing a longneck from the refrigerator unit under the counter then popping the top.

I chuckled as she slid it across the bar to me. I wasn't much of a drinker but tonight I needed what the bottle could give me.

A break.

Cold beer hit my tongue at the exact same moment the sound of light, flirty female laughter filled the bar. I paused, the bottle still at my lips.

It was her. The girl with the eyes.

The moment I walked in, I had spotted her. She was sitting at a center table with her long legs crossed underneath. The tiny sundress she wore looked out of place in a room full of jeans and plaid shirts. Pearls were in her ears and a tiny diamond necklace was around her neck.

Too rich for my taste.

Dark hair fell down around her shoulders like black silk against porcelain skin. Her legs went on forever and she was curvy in all the right places. Her cowboy boots were handcrafted, probably from one of those damn boutiques that were popping up downtown. But her eyes – god, her eyes were amazing. They were a clear green, like new grass on a spring day. I had never seen such vivid, gorgeous eyes before. It was hard not to stare.

She looked like a beauty queen, on display for all to see. Only one thing came to mind when I saw her - high maintenance.

And guys like me didn't go near girls like that.

I was flat broke, giving all I had to the farm. If the girl was from around town, I wouldn't have known it. I was too busy trying to make ends meet and helping my parents to care what went on around here. My dad was buried so deep in debt, I was afraid he wouldn't see the light of day for years. Now here I sat, wasting away the last few dollars I had on beer and bad music. But I gotta say the other entertainment wasn't that bad.

I had watched the girl with the boots and eyes for the past hour. She flirted. She danced. She hung on cowboys twice her age. She might be gorgeous but she was a party girl. There was only one thing she wanted and it looked like there were plenty of volunteers to give it to her.

I took a drink of my beer, trying to concentrate on something else and not stare at her long legs and hourglass figure. Usually I didn't like women like her – ones that soaked up attention and craved a little action from cowboys like me. I was more the girl-next-door type.

And this girl wasn't it.

"Tessa, another?" someone called out behind me, walking up to the bar.

Speak of the devil.

I kept my eyes on my beer and my fingers cupped around the longneck as the girl squeezed between me and a longhaired cowboy. Her sundress brushed against my outer thigh, the fabric gliding against my worn-out, old jeans. I shifted out of the way, readjusting my crotch at the same time. *Shit.*

"Bartender!" the girl shouted, leaning on the counter. It pushed her tits up and made the edge of her sundress slide down enough to catch my attention.

I paused with the beer bottle halfway to my mouth. My gaze drifted across breasts just the right size to fit in the palm of my hands and down to the girl's long, tanned legs.

"Bartender!" the girl called out again, waking me up from whatever hold her body had on me. I averted my eyes and hurried to take another drink, keeping my face in the shadows of my hat.

Yeah, I didn't do women like her but I wasn't blind. The girl was gorgeous and damn if she didn't have the perfect body. Long legs. Full, bouncy breasts. Tall. Tan. Slender. She was a supermodel in cowboy boots. Only someone forgot to tell her she didn't belong in a place like this, whoring around men that couldn't afford her and cowboys that shouldn't touch her.

The bartender ignored the girl, about the only person in the room doing it. I heard the girl blow out an aggravated breath. Just when I thought she was going to relax and wait her turn, she got a second wind.

"Who does a girl have to blow around here to get a drink?" she shouted, looking down the bar at the bartender.

I shook my head and chuckled. I couldn't help it. The girl had guts, I'd give her that.

She flipped her hair around and looked at me with one eyebrow arched high. "Can I help you?" she asked, her voice dripping with attitude.

"No ma'am, but maybe I can help you." I motioned to the bartender with a lifting of my chin.

The woman behind the counter saw me and headed my way. Her name was Jo and she was bartender, bouncer, and owner of Cooper's. Tough-as-nails and grittier than dirt, I had seen Jo break up more than one bar fight. Sometimes she used a baseball bat and other times it was a sawed off shotgun, but she was always unafraid of drunk cowboys or their swinging fists.

I kept my eyes off the beauty queen beside me and watched as Jo moved our way. I could feel the girl eyeing me, sizing me up with haughtiness. I didn't mind. Wasn't like I hadn't looked my share of her too.

"What can I get for you? Just one more?" Jo asked with a smirk, her round cheeks red from exertion.

The corner of my mouth lifted in a crooked grin. "No ma'am. Just whatever she would like," I said, nodding at the princess beside me.

Jo looked the girl up and down. "What can I get for you?"

"Two tequila shots," the girl said, tapping her long nails on the scarred bar top.

"You underage?" Jo asked, frowning. "I ain't serving kids in here."

Beauty Queen stuck her perfectly shaped chin up in the air. "I'm twenty-one."

Jo snorted. "And my name's Martha Stewart. Let me make you a damned two-layer cake full of bullshit."

Beauty Queen stuck her chin up higher. The girl was going to get a crick in her neck if she kept that up.

"If I wanted bullshit all I'd have to do is look at your liquor selection. I asked for two tequila shots. Think you could manage that?" Her words dripped with sickly sweetness.

Jo didn't blink twice. She grabbed two shot glasses and flipped them over on the counter, giving me a sharp look.

"If you're buying her these, she's your responsibility. You hear?"

I nodded and watched as Jo grabbed a bottle of Jose Cuervo and filled up the glasses. Her gaze went from me to the girl with annoyance. When the glasses were full, she pushed them toward us with another frown.

"I'm putting it on your tab and adding a generous tip for myself for putting up with Miss High-and-Mighty here." She nodded toward Beauty Queen. "Keep her in line, cowboy."

"Yes, ma'am," I said against my better judgment. I grabbed my own beer and took a long drink as Jo walked off. I had a feeling I would need it.

Out of the corner of my eye, I saw Beauty Queen reach for the shots and glance at me with those big cat eyes of hers.

"Thanks for the drinks, but I'm not blowing you," she said, her voice sounding like sex on a stick.

I almost choked on my beer. The girl might look like a sex kitten but she had the mouth of a sailor.

But two could play at her game.

I pushed the brim of my hat back and surveyed her, letting my eyes slide over her body with blunt appraisal. "Well, ma'am, I'm not much for buying a blow job with drinks, but I have a feeling you usually give them away for free."

Surprise made her green eyes go round. She covered it up quickly but I still saw it. That's when I knew she wasn't used to a man calling her bluff.

She grabbed the drinks and turned away, flipping her long, dark hair over her shoulder and muttering something about me being a jerk. I let her go. It was fun while it lasted but I wouldn't touch Miss Beauty Queen with a ten-foot pole. Well, maybe I would but it wasn't going to happen in this lifetime.

Just when I thought she would disappear, she stopped right beside me. Her breast rubbed against my arm, sending spikes of heat through me. That little sundress of hers brushed up against my thigh again, burning me from the inside out. When she leaned closer to me, I froze.

"For you, I might just give one away for free," she said in a sweet, sultry voice. "But for now, keep dreaming, cowboy."

~~~~

I tried not to watch her but it was hard not to stare. She danced every slow dance and flirted with every man between the ages of 21 and 80. By midnight one man had claimed her, a tall fellow with a brand new hat and asshole written all over his face.

But it wasn't my problem.

I pulled out some cash to settle my tab, ready to call it a night. About that time Beauty Queen's laughter rang out in the bar. It sounded a little forced. A little too fake. I stole a glance at her from under my cowboy hat, something telling me there was trouble brewing.

But I was wrong.

New Hat Asshole had an arm around Miss Beauty Queen's waist, holding her close. His mouth was near her ear and his hand was easing down her back, heading for her bottom. And she seemed to be enjoying every moment of it.

She leaned into him, pressing her breasts against his chest and letting that little dress of hers slide against his leg. He held her tight and nuzzled the skin below her ear, pushing her dark hair back at the same time.

I turned away, feeling the sudden need to leave. I wasn't one for jealousy but I felt it right then and there. I wanted to touch her. Be the one to taste that little delicate spot right below her ear.

Agitated, I dug money out of my wallet and settled my tab with swift movements. I had to get out of there. The girl was affecting me more than she should. I needed to wipe her from my mind quick.

I headed for the exit like the devil was on my tail, enticing me with an angel in cowboy boots. A woman who probably tempted guys and stole hearts.

Rain and thunder greeted me as soon as I walked out of Cooper's. It was coming down in buckets, turning the gravel parking lot into a mud hole. I ducked my head, held onto my hat, and took off running for my truck. Water splashed around my boots and soaked the bottom of my jeans as I headed across the parking lot. By the time I climbed into my truck, I was drenched. I took off my cowboy hat and smoothed my wet hair back. Through the downpour beating on the windshield, I saw a group of people leaving the bar.

I didn't give them much thought as I started my truck and pulled out of the parking space. My mind was on how the rain would slow down work on the farm tomorrow. But as I drove down the aisle of jacked-up trucks and farm vehicles, I glanced in my rearview mirror. That's when I saw her. Miss Beauty Queen. She was standing beside a little sports car. The hood was popped open and she and another girl were peering down into the engine. Both of them were soaking wet.

I slowed down, my conscious nudging at me. Rain? Two girls with a broken-down car?

"Shit," I muttered, slamming the truck into reverse. I backed it into a nearby parking space and threw it into park.

Thunder cracked overhead but the harsh rain turned into a soft drizzle. I saw New Hat Asshole stroll over to Miss Beauty Queen's car. His stride was cocky and he had a shit-eating grin on his face. Something about him didn't sit well with me. He walked over to Miss Beauty Queen and put an arm around her waist, just like he owned her. But I had a feeling no one had the right to her. She seemed to be nobody's and everybody's at the same time.

He started to pull her toward his truck, keeping an arm around her and speaking low into her ear. I saw her reluctance. Saw the way she looked back at her friend with uncertainty. Through the drizzling rain, I even saw the worry on her face. It was there a second then gone, replaced by an arrogant look again. I had a feeling she wasn't afraid of anything. Certainly not some guy she had been leading on all night.

I must have been right because she gave New Hat Asshole a sweet, sugary smile and looked up into his eyes with boldness. He returned the smile and tightened his arm around her waist.

Miss Beauty Queen put a hand on his chest, keeping him at a safe distance, but he didn't take the hint. He ducked his head and whispered to her, causing rain to drip off his cowboy hat onto her. She stiffened and tried to ease out of his arms but he wasn't letting go. He started tugging her toward the parked pickup trucks nearby, leading her away from her friend and their broken down car.

But Miss Beauty Queen wasn't going to give in so easily. In the middle of the parking lot, she started resisting, pulling away from him. I saw her motion at her friend, saying something heated and angry.

Her friend jumped to attention and started to run to her friend's rescue, but before she could get there another man appeared. This one bigger than New Hat Asshole and much more deadlier looking.

"Goddamnit," I muttered. I didn't want to do it. I usually kept my nose down and stayed out of other people's business. But Jo's words rang in my ear – '*She's your responsibility.*'

And I took my responsibilities very seriously.

I grabbed my hat and smacked it on my head as I opened the truck door. The rain was now coming down in a fine mist. I kept my eyes on Miss High-And-Mighty and headed her way, silently cursing my stupidity. *I should just get back in my truck and leave. The girl's nothing but trouble.*

But I couldn't seem to walk away.

When I got close enough I could hear them arguing.

"We're fine. Right, Tessa?" Beauty Queen said in her amazing, seductive voice, trying to pry New Hat Asshole's arm from around her waist. "We don't need any help. We'll just call a wrecker."

New Hat Asshole ignored her attempts to escape and just grinned. "Come on, sweetheart, we'll give you a ride. Isn't that what you were offering anyway?"

Beauty Queen's eyes lit on fire. She was soaking wet, reminding me of a drowned cat ready to scratch someone's eyes out. Black mascara ran down her face, leaving dark streaks on her porcelain skin. Her hair was stuck to her head, hanging down her back in wet strands. I would have laughed any other time because, god she looked cute, but the asshole was refusing to let her go. I didn't care if she had led him on, when a woman said no, a man should listen.

"I think the woman doesn't want to be touched," I said, walking up to them. Rain dripped down the brim of my cowboy hat but it didn't stop me from staring daggers at the asshole.

New Hat looked me up and down. I was younger than him by ten years or so but there was no question who was probably stronger. My body was leaner with more sinewy muscle thanks to years of hard work on a farm. But I wasn't a fool. No way in hell would I throw a punch for Miss Beauty Queen.

But I sure as hell would stand up for her.

"This is none of your business, cowboy," New Hat Asshole said, full of piss and vinegar. "Mosey along."

My jaw clenched hard. I readjusted my cowboy hat, pulling the brim even lower. Anything to keep my hands from strangling him.

"She may not be my business," I said, nodding toward Miss Beauty Queen. "But your unwanted hands on her are."

New Hat Asshole sized me up again, taking in my scuffed boots and worn clothes. I kept my expression neutral, letting him look his fill, aware his grip on her hadn't loosened. *Let him figure out if he could take me.* Only I knew the truth.

I stood relaxed. Waiting. Watching. Ready to do what I had to do to protect a woman – any woman - from an asshole like him. But Beauty Queen had plans of her own and it didn't involve me coming to her rescue.

"Let me go, asshat!" She raised one small fist and jabbed him hard in the nose.

He howled and grabbed his face, releasing her. But she wasn't done yet. Her sundress rose higher, exposing her tanned, firm thighs as she raised her knee then slammed the heel of her boot down on the man's instep.

"OWWW!" New Hat Asshole screamed, dancing around on one foot while holding his nose with the other. I wanted to laugh but all I could do was stare.

Thunder clapped over, matching the hell that was standing in front of me. Fire spit from Miss Beauty Queen's eyes and anger poured off her. She tossed her wet hair behind her shoulder like she was walking down Fifth Avenue instead of standing in front of a redneck bar. With no thought to her safety, she got in the guy's face.

"Try to touch me again and I'm going to bury my knee in your little balls and make you squeal like the pig you are. Got it?" she said with a sweet smile on her face.

New Hat Asshole glared at her from underneath his wet, soggy cowboy hat. His nose was red but looked fine, unlike his pride. I saw his hands clench into fists, seconds away from exploding and grabbing her again.

Guess it was time I broke up this little party.

I took my time, stepping between Miss High-And-Mighty and the man that looked like he wanted to beat the living hell out of her. Can't say I blamed him for being mad – the girl was trouble with a capital T – but he would have to go through me in order to touch her again.

"I think the girl got her point across," I said to New Hat Asshole, trying to ignore the heat of Miss Beauty Queen's body so close behind me. "Walk away while you still can."

The man stood up straighter, favoring his injured foot and wiping his nose. He looked over my shoulder at the girl, the contempt rolling off him like the raindrops falling down his hat.

I watched him and his friend closely, knowing guys like them didn't take too kindly to being one-upped by a girl like her. And I was right. New Hat Asshole suddenly shot around me, going right for her. But I was quicker. I stepped in his way, blocking him and keeping her safe behind me. My gaze never left him. He was in my sights and I was about to pull the trigger.

"You got three seconds," I said, my voice low and menacing.

He popped his knuckles then smirked. "And what happens in three seconds, cowpoke?"

I shrugged, cutting my eyes over to the front of the bar. "That."

He turned to look the same time we all did.

In the misty rain stood Jo, staring down the barrel of a shotgun. It was pointed straight at New Hat Asshole, unwavering in her solid, steady hands.

"Get off my property, boys!" she shouted, cocking the gun for effect. "Now!"

I looked back at New Hat. He was scowling at Jo, looking her up and down. I started to think he didn't have a brain in his head and was going to test her, but he took a step back instead, nudging his buddy.

"Let's go," he said, sliding his eyes over to the Beauty Queen behind me. "The bitch ain't worth it."

He and his friend backed away, keeping their eyes on Jo and me until they were a safe distance away. As soon as they were, they turned and took off for their truck, moving fast in the drizzling rain.

I watched them go, keeping Miss Beauty Queen at my back and her friend within an arm's length of me. As soon as the asshole's truck pulled out of the parking lot, I relaxed and turned to Jo.

"Thanks," I said over the sound of thunder in the distance.

Jo lowered the gun and jerked her double chin toward

the road. "Y'all git home before you cause any more trouble."

I tipped my hat to her in response and turned to face Miss Beauty Queen. I didn't know what I expected to find but it wasn't her frowning at me.

"Ugh," she said, rolling her eyes. With a swing of her wet hair, she spun around and started across the parking lot, followed by her short, round friend.

I had a perfect view of Beauty Queen's little dress clinging to her curves. The material was soaking wet and see-through. I swallowed hard, seeing the roundness of her ass underneath the thin cotton and the space between her legs.

"Shit," I repeated for the hundredth time since meeting her.

As I followed them to their broken down car, I had a feeling the night was far from over.

And her and I were far from done.

Chapter Four

-*Cat*-

The rain was coming down in a fine mist. The thunder was loud and the lightning close. And me? I was shaking in my damn boots.

Daryl had been nice. Decent. But then he changed. When he demanded I pay for the drinks he bought me with a quickie in the men's bathroom, I balked. I did many things but I suddenly didn't want to do them with him.

Knowing when I was in over my head (because I had been there many times before), I grabbed Tessa and left, only to find my car wouldn't start and Daryl had followed us outside, still wanting payback for those drinks.

Now here I was - soaking wet, stuck in the parking lot of a rundown bar, and just wanting to go home.

"*Please* tell me that did not just happen," Tessa said, hurrying to match my pace as we headed to my little car.

I lengthened my stride and clamped my teeth together tightly. "I wish I could but it just did."

"Damn," Tessa said, pushing her blonde, dripping wet hair out of her eyes. "No strike that. Double damn. I mean *fuck*, Cat, you really know how to pick them."

I sighed, glaring at her from underneath my spiked lashes. "Don't start, Tessa. Let's just get my car running and get the hell out of here."

"Agreed." Tessa glanced behind us and dropped her voice to a whisper. "So…who's the cowboy?"

I looked over my shoulder. The guy from the bar was following us. His head was ducked and his face was hidden under his hat, but I had gotten a good look at him earlier. When I did I had gone still, struck silent for the first time in my miserable life. The guy was just that good-looking.

And irritating.

"I have no idea who he is." I shrugged. "Who cares?"

Tessa sneaked a peek again. "So why is he following us?" she whispered in a loud voice, looking him up and down.

I heard a chuckle behind me and I swear my face turned beet red. It almost made me stumble, catching me off guard. *When was the last time I blushed? Or got rattled by a guy?* My answer was clear-as-day. The last time was a year ago.

When I had to watch a man be buried. Luke.

I silently cussed the rain that splashed around my boots. I cursed life and my very existence. I swore obscenities in my head at the cowboy who had saved me from Daryl. I did it all to take away the pain and hide my tattered soul.

With anger in my step, I hurried to my car. It was a three-year-old BMW. My baby. The hood was popped open. Big fat raindrops made pinging sounds on the exposed engine. I stopped at the front end and peered down, cursing the storm, the car, Daryl, and myself.

Always myself.

"What's wrong with it?" Tessa asked, looking down at the engine too.

I shrugged. "How the hell should I know? Its been making some weird noises."

The cowboy appeared beside me. I looked him up and down, a scowl on my face but a glimmer of awareness sparking in my body.

His hat still hid his face, shielding his eyes from me. His wet shirt was plastered to his body, outlining solid, lean muscles. Low-slung jeans hugged his legs and hips. From underneath his hat I could see dark strands of hair against his tanned face and neck. But it was what was hidden under his cowboy hat that had caused me to draw in a shaky breath earlier.

His face was perfect, all chiseled angles and strong features, but his eyes…his eyes were amazing. They were the color of the sky on a stormy day. The color of my favorite cashmere sweater. They were the color of Luke's headstone the day we buried him. The color I felt everyday since. When the cowboy looked at me in the bar, the crystal gray of his eyes had shocked me.

And that was hard to do.

I stiffened when he stepped closer to my side. His arm brushed along my abdomen as he reached past me to fiddle with something in the engine. I tried to keep my focus on what he was doing but finally gave up and let my gaze travel down his back instead. Fat raindrops hit his already soaked shirt and molded it even more to the well-defined muscles in his back.

He was hot but he was not my type. He didn't gawk at me or try to flirt when I had talked to him at the bar. He had kept his hands to himself and seemed uninterested, at best. I liked men to pay attention to me. I fed on it, survived because of it. Then why did parts of me clench and grow wet when I looked at him? When I felt those gray eyes on me?

I cleared my throat, irritated with him for affecting me so strongly.

"You plan on telling us your name or you just gonna fix our car, mute-like?" I asked, the bitch in me coming out. My go-to defense mechanism.

The cowboy checked one last wire in the engine then straightened, still staying close by my side. When he looked at me, his eyes didn't drop down to my breasts or run over my thighs and legs. Most men would have salivated at the sight of my see-through dress. It's what I expected. What I counted on. Instead, the cowboy stared straight into my eyes, seeing *me* not my body. *Me*.

And I didn't like it at all.

I gritted my teeth. "Name?" I snapped, curling my lip up. "You got one?"

The corner of the cowboy's mouth lifted in a lopsided smile.

"Yes, ma'am. It's Cash," he said in a deep voice that washed over my skin and down into my core. It was both smooth and rough. Gravelly and perfect. I had no doubt that his voice alone could make a woman scream in ecstasy and come in seconds.

Speaking of…a shudder passed over my body. I blamed it on the rain. No way in hell would I acknowledge it was anything else.

Without another look at me, he leaned over again and did something to the engine, dismissing me like I was unimportant.

I glared at his back, hating him. Despising him. Not understanding why I was interested in him. I didn't chase guys; guys chased me. I collected them like I collected shoes. When I got tired of them, I tossed them to the side and moved on to the next one. Just to fill a void and help me to forget.

The cowboy finished whatever he was doing to the engine and straightened, looking straight at Tessa and ignoring me. "Turn it over and see if it starts."

Once again, his voice made me burn with need and squirm, more than my dress becoming soaked.

Tessa's eyes gleamed with love and devotion at him as she jumped to attention like the good little girl she was. I rolled my eyes as she hurried to the driver's side, slipping once in her wedge heels. She had my keys since I had drank one too many but right now I wanted to kill her for leaving me standing alone with the cowboy.

He – Cash – continued to ignore me. He laid both hands on the car and studied the engine like he expected it to talk to him.

I crossed my arms over my chest and tapped my foot, annoyed. Most men ate out of the palm of my hand, but he didn't seem to care who I was or what I looked like. Sure, I was soaking wet and my makeup was probably nonexistent thanks to the rain, but I knew I still looked good.

At least good enough for this cowboy.

Okay, yeah I was pissed. The guy was ignoring me and I wasn't used to being ignored. My dad gave me whatever I wanted and men never told me 'no'. My older brother was the only man that actually stood up to me, calling my bluff and telling me I was full of shit when I was.

But no man ignored me. I made sure of it.

The engine popped then roared to life, startling me. I heard Tessa squeal from inside the car, almost bouncing up and down in the seat. I frowned. How she could be so happy all the time? I didn't understand it. Of course she didn't bury someone she loved a year ago. She hadn't seen him lying on the ground, bloody and broken, knowing it was her fault.

I had.

I blinked, the disturbing image disappearing as Cash slammed the hood shut.

"You're good to go. Night," he said, tipping his hat then turning and walking away.

I spun around, speechless. I wanted to call out to him, get his attention. Prove I could. I didn't want him to leave. There I said it. *Ugh. What was wrong with me?* He was the first man to show no interest in me. For that, he got my undivided attention.

"Let's go!" Tessa yelled, sticking her wet, drenched head out of the driver's side window and waving at me with impatience.

I ignored her and watched the cowboy stroll away.

"Jerk," I muttered, frowning. I hated that my heart was pounding. That I suddenly wanted something, but he was not offering it to me.

Abruptly he turned, his gaze going straight to mine.

"You gonna tell me your name, or just let me walk away, mute-like?" he asked with a cuter-than-hell lopsided grin.

I blew out an aggravated breath. Outside I knew I looked irritated but inside a tiny thrill went through me.

"Cat," I called out over the sound of the soft rain. "My name's Cat."

Cash's grin grew wider, his gaze warm. "Fits you."

Something twisted inside me, something I hadn't felt in a long time. I turned and headed for the passenger side of the car, fighting the urge to run. I was reaching for the handle when I glanced back at Cash.

He was walking backwards, watching me. This time his gaze dropped down my body, taking its time, traveling over my rain-soaked dress. Finally he met my eyes again.

"It was nice meeting you, Cat. See you around." He tipped his hat at me then turned and strolled away.

Disappearing from my life forever.

Well, maybe.

Chapter Five

-Cat-

Two Days Later

"Yᴏu little brat! Get the hell back here!"

"Make me, ass-wipe!"

I woke up to the sound of fighting. Loud male voices boomed throughout the house.

"You little shit!"

"Fuck off!"

I groaned and rolled over onto my stomach, pulling a pillow over my head. It didn't help. I could still hear them.

"Dad said—"

"I don't care what Dad said! He's not here and I am. If I tell you to clean up your shit, you're cleaning your shit!"

The sound of booted feet running on hand-scraped, hardwood floors followed. A door slammed somewhere, shaking the pictures on my wall.

I groaned again and rolled over, tossing the pillow to the foot of the bed. *Could a girl not get a decent night's sleep around here?*

Bright sunlight streamed in through my bedroom window, making me squint then wince when I tried to open my eyes. I picked up a small, satin pillow and threw it across the room, missing the window by at least a good foot.

"Cat, get your ass out of bed and make breakfast! It's your turn!" A deep voice boomed down the hallway. "NOW!"

I moaned and rolled over onto my side. My phone caught my eye. It blinked obnoxiously at me from the nightstand, letting me know I had a text. I grabbed it, wishing I could just go back to sleep instead. But that wasn't a possibility with my two brothers fighting and someone sending me pictures of…

I sat upright, my phone clutched in my hand. It was a text from Tessa with a picture of me dancing on one of the tables last night.

"Shiiiiit."

The fog of sleep left me. My mind sorted through all the fragmented memories of last night. Tessa and I had drove to another town almost an hour away. We hit the first bar we came to, a place just one step up from Cooper's. The music had been loud and the place packed. They had been given away free tequila shots to any girl that danced on a table and showed her boobs. Of course I was one of the first ones. People didn't call me wild for nothing.

I started typing, my fingers flying over the tiny keypad.

WTF, Tessa?

A second later she responded.

Morning, sunshine. How u feel?

I answered, hating to be reminded of the sunshine that was now causing a headache to form right behind my eyeballs thanks to all the drinks last night.

Feel like crap. Erase that pic. Now.

She responded right away.

Done. Nathan home?

I rolled my eyes then wished I hadn't, the headache now a full-fledged throb. Every girl between the ages of ten and ninety had the hots for my older brother, Nathan. He was cute and nice and everything I was not. Even

Tessa, someone that swore to love Junior until her dying day, would have Nathan's baby if he asked her to.

I started typing again, wincing when I blinked.

Yeah, he's home. Yelling at me right now.

And he was.

"CAT! GET UP!" he shouted.

I groaned and tossed the phone in the middle of my bed. I knew Nathan wouldn't stop yelling until I made an appearance. That meant I had to drag myself out of bed.

I pushed the covers back and swung my legs over the side. Cool air blew across my bare legs as I stood up. I was only wearing a skimpy t-shirt and panties. I don't remember changing into them last night. Oh, well.

I padded across my bedroom, twisting my long hair up into a messy bun at the same time. I didn't pay attention to the dirty clothes covering the floor of my room. At some point I had thrown them there, four hundred dollar dresses and six hundred dollar purses. Uncared for and discarded, just like trash. My dad bought them for me, his way of making up for his absence and lack of parenting. If he had asked me what I wanted, I would have told him I would much rather have him home than a fancy dress or designer handbag. But that was never going to happen so I accepted the gifts and smiled, acting like the perfect daughter for the so-called perfect father.

In the god-awful perfect life.

I slung open my bedroom door and walked out, glad to be out of the sunshine and in the hallway where it was dark. A quick glance to my right told me that my younger brother, Tate, was in his room, the closed door the one he had slammed minutes ago.

I didn't bother knocking on it. Instead I turned and headed down the hallway. The expensive hardwood floor felt cold beneath my bare feet, making me miss the thick carpet that once lined the house. My dad's third wife – my second step-mom – insisted that all the carpet be pulled up and replaced with wood specially selected and lumbered for her. It had cost more than most people made in a year, but I wasn't supposed to know that. My dad didn't and I'm not sure he ever found out either.

I walked past their room – well, my dad's room now. He left the third wife for a younger version, but they weren't married yet. One day he would call and tell us that he had married Bambie or Barbie or whatever her name was. When you own the biggest oil drilling business in Texas, you could do whatever the hell you pleased.

I passed the other bedrooms – six in total and that was just upstairs. Despite the headache lingering behind my eyes, I jogged down the stairs, making my messy bun bounce with every step. I crossed the living room, noting the empty pizza boxes and Coke cans everywhere. We had a housekeeper but Tate had chased her off last week when he put a barn mouse in her apron pocket. Guess she didn't share the same love of animals as he did.

I entered the kitchen a few seconds later with murder in my eyes. It was too early to cook. Too early to be awake. Too early to face Nathan and his bossiness. Just too damn early.

I found my older brother leaning against the kitchen island, staring at his phone. He had one ankle crossed over the other, looking relaxed and *GQ* ready like he always did. We were cut from the same cloth, him from Dad's first wife and me from his second. But Nathan and I were about as different as night and day. He had blonde hair and I had dark. He was good while I was bad. He was loved by all while I was scorned by most.

Despite the differences, we were very close. Nathan had a hard exterior, a take-no-prisoner's attitude most of the time, but he loved me no matter what I had done in the past or what I did now. I loved him just as equally, even though he could be an ass sometimes, especially in the mornings.

"About time you woke up," he mumbled when I walked in, still studying his phone.

"Whatever. I need coffee." I pushed past him to the gourmet coffeemaker on the counter. He moved out of my way, pocketing his phone.

"What's for breakfast? It's your turn to cook," he said, watching me open up a cabinet to search for a clean coffee cup.

I looked over my shoulder at him. "Really? Cook? Can't y'all eat toast or something?"

Nathan walked over to the industrial-sized refrigerator and pulled open one of the doors. He started studying the contents inside. "We agreed that we would take turns making breakfast, Cat. It's your turn. Deal with it."

I sighed. Nathan liked his rules. I just didn't think when I returned home for the summer that I would have to follow them.

"Fine. I'll cook," I grumbled, watching the coffee sputter from the machine into my cup. As soon as it was done, I added sweetener and stirred it, needing the dark stuff like some people needed crack.

"We've got crap," Nathan muttered, sticking his head in the refrigerator. "Not a stick of butter or an egg to fry."

I took a sip of my coffee, watching as Nathan opened up the freezer and glanced at its empty shelves.

"Yeah, we've got shit." He shut the door and glanced at me. "Unless we count you because you look like shit, Cat."

I stuck my tongue out at him but he just grinned.

"What did you do last night? Drink half the liquor in town?" he asked.

"Nope but tried." I smiled smugly and lifted the coffee cup to my lips to take another sip.

"What are y'all talking about?" my younger brother asked as he barged into the room. "What did you try, Cat?"

"None of your business," Nathan said, leaning against the counter and crossing his arms over his chest.

Tate scowled at him. "I ain't talking to you, Nathan." He opened up the fridge, sticking his head in just like Nathan did seconds ago. A second later he slammed the fridge door shut and turned to glare at me. "We've got crap, sis, and I'm starving. You gonna let me turn into a bag of bones?"

I set my coffee cup on the counter and headed toward him, eyeing him from the top of his brown, shaggy hair to the bottom of his torn-up, brown boots. He eyed me warily, looking like he might bolt and run any second.

With the help of a nanny I had raised Tate when his mother – another one of my step-moms – cut and run when he was only six months old. Nathan and I were his family. Not the dad who was never around or the mom who shouldn't have had a baby in the first place since she was only twenty years old when she had Tate. Nope. We were it – Nathan, Tate, and me. A perfect little, screwed up family.

When I got closer to Tate my nose started twitching. I took a big whiff. The smell of cow manure lingered on him, mixing with the sweet smell of freshly cut hay.

"You smell like cow shit, Tater Tot. Go take a shower and we'll go to town for food," I said, catching another smell of him.

Tate scowled, fury shooting from his eyes. "My name *ain't* Tater Tot and I don't stink." He frowned and eyed me cautiously. "You're the one who stinks. You smell like the inside of Grandpa's wine bottle. *You* go take a shower, Cat, then we'll go."

Nathan chuckled, not helping me much. Ignoring him, I crossed my arms over my chest.

"Fine," I told Tate. "But you're going with me to carry the groceries. That's your punishment for smelling like a cow pasture this early in the morning."

"Yes, ma'am," Tate said, saluting me as I turned back to my coffee.

I froze, my hand reaching for the coffee cup. Not many people said *yes ma'am* anymore but I suddenly remembered one man who did.

A cowboy with a low brimmed hat, standing in the rain and smiling at me.

~~~~

"Damn, it's so fuckin' hot. You could fry a goddamn egg on the hood."

I ignored Tate's cussing and eased our old farm truck into an empty parking space in front of Craig's Discount Grocery. My BMW was on the fritz, the engine a goner. Who knows when I would get it back so in the meantime my ride was a dirty pickup.

The metal Craig's sign stared back at me through the windshield. The letters were old and faded, matching everything else in this pitiful little town. Why my dad insisted on keeping our family home here, I didn't know. Sure, *when* he was home he liked to veg out on the porch, but there wasn't much left here for me.

Not anymore.

I swallowed past the lump in my throat, suddenly hating this little town even more.

"You gonna sit there all day or we gonna get some food?" Tate asked, staring at me from across the truck.

I paid no attention to him and turned the rearview mirror down so I could look at myself. Big, dark sunglasses stared back at me, hiding my eyes. I pushed a loose strand of hair behind my ear then double-checked my messy bun.

"Shit, Cat, it's just the grocery store," Tate whined, his voice breaking. "It ain't some damn beauty pageant."

I licked my full lips then turned the mirror away.

"Stop cussing," I said, grabbing my purse and opening the truck door. "And stop being so bitchy."

Tate grumbled under his breath as we got out. Heat from the asphalt rose around us, warming my legs and burning my toes left exposed in my wedge heels.

I slung my little purse on my shoulder and started across the parking lot to the store. Tate jogged to catch up with me. We passed little ol' blue-haired ladies pushing squeaky carts to their cars and tired looking moms carrying dirty, bare-footed babies on their hips. Everyone looked exhausted, every bit of energy sucked from them thanks to the high humidity heat.

I pushed my sunglasses higher on my nose and lengthened my strides, ignoring everyone around. Cool air enveloped me as soon as I stepped into the little discount grocery. So did the smell of mildew. The place was still stuck back in the 1950s, with old cash registers and ancient, rusted carts. It still smelled just as bad as it did when I was a little kid, walking through the doors with my high-maintenance mother. We were stared at then and I was stared at now. *Guess nothing's changed in this small town.*

"Cereal. Cereal. Cereal," I muttered to myself, reading the drooping signs above each aisle and ignoring the stares of people in the checkout lanes. I could feel their eyes watching me. Judging me. Following me. *Let them stare. Let them whisper behind their hands, telling each other, "There goes that Phillips girl. The one that got that boy and girl killed."*

I stuck my chin higher and threw my head back. Put a little more swing into my step. It's what I did. A way to fight back. Prove the rumors couldn't get to me, even if they were true.

Tate followed close behind me. "I ain't eating cereal," he said when we turned down the breakfast aisle. "I need a workingman's breakfast. Eggs and bacon. Maybe some biscuits."

"If I'm cooking, you're getting cereal."

Tate mumbled some colorful curses under his breath.

I gave him a warning look over my shoulder before grabbing two cereal boxes. "Cheerios or Fruit Loops?" I held up both.

Tate studied them, his eyes level with mine. For a twelve-year old, he was tall.

And way too cocky.

"I'm not two, Cat. I wanna eat bacon like a man," he complained, his freckled nose scrunching up as he turned and walked away.

I rolled my eyes and set the box of Cheerios back on the shelf, keeping the Fruit Loops. Minutes later, I found Tate in the meat aisle, studying two different packages of bacon.

"Peppered or regular?" he asked, his eyebrows furrowed in concentration. The kid took his eating seriously.

"Peppered," I said with boredom, glancing around. "Just hurry up—"

Shit.

It was him. The cowboy with the stormy gray eyes and the crooked smile. The guy that made me madder than hell and hornier than sin.

He was standing a few yards away, talking to the butcher behind the meat counter. One of his knees was bent and both of his hands were resting on the counter. He was wearing that damn cowboy hat again. The one that looked trampled and beat up. My heart skipped a beat when I saw it. There was just something about him and that hat that made me weak in the knees.

Not that he would care. He hadn't seemed all that impressed with me the other night. The thought still made me mad. I wanted to stomp over there and rip the fuckin' hat off his head. Toss it to the ground just to see what he would do. I didn't like feeling vulnerable and I didn't like being ignored.

In fact, I refused to be either.

I narrowed my eyes at him. He laughed at something the butcher said, his laugh too sexy for someone so aggravating. When I heard it I felt like someone had slammed me against the wall, knocking the sense out of me. And that's just what happened when I looked at him.

The sense was knocked out of me.

He turned his head just a little, enough that he saw me. His smile slipped just a smidgen and recognition filled his eyes. He forced his grin back in place and looked directly at me.

I felt those headstone colored irises pierce mine, sending a jolt through me. The bad girl in me hoped his gaze would travel up and down my body, but it never did. He kept his focus on my face, never wavering as he dropped his hands from the counter and started walking toward me.

Oh, fuuuuuck!

"You hear me, Cat? I'm buying hot dogs too," Tate said behind me, interrupting my cowboy-induced trance.

"Yeah. Whatever," I said with a dry mouth, watching a nympho's dream approach me.

He had a swagger. Yeah, that's what I would call it – a swagger. Each step was measured. Sure. Slow and precise. My palms grew sweaty. My heart raced. My breath hitched.

And it all scared the hell out of me.

I stuck my chin up and cocked my hip to the side.

"Hello, cowboy." I smiled in what I hope was a sarcastic, smug smirk that let him know he was the last person I wanted to see. "Lucky you meeting me here."

The cowboy's grin only grew wider as he sauntered toward me.

"Who the hell is he?" Tate asked from behind me, his voice raising an octave then dropping.

"A guy," I muttered out of the corner of my mouth.

"No shit," Tate said sarcastically, eyeing the cowboy up and down. "You know him?"

I swallowed hard, my mouth still dry as a desert. "Yeah." I let my gaze travel over the cowboy's dusty jeans and dirt-encrusted boots. "I mean no," I backtracked with a small shake of my head. "Not really."

Tate grunted, his new form of conversation. "Whatever. Girls are confusing as hell. I'm gonna go hunt me some eggs. Meet you up front."

My gaze stayed on the cowboy as Tate walked away. My knees felt weak. My face felt hot. I wanted to take a step back. Run after my little brother. Hide from the feelings coursing through me.

But I was Catarina Phillips. I didn't run from anything and I wouldn't start now.

I stuck my chin up higher as the cowboy got closer. A couple of feet away, he stopped. The air crackled. I forgot how to breathe. Pure, unadulterated anticipation froze me in place.

He was taller than me and I was tall for a girl. The top of my head reached his chest, giving him at least a good foot on me. He looked strong, with toned, lean muscles. His body was sleek and a dangerous vibe seemed to radiate off him.

My gaze dropped, just a fraction. It traveled over his full lips and down his chiseled jaw. It stopped at the small hollow at the base of his neck, left exposed by his open shirt collar. I had a flitting image of me pressing my lips to that spot. The thought just made me mad.

"Cat," he said in greeting, giving me a short nod. His voice like the softest silk money could buy. My name on his lips had the ability to send a shiver through me.

I hated it.

"You remembered my name? I'm surprised," I said with a nasty smirk, crossing my arms over my chest and then tapping my foot. "I thought you might have been too busy playing the mute knight in shining armor the other night to remember me."

One of his eyebrows lifted. His gaze shot down to my tapping toes, his brow quirking up even more.

"Yeah, well can't forget a cat with claws," he drawled, his eyes moving up my body slowly, laughter in them.

I bristled. He was enjoying himself at my expense. Time to show him who he was messing with.

I glanced down at his dusty, old boots. With a look of contempt, I raised one finely arched eyebrow.

"Sorry cowboy, but I forgot your name."

He chuckled, low and deep and averted his gaze, rubbing the tip of his nose with his index finger in a nervous gesture.

Good, I thought with smugness. He made me hot and bothered; I'd make him nervous. *Serves him right.*

But when he raised his eyes, looking at me from beneath his cowboy hat, I was the one who grew nervous. I sucked in a breath. They held something that shook me to my core.

Desire.

I looked away, afraid to see what was staring me in the face. Sure, I used men. They gave me what I needed – a distraction. But something about the cowboy was different. In the very short amount of time I had known him, I felt threatened. Exposed. It was a silly notion but I couldn't shake it.

So I did what I did so well. I reached down deep, into the part of me that only knew coldness and pain. I wrapped the feelings around me, covering up what I didn't want anyone to see. When I glanced back at the cowboy, I found him watching me carefully. Our gazes locked. His with humor, mine with anger.

"Cash. My name's Cash," he said, all traces of desire gone. Only humor remained.

"That's right – Cash. My dad's favorite word," I whipped.

That eyebrow of his shot up again. "Excuse me?"

"Nothing." I shook my head. "So, Cash…what are you doing? Buying meat?" I glanced around him at the butcher who was filling the refrigerated bin with chunks of steak.

Cash followed my gaze, looking at the man over his shoulder. "Nope, selling more like it," he said.

"Selling?"

He glanced back at me. "Yeah. Beef, straight from my family's ranch. Best tasting meat around."

I didn't comment because I really didn't care what he was doing here or how his meat tasted. I just wanted him to stay away from me so I could go back to being me. Numb and wild.

"Well, I've gotta go…" I turned to go, hoping I never saw the cowboy again. I didn't want to feel that twinge of curiosity that had appeared since the moment I met him. Didn't want to listen to my body beg and plead to get closer to him. But more than anything, I didn't want to experience feelings that should be dead.

"Nice seeing you again, Cat." My name sounded like he was tasting it on the tip of his tongue. Like he was getting ready to devour it and make it his.

I forced a smile on my face then turned and walked away. I fought the urge to look back. To run to him and have my way. Instead, I continued walking.

I ignored the two little old ladies watching and whispering behind their hands nearby. I ignored the pimpled stock boy that almost dropped two cans of soup when I strolled past him. I ignored them all. Everyone in this miserable little town.

Including my quickly beating heart.

I was a safe distance from Cash - at the end of the refrigerated aisle down by the butter and biscuits - when his deep, throaty voice called out to me.

"Have dinner with me tomorrow night."

Surprise and shock made me almost miss a step. I regained my composure and turned, ignoring the little old ladies and the stock boy studying my legs. I ignored the mother with the newborn, pushing a cart past me, and the announcement overhead, talking about the price of pears. I ignored them all, but not the cowboy.

He stood in the same spot, one hip cocked, his hat pulled down lower. He looked out of place in the grocery store, a rough and tumble cowboy from a different era. One that was better suited for the 1800s, sitting on the back of a horse with six-shooters hanging from his belt, than in a rickety old store that was having a one-day sale on toilet paper.

My inner bad girl screamed and stomped her feet, demanding that I tell him to fuck off. I didn't need someone like him, with his dusty boots and broken in hat. I didn't need anyone.

But then there was the other part of me. The part that I had tried to bury in the ground with Luke. The part that could love and hope and dream.

The part I hated.

"And just what's in it for me, cowboy?" I asked loudly, being that reckless girl again. The one that refused to love but loved to cause trouble.

Cash walked toward me slowly, taking his time. His gaze was heated under the brim of his hat, studying me. Staring at me. Locking me in place.

The young mother watched nearby, ignoring her crying baby. The little ol' ladies stood still, their puckered lips pulled down in disapproval. The stock boy pulled at his stiff collar, watching the show play out. Cash never noticed them and neither did I, too focused on each other to care who was listening or watching.

When he got close enough, I could see the heat blazing in his eyes.

"What's in it for you?" he asked, his voice a low rasp. "Guess that depends on what you want, Cat."

He stopped right in front of me, the toes of his boots very close to the edges of my wedge high heels. I could smell the outdoors on him. It was a scent that reminded me of clear skies and early summer mornings.

"What if I want everything?" I asked, jutting my chin out.

His lips twitched. "Well," he said, tilting his head to the side and studying me from underneath his hat. "Just tell me and it's yours."

Jesus H. Christ, his words could make a girl wetter than Florida in a tropical storm. I nibbled on my bottom lip, feeling completely insane that I was contemplating having dinner with him.

I took a step back, needing my distance. Needing to take control again. Best way to do that? Shock him.

"Well, I'm not sleeping with you," I said. "At least not yet."

The old ladies nearby gasped and the stock boy snickered but I didn't give a damn. They could thank me later for giving them something to talk about.

Cash grinned, looking like he was enjoying our little back-and-forth play. "Well, I'm not asking you to sleep with me. At least not yet."

Fire crackled along my nerve endings. I felt it spread from the tips of my toes to the top of my head. *Holy hell, when was the last time a man could do that to me?*

"Dinner. That's all I want, Cat," he said, all humor gone from his voice. He never took his eyes from mine, never looked down at my chest. It was something I was beginning to like about him.

I shook the thought away, disgusted with myself. He might be polite and different than other men, but he could only be one thing for me. Just another good time. Another roll in the hay. Another way for me to avoid feeling anything. I could handle that. I just couldn't handle anything more.

"201 Chester Road," I said, taking a step back then another, almost running into one of the little old ladies who was eyeing my short shorts with distaste.

"Is that your address?" Cash asked, one corner of his lips lifting higher.

I nodded. "Think you can remember that, cowboy?"

Cash's lopsided grin grew. He shrugged and stuck his right hand in his rear jean's pocket.

"Well, ma'am," he said, peering at me from beneath his hat. "I don't think I'll ever forget a thing about you."

I smirked. "Good. That's the way it should be." With a flounce, I turned and walked away, swinging my hips for his pleasure.

"8 o'clock," he called out in that amazing voice.

I glanced over my shoulder and gave him my best perfected smile. One meant to seduce and destroy. Make men crawl and beg. "Make it 7. See you then, cowboy."

Turning back around, I headed for the front of the store. Anyone who passed me would say they saw a tall, dark-haired girl with sin in her eyes. Someone who had signed on with the devil, ready to break hearts and steal love. Throw it to the curb like it threw her.

They would see a girl that was going nowhere but down and taking every last man with her, even the lone cowboy standing nearby.

Chapter Six

-Cash-

What the hell was I thinking, asking Miss Beauty Queen out? She wasn't my type and I sure as hell wasn't hers. But when I saw her standing in Craig's Grocery, those long legs of hers going on forever, I knew I couldn't let her walk away again.

I peered out the window, looking for her house. There was nothing but acres and acres of pastureland on either side of me, not the kind of place I pictured Cat to call home. For some reason I imagined her living smack dab in the middle of town, surrounded by everything she could possibly snap her fingers and get.

I almost missed her house, which was surprising because it was massive. A long driveway led up to the enormous home, looking like something out of one of those fancy magazines. There were windows everywhere on it. More glass than I had ever seen in one house. The roof was flat and the walls were all angles and sharp corners. The modern architecture looked strange and foreign sitting in the middle of a Texas wasteland, surrounded by dry pastures and smelly livestock. But to each their own, I guessed.

"We're not in Kansas anymore," I muttered to myself, peering closely at the house as I pulled up into the long driveway.

I parked my truck near the house and cut the engine off. After taking a deep breath, I got out. I was nervous as hell. Antsy as shit. I chided myself as I headed to the front door. I wasn't a chicken. I was a grown man. I could handle a girl with fire in her eyes and wickedness to her step. And if I couldn't? Well, I just hoped I could walk away in one piece.

I might be crazy but there was just something about Cat I wanted to experience. Call it basic, thinking-with-my-dick lust or an urge to have what was probably bad for me. Whatever it was, I wanted to know her. Touch her. Find out what was behind those green eyes and seductive smile.

I wanted her. Period.

I raised my hand to knock on the door. Whatever happened between her and me, I could handle a little Cat like her, sharp claws and all. The fight would be sweet but damn, I think it might just be worth it.

At least one time.

Chapter Seven

-Cat-

I turned, glancing over my shoulder at my reflection. The dark red chiffon halter dress I wore hit me above the knees and outlined my body perfectly. It was backless, just begging for a man's fingers to run over me. My hair, dark against the paleness of my skin, fell across my back in waves. Tiny diamonds dotted my ears and sat in the hollow of my neck, both a gift from my dad when he missed my sixteenth birthday.

I smoothed a hand over my hip. *I'll have the cowboy tongue-tied*, I thought, smiling. *Tongue-tied and putty in my hands.*

"So who's the guy?"

I whipped around, my hair falling over my shoulder. Nathan was leaning against the doorframe, staring at me with curiosity.

"He's just a guy," I said, avoiding Nathan's eyes as I headed toward my walk-in closet. Ever since I returned home, Nathan had been keeping close tabs on me. It was irritating as hell. Not because he cared. Because he cared too fucking much.

He knew my past. He knew what I had done. I didn't want him to worry about me and I sure as fuck didn't want his or anyone's sympathy.

Nathan was quiet, watching me stoop down to toss a University of Texas t-shirt out of the way in my closet so I could search for my strappy high heels. *Where the hell were they?*

"Where'd you meet him?" Nathan asked, his calm voice edged with danger. "A bar?"

"Does it matter?" I retorted.

I found my heels under a pair of skinny jeans on my closet floor and pulled them out. As I slipped them on, I looked over at Nathan and raised one eyebrow, daring him to comment. When he didn't, I walked over to the full-length mirror and checked my reflection one last time.

"You're my sister, Cat. It matters," Nathan finally said, pushing away from the doorframe and walking into the room. He stopped a few feet behind me and stuffed his hands in the pockets of his jeans, staring at me in the mirror.

He had perfectly arranged, unruly hair and a chiseled chin. He got our dad's looks and his mother's personality. Girls always drooled over him but he was just a pain in my ass. The nosy kind.

"Get a life, Nathan. I can take care of myself," I snapped.

Nathan snorted. "So you say. Just be careful, Cat. Okay?"

I smiled sweetly at him. "I'm always careful, Nate. Cross my heart."

"Yeah, right," Nathan scoffed. "And exactly how many guys have you been with since Luke died? Five? Ten? Twenty? What's the number, Cat? I know what you're doing. I'm not blind or stupid."

I froze, reaching for my little Gucci purse. "I'm fine, Nathan," I mumbled. "Just back off."

I grabbed the purse and spun around. Without looking at him, I walked to the other side of the room. I just hoped the anguish didn't show on my face.

I started tossing clothes off of my nightstand, searching for my cell phone and praying Nathan would get the message and leave.

He didn't. In fact, he became even more persistent.

"Come on, Cat. You're fine? Really? You said the same exact thing the day of Luke and Jenna's funeral. You need to face facts. You're not okay. You haven't been for a year. You're screwed up, little sister, and I'm not going to sit back and watch you destroy your life."

My throat closed up. I didn't want anyone to care. I was too far-gone. Nathan was only wasting his time.

"I said I was fine and I am," I said sharply, hoping he couldn't see the truth in my eyes. I grabbed my cell phone and swung around to face him. "I'm just perfect like always."

Nathan met my glare with one of his own. His eyes were full of warning. Mine was just full of spite.

"Just be careful. Guys are assholes," he said.

I smiled caustically. "But I'm a bitch."

And I was. It was the only way I could protect my heart and not feel one damn thing.

~~~~

The doorbell rang, the musical tone echoing through the house like little chiming bells. I headed for the front door, followed by the sound of Tate's heavy boots.

"But do you know where he is?" he asked from behind me, sounding whiny.

"He's in Dubai on business. If you need something tell Nathan," I said over my shoulder. My little brother had cornered me as soon as I came out of my room, antsy about something. It was no telling, knowing him.

"I ain't going to ask Nathan for shit," Tate grumbled. "Shit, no."

I curbed my irritation at his cussing and turned around to face him. "What do you need, Tate? Maybe I can help."

He frowned then glanced over at the front door. "Nah. You don't got time. Plus, I ain't telling you. You'll just think it's stupid."

I crossed my arms over my chest. "Try me."

Tate shook his head, making his bangs fall into his eyes. "No way."

"Fine." I turned back to the door. "Don't tell me. Dad will call when he gets a chance. Until then it's just us, Tater Tot. Deal with it."

Before he could respond with some smartass comment, I opened the front door.

Cash stood on the other side. He was clean-shaven and god, was he gorgeous. His stone-cut jaw was smooth, recently shaven. I wanted to reach out and run my fingers over it. See if it sent shivers over my spine just like it did when I stared at him.

His light brown hair was shorter – just cut if I had to guess. It was styled in a messy, I-just-fucked-you-silly kind of way.

The shirt he wore was cut for his body, outlining taut muscles and a sleek frame. His jeans gave sexy a whole new meaning. I wanted to stand between his legs or better yet, feel the rough material against my bare thighs, rubbing over me just right. The thought almost made me quiver.

But it was his eyes that rattled me. They made me question my sanity. Examine my wisdom. Second-guess my resistance to him. When he looked at me, I felt something snap inside me.

"Hello, Cat."

I let his voice wash over me, warming me like liquid fire. I wanted to soak and swim in it. Close my eyes and let it consume me. Instead I smiled and took a slow step toward him.

"Hello, cowboy. Where's your hat?"

Cash's lips turned up in a lopsided grin. "In the truck. Wouldn't leave home without it." His eyes made a quick pass over me. "Are you ready?"

Before I could respond, Tate pushed past me. "You're taking my sister out? The guy from the meat department?" he asked, crossing his arms over his chest and standing guard in front of me.

Cash glanced from me to Tate, not flinching at Tate's scowl. "Yes, sir. If that's okay with you?" he said with sincerity.

Tate seemed startled but recovered quickly. He gave a short, curt nod. "Yeah. Okay. Just…just know if you hurt her, I'll break your face."

Cash's eyebrows shot up and the corners of his mouth twitched but he kept a straight face. "Well, I promise not to hurt her if you promise to keep her safe when I'm not around," he said.

My heart skipped a much-needed beat. No one had ever said anything like that to one of my brothers. No one had ever asked permission to date me or promised to not hurt me. I didn't know what to think. What to feel. I was confused and scared and damned well loving every single moment of it.

"Do we have a deal?" Cash asked, sticking his hand out for Tate to shake.

Tate hesitated only a second before putting his hand in Cash's. "Deal."

As they shook hands, Cash's attention moved to me but his words were for Tate.

"I'll take care of her. Promise."

The air between us seemed to come alive, stripping me of all thought. I wanted to step closer to him. Press my body against his. Touch him with my fingertips and beg him to touch me.

It made me mad. I called the shots. Men were supposed to worship me, not the other way around. It was time this cowboy learned his place.

"Enough chitchat. Let's go." I pushed past Tate and then over to Cash. My arm brushed his chest as I passed him on the threshold. His hard muscles tensed, enough to let me know that I had an effect on him. Good.

With a smug smile, I headed down the stone path. I heard him say goodbye to Tate then follow me. Knowing Cash was behind me sent a tingle over my skin. I could feel his eyes on me, running down my back, traveling over my ass. I could sense them touching on my legs, wandering down to my heels then slowly traveling back up. Getting his fill. Taking his time. Just like I wanted to do with him.

I resisted the urge to bolt when the stone walkway opened up to the driveway. That's when Cash started walking beside me. I ignored him as best as a girl could, considering he looked like a recovering sex addict's worse nightmare. I did my best and focused on the faded red pickup truck that sat next to Nathan's car.

"So where are we going?" I asked, stopping beside the truck's passenger door.

"Where would you like to go?" Cash asked, reaching around me to open the door.

"Hmm." I thought about it as I started to get in but then all thought left me.

Cash touched my arm, stopping me from climbing into the truck. My skin tingled. My breath hitched.

He didn't seem to notice. He slid his hand from me and reached inside the pickup. His knuckles brushed against my waist. His scent, so warm and manly, wrapped around me.

I was trapped against the truck, one of his hands on the vehicle, the other reaching inside to move his hat out of the way on the seat. I wasn't sure if it was the perfect place to be or the worst place in the world. I wanted to reach out and touch him. Kiss his neck that was only inches from me.

Shit. My control was slipping. That was a scary thing for me.

Cash took his time, standing up slowly. His fingers brushed against my hip as he pulled his hand out of the truck. It sent jolts along my nerve endings and made my heart beat faster. Shitty little thing.

I put on my best, queen-bitch face, and pushed my feelings away. With a seductive smile, I took a step toward him, refusing to acknowledge the buzz of excitement that went through my body.

"Listen, cowboy," I said in a voice meant to make a certain part of him stand up and pay attention. "If we're going on this *date*, we've got to get a few things straight."

"Okay." Cash grinned. "I like rules. Tell me yours and I'll tell you mine."

Shimmers of need ran through me. My imagination went haywire. I reached out and grabbed his shirt then tugged him to me. He planted a boot on either side of my legs, grabbing the doorframe and truck to keep from falling on me.

"Number one is I hate dates," I said, hating the way I felt nervous at his closeness. God, he was even more gorgeous up close.

Cash chuckled, looking down at me. "You and me both, Cat."

I smiled. The muscles in his arms tensed when he saw it. His grin slipped and his gaze dropped down to my lips. The air left my lungs and seemed to evaporate from the atmosphere, making it hard to breathe. I wondered if Cash had the guts to take what most men would die to have.

And apparently he did.

He took a step closer, backing me into the door. His hips touched mine. His voice turned smooth, like the fine whiskey my grandfather used to drink.

"And what's rule number two?" he asked, his gray eyes peering into mine.

I licked my dry lips. "Well, rule number two is no kissing on a first date."

Cash nodded slowly. "Okay. I can deal with that," he said, not flinching when I tightened my hand on his shirt. Thankfully my hand didn't shake but inside I was trembling. Only one way to fix that – prove it was nothing.

I gave him a seductive smile and let go of his shirt. I moved my fingers down until they rested against his stomach, inches from his belt buckle.

"But the thing is I like to break the rules, cowboy," I whispered.

Before I thought better of it, I grabbed the back of his neck and pulled him down to me. It was time to take control and show him who was boss. But I was in for one hell of a surprise.

His mouth captured mine with fierce possession. He took control. Tasting me. Experiencing me. Stamping me as his. It was hot and aggravating and fucking amazing all at this same time. There was no hesitation. No uncertainty. No shyness or holding back. This man was in charge.

And I had no hope of winning.

His body fitted mine like a glove, from top to bottom and everywhere in between. I was crushed against the truck, metal on one side and pure male hardness on the other. His lips slanted across mine like it wasn't our first kiss but our millionth. Gone was the cowboy who smiled and grinned like a good ol' boy who wouldn't hurt a fly. The man that kissed me was a man on a mission. A man not to tease.

I started to doubt my decision to kiss him, wondering if I would be able to walk away in one piece. But his hands stayed a safe distance from my body, leaving me safe. His lips were all I needed. All I desired and more.

I slid my hand around his neck, pulling him to me more. His skin was warm. Strands of his hair teased the top of my fingers. I wanted to touch him everywhere and desperately wanted him to touch me.

The thought sobered me up. I tore my mouth from his, letting go of his shirt and dropping my hand from his neck at the same time.

"Shit," I whispered, touching my lips. They felt swollen and used, abused and more.

"That's one rule broken. Have any others?" Cash said, his mouth close to mine. The muscles in his arms flexed as he kept me trapped against the truck door.

I lifted my gaze to his, looking him in the eye. "No. Do you have any rules?"

Cash's mouth curved upward. "Yeah, I do. Maybe one day I'll tell you or better yet, show you."

He dropped his hands away and took a step back, his eyes pinpoints of gray heat searing me. I stood shock still, my body sparking like a live wire dropped in water. He was dangerous. Hazardous to my well-being. I hadn't felt this way around a man since Luke.

And that scared me.

"Ready to go?" he asked in a low voice.

I nodded, running my tongue over my lip in stupid awe.

He grinned, seeing me do it, but didn't say anything. He just waited patiently for me to climb in the truck. With my heart beating out of control, I did, careful to keep my dress tucked around me.

Cash shut the door as soon as I was in and started around the truck. A second later he was sliding into the driver's seat. I didn't have to look at him to feel him near me. My subconscious was drawn to him. My body was craving him. I suddenly had no control and that was terrifying to me.

I looked down at my hands, clenched tightly in my lap. They were shaking. *Shaking, for chrissake.* My head was spinning and my mind was in turmoil. What I was feeling was wrong and I had no right to it.

None at all.

"So where would you like to go?" Cash asked from the driver's side, gazing at me with calm composure.

I felt myself stiffen, my decision firmly in place. I needed to take control again. It was that simple. I had to put him in his place. Build up and fortify the wall that I kept between me and every man I met. I had to prove that I didn't want him. The best way I knew how to do that was to remind Cash who he was and who he was with.

And why we didn't belong together.

I knew exactly how to do it.

"Take me to Dallas. I know the perfect place," I said with secret smugness. What better way to prove that I held the upper hand and was untouchable by someone like him than to go to a luxurious restaurant with a hundred dollar price tag per plate? Oh, yes. He would feel embarrassed and out of my league. I would have him under my thumb, right where I had most men. I would be in control, getting what I wanted with no strings attached.

And I would walk away unscathed.

Feeling nothing.

Chapter Eight

-*Cat*-

Cliché was posh, outrageously overpriced, and intimate. The lighting was low, giving the tables and their occupants privacy. White tablecloths adorned each table and artfully folded black napkins were placed on expensive appetizer plates. The menu boasted extravagant foods, from oysters and squid to duck and quail. The wine list started at triple digit prices and the champagne list was extensive. It was in the heart of Dallas, one hour away from our little hick town and worlds above what most people could afford.

Cash didn't bat an eye when I told him where I wanted to go. He also didn't flinch when he handed the keys of his beat-up truck over to the valet and watched him drive it away. But he did tense when we walked into the restaurant and the maître d' greeted us with a look of revulsion, glancing down at Cash's boots and jeans.

"Ah... Mmm..." The man twisted around, looking flustered and not sure what to do with a cowboy in his restaurant. Jeans and boots might be the normal attire for people in the state of Texas but in this restaurant, suits, ties, and even tuxedos were the only acceptable style of dress.

The corner of my mouth lifted in a satisfied smile, happy that my plan was working. But when I looked at Cash my breath was stolen.

He stood next to me, a man cut from stone and made from perfection. Intensity lined his body. His hand hung loosely at his side, his fingers long and powerful against his jeans. I imagined them on me. Running down my body. Driving me crazy.

"Ahem."

I blinked. The maître d' was staring at me expectedly.

"Sorry," I said with a nervous smile, hoping no one could see the sudden flush on my body.

"Yes, well…" The maître d' gave Cash another perusal then sniffed with distaste and averted his eyes, focusing on me. "Two tonight?"

"Yes," I answered.

The man turned with a flourish and motioned for us to follow him. We entered the dining area. Men in dark suits and women in slinky dresses ogled Cash as he walked behind me. They stared with blatant disapproval at his clothes and frowned with disdain at his boots.

I smiled smugly. It's what I wanted, for him to feel awkward and beneath me. If I proved he didn't belong in my world then I could prove I didn't belong with him. I could compartmentalize him and any emotions he invoked in me.

But that idea went out the window a second later.

As the maître d' led the way between the tables, I felt a hand on the small of my back. Every inch of me came alive. My dress provided only a thin veil between Cash's fingers and my skin. His touch was strong yet gentle. Innocent yet intimate. I felt possessed and protected. My control started slipping. If I lost it…if I let my guard down…I might feel something.

And that wasn't an option.

The maître d' led us to a secluded table in the corner. Cash never removed his hand from me the entire time there. It stayed on my waist, searing me through my dress. Torturing me as it slid around to my hip. I seethed. I wanted it off. It threatened me. But for some reason I couldn't push it away.

My heart pounded as his arm brushed across my back. Shivers moved down my arm when his crisp shirt rubbed against me. When we reached the table, his fingers skimmed over my waist, leaving me so we could sit down on the overstuffed, plush seat for two.

The corner was secluded, made for intimacy and situated for secrecy. Heavy black drapes separated us from others. Red velvet lined the wall behind us and the single black leather seat hugged our bodies and kept us close together.

Cash sat down beside me. His thigh rested against mine, his arm brushed against me as he moved. Sitting so close to him made me feel cocooned. Safe in our little secret enclosure. It was an unusual feeling for me, one that made me nervous and put me on edge.

"For you, madam."

I forced a gracious smile at the maître d and took the menu he offered. He gave one to Cash without comment, refusing to look at him. With a sniff, he turned and walked away.

Cash studied his menu a second then laid it on the table in front of him. I took a little longer, afraid to face what was becoming my new problem.

Resisting him.

"Nervous?" he asked, watching me.

My heart quickened but I remained calm. I put my menu on the table and looked at him, knowing I had to lie.

"Not at all. You?" I asked, proud my voice didn't waver.

He put his arm on top of the chair behind me, a movement that instantly brought him closer to me.

"Yes, I'm nervous as hell. You're beautiful, Cat, and I'm here with you," he said in a low, raspy voice.

My breath hitched and I felt myself falling. I didn't like it at all. *Don't let him get to you. Keep your guard up. Flirt but don't feel.*

I gave him a suggestive smile, hoping he couldn't read my mind. "You should be nervous, cowboy. I'm dangerous."

The corner of Cash's mouth shot up in a smirk. He leaned closer and his voice dropped to a whisper.

"Well, I think I can handle one tiny, little pussy cat even if it means getting a few scratches," he said.

I opened my mouth to respond but clamped it shut when a waiter appeared at our table.

Cash removed his arm from the back of the chair and turned his attention to the tuxedo-wearing waiter. I grew aggravated at his easy smile and relaxed composure as he answered the man's questions and smiled politely.

He shouldn't feel comfortable here. He should feel out of place. Forced to see that he didn't fit in my world. But instead I was the one feeling disoriented.

I listened as he ordered quail like he did it every day. I ordered the veal, sounding more confident than I felt. If the waiter noticed the tension, he didn't reveal it. He filled our glasses with chilled bottled water and left us alone in our private, secluded corner.

I put a napkin in my lap then took a drink, watching Cash out of the corner of my eye. His jaw tightened as he watched the other patrons. I wondered what he was thinking and then wondered why the hell I even cared. As long as he started to believe that asking me out was a bad idea, he could think whatever he wanted. I needed him to believe that because if he didn't, I was afraid I was in trouble.

Cash caught me staring at him. He turned his gray eyes on me, making me shiver.

"So tell me, Cat, what's your real name?" he asked.

I blinked, ending the trance I was in. "Catarina," I answered, putting my glass down. "I was named after my mother's abuela."

"I like that. Catarina."

He tried out my name like he was considering owning it. He might as well have been saying, 'I want to fuck you' or 'I want to lick your pussy.' It had just as much effect on me.

Cash didn't seem to notice how his voice alone was an aphrodisiac to me. He took a small sip of his water then set it on the table.

"What do your parents do for a living?" he asked, keeping his gaze on me.

I cleared my throat and my thoughts. "You've never heard of my father, the all powerful Matt Phillips?" I asked, covering up my nervousness with a smart-aleck attitude.

Cash shook his head. "Nope. Should I?"

I scoffed. "Well, just about everyone in the county knows him."

Cash ran a finger over the sweat on his water glass, catching a drop on the pad of his thumb. Fuck, that was hot.

"I'm not everyone, Cat," he said, his voice oozing sex.

I suddenly felt warm. Very warm and…wet.

A tiny smile lifted the corner of his mouth. He dropped his hand away from the glass, turning his full attention on me. "Tell me about your dad."

I tucked a curl behind my ear. "Well, he's an oil tycoon. The biggest around."

"And?" Cash prompted when I didn't say anything else. "Are you two close?"

I played with the edge of the napkin in my lap, uncomfortable with the conversation. "Not really. He travels a lot."

"What about your mom?" Cash asked, his gaze dropping to my fingers on the napkin. "Are you close to her?"

I laughed sarcastically. "My mother? Uh, no. She didn't like me from the moment I was born. But it doesn't matter. Her and my dad divorced. She lives in New York City now with her boyfriend. I never see her."

Cash's gaze darted up to mine. "Never?"

"Nope. I just don't fit into her life. At least that's what she told me." I let go of the napkin, becoming frustrated with all the questions. They picked at a scab that would never heal.

"Shit, that's awful," Cash said with sympathy. Something I didn't want from anyone.

I shrugged, becoming defensive. "Not really. I've never known anything different."

"So you have one brother?" Cash asked, studying me closely.

"No. I have two. Tate and Nathan. You met Tate. He's the youngest. Nathan is—" I stopped myself. What was I doing, telling Cash all about myself? I couldn't let him in my world. I kept that part of me safe. Locked away. What the hell was happening to me? I never told men anything. It was always just fuck and leave. Wham bam, thank you. But when Cash looked at me, I felt different.

And that was disturbing.

He started to say something but paused, his eyebrows

drawing together. "Wait. Nathan Phillips? That name sounds familiar. Did he go to Central High?"

"Yes. He was two grades ahead of me."

Cash's gaze dropped down to my lips then back up, a movement so fast I almost missed it. "So where did you go to school?" he asked. "I was a loner but I would have known if someone like you was in one of my classes."

I shifted in the seat, wondering why my shitty little heart wouldn't stop pounding and why the simplest words Cash said caused it.

"I went to private school in Dallas," I admitted. "Nathan chose to stay here."

"Hmm. Figures."

I frowned. "What's that supposed to mean?"

Cash leaned even closer. "It means that I had a feeling you're a spoiled little rich girl. Your daddy is a bigwig. You probably get everything you want when you want it, including going to a private school."

"So what's your point?" I asked, growing angry.

Cash's eyes turned darker, piercing mine. "The point is – what do you want with a guy like me? I asked you out but I want to know why you agreed to go. I'm not one of those men you can lead around with a shake of your ass and a cock-teasing smile, Cat."

I clenched my hands tightly in my lap, fighting the wave of fury building in me. From the moment I met him he made my hands shake and my heart race. He pissed me off one moment and made my panties wet the next. It made me mad and afraid and questioning my own sanity. I became angry and annoyed and fucking tired of playing nice.

I reached out and ran my hand along his thigh, letting my fingers slide over the muscle. "So why did you ask me out then? To see if I'll go down on you or to find out how I taste?"

A muscle ticked in Cash's jaw.

"Maybe I just want to know what's behind that pretty face and perfect body," he said in a whisper, leaning dangerously closer to me. "Or maybe I want to know why sometimes that beautiful mouth of yours is turned down in sadness."

I flinched, his words hitting too close to home, but Cash wasn't done yet.

"I won't lie to you," he said, putting his hand on my thigh. "I want to find out how you taste. How you sound when you come. But before we get to that stage, maybe all I want to know is if you'll kiss me again."

I opened my mouth to respond. To say something smartass and sassy. But Cash's fingers tightened on me, inches from the insatiable part of my anatomy.

"Is that all you want?" I whispered, hoping he would say more but afraid he would.

Cash seemed to think about it a second then he shook his head slowly. "No. What I really want to know is why I don't load you in my truck and take you home. Leave you on your doorstep and say adios and good riddance. You're not my type, sweetheart, and I'm not yours. You're high maintenance and a brat and I shouldn't even want to be around you."

Unexpected hurt filled me. It was a feeling I didn't expect. One I refused to acknowledge.

He ran his hand down the outside of my thigh, pulling me closer and putting his mouth near my ear.

"But for some damn reason I'm here, Cat. I want to be around you. I want that and so much more," he said in a hoarse whisper.

The waiter cleared his throat, suddenly appearing at our table. I wanted to both curse him for interrupting and breathe a sigh of relief.

Cash slid his hand from me and turned his attention to the man. He gave him a warm, friendly smile. I attempted to do the same but failed miserably.

I stared down at the veal as the waiter placed it in front of me but I wasn't really seeing the food. I was seeing the mistake I was about to make. The dare that I was about to take.

I needed to put a stop to it immediately for my own sanity.

When the waiter walked away, I looked at Cash. He was studying the artfully arranged food on his plate with a frown. It didn't ruin his features. It just made him all that more irresistible. I wanted him. Not in a fuck-and-leave kind of way. Nope.

And that made me mad.

"You don't belong here, Cash," I said in my best mean girl voice. I had to protect myself, even if it meant being mean to him.

He snapped his eyes up to mine, his food forgotten. "What?"

I sighed and plowed ahead. "You're right. I'm not your type and you're not mine. You don't belong with me and you don't belong in a place like this." I said it with conviction, growing angrier with myself by the second. It was damn better than feeling anything for him.

I threw my napkin beside my plate and started to get up. Cash's hand shot out, grabbing my wrist and keeping me in my seat.

"Cat, listen—"

I shook my head, trying my hardest to ignore the ache in my chest.

"No, don't," I said as cool as I could. "I'm going to the restroom. When I come back, I don't expect you to be here. It's better this way."

Before he could argue, I pulled my arm away from him and grabbed my purse. As I walked away, I felt a rush of agony.

But I knew it was for the best.

Chapter Nine

-Cat-

My heels clicked across the black marble floor in the swanky bathroom. I headed straight to one of the square sinks that lined both sides of the restroom, almost running into a middle-aged woman walking out.

"Shit!" I swore, slamming my Gucci purse on the counter. I planted both hands on the granite countertop and stared at my reflection in the mirror.

My cheeks were tinged pink. My lips were parted slightly, my breathing erratic and quick. My dark hair fell over my shoulders, and my eyes flared with something akin to desire. I didn't recognize myself and that freaked me out.

I reached for my purse and pulled it toward me, cursing under my breath. I wasn't some damn good girl. I would eat my dinner, pay the bill, and call a taxi. I needed to get away from Cash. He threatened me. I was used to backseats and one-night stands. Not cowboys and words that could break me.

With my mind made up, I pulled out a tube of lipstick and applied some on my lips. After that, I combed my fingers through my hair quickly and forced myself to calm down.

Two blondes entered the bathroom as I was shoving my lipstick back into my clutch. They chatted as they checked their makeup in the mirror, paying little attention to me. I adjusted the strap of my dress and kept an eye on them, wishing they would just leave. After a minute or two they did.

I let out the breath I had been holding and relaxed. *I just need to be alone.*

I closed my eyes and took a deep breath. It was the first time since Luke that I had felt something for a man. Sure, I wasn't a saint but other men were just a means to an end. An easy way to forget what I had done and lost. But Cash was different than the others and the effect he had on me was profound.

I heard the bathroom door open but I kept my eyes shut. The stuck-up snobs here could gawk all they wanted at me. I needed just one more second...

"Cat."

I snapped my eyes open, drawing in a breath. I found Cash staring at me in the mirror.

"What are you doing?" I asked in a raspy whisper.

He didn't answer. Instead he reached up and flipped the lock on the bathroom door, his eyes never leaving mine.

My heart started racing. I spun around, putting the counter at my back.

He started toward me, taking his time. His gaze was scorching, sweeping over me with forced restraint. The muted lights in the bathroom made him look dangerous, an animal ready to strike. He was suddenly not the cowboy who smiled and said *yes, ma'am* politely.

He was the man who had kissed me with need. The man that wanted much, much more and I was at his mercy.

He stopped a foot from me, his stance relaxed, so damn sure of himself. The smell of his aftershave wrapped around me, giving me the false sense of security. His eyes held the promise of things a good girl should fear.

But I wasn't a good girl.

I jutted my chin up, refusing to cower. "What do you want, Cash?"

He didn't answer, just stood there and stared at me with a dark look that seemed to see my deepest, darkest desires.

I felt a stirring of panic. To cover it up, I rolled my eyes and grabbed my purse. "Whatever." I wasn't in the mood for some kind of mind fuck.

I started to go around him but his hand shot out and grabbed my arm, stopping me.

"Cat," he growled.

"What?" I snapped, jerking my arm away from him.

"You've got some nerve."

I frowned. "And you've got some nerve walking in the ladies restroom, Cash. You don't belong in here. Just like you don't belong out there. Leave." I pointed to the locked door.

Warning bells went off in my head when I saw the tick in his jaw but it was too late.

"Screw it," he hissed between clenched teeth.

He shoved his hand under my hair and yanked my mouth to his.

I inhaled sharply. His kiss was punishing. Bruising. He devoured me. I made a feeble attempt to push away from him but his fingers tangled into my hair, holding me tightly.

His tongue dipped inside my mouth, hot as it urged mine to play. He grabbed my wrist and held me against the counter, grinding his hips into mine. I gasped and he took advantage of it, thrusting his tongue further into my mouth. The hardness under his jeans pushed into me, making parts of me grow damp and achy.

He bit my lip brutally then sucked at it gently, making a small cry escape from me. *Fuck, the man knew how to kiss.*

He was control. Heat. Desire. Passion. He was everything in one perfect package and more.

Without warning, he grabbed me around the waist and lifted me up, sitting me on the cold granite counter. The coolness against my thighs made me suck in a shuddering breath.

Cash ran his hands along the outside of my thighs, grasping them tightly.

"You were right, Cat. I don't belong in this place," he said in a low whisper. "I belong here instead."

He jerked my legs apart and stepped between them. The counter was low and he was tall. His crotch fit perfectly between my legs. Right where I needed him. Right where I had to have him.

He shoved his hand under my hair again and grasped my nape, dragging my mouth back to his. Raw desire made the kiss hard and fast. There was no tenderness, no hesitation, and no mercy. That man was gone. There was only taking and giving. A man that knew what he wanted and was going after it.

I grabbed a handful of his shirt and yanked him closer, moaning when his cock hit my crotch behind his jeans. It was just the hint he needed. He reached under my dress and hooked his fingers in my panties. Breaking the kiss, he yanked the little swath of material down my legs, his eyes staying on mine with intensity.

I could come from his gaze alone, but I wanted something more. I wanted him in me. It might be wrong but it was who I was. Who I had to be.

I reached out, pulling him back to me. He groaned and settled between my legs. I didn't think about being in a public bathroom. I didn't worry about someone unlocking the door and walking in on us. I only thought of him fucking me.

With crazed frenzy, I reached for his belt buckle. In seconds I had it undone and his fly ripped down. I pushed his jeans aside and plunged my hand inside, wrapping my fingers around him.

Holy fuck. He was big and long and for one unbelievably insane second I wondered how he would ever fit in me.

"Second thoughts, princess?" Cash asked in whispered rumble, the side of his mouth quirking up.

"Hell, no," I breathed.

He hissed and took my mouth again with his as I started to move my hand up and down on his cock. He was hardness draped with silk, so wide my fingers barely met around him. I ran my palm up, catching the drip of precum on his tip with my thumb. I smeared it over him before sliding back down. His fingers tightened on my hip, digging into me painfully.

"Condom. Do you have a fucking condom?" he asked, tearing his mouth from mine. "God, please say yes."

"Yes."

I reached for my purse and dumped the contents on the counter, not caring if my lipstick rolled away or my wad of cash fell on the floor. I grabbed the little silver package I always carried with me. A girl had to be prepared nowadays.

"Put it on me," he demanded, thrusting his cock up into my hand.

Willing to do anything he asked, I let go of him and tore the package open, letting the wrapping fall to the floor. He hissed when my fingers closed around him again, holding him tight before moving up and down. When he started breathing harder, I stopped and unrolled the condom on him, wondering if the damn thing would even fit.

He held still but I could see fire in his eyes. His fingers on my thighs tightened, encouraging me to continue. I did, torturing slow, enjoying the feel of him in my hand.

As soon as the condom was in place, his mouth captured mine again. He wrapped an arm around my waist and dragged me to the edge of the counter. The head of his shaft pushed against me, seeking entrance into my pussy. I trembled, the anticipation and need almost killing me.

He groaned and gathered the hem of my dress in one strong fist. With a jerk, he shoved it up around my waist. It left me exposed to the air and to him, making the damp part of me all that more sensitive.

"Where do I belong?" he growled, his dick nudging at me.

I licked my dry lips. "In me."

With one hard thrust, he impaled himself into me.

I cried out, throwing my head back. *Oh, Jesus.* He was big and wide... *Oh, god.* His cock was so long and thick that I felt torn in half. There was pain and there was pleasure. I knew what we were doing might have repercussions I may not be able to handle later, but I didn't give a damn. He felt *good* inside me.

He withdrew then thrust back into me hard. *So fucking hard.* It made me moan and whimper, hating the exquisite torture but suddenly addicted to it.

My body clutched his as it pounded in and out of it. I cried out as he moved faster, biting my lip until I tasted blood.

His hand snapped out and grabbed the back of my neck, yanking my mouth to his and silencing my cries. He started plunging into me, going harder and deeper. Picking up speed and destroying my pussy.

I whimpered and gasped, holding onto him for dear life. He held me tightly, controlling my body and taking what he demanded. His hips jerked against me, driving his hardness into me roughly. He wasted no time and he wasn't gentle. That cowboy was gone. The man that was fucking me was brutal, passionate, and fierce.

And, god, he was killing me.

As if he could read my mind, he suddenly slowed down. He tore his mouth from mine, sliding his cock into me. "Open your eyes."

I did, slowly lifting my eyelids. What I saw was the mirror behind him - the one on the opposite wall. I saw him between my legs, his jeans around his hips as he moved in and out of me.

"You see us, sweetheart?" he asked, pulling out then sinking deep inside.

I nodded, unable to talk. Unable to think straight.

"Good. Keep your eyes open. I want you to remember who's in you. Someone like me."

He slammed into me again, picking up speed. He took possession of my mouth once more. His kiss was hard and fast, matching his cock thrusting in and out me. He held me tight and drove into me faster and faster like he couldn't get enough.

I gasped against his mouth and rocked against his body, feeling the ecstasy build in me. He pumped harder and harder, sensing I was almost there. My orgasm built. When it hit me, I screamed.

Cash swallowed the sound with his mouth, owning it and damn well taking it. His hands dropped down to my hips, holding them steady as he raced for the finish line too.

His fingers dug into my skin as he slammed into me. Once. Twice. "Oh, fuck!" He growled against my mouth and thrust deep, going suddenly still.

We stayed that way forever - him between my legs and his dick buried deep inside me. We breathed hard. Every inch of me pulsated, each nerve ending awake.

Slowly, I became conscious of the coldness of the granite counter under my bottom and the muted sounds of the restaurant in the distance. I saw his backside nestled between my legs in the mirror. A stranger's ass between my thighs. It was a harsh wakeup call. One I didn't want to face.

I pulled my arms from his shoulder, untangling myself from him. His eyes were gray pools of emotions as he looked at me, maybe seeing me for what I really was.

A girl that had sex on the first date and in a public restroom.

I had never felt shame before but I did just then. I avoided his eyes and pulled away from him. He let me go, easing out of me gently. I suddenly missed him in me. The thought was terrifying. It was something I had never thought of before when I was with a man. So why now and why him?

He kept his gaze on me as he lifted me off the counter and pulled my dress down. I wanted to cry at his tenderness and beg for it to disappear. I couldn't handle it. I could barely handle the man that had walked in here - controlling, domineering, and seductive as hell.

I averted my eyes as he removed the condom and threw it in the trash then zipped up his jeans. I had never been embarrassed by such an intimate act but something about Cash doing it affected me. For the first time in my pitiful life, I was embarrassed for the girl I was.

Cash picked my panties up from the floor and offered them to me. I reached for them, still refusing to look at him, but the domineering man wasn't gone yet.

He grasped my wrist, not allowing me to take the panties from him.

I raised my eyes to his. He gritted his teeth and took a step toward me, trapping me between him and the counter again. His body brushed against mine, making the need he had just extinguish minutes ago flare to life again.

He slid his hand around my nape, drawing me toward him one more time.

"Jesus, Cat," he whispered, lowering his head and touching his lips to mine.

I stood still as he kissed me, wondering what the hell he thought he was doing. We fucked. It was supposed to be over now. A wham-bam-thank-you-ma'am kind of date. But I was afraid we were far from done.

His mouth was gentle. Tender. I felt worshiped when minutes ago I felt claimed. He kissed me like he cared. Like I was his.

Not just his for tonight.

Too soon his lips left mine and he let go of me, taking one step back.

"Come have dinner with me," he said in a voice that oozed sex but promised he would be nice. "Please."

I should have said no. He was every woman's dream with his boyish, flirty grin and drop dead perfect body. He had been a living, breathing sex god between my legs, unquenchable and demanding. Nothing like I expected. But I wasn't a typical woman and I didn't dream. Not anymore. He wasn't the type of man I went for. Not since Luke at least. But for some stupid, insane, totally fucked-up reason, I nodded, agreeing to go back to dinner with him.

He swept his eyes over me one more time. Desire mixed with possession threatened to destroy my will to behave. It made the parts of me that were tender and sore start to ache all over again.

Without another word he turned and walked away. My body screamed for him to return to me even though I refused to let my heart unfreeze.

I'm in trouble, I thought as I watched him unlock the door and walk out. *I'm in so much fucking trouble.*

I was left standing alone in a public restroom, my body used, my pride wounded. I had always held the upper hand. Men bent to my will. I always called the shots. But Cash had just turned the tables on me.

I wondered if I had made a big mistake. I had done a lot of things in my life but something about being with Cash had felt final, as if I had crossed a threshold I couldn't return from.

I had carefully constructed a cold, heartless wall around myself the day Luke died. But now Cash threatened to bring it crumbling down.

Exposing the rawest part of me. My soul.

~~~~

I smoothed my dress down as I walked through the restaurant. I didn't blush when people stared at me. I didn't worry if they saw the wrinkles in my dress or guessed what I had been doing in the bathroom with a boy I had just met and sure as hell didn't love. I didn't care.

I stiffened my spine and became the girl I was again. Cold, brash, and damaged. It was how I faced the world when people were watching me.

I ignored the quiet chatter in the restaurant and headed for the table. My heart beat quicker when I saw Cash. He was reclining in the seat, one of his long legs stretched out under the table. The tip of his boot was exposed from underneath the expensive tablecloth, a kind of in-your-face to the snobby wealthy patrons that looked down their nose at him.

His gaze ran down my body as I approached. My skin heated, imagining he could see how wet I still was and how tender the area between my legs remained.

When I arrived at the table, he rose to his feet and moved aside so I could sit down. His hand touched my hip, curving around to the small of my back, as I moved past him.

When I sat down, he was there immediately, next to me. The smell of his aftershave seemed to invade my senses. Plunge me into chaos once again. He kept his eyes on me but hid his emotions. In the small amount of time I had been around him, I learned that he was good at doing that when he wanted to be.

I crossed my legs under the table carefully, super aware of the ultra sensitive spot his cock had just been in minutes ago. My legs caught his attention and a spark lit his eyes. It made a tingle run through me. I reached for my glass of water, needing to do something with my hands, but Cash's voice stopped me.

"Talk to me, Beauty Queen," he demanded hoarsely.

I drew my brows together and took a sip of water. I was unsure if I should be offended by his nickname for me or proud of it.

The water helped calm me. I put my glass down and picked up my fork.

"What do you want to talk about?" I asked, stabbing a bite of veal but wishing I could stab some sense into me.

Cash cleared his throat. "How about we talk about what we did in the bathroom."

I stuck the cold veal in my mouth and chewed slowly, afraid of facing the truth. The best way to deal with that was to lie.

"How about we don't because it was nothing," I whipped back, staring at him and covering up my fear with attitude.

His eyes flared. I saw that muscle tick in his jaw again and knew I hit a nerve. Good.

I stabbed another piece of veal and smiled around the bite. But once again Cash was full of surprises.

He turned cold gray eyes on me, the muscle in his jaw clenching harder.

"You're right," he said, his voice hard and menacing. "It *was* nothing."

Shock vibrated through my body. Yeah, I had no right to be surprised – I did say it first - but I was the one that was supposed to be aloof and caustic. Not him. I lured men. I used them. Not the other way around.

Cash met my eyes, the coldness in his challenging. His body was coiled tight. I watched as he angrily grabbed his glass of water and took a long drink, looking like he was trying to calm himself down. When he swallowed, it caused the tendons in his strong throat to flex. It was hot as fuck, but not as hot as what he did next.

Composed, he set his glass down and looked at me. I fidgeted in my seat, refusing to meet his eyes, but he grasped my chin, forcing me to look at him.

His eyes dropped down to my mouth and he whispered words that would stay with me forever.

"It was the *best* nothing I've ever had, Catarina."

Then he kissed me again.

Chapter Ten

-Cash-

I was madder than hell but satisfied like never before. We had fucked. Screwed. Damn, it had been amazing. The best moments of my life.

Cat's mouth had sent me over the edge. She had smarted off, telling me I didn't belong at that snotty restaurant or with her. I had lost my freaking hold on sanity when I saw her get up and leave. I was always so calm but tangling with Cat had left me with some claw marks.

I had followed her to the bathroom like a mad man. I stood between her legs like a crazy person, getting what I wanted. The sex was dirty, no-holds-barred. I had fucked her right there. If we were kicked out of the place, so what? I damn well had to have her.

We finished the rest of our meal in silence. I tried to make small talk. Ease some of the tension. I told her about my sister, Keely, who was going to the same college as she was. For the most part, the conversation stayed neutral, carefully staying clear of anything too personal. We were both skirting around the inevitable, the reality of what we had done.

When the waiter delivered the bill, I didn't even flinch when I saw it. I pulled out a credit card and slid it onto the little silver plate. I would make payments on it later.

Cat opened her mouth to argue but I glared at her. Pissed at myself for fucking her on a first date. Angry that I wanted to do it again. And insulted that she thought I would let a lady pay.

"Don't even try, Cat," I said, scowling when she attempted to grab my credit card.

She frowned. God, she was stunning even with her full lips turned down.

"But it's a lot, Cash, and I know you—"

I cut her off. "I pay. Period."

She relented and I felt a surge of satisfaction. I had a feeling she didn't let many men call the shots so easily. I wasn't one to boss women around but something about her submitting to me caused my dick to jump to attention.

Outside the restaurant, the air was heavy and humid. We waited silently as the valet brought my truck around. Cat stood close by me, making it real hard not to touch her. I grew antsy. I was ready to get out of there. Expensive dinners that looked like damn art and uppity people who stared at me too much weren't my thing.

Being alone with Cat suddenly was.

In minutes we were in the truck and back on the freeway, heading home. Again we didn't talk. What was there to say? *Oh, thanks for letting me fuck you back there. I really enjoyed it. Wanna do it again?*

I tightened my hands around the steering wheel, growing irritable. *Since when did I lock girls in restrooms and have sex with them? Demand that I belonged between their legs? Had I lost my mind?*

I ran a hand through my hair, frustrated. I was screwed beyond hope. Resisting Cat was impossible, but I wasn't sure what I was doing with her. She was spoiled, wild, and a little too self-absorbed for my taste. In the short amount of time I had known her, she had irritated the hell out of me and drove me to do things I wouldn't normally say or do. I wanted to strangle her one moment and find out what made her tick the next. It was a problem but I damn sure wasn't looking for a solution.

I glanced over at her, just needing to look my fill again. The lights from oncoming traffic played across her face. She looked like an angel but I wanted to love her like the devil even if it meant damning my own soul.

"Let's go somewhere else," I said suddenly, breaking the silence. Where the hell that had come from, I didn't know. I just wasn't ready to take her home yet. Something was telling me when I finally did, it would be the last I would see of her. I wasn't ready for that yet.

"Where do you want to go?" she asked, her full lips lifting in a sensual smile that made my dick ache to slide along them.

"Well, you took me to your neck of the woods, let me take you to mine."

~~~~

The trees were just blurs as we flew down the road. We were back where no traffic jams occurred (unless you count the local church letting out on Sunday) and the most exciting thing that happened was the high school winning a football game every now and then. There were no waiters in tuxedos and the only fancy meal you could get was a fried chicken basket from the local diner.

It wasn't the big city but it was home.

The wind whipped through the open window, hitting me like a tornado as shadows zipped by on both sides of the truck. Empty pastures and barbed wire fences were nothing but streaks as we flew down the dirt road. You could take your fancy restaurant and shove it. There wasn't anything quite like driving down an old dusty road with a drop-dead gorgeous girl beside me.

In minutes a large lake appeared in front of us. It was Turner's Lake. Local swimming hole in the summer and the perfect fishing spot year round. It was also a secret place for kids to party, despite the county's best intentions to keep them out.

Tonight the lake water sparkled under the moonlight. The place was packed. Parked cars and trucks were strewn all over the open field. The tall grass had been crushed by feet and tires. Someone had started a bonfire near the lake's edge and a large group had gathered around it, most of them holding beer bottles and red plastic cups. Loud music played from somewhere, sounding suspiciously like country music.

I slowed the truck down, passing cars and jacked-up pickup trucks. Finally I found a place to park and eased into the spot.

The sounds of laughter and music drifted inside the truck. I shut off the engine and glanced at Cat. She was staring at me, a closed off look in her eyes. I wanted to reach across and touch her, run my thumb over her lower lip. Instead I stayed in my seat and put my cowboy hat on my head.

"This okay?" I asked, nodding at the bonfire.

Her gaze darted to it then back at me. "Yeah. Your neck of the woods isn't too bad."

I gave her a lopsided grin. "Well, sweetheart, I don't really care where we're at. A fancy restaurant or the middle of nowhere. It doesn't matter if you're with me."

Before she could respond, I opened the door and got out.

I had done some crazy, insane things in my life – riding bulls, going toe to toe with rattlesnakes – but admitting that to Cat might just be the craziest one.

~~~~

Tall weeds whacked at my jeans as I followed her across the field. The moon was full, like a giant bulb in the sky. It gave me just enough light to see the crowd milling around. They were doing what twentysomethings did in the country – hang out and drink.

A few of them glanced at Cat and me, checking out the newcomers. I didn't give them much thought as we headed to the bonfire, the large flames drawing us like moths.

"Cat!" some girl screeched when she saw us. She started running toward us, her perfect blonde hair flying behind her. I recognized her as soon as she got closer. It was the girl from the bar. Cat's friend.

As soon as she reached Cat, she threw her arms around her neck and squealed with delight.

"What are you doing here? I didn't know you were coming! Junior is here so hush-hush about the other night. Come on, you have to meet someone," the girl said, talking a hundred miles a minute.

Cat gave me a quick look over her shoulder as the girl pulled her away. The little dress she wore swooshed from side to side, tempting every man present. I saw a few of them watch her, eyeing her ass. If she noticed, she didn't show it. She followed her friend to a truck parked a few yards away, those legs of hers taking away what I had experienced and craved again.

I wanted to run after her like a dog with his tongue hanging out, desperate to be petted. Instead I joined the other guys around the bonfire, silently cussing the heat, the humidity, and damned near everything else in frustration. I couldn't keep my hands off Cat. I didn't see her as long term but right now short term was looking better and better.

Some of the guys I knew from high school were standing around the fire, drinking beer. One of them handed me a longneck, lukewarm but wet. I popped the top and took a long sip, needing it after the night I had.

"I tell you if they go to war, I'm signing up," some good-ol'-boy said on my right, spitting a wad of tobacco into the fire.

I listened to their conversation with vague interest and watched as the flames spit and sputtered, reaching high into the sky. There was still talk on the news that things were tense in the world. Military was on standby. There had been some small skirmishes involving U.S. soldiers around the world. Relations with other countries were strained. Things did not look good. But when had they ever?

"They got to draft my ass," some guy said on my left. "I ain't dying for nobody."

"You'd die to get your dick in Tessa's twat," some other fella teased, howling with laugher at his own joke.

"True dat," the first guy said, lifting his beer in a silent toast before taking a drink.

I half listened to them, taking another pull on my drink and waving off a mosquito buzzing around. A few yards away a bunch of girls laughed, Cat being one of them.

"What about you?" someone asked me from across the fire, jerking his chin my direction and swaying slightly on his feet. "You ready to fight?"

I lowered the longneck and held it between my finger and thumb, tapping it against my leg as I watched him warily. I had noticed him when I first walked up. He was drunk and mean looking. About my age but twice my size. That was saying a lot since I was tall and lean, all muscle and no fat, thanks to hours working outside with my bare hands.

"Well, I reckon if I've got to fight, I'll fight," I replied, a simple answer to a simple question. My dad had taught me to be afraid of nothing, including guys like this one. He also taught me to survive, to do what had to be done in order to keep those I loved safe. If that meant going to war, I would go to war. Gun in my hand. Pride on my shoulders. No fear in my heart.

The drunk guy across the fire squinted at me. "You come here with Cat?" he asked, belching halfway through the question.

The hair on the back of my neck stood up, protectiveness rising in me. "Yep," I answered, watching him carefully across the bonfire.

"You dating her?" he asked. His voice had an edge to it that spelled trouble.

I felt every muscle in my body tense, something akin to anger igniting in me. I pushed the brim of my cowboy hat back with the mouth of my longneck, keeping my face neutral.

"Guess you could say that," I drawled.

The guy puffed up like a damned porcupine. "You know that's my ex-girlfriend? The one you're fucking."

I sighed. I wasn't one for throwing punches but, hell, I felt one coming on.

"Really? Sorry about that man," I said, keeping my voice calm. Void of any possessiveness I felt. "No hard feelings."

The guy rolled his shoulders, almost crushing the red cup in his hand.

"Yeah, no hard feelings." He forced the words out

between clamped teeth, making the veins stick out in his neck.

I nodded and took another drink of my beer, watching him closely. He stared at me, his fist clenching and unclenching at his side. He looked like a big bull, full of meanness and waiting to attack. I had seen one go on a killing spree once, fire in its eyes and deadly precision in its horns. This guy was that bull, out for blood. I just happened to show up with something he still considered his.

And like me, I had a feeling he would kill for it.

No one spoke. The other guys watched us, waiting for something to happen. Someone tossed an empty beer can in the fire, grumbling about needing to take a leak. Another guy picked up a good-sized tree limb and threw it on the fire, sending sparks up into the sky.

I just stood there, nursing my drink, trying not to think of Cat with the guy across from me. Outwardly I appeared calm. Cool. Inside I was on edge. Fuming. Ready to strike.

And I didn't have to wait long.

I finished my drink and decided to head for where Cat had disappeared. That's when it happened.

I was only a few feet from the bonfire when the air seemed to change. A sense of warning crackled in it. I felt the hair rise on the back of my neck. I started to turn, ready to go on the attack, but something solid slammed into my back. The force took me to the ground, knocking the air from my lungs and taking me down hard.

Smack!

My chin hit the dirt, scraping the skin raw. My cowboy hat went flying. Shouts broke out around me, the only sounds I could hear.

A punch landed in my back, right above my kidneys. *Shiiit!* I wanted to howl with pain. Instead I fought like a rabid dog cornered in a cage.

I rolled over with my fists swinging. Each punch was calculated, precise. I buried my knuckles in the big guy's gut and then in his chin as he kneeled above me. Cat's ex grunted and swayed, but stayed locked in place.

"Little shit, fucking with my girl," he snarled with a drunken slur, raising his arm high. "I'm gonna leave you crying for your mama and take that sweet little ass of hers home with me."

He swung and caught me in the nose. My head snapped to the side, sending pain shooting through my neck and blood spurting from my nostrils, but it didn't stop me. I got in a good punch to his throat. Damn, the guy's neck was even solid muscle. He recovered quickly, drawing his arm back and swinging.

I was faster this time. Getting to my feet, I clipped his chin, putting power behind it. My knuckles hurt like hell but the punch knocked the big guy's head back and probably loosened some of his teeth.

I wasn't finished yet. I buried my other fist in the side of his jaw, snapping his head to the left. His eyes rolled back in his skull and he swayed a second but didn't go anywhere. Shit, the guy was a tank.

I swung again. Sure, I had a five-inch knife hidden in my boot, but I didn't need it. All I needed was a little more power and some muscle. The alcohol the asshole had consumed would do the rest.

This time my punch worked. The hit to his solar plexus was all it took to take him down. The guy fell to the ground with a grunt, flattening the weeds and grass beneath him. A few grasshoppers hopped out of the way, almost losing their lives under his big body.

I was breathing hard and still itching to fight, but I forced myself to calm down. My hat was still on the ground a foot or so away. I bent over and grabbed it, noticing for the first time that we had an audience. The onlookers stood around, sipping their drinks and watching the show.

I smacked my cowboy hat against my leg a few times to get the dirt off before sticking it on my head. Sweat dripped down my face along with some blood. I wiped both away. It wasn't the first time I had bled at a party.

"Shit, man. Take him out, why don't ya?" some guy said on my right before taking a drink of his beer.

I didn't bother responding. The peckerheads could kiss my ass.

I returned my attention back to the guy on the ground. I stood over him, my boots inches from his ribs. Sniffing back a drop of blood, I glanced around then squatted down by him. The guy was groaning, rubbing his belly like he had the mother of all bellyaches.

"You okay?" I asked, my voice hard but calm. My gaze stayed on the onlookers but my words were spoken low, only for him. I wanted to beat him to a pulp just knowing that his big, beefy hands had been on Cat, but I fought fair and square, treating my enemies with respect.

"Screw you!" he hissed, spittle coming out of his mouth as he held his stomach. "Motherfucker!"

I nodded and reached out, patting him on the chest. "You're good." I started to get up but stopped. Leaning toward him, I added one more thing. "By the way - stay the *fuck* away from Cat."

Before he could say anything, I rose to my feet and pulled the brim of my hat down low. I turned to walk away, knowing the guy wouldn't try anything again, but a voice that had cried out in orgasm while I fucked her on a bathroom counter stopped me.

"What the hell are you doing, Cash?"

I glanced over my shoulder. The moon was bright enough for me to see Cat push her way through the onlookers. She stopped inside the circle, frowning but still looking gorgeous doing it. Crossing her arms over her chest, she glanced down at her ex, now being helped to his feet by a friend. Her gaze shot to mine, running over the blood dripping from my nose and my bruised face. Her eyes filled with something I didn't expect.

Worry.

I watched as she raced toward me, determination on her face. *Oh, hell.* I hadn't been afraid of her ex but shit, I was afraid of her.

She grabbed my hand as she walked by, never slowing down or messing a step. Her strides were long and rushed as she led me to the truck. Her hand fit perfectly in mine, small and dainty in my large and rough one.

I knew at that moment that I would follow her anywhere.

At the tailgate Cat stopped. She let go of my hand and took a step closer. Her eyes roamed over my face under the moonlight.

"You're bleeding," she said with concern.

Not one to take things too seriously, I wiped my nose and looked down at the drop of blood on my hand.

"Yep," I said, trying my hardest to keep my gaze anywhere but on her lips.

Cat reached up and ran a finger along my chin. It was gentle, almost tender. Nothing like what I expected from her. It caught me off guard and made me weak in the knees, but a second later the girl I knew returned.

She grabbed the brim of my cowboy hat and pulled it off my head. Before I could react, she grasped the front of my shirt and yanked me to her. Her lips found mine. My heart found hers.

She wrapped a hand around my neck, dragging me closer. Her tongue started playing tag with mine. My hat still dangled in her hand but she could have the damned thing. I would give her everything I owned if she just kept on doing what she was doing with her mouth and tongue.

When she licked the corner of my mouth, I lost it. I grasped her upper arms and hauled her closer, kissing her with greed and harshness. I swept my tongue into her mouth and tightened my fingers on her, afraid either she would run or I would bolt. We were just that wrong for each other. She was a helluva long way from what I needed.

But she was what I had to have.

Cat drew my tongue deeper into her mouth, sucking on it. *Damn, the girl knew what she was doing.* I dropped my hands from her arms and grasped her waist instead, pulling her flush against me. I was probably holding her too tight but she wasn't complaining and I wasn't letting go. Never before had a girl drove me so damn crazy. And never before had I wanted to fuck a woman again so soon after the first time.

Cat must have read my mind because she tore her mouth from mine, breathing heavily.

"I think I need to be reminded where you belong," she mumbled, her green eyes vivid with need. "Show me again, cowboy. Teach me a lesson for forgetting."

I moved one hand down her waist to her inner thigh. "You are so goddamn bad. You think you can handle me again so soon?"

She bit her lower lip and peered up at me through her long, dark lashes, her face flushed under the moonlight. "Oh, yeah. Just promise me you won't be gentle."

My cock threatened to bust my zipper. Time to get serious.

"Princess, I'll do whatever the hell I want. But if you don't get in the damn truck, what I did to you in the restroom is going to look G-rated compared to what I'll do to you out here." My voice sounded hoarse and demanding. Nothing like myself.

"Promise?" she asked with a smile on her face.

Damn, I wanted in her.

With a teasing grin, she put my cowboy hat on her head and pulled the brim down low, tipping the hat at me like I had done so many times to her. I watched with a dry mouth as she turned and walked away.

God, she was sexy. She gave me a look over her shoulder that promised heaven in a hell of a bad way. I was unable to take my eyes off her body as she headed toward the passenger door. Her dress swung from side to side, the edge of it dangerously close to her ass.

I ran a hand over my jaw as I watched her, feeling another drop of blood ooze out of my nose. I could be lying on the ground with a bullet in side - drawing my last breath and about to meet my maker - and I would still stare at Cat in awe, amazed that a woman could look as perfect and desirable as her.

When she reached the passenger door, she turned and smiled again at me. Her lips were full and a deep rosy pink, the perfect shape and size for every man's wet dream and darkest desire.

And her eyes? They turned up at the corners just like a cat's, framed by long lashes that were the color of midnight. It was the look in them that rocked me to the core. It promised all kinds of things and none of them sweet or nice at all.

"You coming, cowboy, or you just gonna stand there and stare at me all night?" she asked, raising one finely arched eyebrow and smiling at me seductively.

I grinned. There she was again – the Cat I had come to know and expect. What the hell I was doing with her I didn't know. What the hell I expected, I had no idea. All I knew was that I couldn't keep my hands off her.

And I was tired of trying.

Chapter Eleven

-Cat-

My dad once said that if a man loved a woman, he would take a hit and get back up, willing to shed a little blood and lose a little pride for the woman he loved. I'm not sure my dad had ever done anything like that for a woman, but Cash had just done it for me. I knew he didn't love me and never would, but seeing him on the ground, with blood dripping down his nose, something melted in me.

I couldn't help but stare at him as he climbed into the driver's seat. His profile was all sharp angles and smooth planes. His jaw was sculptured. His jeans were dirty and grass stains marked his knees and thighs.

It made me squirm with need, remembering his legs between mine in the restroom. The roughness of jeans had rubbed the sensitive skin of my thighs, driving me nuts. I wanted to feel them again between my legs, moving against me as we made love.

I bit my lower lip, wondering what the hell I was doing, contemplating having sex with him again. Something told me one time with Cash was a fluke. Twice was trouble.

I reminded myself that he was just another roll in the hay. Another man to use to take away the pain. It was who I was. Who I had to be. I had managed to bury my emotions for a year now. I had used men that were sweet and men that were assholes. Men that were looking for love and men that didn't even want to know my name. Each and every time I walked away unscathed.

Unattached. Unattainable. And being with Cash would be no different. I would make sure of it.

Time to prove it.

As soon as he slammed the truck door closed I was in his lap, straddling him.

"Fuck waiting," I groaned. I lowered my head and kissed him, taking his mouth with desperation. His cowboy hat was still on my head, shadowing our faces from the outside world.

His body was hard under mine, feeding my desire for him. I deepened the kiss, craving more and wanting to prove my crazy racing heart meant nothing. He was just a guy and I was just a girl. We had chemistry and it was just a matter of experimentation. We fed each other's needs. Nothing else.

I urged his tongue into my mouth. I could taste blood from his cut lip and it just turned me on more. I moaned, wanting his hands on me. Needing his hands on me. But they stayed by his sides, resting on the seat.

· I ran my tongue over his split lip, reaching down for his hand.

"Touch me," I whispered against his mouth, placing his fingers on my hip.

Pleasure pulsed through me when his palm slid up my side to my ribs, spanning my entire side. His thumb rested right below my breast, left braless and bare under my dress.

"Where do you want me to touch you?" Cash asked, his voice rugged in the quiet of the truck. "Here?"

He made a slow pass across the bottom of my breast with the pad of his thumb.

I sucked in a breath. "That's good, but higher."

"Mmm. Yes, ma'am."

His thumb moved higher, gliding over my nipple. The sensation traveled through my body like a bolt of lightning through my veins, electrifying me.

"God, that feels good," I whispered, arching into him. "Do it again."

My words must have sent him over the edge. He reached up and yanked his hat from my head then threw it to the seat beside us. With roughness born out of need, he thrust a hand into my hair and yanked my head down.

But he didn't kiss me. His lips didn't touch mine. Instead his gray eyes stared at me with raw intensity.

He ran his thumb over my nipple again, slow and sensual, taking his time. I shuddered, every nerve ending in my body going haywire. Every ounce of me hungry for more.

I tightened my legs around him, a reflex I couldn't stop even if I tried. The muscles in his legs were hard and powerful against me. My dress rose higher, the silky material too abrasive against my overheated, sensitive skin. I wanted it off *now*. I couldn't take it anymore.

I grabbed a handful of his hair and kissed him again, unable to resist. My body fit against his too well and my heart thundered in my chest too fast to not take what I wanted.

I wanted to scream with frustration and tear him apart with anger when his thumb stopped traveling over my nipple. But then he cupped my breast. Oh, god. He didn't just cup it. He owned it. It drove me crazy and left me senseless, aching for more.

I moved higher up his body, wanting to get closer. Wanting to feel the hardness under his zipper. Wanting him to give my neglected breasts some much deserved attention.

"Not here," he whispered against my mouth, his hand squeezing my breast gently.

I sucked in a breath as his thumb made another pass over my nipple.

"Then where?" I asked around a moan as heat flared in me. "I'm about ready to fuckin' implode."

Cash chuckled and dropped his hands to my thigh. "Such a dirty mouth for such a beautiful girl," he said in a husky voice, sliding his fingers under the edge of my dress. "What else can it do?"

I drew a sharp breath. "Oh, all kinds of things. Why don't you take me somewhere and find out."

He let out an animalistic growl and captured my mouth again with frenzy. His lips were demanding as they forced mine apart. I grasped a handful of his shirt again and held on tight.

His hands slid from under my dress and grasped my hips firmly, holding me still when I tried to rock against him. I moaned with irritation and tried it again. He clenched me harder and tore his mouth from mine.

"Let's get out of here," he said in a strained voice, lifting me off him like I weighed nothing.

I plopped down next to him, surprised. There was no pride or satisfaction or a crap load of arrogance in his eyes like most guys had when they knew they were going to get some from me. There was only calmness and that did something significant to me.

He shifted his gaze away and started the truck. The engine rumbled and my body vibrated. I was flushed and warm and just wanted to get alone with him.

He threw the truck into reverse and backed out of the parking spot, spinning the tires just a little. The silence between us hummed with eagerness. Anticipation made me squirm in my seat.

I glanced at him out of the corner of my eye. His wrist rested on the top of the steering wheel casually as he maneuvered the pickup through the maze of parked vehicles. The muscles in his arm were all angles and rugged ridges, sinew and strength in every line. I wanted to reach out and touch them, feel the power under my fingertips. But I resisted for now.

He caught me staring and turned to look at me. There was craving in his eyes. Pure unleashed hunger. His jaw tightened. Sexual energy arched between us.

He focused back on driving and I refocused on breathing normally. In seconds we were barreling down an old country road, leading us further away from the bonfire but keeping us near the lake's edge.

The woods became thicker, the country road narrower. Just when I thought we would drive forever Cash turned the wheel. The truck's headlights flashed across the lake, visible through the trees. He stopped the truck and cut off the engine, plunging us into darkness.

Cash reached for me but I beat him to it, straddling his lap in seconds. My lips met his with desperation, hurried and frantic.

He thrust his fingers into my hair and held on to me tightly. His teeth clashed against mine, bruising my lips and making me whimper.

"Sorry," he whispered, softening the kiss and loosening his hand from my hair.

"Don't be gentle," I said breathlessly. "Take me, cowboy."

My words sent him over the edge. He groaned and fisted my hair painfully. His tongue slipped past my lips and into my mouth, ravaging me. It drove me mad. I was at his mercy, his to conquer and control. It's what I wanted and he demanded to get.

I kicked off my heels and wiggled in his lap, hating his jeans. They hid what I wanted under them. I hated my dress also. It kept my slick wetness away from him. I hated clothes period. They should be outlawed around him.

I reached for his belt buckle. "Take it off," I demanded, tugging at the piece of metal.

"No," he whispered against my mouth, his fingers digging into my hips.

I moaned, frustrated. "Why the fuck not? We're alone. We're horny. Let's do this," I whined, my lips brushing against his. "I want you in me. I think I'm addicted to it."

Cash tightened his fingers on my hips. "I fucked you in a fancy restaurant, Cat, but now I want to fuck you under the stars. That's more my style, sweetheart. You had yours and now it's my turn to have mine."

I wiggled against the hardness under his jeans. "I don't give a damn where we do it—"

"But I do, Catarina."

He let go of my hip and opened the driver's side door. I looked out into the darkness, seeing nothing but woods and the distance glow of the bonfire through the trees.

Before I could ask what he had planned, Cash lifted me out of his lap and sat me down in the seat next to him. He got out of the truck but then stopped. His gaze ran over me, stopping at the hem of my dress. It was riding high on my thighs.

Feeling naughty and impatient, I reached down and pulled the dress higher and higher, not stopping until the edge of my panties were showing. As soon as they were, I ran my hand down between my thighs, tempting him. Men didn't call me a tease for nothing.

Cash's eyes burned. "I don't think so, sweetheart."

His hand snapped out and grabbed my ankle, yanking me toward him. I squealed in surprise as he dragged me across the seat, the leather hot against my naked thighs. As soon as I was near the edge, Cash hooked a finger in the waistband of my panties and yanked them down.

I gasped but he didn't stop until the little stitch of lace was off of me. He flung it to the floorboard next to my heels. With a growl, he stepped between my legs and buried his hand in my hair, dragging my mouth to his.

Every nerve ending in my body quavered and quaked as his lips dominated mine. His tongue thrust inside to prove just who called the shots and who was in charge.

"More," I rasped, reaching for his belt buckle. "Give me more."

His fingers tightened in my hair, pulling my head back.

"I knew you were spoiled," he hissed, lowering his mouth to my neck.

His hand delved between my legs but the only thing I got was frustration. His fingers stayed on my thigh, denying me what I wanted but driving me senseless anyway.

My neck was arched and he took advantage of it. He kissed the sensitive skin, alternating between licking and biting my neck. I thought I would die a slow, painful death, waiting for him to do something with his fingers, but he just kept them inches away from my wetness.

"Cash, touch me dammit," I demanded, wrapping my arm around his neck and drawing him closer.

His mouth left my neck and traveled up over my jaw to my lips again.

"Little Beauty Queen's begging? Why do I think this is a first?" he whispered against my mouth, his fingers oh so close to my opening.

"Damn you," I said breathlessly, unable to control my breathing.

Cash chuckled, low and throaty. "Sweetheart, I was damned the moment you walked in that bar."

I snapped my eyes open, ready to raise hell, but he wasn't going to let me argue. He took my mouth with violent need, ravishing it. Any thoughts of being angry disappeared as he kissed and sucked at my lower lip, sending spikes of desire through me.

He moved his hand down to the back of my knee. His fingers caressed the sensitive skin there, sending a tremor over me. I was lost in the feeling when suddenly he grasped the underside of my knee and lifted my leg, parting me even more.

Please, oh, please fuck me. The words never left me but I tingled and burned, waiting for him to touch me. To fill my pussy with his fingers and then with his cock in me.

But he did neither. Instead he hooked my leg around his waist and then the other, sliding his hand along my outer thigh and bottom. With no effort at all, he lifted me out of the truck, his lips never leaving mine, my legs wrapped around his hips.

I squealed against his mouth and wrapped my arms around his neck. He chuckled, low and deep, and held me tight. With an arm around my waist, he reached down and pulled a blanket out from behind the driver's seat.

I threaded my fingers in his hair and swept my tongue over his bottom lip as he carried me to the rear of the truck. His jeans scratched my bare thighs and his belt buckle poked into my lower stomach. Each roll of his hips sent waves of pleasure through me.

At the rear of the truck, Cash popped open the tailgate and lowered it with one hand. Dropping the blanket on top, he eased me down.

"God, Cash, do I have to beg?" I asked on a hitched breath, tearing my mouth from his as his fingers eased under my dress again.

He laughed, a sound so deep and throaty that I shivered.

"I *would* like to see you on your knees, princess."

He didn't have to say more.

Chapter Twelve

-*Cat*-

I jumped off the tailgate and reached for his belt buckle, dropping to my knees in the grass at the same time. His hands buried in my hair, urging me on, as I got the buckle undone and pushed it out of the way. I licked my lips and reached inside.

But then he stopped me.

Cash grabbed my upper arms and jerked me to my feet. That's when the cowboy who had taken a bloody nose for me, that saved me in a drenching rain and screwed me in a public restroom, became a mad man.

He had me on the ground in seconds, the blanket somehow appearing under us. He was desperate and greedy. Oh so eager and crazy for more.

He gathered the edge of my dress in his fist and pushed it up my body until my breasts were bared. The night air made them pucker but it was Cash that made them ache. He cupped one in his hand, squeezing it gently.

"You're beautiful," he said, running his thumb over the rounded curve. "Perfect like I knew you would be."

It wasn't the first time I had heard a man say those words, but when Cash said them I felt special. Worshipped. Loved. It frightened me. I didn't need someone to care for me. What I needed was a good fucking.

"Stop talking, Cash," I demanded, playing the part of a horny, cold-hearted bitch so well. "I'm getting bored."

Cash grinned, clutching my breast possessively. "Well, can't have you getting bored now can we?"

"God, no," I said in a hushed whisper as he leaned over, his mouth going dangerously close to my nipple.

"What is it about you, Cat?" he whispered, his breath rushing over the rosy peak of my breast. "You're a little hellcat with sharp claws and a nasty mouth. I should run but God help me, I can't."

I didn't get a chance to respond. He lowered his head and took my nipple into his mouth.

I arched off the ground, sensations shooting through me. Cash sucked and nipped, twirling his hot tongue around my nipple. Again and again he did it, never giving me a moment's rest.

I whimpered, foreign sounds escaping past my lips. My body quivered. I wiggled and arched into his mouth, greedy for more. *Jesus, I've never...I've never had a guy's mouth do this to me.*

He drew my puckered tip into his mouth and bit it gently. I cried out, the orgasm coming on hard and fast. Unexpected sensations rocked my body, shattering me.

Cash didn't stop, even when I tugged at his hair, trying to pull him away. I couldn't take anymore. Surely, I would die.

But he just continued, taking my whole nipple into his mouth. It sent wave after wave of ecstasy through me. He teased and toyed until I was an exhausted mess.

Little mewling sounds escaped me. I was dying. Unable to take anymore. Cash had made me come with just his mouth.

I grabbed the sides of his face and tugged his head away from my breasts. He let go of my nipple with a pop and glanced up at me, a question in his eyes.

"You bored now?" he asked, a challenge in his voice.

I licked my lips, breathing out of control. "No, but I'm in trouble."

I fisted a handful of his hair and pushed his head back down, forcing him to give my other breast some much needed attention.

He obligated, closing his mouth around my entire areola. I gasped as he sucked then flicked his tongue over the tip. It fueled the fire in me again.

He ran his fingertips down along my stomach, sending shivers over my skin. He grazed my belly button in a leisure path, taking all the time in the world to touch me. It made my skin come alive, but what he did next made a sharp cry escape me.

He slid his fingers between my legs like they were finally finding their home. I closed my eyes and threw my head back as they glided over the sensitive, wet area of my pussy. His mouth left my breast and trailed up my neck. His fingers played with me, running over my opening and then to my clit. His tongue darted out to taste the skin of my neck, my jawline, and then my mouth.

When his tongue delved past my lips, his fingers plunged into me. *Finally.* My back came off the ground. A cry tore from me. He swallowed it with his mouth and worked his fingers in and out of me. It felt amazing.

I reached between us for his cock, shoving my hand in his boxer shorts and wrapping my hand around him. I needed him. God, I needed him so bad.

He hissed as I started moving my hand up and down on him. He was ready and I was wet. My dress was sticking to my skin with the heat, but I didn't want to waste precious seconds pulling it off. I wanted him in me instead.

I let go of him and shoved him to his back. He fell back with a grunt, his fingers leaving me. His gaze roamed over my body as I threw a leg over him, straddling his crotch. I rocked against him then leaned over, kissing him passionately.

Cash reached up, pushing my hair out of the way. He kept his hand on the back of my head, slanting his mouth across mine. I felt lost in his kiss, almost loved by his tenderness. It was a false feeling. A lie. The only thing that could ever exist between us - the only thing I could ever feel for him - was lust.

I reached down, grasping his cock. It was time to prove it was just about sex.

Cash tightened his fingers in my hair. "We need protection," he whispered.

I gasped in surprise when he flipped me onto my back. He was on his feet in seconds, striding to the truck quickly.

I watched, wide-eyed and lustfully, as he stalked away. His jeans were unbuckled and his shirt was untucked. He leaned inside the cab of the truck, the solid muscles in his back flexing with the movement. A second later he was striding back to me, his eyes a piercing gray as they stared at me on the blanket.

He dropped down beside me, his gaze running over my exposed body. I watched, almost salivating, as he grasped his dick in one fist and rolled the condom down on it with the other. His large fist around his long, thick cock was the hottest thing I had ever seen.

With the condom in place, he turned to me. He leaned over me, pulling me close and touching his lips to my stomach. A tremble shook me as he ran his tongue slowly and leisurely across my skin, marking me with his mouth. The coarse stubble on his chin burned me as he kissed a lazy path down my body, taking his time. Memorizing every inch of me.

But when his mouth grazed my hip, I froze.

"What's this?" he asked, running a finger over the tattoo on my hip.

I stopped breathing. I knew what he was looking at, what he had found and the full moon gave him enough light to see. A heart tattooed right on my pelvis and below it a teardrop with Luke's initials.

"It's a tattoo," I whispered, afraid to look at him. Afraid to see his mouth so close to the heartbreak inked on my skin.

"I know it's a tattoo, princess," Cash growled playfully, leaning down to bite at the heart.

I jerked away. The tattoo represented death and loss. Heartache and pain. It reminded me every day not to love or care or give a damn. Cash touching it threatened to break me.

He eased off me but ran his fingers over the heart again.

"Why the tear?" he asked in a whisper, watching his thumb make a slow track across the tattoo.

I stared up at the midnight sky, not wanting to answer.

"Cat?"

I drew in a breath. "It means my heart's crying."

Cash went still. I could feel his palm flat against my hip. Warm. Possessive. Tender.

"Why is your heart crying? For L.C.?" he asked, touching the initials branded into my skin.

I flinched. "Yes," I answered, my throat thick. "And that's why the heart's black. Because it's dying for L.C."

Cash lowered his head, not bothering with words. I didn't need them anyway. I knew from experience that they couldn't heal me or make me love again. Nothing could.

But I was about to find out that I was wrong.

Cash kissed the tattoo, right in the center of the heart.

"I'm sorry," he whispered, his breath warm on my skin. "But maybe I can make your heart come alive again."

He suddenly rolled over, taking me with him. My dress fell down around my thighs as I landed on top of him. He ran his hands down my sides to my waist, bunching the material up high on my body. With one push, he plunged into me.

I cried out but he kept a tight hold on my waist, stretching me with his cock. Making me whimper with his length and width.

"Stay still, sweetheart. I want to feel you clench me," he demanded, running a hand down my spine to cup my ass as he pulsated deep in me.

I nodded and bit my lip, fighting the urge to move.

He groaned with satisfaction and pulled me down, putting his mouth near my ear.

"Good. Now let's pretend, Cat," he said, his voice a deep rumble in my eardrum. "Right here, right now, you're mine and I'm the only one that can have you. Just once more."

"Yes," I said breathless, willing to agree to anything if he would just start moving in me.

Cash tightened his hold on my ass, keeping me still when I tried to roll my hips. His voice rasped in my ear again.

"Say it."

I swallowed past my dry throat, not sure I could utter a single word. He was so big in me, so encompassing. I was forever spoiled.

"Cat?" he said again, tightening his fingers on my bottom to get my attention. "Promise me."

"I promise," I whispered, out of my mind with need.

He tightened his fingers on me, holding me in place, as he withdrew slowly then plunged back into me.

I threw my head back. "Oh, god. Oh, god," I whispered as I moved on top of him.

He let me set the pace, a hard and fast one. I lost awareness of everything. The stars. The moon. The water lapping at the edge of the lake. All I knew was him and his cock filling me.

"Talk to me, Beauty Queen. Tell me what you need," he instructed, thrusting into me slower, drawing out the torture. "Do you want more?"

I breathed harder, trying to keep my wits as he slid out gradually, inch by torturous inch, only to ease back into me. It was delicious. It was heaven. It was hell in its meanest form.

"More? Cowboy, I want it all," I managed to say.

At my words, he wrapped an arm around my waist and flipped me over onto my back. I wrapped my legs around his hip and dug my nails into his back as he started pumping into me, hard and fast.

I reached up and brought his head down to mine.

"Make me forget, Cash," I whispered against his lips, the words slipping out before I could stop them.

Cash plunged up into me and buried his fingers in my hair, holding my head steady as his mouth went to my ear. "I'll make you forget everyone, Cat. Everyone who's ever touched you before."

He started moving faster. With each thrust my breasts came close to his mouth. Finally he latched onto one. His tongue and teeth found my nipple.

And that's when I exploded.

The orgasm hit me. I went flying, rocketing out of control. I shouted a nonsensical word I can't even remember. It sent Cash coming right after me.

His mouth left my breast and moved to my neck as he jerked, trembling and riding out his own release. His lips moved against my skin, murmuring words I couldn't hear, as he shuddered then stilled deep inside me.

We stayed that way forever, my body still clenching him tightly. He was breathing hard, holding his weight off of me. Our eyes locked. I let my guard down and let myself feel for a minute. Just one.

Then reality intruded.

The wind shifted and sounds of the bonfire party drifted our way, reminding me of another night. Another party.

Another boy who had made me cry out with need.

It was a slap in the face. A shock to my system.

I blinked, my body going stiff. *What had I done? What the hell had I just done?* Yes, I fucked around but being with Cash was different. I couldn't put my finger on why but it just was and that scared the hell out of me.

I pushed Cash off me, crawling out from under him. I couldn't get away fast enough. He represented all I hated. Love. Tenderness. Caring. It was all a load of shit and for one moment in time I had let myself consider rolling around in it.

I was such a fool.

I crawled away from him, pulling my dress down at the same time. Cash reached for my ankle, his warm fingers sliding around the fragile bone.

"You okay?" he asked, his voice hushed in the night.

I resisted the urge to kick his hand away.

"I'm fine," I said in a clipped tone, averting my gaze from his.

"You don't seem fine," Cash said, running his thumb gently over my ankle. "Did I hurt you?"

I scoffed. "Nobody can hurt me, cowboy."

Piercing gray eyes stared back at me, looking so deep in my soul that I wanted to crawl into the lake and swim away. He looked too good. Too *real*. His hair was messy and he had dried blood on his face. His lean, athletic body was relaxed, his sleek muscles at ease. He was gorgeous and I could almost picture myself falling for him.

But then I remembered Luke.

I yanked my ankle away from Cash and climbed to my feet. *I can't do this.*

With angry strides I headed for his truck. Grasshoppers hopped out of my way and grass poked through my toes. I heard Cash buckle his belt and arrange his clothes. I didn't care if he followed me or not. I would walk the fuck home if I had to.

"So stupid. So goddamn stupid," I murmured, blinking hard and fighting tears.

"Cat. Hold up," Cash called out, jogging to catch up to me.

"Take me home, cowboy!" I called over my shoulder. My heart started beating quicker when I realized how fast he was gaining on me.

I lengthened my stride but it was too late. He reached out and grabbed my elbow.

"Don't touch me," I snapped, spinning around. The tears in my eyes betrayed the harshness of my words.

"Too late for that," Cash said, staring down at me with intensity, refusing to back off. "You want to tell me what's wrong?"

"Not really."

"Cat," Cash said, his grip on my elbow not going anywhere. "Talk or we'll have another go on that blanket."

I jerked my elbow out of his hold, glaring at him. "Are you threatening me?" I asked, my voice gaining strength. "Because if you are, you don't know who you're messing with, cowboy."

He gave a short nod. "Yeah I do. You're a spoiled, little rich girl that is used to getting her way. Now, tell me what's wrong."

I stuck my chin up. "Take me home," I insisted, spinning around and heading for the passenger side of the truck. "Now!"

Cash didn't respond and I didn't wait for him to. I yanked open the truck door and climbed inside.

A second later, he appeared at the driver's side. He stuffed the blanket back behind the seat with stiff, jerky movements. Without looking at me, he got in the truck and shoved the key in the ignition.

I ignored him and smoothed my dress down. I had to remember who he was. Another notch. Another fuck. Just another man in a line of them. It was the only way I could protect myself.

I took a deep breath. I was back to being me. Cold and cynical. A bitch in heels.

And like the gossips in this little hick town said - I did it well.

Chapter Thirteen

-Cash-

I ran my hand through my hair, annoyed.

When I walked into that swanky restaurant's restroom, I knew being with Cat would be a quick lay, plain and simple. I would get what I wanted and so would she. But I didn't count on a second time. Now I was questioning my decision.

I glanced over at her. She was staring straight ahead, her long dark hair cascading down her chest in messy waves. Her delicate jaw was set, the memory of kissing it almost sending me swerving off the road. She must have caught me staring because she stiffened and snapped her head around, glaring at me.

I alternated between watching the road and watching her, worried she would turn on me like a rabid animal. I had somehow managed to piss her off and I wasn't sure how.

Then I remembered the little black heart tattooed on her hip. Who was L.C. and why was her heart crying for him? I couldn't imagine a girl like Cat inking her body with a guy's initials but stranger things had happen.

Like me having her…twice.

I let out a breath of resignation. I either had made the worst mistake of my life or the best. I had a feeling with Cat the line between the two was gray and a little faded.

I reached for my cowboy hat, lying on the seat between us. I put it on and pulled the brim down low, a little trick I had for hiding my emotions.

Frustration made my foot heavy on the pedal. I floored the gas, aggravated. The truck revved, the exhaust loud in the night.

The awkward silence between Cat and me was about to drive me crazy. I reached over and turned up the radio. The sound of two broadcasters filled the truck, loud and clear in the night.

"U.S. authorities say the threat is real. Americans should be concerned. What do you say, Martin? You agree?"

A man – must be Martin - cleared his voice. *"Well, Gary, my contacts in the White House are concerned. They have ample evidence that our enemies are in possession of new, specialized weapons of mass destruction and are ready to use them. The intelligence reports are staggering and frankly, quite frightening. So yes, we should be worried."*

"Haven't we heard that before, Martin?" Gary asked, sounding bored. *"I mean, come on! Do these countries really have the power to take the United States down? And some people are asking if the talk of war is just another ploy by the President to help his reelection campaign. Your take?"*

Martin sighed. *"Gary, I wish it was only for political reasons but consider the following: We have Russia threatening us and our allies. They are being very vocal about their firepower. We have China meeting with foreign diplomats in secret, their patience with America spent. We have North Korea manufacturing weapons that worries our government. We have terrorists in the Middle East killing U.S. soldiers on a daily basis and increasing their violence toward us, including here at home. We have sleeper cells right here in the Unites States that are growing and becoming an entity we can't control. How can anyone ignore these facts? I can't. The White House can't. And the average American shouldn't either."*

Gary didn't respond right away. When he did his voice was dead serious. *"Will the President raise the threat level to red?"*

"I don't know, Gary." Martin said. *"But even if he doesn't the American people need to pray. We need to pray real hard."*

I reached over and turned off the radio. The last thing I wanted to listen to was chatter about a pending war. I had one building right here next to me.

I glanced over at Cat. "You gonna talk to me or you just gonna sit there and pout?"

Cat rolled her eyes and crossed her arms over her chest. "I'm not pouting, Cash. Get over yourself."

I grinned. I couldn't help it. "Looks like pouting to me," I said, eyeing her up and down before focusing back on the road. "But whatever it is, you look beautiful doing it."

Cat sighed. "Just take me home, Cash."

I wasn't going to argue. She wanted to go home? I'd take her home. I mean, who was I trying to kid? The reality was we went together like oil and water. Sure, we fucked like rabbits and hell yeah I would do it again and again with her, but it was more than that.

It was everything about her I wanted.

I wanted to learn her fears and dreams and what made her tick. I wanted to know her past and what she wanted in the future. I wanted to know everything there was, but I had a feeling Cat didn't let people in, especially a man like me.

We didn't talk the rest of the way to her house. The miles flew past us, the inky darkness growing deeper as the humidity and the heat lessened.

I pulled into her long driveway and cruised up the incline, stopping near the stone path that led to her front door.

Cat sat still, staring out the windshield when I glanced over at her. She made no move to open the door and get out. I wasn't sure if that was a good sign or a really bad one.

Time ticked by. One minute. Two. I didn't move, watching her under the shadows of my hat. She took a deep breath.

"His name was Luke."

I didn't need to be told what she was talking about. I remembered the initials tattooed on her body.

"You loved him," I stated simply, more a statement than a question.

She finally looked over at me, her eyes dark in the night. "Yeah, and that's the problem."

Without another word, she opened the passenger door and got out.

I watched her grab her little purse off the seat, her gaze lifting to touch on mine briefly. I recognized the pride and haughty attitude behind her green irises, but there was also hurt in there too. Lots of it.

She averted her eyes from me and turned. She didn't wait for me to get out of the truck. Instead, she walked away, heading down the path leading to her front door.

I took my time getting out. *I should just hit the road. Chalk this one up to a good lay and nothing else.* But my dick was leading me around like a puppet on a string. I couldn't shake the feeling that Cat was branded on my body and soul, just like that damned initial on her hip.

Shit, I was in over my head here.

I caught up to her halfway down the walkway. "Cat, wait—" I reached out to touch her arm, not ready for her to leave me yet.

She cut me off, whirling around to face me. "Let's get something straight, cowboy. We fucked. Twice. It was fun and exciting and hell yes, it was earth shattering, but that's it. There's no love. No handholding. No you and me and definitely no future or a third time. Got it?"

She had a fighter's stance, her feet separated, her body stiff. But me? I was relaxed, one hip cocked, my face hidden under my hat.

"You done?" I asked, my voice hard. She expected me to fight, argue with her, but I didn't. I had never begged a woman for anything and I wasn't about to start now.

She drew in a ragged breath and took a step closer. "Hell, no. I don't love, Cash, and I don't care. You're wasting your time with me so you better leave."

The thought of walking away from her made me mad. I grabbed her arms and had her up against the outside of the house in seconds.

A tiny moan escaped her when I pushed my body against hers. The sound sent satisfaction through me and need spiking in my blood. I was getting drunk on her closeness and stoned on her beauty. I knew she wasn't good for me, but sometimes what isn't good feels damn right.

I grasped her neck and pulled her toward me, wanting her mouth. Seeking what wasn't mine but had been for tonight.

Cat sucked in a breath and put a well-manicured hand on my chest, stopping me.

"What are you doing, Cash? I said there is no you and me."

I paused, lifting my gaze from her lips to her eyes. "Well, then" I whispered. "Consider this a goodbye."

I took her mouth, feeding my craving. I tasted her and wished to God I could have her again and again.

Her body was soft against mine, a temple I knew I shouldn't touch but I sure as hell wanted to worship. I curved my hand around her hip, holding her steady as I deepened the kiss, eager for more.

Her lips parted, letting me in. I didn't know if she did it on purpose or just as a natural response to a man's lips, but I was going to show her just how I felt.

I swept my tongue into her mouth. There may not be any '*her and me*' but until she walked away, she was mine.

She moaned against my lips. It was just what I wanted to hear. I tore my mouth from hers and tightened my fingers on the back of her neck.

"Luke was a lucky man, but I'm here now and he isn't," I said hoarsely.

Cat's body grew stiff. "Damn you, Cash," she said, her breath mixing with mine. "Damn you to hell for saying his name."

She wiggled out of my arms and shoved past me, knocking me back a step. Her strength was no match for mine since I was twice her size and about a hundred pounds heaver, but I didn't lift a hand to touch her.

At least until she got two steps away from me.

I reached out and grabbed her elbow, my jaw set against what I knew was coming.

Cat spun around, fire and ice mixing in her eyes.

"You'll never be Luke, Cash," she said, her voice sounding like silk but her words cutting into me like knives. "And I'll never be in love with you."

I met her toe to toe, unafraid, a little pissed, and raring to show her just who I really was under my cowboy hat.

"Well, ma'am," I said, my voice as cold as hers. "Tell me where Luke is now? Not here. Not having you twice in one night. That was me between your legs, Cat. Not him, sweetheart."

Cat opened her mouth then clamped it shut. Her eyes sparked hate and loathing and all things I imagined hell could come up with.

I ignored it all and leaned toward her, smirking and not even close to being done. "If you love him so much than why did you fuck me?"

She blinked, the anger vanishing from her eyes. That's when I noticed it. Her green irises were drowning in tears.

The fury left me in a whoosh. I felt like I had been gutted, my heart ripped from my body. Her pain had a sharp edge to it, digging into my bones and hollowing out my soul.

"Cat, listen, I'm sorry," I said, reaching out to touch her.

She jumped back, out of my reach. "Stay away from me. Just stay the hell away."

She turned and hurried away. I didn't try to stop her. I let her walk, knowing I would never see her again.

Chapter Fourteen

-Cat-

I shut the front door with a soft click. The shadows of the entryway surrounded me. The hum of nothingness greeted me. My chest felt tight and my lungs constricted. I couldn't breathe. Couldn't think. Couldn't feel anything but pain.

Cash had said Luke's name.

I slumped against the massive oak door and let my purse drop to the floor. *What have I done? I let myself feel something.*

I slid down to the floor, the door at my back. Tears were in my eyes but I refused to let one fall. Only the weak cried and I had proved I wasn't one of the weak.

Or was I?

I could still smell the scent of grass in my hair and taste the lasting effects of Cash on my lips. I could still feel the rawness between my legs, the ache of having him in me not once but twice. He had pushed past my barriers. Past the wall that kept memories of Luke in and everyone else out.

And I had let him.

A single tear made a slow streak down my cheek, warm against my skin. My vision became blurry. I blinked and another tear fell.

I loved Luke. I always had and I always would. He had been everything to me. My best friend and my better half. We had been young but we had been in love.

At least until he died because of me.

I stared into space, trying to remember what it had been like to lie in his arms, to feel his body against mine. The image was fuzzy, replaced instead with Cash.

I drew in a shaky breath. I couldn't fall for someone, never again. Luke was dead, buried in a cold, dark grave. Putting him there had almost killed me.

I swore I would never leave myself open to hurt or love again and here I was, tempted by one but in the grips of another.

I angrily wiped the tears off my face, hating them. I was the daughter of the most influential businessman in Texas and my mother was the queen bitch. I was cold and calculating. I *used* men, for god's sake. I shouldn't feel something for some random cowboy I met in a honkytonk a few days ago.

But I did and that's what worried me.

My phone vibrated in my purse, interrupting my pity party. I wanted to ignore it, afraid it might be Cash, but the little humming noise mocked me.

I grabbed my purse with aggravation and dug my phone out.

What were you doing with the guy from the bar?

The text was blurry thanks to my tears. I swiped them away and read it again. It was from Tessa. I was reluctant to answer but knew if I didn't she would be messaging me all night.

Don't feel like talking. Later.

I typed then hit send. A second later my phone vibrated again.

Tell.

Pain squeezed my heart as I typed three little words.

I miss him.

Tessa didn't respond right away. I held the phone tight, my fingers gripping the hard case painfully. I needed her to reply. I wanted someone to talk to. Someone to assure me that I would be okay.

The phone buzzed again.

I take it u fucked the cowboy?

The words hurt because I saw the underlining meaning. Tessa knew what I did in the name of grief.

I flung the phone in my purse, tired of Tessa's shit. I didn't need her telling me that Luke wouldn't want me living like this. I knew that. I lived with the knowledge every day. I didn't need Tessa telling me what I was doing was wrong. She just didn't understand. The alcohol...the parties...the men...they were my way to forget. My distraction from the pain.

My phone vibrated again but I paid no attention to it. Instead I pushed myself to my feet. My dress stuck to my body and my panties were a lost cause. I ached in all the right places and still throbbed deep inside from Cash's width and length. I just wanted to get to my room without being discovered by Tate or Nathan. I couldn't handle seeing the pity on their faces if they saw me or my tears.

I grabbed my purse and started down the hallway. I was careful not to make any sounds as I walked through the house.

The second floor was dark and empty when I got to it. I rushed to my room, yanking out my earrings as I went. As soon as I shut the bedroom door, I slipped off my heels, leaving them where they landed.

Next was my dress. I pulled it over my head and left it on top of a discarded pair of four hundred dollar jeans. I padded through my bedroom in nothing but my panties, heading for my private bathroom. I couldn't get there fast enough. I needed hot water to wash away the scent of Cash on me and the wetness left between my legs.

In the bathroom I turned the hot water on full blast. The room quickly filled with steam as I shoved my underwear down my legs and stepped out of them.

I tried not to think about how many times Cash had yanked them down. About how it felt when he ran his hands up my legs.

Scalding water made me hiss when I stepped in the shower, but I needed the prickles of pain it caused on my skin.

Closing my eyes, I turned my face to the spray. Needles of water hit me and took away the tears. But instead of helping me to forget, it brought back memories.

A rainy night. A car. A tree. And blood. Lots of blood.

Chapter Fifteen

-Cat-

*T*he house was little. Too small for the amount of kids in it and too old to withstand the loud music and spilled drinks of the party.

I was leaning against a faded, tattered couch, sucking down a wine cooler. My best friend, Jenna, stood beside me, checking out the guys and drinking herself silly. She was a judge's daughter, born with a silver spoon in her mouth just like me. Her mama was a real estate agent in Dallas, selling high rises and earning the big bucks to support her twenty-three year old pool boy who rocked her world.

Then rocked Jenna's on the weekends.

Jenna and I had recently graduated from private school in Dallas, top of our class in every way. She had come home with me for the weekend, both of us looking forward to parties and drinking with no rules or parents around. She was a city girl, through and through, but she was enjoying all the cowboys and ranchers' sons in town.

Speaking of a rancher's kid, my eyes caught a movement in the doorway. A tall, muscular guy walked in, his gaze going around the room with measured precision. I watched him and raised the wine cooler to my mouth to take another long drink.

He was good looking, built like a quarterback and confident in every way that counted. I knew that he had a badass tattoo on his shoulder and a scar on his hip. I knew that his favorite color was army green and his eyes were a bright, bright blue.

His gaze skipped around the room. I stayed still, waiting and watching for him to notice me. When he did, he smiled. It was the sexiest thing I had ever seen. I loved him. I might have loved him from the first moment I met him, back when we were thirteen.

He started toward me, at least a head taller than most of the people in the room. My vision faded for a second but I blinked and it cleared away. The effects of the wine cooler were hitting me harder than I thought they would on an empty stomach.

I didn't pay any attention to Jenna as Luke headed my way. If I could go back in time, I would slap the girl I had been. Tell her to put the drink down and pay attention to her best friend. It would be the last conversation they had together. The last moment Jenna made me laugh.

I pushed away from the couch and tried to blink away the spinning room. It wasn't working but Luke would save me. He always did. With him I felt loved and cared for, something I had never felt before unless you counted Nathan stepping in and taking care of me when I was younger.

Luke strolled over to me, his grin widening.

"Hey, babe," he said when he got closer. He ran his hand around my waist, pulling me into him. "Missed you."

"How much?" I asked, pressing my breasts into his chest and smiling dreamily, thanks to the number of drinks I had consumed.

Luke grinned and lowered his head, putting his mouth near my ear. "Let's get out of here and I'll show you."

I didn't waste any more time. I grabbed Jenna's hand. "Let's go."

She argued but I didn't want to hear it. Luke wanted sex and I desperately wanted him too. The party sucked anyway so I was doing Jenna a favor. I was just a good friend that way.

So we followed Luke out of the house. I kept my hand wrapped around Jenna's so she wouldn't escape. We had both been drinking, one of us forgetting to watch out for the other. But Luke hadn't had one beer. At least one of us was sober.

The crowd parted for him, making it a breeze to leave. Outside the ground was wet thanks to a storm that had just blown through and left.

We hurried and followed Luke across the mud-splattered yard, heading for the trucks and cars parked helter-skelter everywhere on the owner's lawn. Music from the house echoed behind us, enticing us to return.

I danced behind Luke, shaking my butt at Jenna then laughing when she started humping me.

Luke chuckled, stopping to wrap his arm around my waist and help me the rest of the way to his car. I somehow managed to put one foot in front of the other, keeping my eyes on his black Ford Mustang parked ahead. It looked dangerous and fast, sending a thrill of excitement through me.

He opened the passenger door and helped me inside. I fell into the seat. My skirt slid up my legs, exposing my panties. I giggled and Luke just grinned, his eyes dropping with hunger to my crotch.

The moment shattered when Jenna crawled into the back seat, making enough noise to wake the dead. I glanced over my shoulder at her, the world swaying as I did so.

She slid across the seat until she was sitting in the middle. She started gabbing about some cute boy at the party as Luke shut my door and jogged over to the driver's side. He dropped down into the seat and started the car. The roar of the engine drowned out the rest of Jenna's words. We hit the dirt road minutes later.

As we raced through the dark, I reached over and cranked the radio up. Jenna started singing along with the music but I had other things on my mind.

I looked over at Luke, catching his eye. He raised one eyebrow and watched me with interest as I slowly unbuttoned the top buttons on my dress until the edge of my bra was visible.

Jenna was too busy to notice. I was too drunk to care that I was distracting Luke.

He watched me, taking his eyes off the road for a long minute.

"God, I love you, Cat," he said.

I smiled, my drunk mind giddy with the power I held over him.

He glanced back at the road just in enough time to turn the wheel sharply and take a curve. I laughed and Jenna was still singing at the top of her lungs. I reached over and cranked the radio up even more, the drunk in me very happy. I had a good-looking boyfriend, more money than God, and parents that didn't care how late I stayed out or who I was with. Life couldn't get any better.

Feeling crazy happy, I rolled down my window. I wanted to feel the air in my hair. The wind grabbed strands of my dark locks, tangling it and yanking it this way and that. Still I wanted more. I had no bounds. I never had.

I unbuckled my seat belt and climbed to my knees. With a tight grasp on the doorframe, I stuck my upper body out the window. The alcohol in my system killed any fear I had. My common sense had been drowned in the bottom of numerous bottles.

The car swerved to the left, but my body swayed with it. I heard Jenna laugh and Luke shout my name but I didn't care. I was free. Free from parents that didn't give a damn. Free from society telling me I was a spoiled brat. I had one man who loved me and that's all I needed. All I would ever want.

The world flew by as we raced down the road. I hung out of the window more, letting the wind slap my hair around.

Luke tugged on my sweater, trying to get me back inside. I paid no attention to him and raised my hands above my head instead, imagining I was flying.

The Mustang swung to the left as a car passed us. I was thrown forward, my stomach hitting the side of the door. The road was a blur feet under me, dangerously close to my head. I screamed but the wind caught it and flung the sound away.

I clawed at the door, trying to get back inside, but the wind was sucking at me, working against my efforts. The only thing keeping me in the car was Luke grasping a handful of my sweater and hanging on tight.

Over the roar of the car, I heard him snap off his seat belt. He leaned further across the seat, one hand on the wheel and one on me. He shouted something then gave me a firm yank.

I fell across the seat, stars appearing in my vision. Luke's shouting blasted my eardrums. He called me fucking crazy. Asked if I was out of my fuckin' mind. I sat up and looked at him, surprised and shaken.

He punched the steering wheel, making me jump. Then he did it again, roaring at me, saying he wanted to wring my neck for scaring him.

I flinched with each punch of his fist, each shout of his voice. The alcohol in my bloodstream was now making me nauseous. Sick.

I could be stupid sometimes. Too wild and headstrong, my grandmother said. I could handle people saying that about me but I couldn't handle Luke being mad at me.

We continued flying down the road at high speeds. Luke pushed the car faster and faster in his frustration. He gritted his teeth and hit the steering wheel hard.

"I fucking love you!" he yelled. "LOVE YOU! And then you pull that shit! What if you died? Huh? How am I supposed to live without you, Cat? Tell me!"

I didn't answer, my throat too thick to respond. I had never seen Luke that way. A single tear rolled down my cheek.

"Shit!" he swore, gunning the gas. "I would fuckin' kill myself if you died, Cat! Kill myself! Do you get that? That's how seriously fucked up I am about you! I want to marry you, but I can't do that if you're fucking dead!"

My heart stopped. I heard Jenna gasp behind me. He wanted to marry me?

"I'm sorry, Luke," I cried, anguish tearing at me. "I'm so sorry!"

He took a deep breath, calming down. When he got himself under control, he glanced at me and said in a calm voice, "Put your seat belt on, babe."

They were the last words he said to me.

I clicked the seat belt into place and then looked up. That's when I saw it. Headlights.

A flatbed truck had swerved into our lane, coming at us head on. We were going too fast on the little two-lane road. The roads were too slick. The rain too recent.

Luke jerked the wheel but it was too late. We started sliding sideways. The Mustang's tires tried to grip the muddy road but failed. Suddenly, the back tires hit the embankment. It was like a powerful right hook to the car.

We started flipping, side over side. Metal screeched. The world turned upside down. It righted itself then did it again, flipping us over and over. We barrel-rolled down the road, our speed sending us flying.

I fell against the door, cracking my head. Jenna screamed and her body hit the back of my seat then the roof of the car. I felt the seat belt cut into my chest as I was slammed up and down, backwards and forwards. The belt bruised me but kept me locked in place when my body wanted to go elsewhere.

They say your life flashes before your eyes but mine didn't. I saw everything in slow motion. Every inch Luke moved. Every way his body flung. Every piece of glass that shattered and flew at me as the car rolled. I saw it all.

Even when the car crashed into the tree.

When I woke up the Mustang was sitting innocently on all four wheels, except it was wrapped around a massive tree.

I forced my eyes open. I must have blacked out. My head hung down, my hair falling into my lap. Something dripped down my nose, landing with a soft splat on my lap. I tried to lift my head, find out what it was, but pain shot through my neck, making me cry out with agony.

I tried again, something telling me I had to move. I needed to find Luke and Jenna.

It took a few tries but I finally lifted my head, moaning at the pain. I moved my arms gingerly, afraid I'd find one broken or a bone protruding.

My chest hurt. Breathing was painful and close to impossible. I pushed the air bag out of the way and reached down, unhooking the seat belt with my slippery, cold fingers.

When I was free, I glanced over at the driver's side, afraid of what I would find. It was folded in on itself. The roof was caved in, inches from my head.

I couldn't see Luke or hear Jenna. There were no moans, no gasps of pain. The silence scared me just as much as not being able to see them. Reaching down, I felt for the handle of the door, desperate to get out. Frantic to find them. It seemed to take all my strength but I finally opened the door.

It creaked, protesting. The outside of the car had been bent and smashed in, looking as thin and pliable as tin foil. I pushed the door open more and fell out, unable to stop my downward momentum.

Prickly weeds and little pieces of gravel embedded into the palms of my hands as I landed on the ground. I clenched my teeth against the pain and pushed my upper body up.

Wind whistled through the trees, disturbing a bird that sat watching me. I pulled myself to my feet, scared but determined. The world spun when I stood up but I managed to stay on my feet.

I used the car as a crutch, hobbling around the side. My knee hurt, feeling like I had the mother of all bruises, but I somehow made it to the road.

And that's when I screamed.

I dropped to the floor of the shower, shaking. The water had turned cold, hitting me like tiny pinpoints of ice. I was still in the shower but in my mind, I was still on that road.

Luke was lying on the center stripe, his body at a weird angle. His eyes were open, staring at the dark sky. Blood coated his head, clumps of it in his hair. I had rushed toward him, tripping over my own feet.

I stared down at my wrinkled fingers in the shower, remembering them cradling his head. I could still imagine the blood coating my hands. It had been warm and sticky. Something I could never wash from my memory.

The sobs that had wracked my body were more painful than the bruises and cuts I had received on my arms and face. I died in that moment. I held the only man I had ever loved, and died.

As blue and red lights flashed across my body, I had held Luke and cried. Jenna had been found yards from the wreck, her neck broken, killing her instantly.

Distraught, I had told the police everything. I didn't care if they hauled me away to jail; I was dead inside anyway.

After that, the rumor mill started. Apparently, one of the first responders shared details of what happened with a loved one, who later told the gossip vultures of the town. Before I knew it, everyone thought I was to blame for Luke and Jenna's death.

And I was.

That night my heart had gone cold, the last bit of feeling in me fading. I wanted to die. If I couldn't, then I swore never to love again. Never to feel again. Never to care. And it had worked.

Until Cash.

My body trembled, freezing from the cold water falling on me. I stared up at the showerhead, blinking against the water in my face.

The answer to my problem suddenly became crystal clear. I had to leave town. Get away from the memories. Get away from Cash.

I pushed myself to my feet, using the tile wall of the shower as leverage. My body shook from the cold and goose bumps broke out over my skin. I hurried and turned off the water. The quiet of the bathroom was disturbing. I needed the sounds of a party, the noises of a bar. I needed laughter and alcohol. Anything but solitude and my thoughts.

I grabbed a plush towel and rubbed myself dry, avoiding the fogged mirror over the sink. After wrapping the towel around me, I swung the bathroom door open, letting my long hair drip down my back.

I could hear the TV downstairs. Something loud was playing with the sounds of gunfire. I rushed into my room and grabbed the first thing I could find to wear – a pair of cut-off sweats with the word *"Sweet"* embroidered across the back. Next, I pulled a tight pink t-shirt over my head and flipped my wet hair down my back. I left my bedroom seconds later, hoping my eyes weren't too red from crying and my lips weren't too swollen from Cash's ravaging.

Even after my shower, my inner thighs felt sensitive, rubbed raw by Cash's body. I still throbbed for him. Need him. God, craved him.

I pushed the thought away as I went downstairs. I buried the feelings deep down under the ugly part of me. There would be another night and another man. There always was and there always would be. I just needed to get my head on straight.

I knew just how to do that.

I avoided the room with the sounds of gunfire erupting from the TV and headed for my dad's study. It was a place that once meant safety and security. Now it held what I needed.

The study was just as dark as the rest of the house. I bypassed the massive, cherry wood desk and headed straight for the place my dad kept his best liquor. I reached behind the mediocre stuff for the clear crystal bottle of vodka, twisting the top off as soon as it was in my hands.

"A lady doesn't drink spirits," my grandmother once said. *"She also doesn't spread her legs for every Tom, Dick, and Harry, Catarina."*

I scoffed. "Here's to you, old biddy."

I gave a silent toast to her memory before raising the three thousand dollar bottle of Russian vodka to my mouth.

The liquid hit my lips and sloshed down my throat. It was smooth going down - as a top dollar, collector's edition bottle of alcohol should be. Whether it came from a rich man's cabinet or a cheap dive bar, alcohol always brought the numbness I needed.

As I waited for it to do its magic, I dropped to my dad's leather chair. Somewhere outside a frog croaked. Inside the sound of the TV blared. But in my dad's study I was safe. Just me, my drink, my sore, used pussy, and my memories.

I slouched down in the chair and propped my feet on the desk, crossing one ankle over the other. *Time to get serious.* I lifted the bottle to my mouth and tilted it up, loving the beautiful sound of liquid sloshing around.

This time the alcohol burned, just enough to make me wince, but I took another drink then another. I wanted to get rip-roaring drunk on my dad's best stash of vodka.

After a few drinks, it still wasn't enough. I could still remember Cash's hands on me and his body claiming mine as if he had a right to.

"Fuck you, cowboy," I whispered, staring off into the darkness of the study. "I don't need you."

I took another long drag from the bottle, tipping my head back further. I drank until I couldn't anymore. Until the voices in my head screamed to stop.

Until Luke's face hovered in front of my eyes.

Pain hit my chest, squeezing the shit out of my heart. It made me gasp, inhaling too much of the filthy rich vodka. With watery eyes, I tore the bottle from my mouth and doubled over, wrapping my arms around my middle as anguish tore through me. I was back on that empty road, kneeling besides Luke's lifeless body again. Screaming for him to return to me.

My fist went to my chest, right over my heart. I hurt so much. So goddamn much. I cried, sobs that I couldn't stop. Wails that I couldn't contain.

I must have been making racket. I heard someone race down the hallway. I couldn't stop the grief that was escaping me in sobs and cries. Couldn't stop it even when the hallway light flipped on, lighting up the study like it was fuckin' Christmas.

A colorful swear word escaped Nathan when he saw me bent over in our dad's chair, drunk and trying to curl myself into a ball and disappear.

"Shit, Cat," he hissed, barging into the room. His long legs ate up the distance across the massive study. He didn't even glance at the vodka bottle I still grasped as he went around the desk.

"What happened? What the fuck did your date do?" he asked, dropping to his knees in front of me. His voice held a combination of fear and anger as he glanced over me, looking for evidence that I had been hurt.

Great, big sobs tore from me, ripping through every ounce of my soul. I hugged myself tighter, needing the physical pain that shot through me as it became harder to breathe. I didn't see Nathan in front of me. I only saw Luke's face and felt guilt for feeling something for Cash.

Nathan grabbed my arms, giving me a hard, rough shake when I didn't answer him.

"What the fuck, Cat? Did he hurt you?" he snapped, his fingers digging into me.

I didn't answer and Nathan became furious.

"Goddamn it! Answer me!" he roared, shaking me again only harder. "Did he hurt you?"

The pain from Nathan's hands finally woke me up and brought me back to harsh, cold reality.

I tore my arms from him, my eyes blazing spitfire. In seconds I went from a sobbing, pitiful girl to an utterly, outrageously mad woman.

I shot to my feet, going on the attack.

"Yes, he hurt me!" I shouted, facing Nathan as he stood up too. "He made me feel! He touched me and made me forget! I love Luke, Nathan! *Luke*! Not a damned cowboy I just met! I hate him! Hate him, hate him, hate him!"

I grabbed the vodka bottle from the desk and flung it across the room. The bottle smashed into the dark red wall and shattered. Clear liquid ran down it in rivers.

Tears of rage swam in front of my eyes. I slapped my hand over my mouth, cutting off a sob before it escaped me.

Nathan turned and stared at me like I had lost my mind.

"Are you finished?" he asked in a harsh voice, staring down at me with irritation.

"No," I said, shaking my head and making the tears fall faster. "I'll never be done. *You* just don't get it."

My gaze stayed locked on the vodka-soaked wall. My dad's prized artwork hung near it. His expensive decanters and bottles of alcohol teased me in my peripheral vision, whispering my name in the darkness. I didn't want to drink them; I just wanted to throw every single one of them against the wall.

Nathan sighed and ran a hand over his head, his anger vanishing. He stepped into my line of vision, forcing me to look up at him or stare at his chest.

I chose his chest.

"Cat, look at me."

I ignored him, something I had gotten good at doing.

Nathan sighed again and stuck his hands in his pockets.

"Fine, don't look at me. I'm still going to say it anyway. It's been one year since Luke died. One. You have every right to grieve but you're strong, Cat. Don't try to check out because of the pain. Luke would want you to be happy. He would want you to find someone to love. So do yourself a favor and let it happen."

Through my carefully downcast eyes, I caught a glimpse of the corner of his mouth lifting up.

"If you don't do it for yourself, then do it for the house and Dad's liquor collection," he said with a smirk.

His words broke through my fog of anguish. I took a much-needed deep breath. Nathan was right. Not about Luke wanting me to love someone. That would never happen. And not about the safety of Dad's precious bottles of overpriced booze. No.

Nathan was right about me being strong.

In order to stay that way I knew what I needed to do. My car was dead, but I had my brother.

I lifted my chin, meeting Nathan's eyes.

"Take me home, Nate."

He stared at me a minute then gave a short nod. "Okay. Tate and I will take you back."

I let out a deep breath. I would return to my college apartment. Somewhere safe. Somewhere no one knew my past. Where memories didn't haunt me and I could forget about a certain cowboy.

And how he made me feel.

Chapter Sixteen

-Cash-

The sun was blazing hot. The kind that went deep into your bones and burned you from the inside out. It had no sympathy, scorching me as I stood under it. Sweat rolled down my back, soaking my jeans and leaving wet streaks on my shirt.

Crows cawed in the tree above me. One flew high above, an inky black spot in the sky. Its wings were spread as it coasted on the air. It's beady little eyes looked down at me with malice, never letting me out of its sight.

I watched it. Like that bird, I was on edge. The muscles in my arms were tense, ready to spring into action. My breathing was measured, my chest rising and falling with minimal movement. I was focused. Controlled. A statue in nature.

But the calmness was a lie.

Inside fury boiled in me. The kind that simmered and festered until it became a problem.

My attention went from the crow to my target. I squinted against the blistering sun. The weight of metal in my palm was an extension of my body. A part of me. My gaze stayed on my mark, judging the distance and anticipating the strike. I became a part of my surroundings, a figure that blended in with the trees. But unlike nature, I wasn't perfect. I made mistakes.

Like Cat.

The anger burst free at the thought of her. I swung my arm, quick and sharp. The knife left my hand. It sliced through the air, end over end. The gleaming sun caught the blade as it spun toward the haystack set some fifty yards away.

I watched the knife with a tightly clenched jaw, welcoming the fury in me. I deserved it. I deserved every damn ounce of it for being such a fool.

Three days, I thought, flexing my fingers with barely controlled anger. For three days I hadn't heard from Cat. I had called, texted, and damned well stalked her but she had ignored all of it.

I had reminded myself that it was only a one-night stand. That I should forget her. I was wrong.

The knife embedded in the haystack at least a foot off center.

"Shit!" I swore. *I'm off my game.*

My strides were long and angry as I headed to the haystack. I had contemplated more than once getting into my truck and showing up on Cat's front porch. I would have but my friend Brody called, listened to me bitch, and then threatened to kick my ass if I drove to her house.

I stopped in front of the haystack and jerked the knife out with anger.

I shouldn't be thinking of her. I shouldn't care if she fell off the face of the earth and I never saw her pretty face again. She was nothing to me but a nice time.

Nothing else.

The knife was cold, heavy in my hand. I ran my index finger over the blade, trying to calm myself down. I knew the weight of a knife in my palm and the sounds of nature around me. Those were things I knew. Things I cared about. Not some black-haired devil of a girl. Not what she did to me or how I wanted to see her again.

Self-loathing made me swear. I rolled my shoulders, trying to loosen up, but that damn crow squawked at me again from high in a tree, mocking me.

I gritted my teeth, ignoring it, but I couldn't ignore the memory of Cat beneath me.

The thought made me furious. I spun around, flipping the knife and catching the point in my palm at the same time. Without missing a beat, I drew my arm back and threw the blade. It sailed through the air, this time with more power.

I watched as it hit the haystack dead center, buried deep in the middle. I let out a breath. My mind might be screwed with thoughts of Cat, but my aim was still good.

I started for the haystack again, feeling better. I was halfway there when suddenly I heard a noise behind me.

I stiffened, all my senses alert. Out in the woods, I was a sitting duck for panthers, trespassers, deadly snakes, and angry hogs. All of which could kill me. I had had my share of run-ins with most of them and I was still here, still standing. This time would be no different.

I spun around, my hands empty of a weapon but my muscles and strength my backup. A man was walking toward me, slow and unhurried in his gait.

My dad.

He didn't say anything at first, just kept his eyes on the ground. I relaxed as he headed my way, not surprised to see him. He had eyes like a hawk and a nose like a bloodhound. He could sense when something was wrong and something had been wrong with me since Cat.

My dad stopped a few feet from me and looked up at the clear, blue sky, ignoring me for the most part. I knew he would talk when he was ready. I just had to give him time.

He eyed the crows in the trees then glanced at the knife in the haystack. His faded eyes stayed on it a while as if he could read all the emotions that had put it there.

Finally, he pushed his sweat-stained Pete's Feed Store ball cap further back on his head and turned his attention to me.

"That hay do something to you?" he asked, motioning to the haystack. His voice sounded like gravel rolling around in a tin can, thanks to years of dust inhaled while plowing fields.

I glanced over my shoulder at the knife. "Just practicing."

He grunted, the normal response he had to about everything. "Seems like more than target practice to me."

He walked past me with his uneven gait. I watched as he pulled the knife from the hay. Flipping it in his hand like I sometimes did, he studied the blade, judging the weight of it in his palm.

"Remember what I told you when I gave you this knife?" he asked, glancing up at me.

"Yeah. I was twelve. You said handle it with care or I'd get hurt."

"That's right," he said, heading back toward me. "I told you that you might be tempted to play around with it, but you had to be careful. Its edges are sharp and its blade long. It could draw blood with just a touch." He stopped beside me and looked down at the knife, running a rough thumb over it. "Lots of things in this life can do that to a man, son. Just remember that."

He offered me the knife, handle first, then walked past me, leaving me alone in the woods once again.

I held the knife with a loose grip. He was right. Lots of things in this world could hurt a man.

Including a beautiful woman.

But she would never make me bleed.

Chapter Seventeen

-Cat-

I dreamed of hell. It came for me, a darkness I couldn't resist. I felt safe as it wrapped around me, dragging me down and taking away the pain. I needed it. I had to have it to keep my heart safe.

My skin burned as the flames of hell licked at me. Drops of sweat trickled down between my breasts, soaking my t-shirt. I shifted, fighting the heat and seeking a cooler spot.

"Where are we?"

The layers of sleep peeled away at Tate's voice. I forced my eyes open. Glaring sunlight blinded me.

I wasn't in hell. I was in the backseat of Nathan's car. It was hot, so hot I was having trouble breathing. I could feel the air conditioning on my face, but it wasn't enough to cool me down.

Hard plastic bit into my ribs. I grimaced and pushed myself up, away from the door poking into my side. My legs were stuck to the leather seat and the window beside me radiated heat. I ran a hand through my hair and stared out the window, seeing nothing but miles and miles of empty grassland. One fence post blended into another and another as we flew by them.

Tate, Nathan, and I had loaded Nathan's car and left our small hometown that morning. They would drop me off at my collage apartment and spend a few days with me. After that Tate and Nathan would return home, minus one sister.

As the miles passed by, numbness engulfed me. I welcomed it. Filled my lungs with it. Breathed it deeply. I reminded myself who I was. The girl that women hated and men loved. The one that didn't give a damn. I just didn't know that when I screwed a cowboy in a bathroom, I would feel something.

I laid my forehead against the hot window and closed my eyes, refusing to open them again even when high-pitched chirps came from the seat beside me.

I flinched with each sound, keeping my eyes squeezed shut. Finally, I couldn't take it anymore. The obnoxious high-pitched tones scratched away at the bitchy side of me.

"You gonna answer that, Cat, or is the ringtone just for shits and giggles?" Nathan asked from the driver's seat, glancing at me in the rearview mirror.

I rolled my eyes and grabbed my phone, answering without looking at the caller id.

"Hello." My voice sounded as irritable as I felt. But underneath it was fear. Fear that I would hear Cash's voice and crumble.

"Hi, Catnip."

I let out a breath of relief.

"Hi, Dad," I said, recognizing the familiar nickname my father had given me. "Where are you?"

"I'm in Dubai, sweetie. Dry as hell here. I've got sand in places I never thought sand could go," he said in his deep, gruff voice that could bark orders at rapid speed or sweet talk a business deal in his favor. "How are you doing, Catnip?"

I shifted in my seat again, seeking a cooler spot on the hot leather. "I'm fine, Dad. Nathan and Tate are taking me back to campus. We're in the car right now."

There was silence on the other end of the line. I frowned, wondering what I had said wrong. My dad was never silent. He always had an opinion and wasn't afraid to voice it.

"Dad?" I asked, wondering if he was still there.

He sighed with irritation, making him sound like he was sitting right beside me instead of thousands of miles away. "Hell, I wish you kids had stayed put. There's been some chatter."

"What kind of chatter? Like government stuff?"

"Yes. My contacts say something is going on. The Syrians and Iranians are up to something. North Koreans too. The government is on high alert but keeping it secret. They're scared, Cat, really scared. And whatever they've heard has got their panties in a wad." He took a deep breath, coughing in the middle of it. "You kids need to stay careful, you understand?"

I furrowed my brows. My dad had contacts in the White House, Congress, and the CIA. He rubbed elbows with the elite, just to get what he wanted for his company. I knew foreign diplomats were in his back pocket and government officials and politicians were on his payroll - under the table of course. You couldn't own a billion dollar oil business without getting your hands a little dirty with bribes and deals.

Most of the time his business trips took him to places and introduced him to men that were dangerous. Rulers of countries and soldiers of warring regions. Men who were crooked behind closed doors and saviors in front of the voting public. If anyone knew what was really going on in the political and world arena, it would be my father.

"Do you understand me, Cat? Stay alert," my dad's deep voice boomed in my ear. "No more trips. No more driving across the state. *Stay put.*"

"Sure," I said, knowing he wouldn't let it go until I agreed. "I'll stay at the apartment."

"Good. Now I've got to go out into the field. I'll probably be unreachable for a few days, but I'll check in when I can. Okay?"

"Yeah. Got it," I answered, watching the land zoom by outside the window. "Do you want to talk to Tate or Nathan?"

"Can't. I gotta go. People are waiting for me. Tell them 'hi.' Okay, Catnip?"

I looked at Tate in the front seat. I could only see his profile but I knew he was hoping…wishing that our dad would pay at least some attention to him. But from the moment he was born, my dad had only ignored him.

"'Bye, Dad," I said, hiding the resentment for the man that had donated his sperm to our mothers and money to us, but never his undivided time or love. Tate needed him. I needed him. He wasn't there when Luke died and he was absent when I started my downward spiral to crazy. But like always, the business needed him more.

I dropped the phone to the seat beside me, disgusted. Tate turned in his seat to look at me. I avoided his questioning stare and glared out the window.

My dad's warning was forgotten, my anger with him dismissed. All that mattered was getting back to my apartment. Forgetting about Cash.

Return to being me.

~~~~

My apartment was on the third floor. It had a balcony, a kitchenette, and one tiny bedroom. It wasn't the greatest but it was decent. My dad had wanted me to get a luxury condo in an upscale area of Austin, but I had put my foot down. I wanted to experience college like a real student, not a filthy-rich girl with her daddy's money.

"You got too many damn stairs in this place," Tate complained as we headed up the building's stairway at a snail's pace. It was sweltering, the kind of heat that made a person move like molasses. It sucked all the energy from you and replaced it with a shitty attitude.

"I wish to God that you would stop cussing, Tate. You're too young to have a mouth like you do," Nathan grumbled with irritation, carrying his duffle bag and my overstuffed suitcase up the stairs.

"I wonder who I learned it from?" Tate whipped back, the heat making him cranky as hell like it did every other person in the city. "You say 'fuck' like every other word, Nate."

"Bullshit," Nathan snapped, dragging my suitcase over a step carelessly.

I tuned them out and trudged up to the third floor landing. The air was thicker that high, hotter. I caught a whiff of stale beer from one of the apartments. It welcomed me like an old friend, wrapping an arm around me and asking me where I'd been. It was a normal smell in the college apartment complex. One that I had missed.

I took a deep breath, filling my lungs with it and city air. Austin was not some little podunk town with old, blue-haired ladies with sticks up their butts or with cowboys with too much shit on their boots. That life wasn't for me. Not anymore.

In Austin, I could disappear. I could be crazy and warped and damn near anything I wanted to be. I could party and drink and sleep with every goddamn man if I wanted to. There was no one to stop me. To judge me. To remind me of the past and things that I had done.

I unlocked the door to my apartment and stepped inside. Cool, artificial air blew in my face from an overhead vent, drying my sweat and welcoming me home.

I flipped on the nearest light. Imported leather furniture and expensive end tables greeted me. I headed straight for the kitchen I pretended I used.

Tate was right behind me. He dropped his bag in the middle of the floor and rushed to the fridge.

"No water?" he asked, flinging the refrigerator door open and sticking his head inside.

"Nope," I said, reaching down to pick up his duffle bag from the floor. "We'll have to make a grocery run later, Tater Tot."

Nathan appeared in the kitchen, rolling my suitcase behind him, one of the wheels slightly off.

"You know there's this thing called a faucet. Last I heard water comes from it. Get your drink that way, Tate," he said to Tate.

Tate gave him an annoyed look. "Last time I drank tap water, it tasted like shit."

"Language, little brother," Nathan warned, heading back out of the kitchen. There were still two more suitcases in the car and a laundry bag full of my dirty, designer clothes waiting to be brought up.

Tate marched past me, grumbling about big brothers with sucky attitudes and the lack of groceries in my shitty apartment. I swear the kid was always hungry.

I sighed. If Tate and Nathan were going to fight the whole time, I needed to get drunk. It was the only way I would survive the two of them in close quarters.

With that in mind, I hurried out of the kitchen and across the living room. Dropping Tate's bag near my leather couch, I headed for the front door. The sooner I helped Nathan bring in the luggage, the sooner I could make my drunkenness happen.

I had only taken a few steps outside my apartment door when I ran smack-dab into a girl.

"Oh my gosh! I'm *so* sorry!" she exclaimed, jumping back.

I recovered quickly, but looked down at her and frowned. She was short and nerdy. Her light blonde hair was limp and flat. Sad-looking curls hung down past her shoulders. Her lips were full and pink, absent of any lipstick. They were pulled back in a friendly smile, showing even white teeth. She wore cheap khaki shorts and a black t-shirt with the words *World of Warcraft* slashed across the front. Her black-rimmed glasses magnified her light-colored eyes, making her appear owl-like. Not one ounce of makeup was on her face, but she somehow managed to pull off the natural look perfectly.

At first glanced, she seemed too bubbly and happy to be normal. *Great. One of those types of people.* I didn't like girls like her. Life just wasn't that great to be overly cheerful. I knew just by looking at her that she had never had to watch her life fall apart, one drink at a time, one man at a time. She never regretted in the morning what she had done last night. Or wish to God sex and men weren't her go-to drug to hide from reality. She was normal and cheerful and all the things society said women should be like.

I disliked her instantly.

"Excuse me," I muttered stepping around her, careful not to touch her again. I didn't want her good girl cooties on me.

"Are you my neighbor?" she asked, sounding too sweet to be real.

I skidded to a stop, feeling dismay. When I left campus a couple of weeks ago, the pimply guy that lived next door had been in the process of moving out. He had graduated with a master's in accounting and was leaving for a new job. At least that's what he had told me while he was hitting on me for the umpteenth time. *So now this…girl…was taking his place? Great.*

"You just came from 304, right?" she asked, pointing to the rusted gold numbers on my door then pushing her glasses higher up the bridge of her nose. "That's next to mine. I'm 303."

I narrowed my eyes. "Yeah. I'm 304," I said, looking her up and down. *Blonde hair. Green eyes.* I cocked my head to the side. *Wait. There's something familiar about her…*

"Hello."

Whatever nagged me about Blondie was forgotten as Nathan appeared. He was hauling the laundry bag behind him as he walked toward us, staring at the girl and checking her out the way only Nathan could – with a James Dean kind of coolness.

His gaze traveled up and down her small frame, taking his time and touching on each of her features. I wanted to roll my eyes. Nathan was a player. Oh, he didn't come across as one, but I heard the rumors. My brother supposedly had game.

I could see the interest rolling off of him for the girl. I wasn't one of those jealous sister types - he could bang whomever he wanted - but not on my watch and definitely not with this girl. She wasn't his type. No way, no how. I was almost sure of it.

I stood my ground, keeping him at bay. Blondie might look innocent but looks could be deceiving. Take me. I looked like a bitch…okay, maybe I wasn't the best example. But still, she could be some strange gamer girl with a tendency toward stalking. I didn't know...

I did have to hand it to her – she had balls. She reached around me with a sweet smile and stuck out her hand for Nathan to shake.

"Hi. My name's Keely," she said, her natural pink lips pulling back in an easy smile.

Nathan stepped around me and dropped the laundry bag at my feet, never taking his eyes from Keely. He took Blondie's outstretched hand and shook it.

"I'm Nathan," he said, looking mesmerized by her.

I felt both ill and awkward at the same time, seeing my brother turn on his charm for my new neighbor. I snorted with irritation and grabbed the handle of the laundry bag. I didn't care who she was or why I felt like I knew her. As long as Blondie stayed out of my way, we were good.

I had more important things to do anyway. There was a cowboy to forget. A dead boyfriend to remember. And a shitload of heartache to bury.

~~~~

The party was in full swing and so was I. I grasped the cup tighter, swaying on my six-inch stilettos. The only thing holding me up was the table behind me, covered with empty plastic cups and a half-eaten bowl of potato chips.

I raised the cup to my mouth, barely making it to my lips for another drink. Cheap vodka slid down my throat, warming me from the inside out. The alcohol would make what I was about to do easier. It always did.

I scanned the crowd, looking over everyone with boredom. The party was a mixture of frat boys and sorority girls. Not really my style but I mixed well with them, especially the frat guys. They liked to drink and party. What else did I need?

Speaking of needing... I needed a man to take my mind off a certain cowboy. Someone not so nice and not so decent. Someone that would prove any man would do.

I pushed away from the table and took a few tentative steps forward. The room spun. That meant the alcohol was doing its job. I was feeling good. Numb to everything. Well, almost everything. Memories still plagued me and thoughts of Cash still lingered. Time to change that.

I took a long drink from my cup and managed to stay on my feet as I went further into the room. The crowd danced around me. I was jostled one way then another as I squeezed past them.

I was halfway across the room when the song changed, something fast and sexy. It's just what I needed to hear. I started dancing, joining the girls and guys around me.

I closed my eyes and held my cup up high, feeling the music move through me. I was in a world of my own that didn't involve thoughts of Cash touching me, kissing me, or making me wish for more.

I forced my eyes back open, hating that I couldn't forget about him. Raising the cup to my mouth, I took a long drink, still continuing to sway to the music. As I did, my gaze automatically traveled over the crowd, looking for a hot, handsome distraction. What I found instead made me frown.

Keely was talking to Nathan. He was inches from her, protecting her with his body from the drunk, sweaty crowd. She gazed up at him with adoration and interest, her light-colored eyes full of happiness.

I had pouted early and thrown a fit when Nathan told me he invited her to the party. We were leaving Tate at home, why not Nathan's new love interest too, I figured. But Nathan had put his foot down and said Keely was going.

I wasn't happy about it and made sure everyone knew, including Keely. But the girl had just looked me in the eyes and smiled. Right then I felt a tiny shred of respect for her. Tiny.

I watched her. She was smiling up at Nathan like he had hung the moon. Her messy, uncombed hair was pulled back in a loose ponytail, making it easy to see her delicate features. Her head was tilted to the right, listening to something Nathan was saying. When she did that, she reminded me of someone…

My blood went cold.

"No way." I pushed the guy in front of me out of the way, not believing my eyes. I knew it felt like I had met her before, I just couldn't figure out when or where. It nagged at me when I unpacked. Picked at me when I took a shower. Pestered me when I dressed. Now I knew why.

I crossed the room quickly, pushing people out of the way roughly. My insides twisted with a sick feeling. When I reached Keely and Nathan, I pushed my way between them.

"What's your last name?" I asked Keely, getting straight to the point.

Her smile wavered. She stared at me wide-eyed from behind her big, ugly glasses. Nathan shrugged and sipped his beer when she looked at him with confusion. He was used to my questionable antics.

I sighed and tried again, growing aggravated. "Your last name, Keely. What is it?"

Keely chewed on her bottom lip as she studied me, then started chewing on a fingernail.

"Marshall. Why?" she asked, mumbling around her finger.

My stomach rolled. The room spun. I felt ill and faint at the same time. *This could not be happening.*

Keely - my brand new, annoying, nerdy neighbor - had Cash's last name.

"And…and do you have a brother?" I asked, barely able to get the words out. I was tempted to take up nail biting myself.

Keely stopped chewing on her fingernail and started back on her bottom lip again, gnawing on it with her teeth. "Yeah. His name is Cash. How do you know—"

I didn't wait for her to finish. I turned away, feeling sick.

"Oh, god. Oh, god. Oh, god." I rubbed my forehead as I walked away. "Oh, holy fucking fuck."

"Hey. You okay?" Nathan asked, jogging to catch up with me. He grabbed my elbow, turning me around.

I couldn't look him in the eye. Nathan had seen me after the night with Cash. He had seen me broken and crying. Seen the war I fought with myself. I didn't want him to worry about me or see me as batshit insane.

So I lied.

"Yeah. I'm okay," I said with a shaky voice.

Nathan looked at me like he didn't believe me, but he didn't say anything. I pushed past him and continued walking, playing like everything was okay when it was not.

Keely is Cash's sister. Keely is Cash's sister. The words kept replaying in my head like a bad song on repeat. I bumped into strangers and was jarred by drunk sorority girls as I pushed my way through the crowd, but I didn't care. Keely was Cash's sister.

I didn't know how I missed it. It was there. In her eyes. In her mannerisms. I had seen it from the first moment I met her; I just refused to acknowledge it. She had the same light gray eyes as Cash. The same tilt of her head as he did. I even saw it in her smile, almost an exact copy of her brother's.

What the fuck is life doing to me? Hasn't it torn me apart and ripped me to pieces enough?

Apparently not. Fate had just played a cruel, cruel joke on me.

Keely had walked into my life.

Just days after I had walked out of her brother's.

Chapter Eighteen

-Cash-

I stared at the ice-cold longneck in front of me. It was my third of the evening. My last attempt to forget about Cat.

She was on my mind again. Hell, when wasn't she? She was the most beautiful woman I had ever seen, but I reminded myself that she had been only a one-night stand.

A thanks-I-needed-that kind of gal.

But after days I still couldn't get her out of my thoughts. It made me cranky as hell. I shifted on my barstool, wishing I could just forget her and her pretty little ass.

I was still thinking of that ass and me cupping it when a loud argument broke out behind me. Some shit about spilt beer. I paid no attention to it and took a long drink of my beer, keeping my back to the fight and my nose out of it.

"Damn drunk cowboys," Jo scowled, watching the men argue as she picked up a dirty shot glass and wiped the counter clean with a dirty rag.

I gave in and glanced over my shoulder, finding two big, bearded guys facing off, one of them so drunk he couldn't keep his eyes open. The other was so wide his belly hung over his belt.

They were yelling, talking smack and looking for a fight. I watched it with a raised brow, wondering when the fists would start flying. Jo wasn't going to wait that long.

I turned back to my beer just in enough time to see her reach under the bar and pull out a metal baseball bat. It was electric blue and had a few scars here and there. I cringed to think where they had come from.

The argument behind me grew in volume, the men now shouting at each other. I watched with a mixture of humor and sympathy as Jo waddled from behind the bar and started to shove past people, keeping the arguing men in her sights and the baseball bat in her hands.

"Break it up, assholes!" she yelled. "Break it up or I'll bust your balls and send them home in a to-go sack!" She smacked the bat against her palm for effect, sending her message across loud and clear.

I looked over at the men, wondering if they were listening. Yep. Both of them were staring at Jo like she had two heads. The argument was forgotten. The spilled beer a thing of the past. Now all that mattered was the tough, gray-haired woman that was as round as she was tall barreling toward them. She had hardness in her eyes and was aiming to crack a few skulls in with her weapon of choice.

The two men took a step away from each other and Jo took advantage of the space, getting between them.

"I know your mama, Gerry," she said to one. "Patched up her black eyes plenty of times when your daddy came around." She squinted hard at him, not afraid of his massive size as he looked down at her. "You think she would be happy to see you right now? All full of vinegar and piss, talking trash to your *cousin*?"

Gerry hung his head down with embarrassment, the fight leaving him. I was surprised he didn't piss his pants. Jo could do that to a fella.

She swung around, facing Guy #2 when he snorted.

"And you, Mr. Piss Poor excuse for a husband," she said, poking him in the chest. "Go back home to your pregnant wife or she's gonna find a new daddy for her next baby."

"Yes, Miss Jo."

She huffed and smacked the bat against her palm again as she watched the two men walk away, the argument forgotten. The crowd went back to its drinking and Jo eyed everyone with unspoken warning, daring anyone else to cause trouble.

I grinned, tipping my hat to her when she glanced at me. The scowl on her face disappeared and a twinkle appeared in her eyes. She loved that dramatic shit no matter how much she grumbled and bitched about the drunks messing up her bar.

She cast one more glance over her shoulder at the crowd and then walked away. When she did, the person behind her stepped forward, catching my attention.

It was him. The man that had cornered Cat in the parking lot the first night I met her. The same man who couldn't take *no* for an answer.

New Hat Asshole.

He was staring at me like he wanted to cut my throat. I returned his glare, daring him to do his worst. I was pissed at Cat for not returning my calls, angry at myself for caring, and damned well tired of trying to forget her. At the moment, I was in a shitty mood.

And then this guy appeared.

His buddy was with him again, standing at his side and staring me down. He was huge, reminding me of one of those wrestlers on TV. His head was shaved but he had a goatee the color of midnight, looking too dark to be natural.

I watched as New Hat Asshole took a drink of his beer, keeping his gaze on me. I tightened my grip around my own beer bottle. I wasn't one for fighting, but this guy had touched Cat.

That made him a dead man to me.

Someone walked between us, blocking my view of him. I took that as a hint from the universe and relaxed. I had to get it through my mind that Cat wasn't my responsibility. She had been mine for only one night. That was it. We were nothing but a one-time – strike that two - screwing. She had said as much that night on her porch.

I turned back to the bar and took a drink of my lukewarm beer. Thirty minutes passed before I downed the last bit in the bottom of the bottle and put it on the counter.

"Another?" Jo asked, grabbing my empty longneck and looking at me with a raised eyebrow.

"No, ma'am. I'm done for the night," I said, laying a ten down.

"Stay out of trouble," she said with a wink, grabbing the money.

I tipped my hat at her and headed for the door.

The sounds of the bar followed me. Loud music. Laughter. The clink of beer bottles. I wanted to hear Cat's musical, teasing laugh instead just like I had the first night I met her. I wanted to see her at the bar again, the little sundress of hers riding up her legs. Or hear her sweet mouth offer a blowjob for a drink, something that probably felt as close to heaven as a man could get.

"Shit," I muttered, hitting the door open with the palm of my hand.

Gravel crunched under my boots as I stepped off the covered entrance. The heat was sweltering. I heard talking off to the side, but figured they were just some people outside for a smoke…that is until I heard the mutter.

"There he is."

The hair on the back of my neck rose and the muscles in my shoulders tensed as footsteps sounded behind me.

"Hey, jackass!"

I glanced over my shoulder. New Hat Asshole and his buddy were tailing me, looking eager to cause some trouble.

"Where's the girl?" New Hat Asshole asked, thrusting his pointy chin at me and following me at a leisure pace.

I just continued walking. Outside I was calm but inside I burned, wanting to send someone to a fiery hell. Rage like I had never felt before took over me, eating at my insides and hollowing out my patience.

"Hey! I'm talking to you! Where's the chick?" New Hat asked in anger, spitting out each word like they were disgusting. "She owes me."

I drew to a stop, keeping my back to them. "She doesn't owe you a thing," I said in a low voice.

New Hat chuckled. "Hell, yeah she owes me and she's got a *goooood* thing coming to her the next time I see her. I guar-on-tee it."

That's it!

I spun around, the control in me shattering. Cat may not be mine, but I wouldn't stand by and let any man threaten her.

My fist caught New Hat in the nose, my knuckles slamming into his face. The sound of flesh on flesh echoed across the parking lot. The crunch of bone on bone was followed by a spurt of blood.

He howled and cupped his face. Blood ran between his fingers. I didn't have time to gloat. His buddy charged me like a bull on steroids.

I stepped out of the way just as he ducked his head and shot toward me. When he got close enough, I buried my fist in his gut. It didn't seem to faze him. He spun around and took a swing at me but I ducked, my cowboy hat flying.

"Fuck him up, Clay," New Hat yelled at his friend. "Make him suffer."

I kept New Hat in my line of vision but watched Clay crack his knuckles then his neck.

"Be my pleasure, Daryl." With a pig-like grunt, he rushed me.

I steeled myself to take him head on, keeping my stance wide. I had already received one bloody nose for Cat. I didn't want to take another.

When Clay got close enough, I threw a hard right hook to his chin. It snapped his head to the side, dazing him. I hit him again and again until he backed away, straggling on his feet.

Without missing a beat, I swung around and punched New Hat (aka Daryl) in the face. He was caught off guard, giving me the perfect opportunity to catch him in the nose again. Bone cracked and pain shot through my hand when it connected with his face, but my only thought was Cat and him touching her again.

Daryl screamed with pain and grabbed his nose, cupping a hand over it. I pulled my arm back to hit him again, but then I heard Clay behind me, lumbering to his feet.

I whirled around just in time to find him charging me once more. I jabbed a short, powerful blow to his shoulder. It pushed him back a step. Just what I wanted. I threw a hard punch to his jaw. His stomach. As the guy kept coming toward me, I kept hitting. His head. His stomach again. The guy was big but I was mad.

When he finally dropped to the ground, I stopped. I was breathing heavy, my chest drawing in deep lungfuls of air. The red haze of anger still clouded my vision as I stood over Clay.

"You son of a bitch! You son of a bitch! You broke my nose! You broke my nose! I'm going to bury you then fuck her!" Daryl screamed behind me.

I pivoted around, finding him lying on the ground, holding his nose and crying like a baby. The thought of Cat walking into Cooper's when I wasn't there and finding this man waiting for her, pushed me over the edge. All the control I had disappeared.

The bar door opened and part of me realized it was probably Jo. I didn't wait for her to jump in with her bat or sawed off shotgun. I rushed toward Daryl. Gravel ground into my jeans and cut into my knees as I skidded to a stop beside him, dropping to the ground. I pulled my knife out of the sheath attached to my boot and grabbed hold of Daryl's bloody shirt. With one yank, I pulled him up and put the tip of the blade under his chin.

"Stay away from her," I growled between clenched teeth.

Daryl stopped wailing. He grew still. His eyes grew wide at the sight of my knife. He looked up at me with fear, his nose swelling to a purple mess.

"Okay. Okay. You can have her," he said, holding up his hands in a sign of surrender. "I...I don't want her anymore. She's all yours."

"You're wrong," I hissed. "She'll never be mine, no matter how much I want her to be."

With that, I shoved him back to the ground and stood up. I flipped the knife around in my hand and stuck it back in its sheath in one smooth movement. Picking up my hat, I put it on then pulled the brim low. Without another glance at Daryl or his friend, I walked away.

It was the first time I had ever pulled a knife on a man. Unfortunately, it wouldn't be my last.

Chapter Nineteen

-Cat-

My grandmother always said the devil lived in all of us. He teased us with gluttony. Tempted us with desire. Won us with lies. If we weren't careful, he would take our soul and destroy it.

I didn't know if that was true, but I had a dark place in my soul. It ate at me, pulling me further down each day. I couldn't fight it. I could only feed it, just like I was doing now.

After finding out that Keely was Cash's sister, I had some shots of tequila. Then I had a couple more. I couldn't help it. Fate had just bent me over and had its way with me. I was screwed, royally and hard. If there was one person Fate liked to fuck around with, it was me.

I poured a trail of salt on my hand and gave the guy standing next to me a sly look. He smiled, almost salivating when I ran my tongue over the salt, licking it up. Once it was gone, I tossed back the tequila, quickly following it with a lime. The tequila burned going down, but I was past noticing or caring that I might be in over my head.

"Whoop! Whoop!"

The frat boys shouted as they watched me slap down the empty shot glass, winning the drinking game we were playing for the second time in a row.

The guy next to me slid his hand around my waist and poured me another drink. I grinned at him but then my favorite song started playing in the living room.

"Let's dance!"

I led the guy through the crowded kitchen, feeling drunk happy. Another drink magically appeared in my hand and I didn't ask how it got there. I held it high above my head so it wouldn't spill and danced like I just didn't give a damn.

In the middle of the living room, I stopped and turned to face my new friend. He had blonde hair that was cut military-style and a tattoo that peeked out from under the sleeve of his shirt. He was a little too buff for me but hey, who was complaining? He was a man and he wasn't Cash. I would feel nothing for him and that's just what I needed.

He ran his hand around my waist, pulling me against his body. We started dancing to the music. The small apartment closed in around us. The thin walls of the building thumped to the music. I danced, pausing every now and then to take a drink of the fiery liquid in my cup.

I was doing a good job of staying on my feet, despite my sky-high heels and the numerous drinks, but then the alcohol finally won out. I stumbled, cursing Jimmy Choo for making shoes I couldn't resist and Jose Cuervo for making some awesome tasting tequila.

The guy caught me with those buff muscles of his. "Hey. You okay?" he asked, holding me upright.

I pulled away from him and gave him a sly look. "I am now."

He smiled back with a toothy grin. All my drunk happiness left me in a whoosh, leaving me stone-cold sober.

His smile wasn't lopsided or sexy in a dangerous sort of way. He didn't have a well-worn cowboy hat pulled low on his head, hiding his eyes from the world and me. His shoes weren't scuffed boots that had seen too many days on a tractor and one too many nights on a barstool.

His eyes didn't remind me of stormy days or a night under the stars.

He wasn't Cash, but I reminded myself for the millionth time that I didn't need the cowboy anyway. I'd prove it.

I eased up next to the guy, letting my body rub against his. He smiled and pulled me closer.

"Are you as tired of this party as I am?" he asked.

My smile wavered but I forced it back. "You read my mind."

The guy grinned even more and moved his hand up my back, skimming it along my spine. "You game for some privacy?"

I looked up at him, wondering if I could go through with it this time. I could always walk away. Be the good girl that falls in love with a guy like Cash. Or I could give in. Break a few hearts and sleep with a few more men to prove I was immune to everything.

I knew what I wanted to do, but I wondered what my heart could handle.

"Let's go." I grabbed the guy's hand and led him out of the crowd before I could change my mind.

What I was about to do was wrong.

But I needed to prove I would be alright.

~~~~

I hit the bathroom wall hard, my back slamming into the towel rack. I winced but didn't stop. My fingers worked quickly to get his buttons undone before I got cold feet. *I need this, I need this, I need this,* I repeated the words to myself. If I said it enough times it would be true.

His tongue slipped into my mouth the minute the last button on his shirt gave way. He shrugged out of it and threw it to the floor. His hands were back on me in seconds. They were rough. Hurried. He was here for one thing and one thing only. The sooner I got out of my clothes, the sooner we could do this and move on.

He popped the button on my Lucky Brand jeans and shoved them open. His hand went down the front, tearing past my lacy, expensive underwear. I fought the panic and resisted the urge to run. I had to prove to myself that I was numb. That Cash did not have a hold on me.

The guy shoved his fingers lower but my jeans were too tight. Frustrated, he backed me toward the sink. I kicked off my heels as I went, sending them flying.

You can do this. You can do this.

The stone counter hit my hip painfully as he pushed me into it. Impatient, he reached around me and shoved bottles out of the way then wrapped an arm around my waist, lifting me onto the counter.

Thoughts of another restroom, another man between my legs, invaded me. My lungs constricted. I suddenly couldn't breathe. I was on the verge of having a mild panic attack, but then the guy touched the tattoo on my hip and everything came back to me.

I flipped my hair behind my shoulder and reached for him. He stepped between my legs and bent closer, kissing me.

It was a sloppy kiss. Too wet. Too hurried. Too messy to be sexy. I held onto the edge of the counter, fighting the urge to vomit. My skin crawled but I squeezed my eyes shut.

It's called surviving. Deal with it!

I held still as he moved his mouth down to my neck, leaving a trail of wetness behind. I shivered, and not in a good way. I wanted to wipe my neck clean with the towel hanging nearby. Maybe even jump in the shower and wash his drool off me.

I pushed the icky feeling away and reached for his jeans. Time to prove that I couldn't feel anything.

The button popped open. His Calvin Klein underwear peeped over the top. The bile rose in my throat. I felt hate so strong for myself that I almost doubled over. Tears popped up behind my eyelids. I blinked them away and started to push his underwear down.

But then the light over the sink flickered.

It was the wakeup call I needed. I froze, my hand going still.

"Come on, baby. It's just a power surge. Happens all the time here," he said against my neck when I pulled my hand away.

He was right. The power to my apartment complex was unreliable. But that wasn't why I stopped. The flickering light shined a harsh reality down on me. For the first time in my miserable life, I didn't want to be an easy girl anymore.

I only wanted to be with Cash and that made me angry.

I put my hand on the guy's chest. "I think we need to stop," I said, pushing him back a step.

He dropped his hand from my side. "You're kidding me, right?"

"No," I said, jumping off the counter and forcing him back another step. "I can't do this."

I circled around him in the tiny bathroom, searching for my shoes. The guy touched my back as I found one and slipped it on.

"Listen, baby—"

I snapped up, the shoes forgotten. I was dizzy and drunk, but I had to keep my head on straight. Guys could be asses when they got a drunk girl alone.

"Get your hands off of me. I'm not your baby!" I hissed, advancing on him. I held one high heel in my hand, ready to use it as a weapon if need be.

He held up his hand and backed away. "Okay. Okay. Shit, didn't know I was about to hook up with a psycho bitch."

I glared at him. "Yeah, I'm a bitch. Tell me something I don't know."

I slipped my shoe on then flung open the bathroom door. Giving him one last dirty look, I stomped out, hoping I never saw him again.

The party had grown. I pushed and shoved my way through the crowd, angry, pissed, and sobering up quick. I needed to fix that quick. I was on my way to the alcohol stash when I saw a blonde girl approach me.

"Hey, Cat."

I held up a hand and continued walking. Keely was the last person I wanted to see. The very last. But she followed me in her little ballet flats. I rolled my eyes and let out a loud sigh. *Shit. The girl just didn't give up.*

"So where's your boyfriend?" I asked her as I shouldered my way through the crowd to the kitchen. If Keely was going to follow me, I would entertain myself and get to know her.

"I don't know what you're talking about," she yelled over the music. "I don't have a boyfriend."

She sounded so innocent and cute. Ugh.

I snorted loudly. "Sure you do," I said, glancing back at her. She was too busy waving away a cloud of cigarette smoke to pay attention to me. She looked so out of place at the party that I wanted to laugh. Instead, I sighed and drew to a stop, turning to face her.

She bumped into me, too busy swatting away smoke to pay attention. When she recovered, she cleared her throat and pushed her glasses up the bridge of her nose, looking nervous and uneasy around so many plastered people.

I drew my brows together. Not only did she look out of place with her flowery shirt and schoolgirl skirt, but she also acted like she had never been to a drunk, put-out-or-get-out frat party. She watched the crowd with a mixture of interest and caution, looking unsure but intrigued.

I had the absurd idea that I should take her under my wing and protect her. Help her shield her innocence against the hoodlums around here. Ridiculous, I know. I mean, I didn't owe her anything. It was her brother I had a problem with. His sister might be Miss Innocent but he sure as hell wasn't. Look how he made love to me. No holds barred. Powerful. Demanding. Taking what he wanted. Shit, was I ever going to get over it?

Not with his little sister hanging around, you won't.

Keely watched wide-eyed as some guy sucked beer from a tube while doing a handstand. I tapped my finger on her skinny shoulder, getting her attention.

"Earth to Keely."

"Huh?" she said, tearing her gaze away from the guy.

I grinned. She was too funny.

"Listen," I said. "My brother likes you. So don't break his heart and I won't break you. Got it?"

She nodded.

"Good."

I left her standing in the middle of the room. I didn't

know where Nathan had disappeared to but she could take care of herself. I had more important things to do.

Like deal with what I couldn't forget.

The frat boys were still at it in the kitchen. Bottles of alcohol and spilled liquor covered the table. When they saw me, they all raised their glasses and shouted to join them in another drinking game. I declined the offer and grabbed a shot glass then a half-empty bottle of cheap tequila. I filled up the glass, stopping only when the liquid reached the top. It would give me just what I needed. Courage. Because I was about to do something crazy.

I leaned against the counter and pulled my cell phone out of my back pocket. Ignoring the party around me, I stared at the little screen. For days I thought about answering Cash's calls or texts. Maybe if I heard his voice, I reasoned, I could prove what I had felt for him meant nothing. I could show myself that it was just lust and close the door on us forever. Maybe Keely was a sign it was time to do that.

My heart pounded as I scrolled through my missed calls. *Tessa. Nathan. Tessa. Tessa.*

Cash.

His number appeared. I took a deep breath.

And hit the call button.

Chapter Twenty

-Cash-

I hit the entrance ramp at full speed. My foot stayed glued to the gas pedal. Without slowing down, I merged onto the freeway. Cars and trucks traveled beside me, keeping up with my crazy speeds.

Fury rolled through me. I flexed my fingers on the steering wheel, glancing at my bloody knuckles. They had been worth it, shedding a few layers of skin and losing a little blood. To think that Daryl or his buddy would touch Cat caused me to lose a little of that calm control that I had been raised to have.

I pulled off my cowboy hat and flung it on the seat beside me.

"Son of a…" I muttered, running a hand through my hair. I called myself every name I could think of. No one had ever made me feel madder than hell one minute and crazy with desire the next. I didn't know whether I wanted Cat again or if I wanted to strangle her neck the next time I saw her.

If I saw her.

I reached over and turned up the radio, drowning out the sound of the truck's engine. I needed something to block the voices in my head, screaming at me for falling for a girl like Cat. Frustration wouldn't leave me alone. Want wouldn't get the hell out of my life.

I ran a hand through my hair again. *I have to get my head on straight. Get my shit together. First things first. Forget her and move on.*

I changed lanes, picking up speed. A streetlight flickered as I passed under it. At the same time my radio went silent, the music suddenly vanishing. I didn't think much of it but I should have.

It was the first sign.

The radio came back on at the same time my phone buzzed beside me on the seat. I reached over and picked it up, glancing at the screen.

It was Cat.

"Hell," I swore. If I was going to forget her, the last thing I needed was to hear her voice again. But no way could I resist.

I clicked on the phone, keeping a close eye on a black car that sped past me. "Hello."

There was static on the other end but I knew she was there. I could feel her, almost sense her by me. Jesus, I was losing my mind but she might just be worth it.

"It's Cat," she said in my ear.

I shifted in my seat, uneasy with the way her voice affected me. It made me nervous as hell and as antsy as shit. I wanted to turn my truck around and race to wherever she was. Tell her I was doing my best to forget her, but so far nothing was working. I needed just one more time between her legs and then I could walk away.

"God, I've been wanting to hear your voice," I said, keeping my eyes on the road but my mind on her. "Are you okay?"

There was silence on the other end of the phone, filled only with static.

"Cash…I think…" Her words faded in and out. "It was a mistake…broken…never again…"

I sat up straighter, my heart pounding out of control.

"Cat, honey, you're breaking up." I pressed the phone

closer to my ear, watching the streetlights blink on and off as the cars raced past me. "Can you hear me?"

Her voice was barely audible through the static. "Don't call me…can't take it…leave me alone…"

The static grew, drowning out her words until I couldn't hear her anymore.

"Cat! CAT!" I shouted, glancing at the phone then holding it back to my ear.

Suddenly, a car flew in front of me. I swerved to miss it, anger and frustration making me hit the gas harder.

"CAT!" I shouted again.

But there was nothing but silence.

~~~~

"Fuck!"

I threw the phone onto the seat beside me just as the roar of my pickup's engine died. The headlights flicked off, going dark. The radio went silent. I looked down at the dash. *What the hell?*

The truck had just lost all power.

I glanced back up and that's when I saw it. Chaos. It was everywhere.

A semi was skidding across the road, jackknifing out of control and coming straight at me. Its trailer crossed the lanes of traffic, taking cars and trucks with it like a broom sweeping up debris.

And I was next in line.

"Shit! Shit! Shit!" I shouted. I jerked the wheel to the left and stood on the brake.

But it was too late.

A station wagon slammed into the front corner of my truck. The impact was bone-jarring. My head snapped to the side, hitting the window. Pain exploded in my skull.

The seat belt cut into my chest, constricting my breathing, as I was thrown forward then backward. If it weren't for that strip of polyester holding me in place, the steering wheel would have left a painful, if not fatal imprint, on my chest.

The sound of screeching tires and the awful noise of grating metal was all I could hear. The smell of gasoline filled my nostrils, making my eyes water.

My truck spun in dizzying circles across the freeway. I wanted to squeeze my eyes shut, block out the spinning world outside the windshield, but I knew I had to be prepared for anything.

The truck flew across a lane and hit the guardrail, crashing into it like it had hit a brick wall. My head hit the window a second time with another crack of pain. I felt the impact down to my bones. Down to every part of my body that pulsated and lived. Fire exploded in my leg as the front end of the truck caved in on itself.

With a heavy, metallic groan the truck stopped, bouncing on its frame. I sat frozen, my hands gripping the steering wheel. My knuckles were white and every muscle in my body was wound tight. My leg felt oddly numb, but I could feel a strange warmth trickle down it.

I wasn't sure how long I sat there, trying to understand what happened. When I finally came to my senses, I dragged in a deep lungful of air then reached down with a shaky hand for the door handle. The door swung open halfway, caught by the dented guardrail. The smell of freshly mowed grass couldn't cover up the scent of burnt rubber and gasoline that surrounded my truck.

I unbuckled my seat belt, grimacing when something hurt in my back. I heard the seat belt unclick and instantly felt relief against my chest.

I started searching the floorboard for my phone, seeing stars with the effort. Finally, I found it under my feet. I grasped it tightly in my hand and eased out the door. Pain radiated up my left leg as soon as my boots hit the ground. I felt a rush of warmth run down my leg, but that wasn't what held my attention.

It was the pandemonium on the highway.

Vehicles were everywhere, strewn all over the place under the moonlight. A semi lay on its side. Boxes tumbled out of its trailer. Another had a dark liquid leaking from it, pooling on the concrete. Cars and trucks were scattered all over the freeway, some of them overturned. A couple of people were climbing out, looking confused and dazed as they glanced around. Further down the highway, I could see the same thing – vehicles stopped everywhere, many of them wrecked or overturned. The strange thing was, none of them had their headlights on.

What the hell?

I started to rush to the road but agony shot up my leg. I hissed and grabbed hold of the truck for support. Shit, whatever was wrong with my leg hurt and was causing it to bleed.

Taking a few deep breaths through the pain, I returned to the driver's side door, gritting my teeth against the throbbing in my leg. Wedging myself in the small opening, I reached inside, searching for what I needed.

The blanket behind the seat.

I tore a length from it and tied the scratchy material around my thigh to staunch the bleeding as much as I could. Next, I reached inside and grabbed my cowboy hat. It had been through hell and back with me. I considered it my lucky charm and wouldn't leave it behind, even if it was just a damned hat.

My fingers curled around the brim. I stuck it on my head then leaned against the truck, favoring my left leg. I was still holding the phone, gripping it tightly in my hand. I glanced down at it. Only a black screen stared back at me. It was dead. I hit the power button. Nothing. Not even a flicker of light. I stuffed it into the rear pocket of my jeans, forgetting about it for now. That's when I heard it.

A bloodcurdling scream.

A girl not much older than myself was standing outside a vehicle a few yards away, screaming her head off. One of her flip-flops was gone and blood trickled down her face in a slow river.

Without thinking of my own injuries, I broke into a shuffling run, hindered by my leg. I felt blood run down into my left boot, but I clenched my teeth and kept my eyes on the girl.

My chest rose and fell quickly, my lungs drawing in short, quick puffs of air as I raced toward her. I remembered what my dad had told me once – *"You see someone in trouble, you help. You see someone suffering, you stop and give them what they need. You be the better man, Cash. That's all I want you to be."*

It was him I was thinking of as I limped quickly toward the car. His words that pushed me on.

"Help them! Help my friends!" the girl cried when she saw me running toward her.

I stumbled past her and over to the driver's door. A man was behind the wheel. He was unconscious. Blood dripped down his forehead from a deep gash in his hairline. I glanced into the backseat, ignoring the loud cries of the girl standing behind me.

There were two girls in the back, probably in their early twenties. One was unconscious. The other was waking up, her eyelids slowly lifting. I turned my attention back to the man behind the wheel. He was a kid, really, maybe eighteen. I reached out and pressed two fingers against his jugular.

The girl behind me grabbed my arm in a strong grip, hysterical. "Is he dead! Oh my gawd, is he dead?" she screamed, her fingers biting into my bicep.

"No, he's alive," I answered, feeling a weak but steady pulse. I unhooked his seatbelt, probably the only thing that had kept him alive.

The man grunted with pain and his eyelids started to open.

"Stay with him," I told the girl.

I limped around the car, glancing around at the other mangled vehicles nearby. *Holy shit, what happened?* I didn't have time to wonder. I could only deal with one thing at a time.

When I got to the passenger side of the car, I pushed the seat forward and wedged myself into the backseat, wincing when my injured leg hit the metal frame of the vehicle.

Fucking two-door.

But I forget about my leg a second later. The girls in the back were a mess. They were covered in blood. I focused on the unconscious one first.

Blood oozed from a gash on the top of her head. I touched her neck, finding her pulse. It was surprisingly strong. She was alive. I grabbed a fast food napkin that was on the floor and pressed it against the wound on her head. It must have hurt because the girl's eyes opened.

"Ouch," she whispered, wincing when I pressed harder.

"I know it hurts." I hated that I was adding to her pain, but I didn't know what else to do.

The girl beside her shifted and gasped. I glanced at her.

"What…what happened?" she asked, looking very confused.

"Don't know," I answered, glancing over her quickly for injuries. She had a split in her head near her temple and a cut above her eyebrow. Nothing serious, from what I could tell. I would say they were lucky, but something was telling me the danger that had caused the chaos was not gone.

In under a minute, I had them both out of the car. Blood still trickled down my leg, but saving whomever I could was my first priority.

All around me, men and women were crawling out of their vehicles. Some were crying, others were shouting for help. Many were walking around, looking puzzled and lost.

But it wasn't the people and wrecked cars that caused a foreboding feeling in me. It wasn't the soft rain that I noticed or the blood trickling down my leg.

It was the quiet and the unnatural stillness that sent unease down my spine.

Something bad had just happened. Something really bad.

Chapter Twenty-One

-Cat-

I held the phone to my ear, hearing only static.

"Cash!" I shouted, but there was no reply. We had a bad connection.

We *were* a bad connection.

I hit the end button on my phone and shoved it into my pocket. "Shit," I muttered under my breath.

I grabbed the bottle of tequila and poured another shot, splashing the liquid over the rim with sloppiness. With a silent goodbye toast to Cash, I tossed back the drink.

And that's when the room went pitch black.

Shouts and silly, girly screams filled the air. I scoffed and reached blindly for the tequila again. *Didn't they know a power outage when they saw one?* I didn't need electricity to get drunk anyway. All I needed was a bottle.

The kitchen was dark and packed full with students. I grabbed the tequila and started toward the doorway, bumping into a few squealing girls along the way. I rolled my eyes and elbowed past them. I just wanted to find a nice, quiet corner where I could snuggle with my new best friend – my bottle of tequila – and get to know it better.

I pushed my way into the living room, stumbling on my feet. Hot air hit me like a hammer as soon as I made it there. Without electricity, there was no such thing as air conditioning. The press of warm bodies only added to the suffocating heat.

I moved on, looking for a private spot. The music had stopped, but in its place was chatter.

"Power's out again. Happens during storms."

"There's no storms tonight, idiot."

"Yeah, on my weather App it says—"

"You're a dumbass. Someone go flip the fuckin' breaker!"

"Holy shit, the lights are out everywhere in the complex! Piece of shit custodian."

"This party is epic, man…"

The voices blended together in my head. I shoved past guys and girls until I came to a wall. I fell against it, cradling the tequila close to my chest. The darkness combined with the alcohol was messing with my equilibrium. I pulled out my cell phone. It had a flashlight on it. *Why the hell is no one using theirs?* I tried pushing the 'on' button but nothing happened. I tried again. Nothing. There was no light. No bright home screen. No little battery picture letting me know that my phone was dead. It didn't make sense. *Oh, well.* I was too tipsy to care.

I pocketed the phone and leaned my head back against the wall. The music might have been dead along with the lights but the party still raged on around me. I wondered briefly where Keely and Nathan were and if Tate was okay back at my apartment, but the alcohol was making it hard to form a coherent thought. It was just what I had wanted. Oblivion.

I took a long drink from the bottle of tequila. After the second one, I slid down the wall, needing to sit down.

My butt hit the carpet and my hand fell to my side. The bottle rolled away from me, spilling liquor on the floor. My head fell back against the wall with a thud, my body going numb. The alcohol was doing its thing. My eyes started to close, but I forced them back open again.

If I passed out, I could forget about Luke and Jenna's death. I could forget about what kind of person I was and how I was so afraid to feel anything for someone ever again.

I could forget about Cash and the threat he poised. About the way he had made me feel or what he had done to my body. I could forget about what I didn't deserve. What I couldn't allow myself to have.

So I did what I needed to do. What I had to do to survive the pain in me. I let the alcohol pull me under and I passed out.

Only darkness surrounded me.

~~~~

I dreamed. I was in the woods, running. Chased by something faceless. The air was thick, the heat harsh. I was sweating, trying to escape from whatever was after me. I heard someone calling my name. Beckoning to me. I swung around. Looking. Searching.

"Cat, wake up."

There it was again. The voice. I needed to hide before he found me, but heaviness kept me prisoner.

"Cat."

My name pulled me to the surface. I groaned, fighting it. The sound crashed into my brain and caused agony.

"Cat, you need to get up. Now."

This time the voice was soft. Whispered. Almost gentle.

I peeled my eyes open to only mere slits. It was the best I could do. My eyelids felt swollen and raw, like someone had rubbed sandpaper on them. Mascara caked my lashes, sticking them together. I tried to remember where I was and what had happened, but I drew a blank.

My tongue felt thick. I groaned and licked my dry lips, instantly recognizing the taste of alcohol. Then I knew.

I was hungover.

I forced my eyes open some more, expecting to be blinded by sunlight or artificial lighting. Both would be excruciating, like needles stuck in my eyeballs, but neither greeted me.

"What's going on?" I asked, wincing when the sound of my own voice hurt my head.

No one answered as I pushed myself to my elbows. Tate was sitting on the foot of my bed, chewing on his thumbnail and watching me with a worried expression. Keely sat near my side, one leg tucked underneath her slim body. She played nervously with a wrinkle in the sheet and stared at me with concern. I followed her gaze when she turned to look behind her. I found Nathan sitting in the overstuffed chair in the corner of my room, looking at me intently.

He leaned forward, resting his elbows on his knees. "We've got a problem, Cat."

I pushed myself to a sitting position and brushed tangled strands of hair out of my eyes.

"If it has anything to do with what I did last night, I don't want to hear about it," I moaned, rubbing a hand over my forehead.

Keely pushed her glasses further up the bridge of her nose. "You passed out."

"Duh," I said, glancing at her from underneath my matted mascara. God, even that hurt to say.

She frowned at me and all the memories of Cash came back. It hurt more than my hangover. Keely looked so much like Cash that guilt and remorse consumed me. It wasn't her fault that I had fucked her brother and fallen for him.

It was mine.

"Enough, Cat," Nathan snapped, looking tense and ready to explode. "Like I said, we've got a problem. We don't have time for your mouth today."

I scowled at him but then backed down. He was upset about something and not much freaked him out. Something was wrong. More than likely I was the cause of it.

"What's going on?" I asked, hoping it wasn't bad. *Did I vomit in his car or dance on a table again? Did they find me half-naked somewhere? That would be the worst.* I scrunched up my face, trying to remember, and caught a whiff of something in my hair. I grabbed a strand and studied it. *Is that fucking dried beer in my hair?*

Nathan let his hands drop between his knees. "Cat, goddamn it, pay attention! Do you remember the lights going off last night?"

I dropped the strand of hair and looked at him. "Yeah. It was a power outage. Happens all the time here."

If they thought a loss of electricity justified pulling me out of a dead sleep, they were wrong.

And all very much on my shit list.

Nathan shook his head, looking suddenly tired. "The power is still off and there's more."

He sounded so bleak that chills went up my spine. I shook the feeling off and reached over to yank the little gold chain that dangled from my nightstand lamp. Nothing happened. I tried again. Nothing.

A feeling of uneasiness slithered between my shoulder blades. I dismissed it. *The lamp's just not plugged in.* Everyone sat quietly and watched as I leaned over, checking to make sure the plug was in the wall socket. It was. *Hmm.*

I pushed myself back up, feeling a little green. Moving made me want to hurl.

"Okay. So let's call the apartment manager. The guy's a sleazeball but he'll know what's going on," I said, picking up my cell phone from the nightstand, wincing when my head pounded and nausea rolled through me.

Keely spoke up, her voice sounding too chipper, all things considered. *Like my headache.*

"I put your phone there last night when Nathan carried you in. I knew you would want it this morning but...but it isn't working either," she said with a shrug.

I didn't believe her. It was the latest iPhone, brand new, expensive, and encased in a gold cover. Something that had worked like a charm last night until...

All the blood drained from my face. My phone had worked great until I had called Cash. *Oh, shit. I called Cash.* I suddenly remembered his voice, his words. The warm, tingly feeling that had washed over me when I heard him on the other end of the line. It all came back to me like a bad dream. Static had ended the call.

But I never should have placed it in the first place.

My face grew hot, guilty for making the one mistake a girl like me never made - calling a hookup afterward.

I looked down at the phone in my hand, my dry mouth suddenly drier.

I had been drunk, I reasoned. People made stupid, dumb phone calls when they were blitzed, calls they would regret in the morning. I regretted this one big time because one-night stands didn't get phone calls afterward from me. It was the golden rule and I had just broken it.

I tried turning on my phone, but it didn't light up. I tried again.

"None of them work, Cat," Nathan said, his voice

sounding so hopeless that I snapped my gaze up to his. Nathan didn't do hopeless. That was my role.

"That doesn't make sense," I muttered. "It's a brand new phone."

Despite the hangover that was killing me, I threw my legs over the side of the bed and tossed the covers back. The world spun when I climbed to my feet but I held onto the side of the bed and stood up.

"What are you doing?" Tate asked around his fingernail as I went over to the corner of my room and started tossing clothes out of the way.

"Looking for my charger. My phone's just dead," I answered.

"It's a waste of time. I told you, none of them work," Nathan grumbled. "Believe me. We checked a million times while you were sleeping off your shit-faced binge from last night."

I felt my face turn bright red with anger.

"Are you really going to give me a hard time about getting wasted, Nathan?" I asked. "Keely, ask him about the last time he got drunk. It's a great story that involves him face down in a stranger's yard with his pants missing."

Nathan rammed a hand through his hair in frustration. "You're such a goddamn pain in my ass, Cat," he muttered. "Listen to me. The phones are fried, the electricity's off, and I have a feeling we're screwed."

He said it with so much finality that it made me madder than hell. Nathan had never given up and he couldn't start now. I gave up. My parents gave up. But Nathan never had. He was a fighter. A warrior. A goddamn machine. If he gave up, we *were* screwed and that made me steaming mad and scared.

I frowned at him, trying to ignore the feeling of fright growing in me. "Don't be such a drama queen, Nathan. It's just a power outage. Maybe some cell towers were affected. So what? We're not *screwed*. You don't know what the hell you're talking about."

Nathan shot to his feet (I did say he was a fighter) and charged across the room. He grabbed my arm and gave me a good shake.

"We're not screwed, huh? Let me just show you how *not screwed* we are." He started hauling me from the room, dragging me toward the door.

"What the hell, Nathan? You're hurting me! Let go!" I screeched. His fingers were leaving imprints on my skin, biting into me. I tried to twist away as he pulled me from the bedroom and through the living room but it was no use.

Tate and Keely followed us as he pulled me toward the front door. I tried prying my arm from him but then I noticed something. The apartment was quiet and, god, was it hot. The air conditioning didn't hum. No light bulbs buzzed in the light fixture.

My t-shirt quickly became stuck to my damp skin. My hair curled up with the humidity. I tried to grab some footing as Nathan pulled me along but it was no use. He was strong.

"I don't know what I'm talking about? Well, let me show you," he roared, flinging open the front door.

He jerked me out into the blistering heat. Sunlight blinded me, feeling like multiple arrows shot through my eyes. I squinted and grimaced, stumbling with the pain that exploded in my head.

Nathan didn't care. He took the stairs two at a time, hauling me with him. I tripped and almost fell. The hot cement burned the bottoms of my bare feet. I didn't have time to cry about it or whine that he was being too rough. I heard voices. Lots of them.

Then I saw the madness.

Chapter Twenty-Two

-Cat-

The apartment's parking lot was full. Not of cars. Of people.

I missed a step and almost fell down the stairs when I saw all the students. They milled around aimlessly. There had to be a hundred of them. Some were in their pajamas. Others were dressed in t-shirts and shorts. They all looked confused, hot, and tired.

A group of blonde-haired sorority lookalikes were standing in a small circle nearby. They were talking a mile a minute as they studied their phones. Their shrill voices rose higher and higher as they disagreed about something. One looked close to tears. Another seemed angry.

Then there was the small group of guys. They were looking under the hood of a beat-up yellow Ford Escort with confusion. A couple of them were arguing. One of the guys started gesturing across the parking lot with his oil-smudged hands, arguing with another kid.

I could feel the tension in the air. Whatever was going on, it wasn't an impromptu block party. It was trouble.

I gaped at everyone as Nathan hauled me across the parking lot. I didn't care if he left bruises on my arm. I was too confused on what was happening.

"I don't know what I'm talking about, huh sis?" he said with hostility, letting me go when we got to his car. "Well, check this out."

He pulled his keys from his pocket and hit the unlock button. Nothing happened. He gave me a told-you-so look then shoved the key into the keyhole and unlocked the car.

The fancy leather driver's seat creaked when he slid behind the wheel. I watched with a sense of unease as he inserted the key into the ignition and turned it. The engine didn't start. The deep rumble of his sports car didn't fill the air. He tried again. Nothing.

Removing the key, he got out of the car and faced me.

"It won't start, Cat. None of these cars will," he said, gesturing around us. "How's that for screwed?"

I glanced at the other vehicles, feeling panicky. *He can't be right. Not everyone could have a dead vehicle.* But then I saw a guy trying to start his motorcycle. He turned the key and stomped on the gas pedal. There was no loud roar. No badass sound coming from the motor. He became frustrated and climbed off, kicking one of the tires.

A few yards away, I saw a girl in bright yellow SpongeBob pajamas sitting on the trunk of her Corolla. She was crying into her hands as some guy tried to start her car. The same thing was happening again and again everywhere – people were trying to start their vehicles.

But nobody was driving away.

That's impossible, right? What are the chances that everyone's car won't start on the same day?

Tate and Keely were beside me, staring at the chaos too. Tate grabbed the keys out of Nathan's hand. "Let me try," he mumbled.

He pushed Nathan out of the way to slide down into the driver's seat. Tate had been driving on the old, dirt roads near our house for the past year. With his typical attitude, he now thought he knew more about vehicles than we did.

Jamming the key in the ignition, he tried to start the engine, wanting to prove Nathan wrong. But again nothing. The car's engine stayed quiet.

Nathan reached inside and grabbed the key. "Told you it didn't work. Believe me now?"

Before Tate could answer a group of guys started racing toward us. They shouted something about looters and needing to protect a store.

Nathan reached out and grabbed Keely, pulling her out of the way just as the guys ran past us. I recognized a few of them. One was the star basketball player for UT. A few of his teammates were with him, looking angry and ready to fight. They were heading around the corner of the apartment complex, their gym shorts loose and their hair wet with sweat.

I knew where they were going. On the other side of the apartment building was a rundown convenience store that had been there forever. It was old and needed some TLC, but underage students could buy beer there without an I.D. I should know. I had been a customer many times over the past year.

A little Asian man ran the store. He was friendly and easygoing, always ready with a cheerful hello. He didn't mind when students hung out in his store, zapping cheap burritos in the ancient microwave or rehashing the loss of a football game over slushies. He didn't even mind giving away a few free candy bars or bags of chips to down-on-their-luck kids until they got their next paycheck.

The store and owner were legendary around campus so if someone were messing with either, the students would fight to protect them. But who would loot it? Looting was something I had only seen on TV. It didn't happen in quiet college towns. So what was going on?

I turned in a slow circle, different scenarios popping up in my head. If a cell tower had collapsed, people would be antsy. God knows we couldn't live without our phones and the Internet for very long. But that wouldn't explain the dead cars. A small solar flare could fry quite a bit. It was an outlandish idea – one you might only see in the movies - but it was possible, according to my science teacher.

Suddenly, I remembered the conversation with my dad. He had said the government was on high alert and we needed to stay alert.

I turned to Nathan. "Dad said—" I never got a chance to finish. Gunfire erupted.

POP! POP! POP!

It sounded like a car backfiring, but it was louder. Closer. Screams erupted, followed by another gunshot.

POP!

We ducked next to Nathan's car, our instincts telling us to take cover. The palms of my hands scraped against cement. Little pebbles dug into my skin. It was the least of my worries. Someone was *shooting*, for Christ's sake.

Keely grabbed my arm, kneeling by me. "Oh shit! Oh, shit! Was that gunfire?" she whispered, her eyes the size of saucers behind her glasses.

I started to answer, but saw Tate climbing to his feet.

"Tate!" I shouted, scrabbling past Keely to get to him.

Nathan was faster. He grabbed a handful of Tate's shirt and yanked him down.

"Are you trying to get yourself killed?" he roared, ramming Tate up against the car. "Stay down!"

I peeled Keely's hold off me and crawled over to Tate.

"It's okay," I whispered, grabbing his arm in a death grip. But I was lying. It wasn't okay. My heart was pounding and my ears were ringing. Someone was shooting and we were out in the open. It was not normal or okay.

I glanced at Nathan as he started to stand up. I instantly knew what he was going to do.

"No! No!" I shouted, reaching over Keely to grab Nathan's arm. I had already lost Luke and Jenna. I couldn't lose my brother too!

My fingers caught his shirt but it didn't stop him.

"Take care of them," he said, nodding at Keely and then Tate. "I'll be right back. I want to find out what's going on."

I fought my panic as Nathan tore from my grasp and took off. I had not prayed since the night Luke died, not even when the priest spread dirt on his coffin and said the last rites over his grave. I didn't believe in God or prayers or hope or miracles anymore. Life just didn't work that way for me. But in that moment, as I kneeled on the hot pavement and watched my brother run toward trouble instead of away from it, I prayed.

I clutched Tate tightly and closed my eyes, shutting out the sounds of crying nearby and the screams in the distance. I didn't open my eyes when Keely grabbed a handful of my shirt. I didn't force them open when I thought of Cash, hoping whatever was happening here was not happening where he was. I just prayed and prayed until I couldn't pray anymore.

But when the screams around me grew louder, I opened my eyes. I could see people running around, looking for cover or safety, but I couldn't see Nathan. I let go of Tate and moved past Keely to look around the car. He had been gone too long.

"Do you see anything? Who's shooting?" Tate asked, easing behind me.

I sat down, careful to keep the rear tire at my back for protection. "I don't know."

I wrapped my arm around Tate's slim shoulders and pulled him closer. Out of the corner of my eye, I saw Keely shaking, her knees tucked up under her. Over the roaring in my ears, I heard running feet and the sound of someone shouting. I squeezed my eyes shut and held on to Tate, wanting to block out everything. Maybe I was just dreaming, a weird side effect of all the alcohol in my system.

Or maybe I was finally in hell.

My fingers tightened on Tate's shoulder, squeezing him to me. I heard the skidding of shoes on asphalt a second before I heard the voice.

"Come on! Come on!"

I snapped my eyes open. Nathan was standing over us - panting, sweating, and motioning for us to get up. His gaze darted around, watching for trouble, as he reached for Keely.

She grabbed his hand and pulled herself up. Nathan tucked her against him and reached for me but I was already on my feet, tugging Tate up too. The sound of gunfire hit again, closer this time.

POP! POP!

Screams burst around us but it wasn't going to stop the four of us. Nathan pushed Tate and me ahead of him.

"RUN!" he shouted.

He didn't have to tell me twice.

We took off, sprinting across the parking lot. The hot pavement blistered my bare feet. Glass tore into my arches and cut my toes but I didn't let it stop me. I ran.

Students were running in all directions, unsure where to go. We dove into the madness, fighting the crowd to get to safety.

I was jarred a couple of times as I headed for the apartment stairs, but I reached back and grabbed Tate's arm. No way was I going to lose him. My feet felt raw and my lungs burned but I pushed on, knowing the only safe place was behind the brick walls of my apartment building. Two more steps and we would be to the stairway. Three flights of stairs and we could slam the door on whatever craziness was going on outside.

But I never got there.

A loud boom shook the ground. It sounded like a bomb exploding. My eardrums popped and my head felt like it would burst. I covered my ears and turned in the direction the explosion had come from.

"Oh, shit! Oh, shit!" I said between numb lips.

Everett Dorm, the student housing across the street, had exploded in fire.

A black cloud of smoke rose in the sky. It looked menacing against the innocent puffy clouds floating by. Bright orange flames licked up the sides of the student building. The roof was one big fireball, the flames almost too bright to look at. Windows burst and shattered as the heat touched them.

People rushed away from the burning building. There were screams and cries. I stood in shock. *This is not real. Not real.* I needed to move but I couldn't. What was going on around me was too surreal to be believable. Too terrible to understand.

Nathan pushed Keely toward Tate. "Get to the apartment! Lock the door and don't open it for anyone. I'll be back!"

Tate caught Keely with one arm, looking at his older brother like he was crazy. Maybe he was. Before I could ask what he was doing, Nathan turned and took off running.

"NATHAN!" I screamed, holding Tate back when he tried to follow his older brother. "NATHAN!"

Nathan either didn't hear me or wasn't paying attention. He sprinted across the parking lot quickly. I watched, my heart in my throat, as he disappeared into the crowd near the burning building.

"What is he doing?" Tate cried, trying to detangle himself from my hold. "What the hell is he doing?"

"He's helping," I said, sounding calmer than I felt. I knew what I had to do.

"Watch him," I ordered Keely, pushing Tate toward her.

She nodded and I took off. Tate shouted for me to stop and Keely yelled that it wasn't safe, but I took off anyway.

My feet were bleeding but I didn't let it slow me down. If my grandmother were there she would have scoffed at the idea of a little brat like me helping others. My dad would have been grinning, proud of his princess. My mother would have looked down her newly constructed nose at me for sweating. But for once in my sucky life, I did what I knew was right. I ran.

The heat from the flames burned my face as I got closer to the burning building. Someone yelled at me to not go any closer, but Nathan was somewhere nearby. We always stuck together no matter what. This time would be no different.

I shoved past people. I avoided falling when someone jostled me.

"NATHAN!" I screamed, getting as close as I could to the flame-filled building.

"Get back! Get back!"

He was running toward me, motioning for me to get away.

The crowd surged around me. The world spun at a dizzying speed. Suddenly, strong hands grabbed my arms.

"Get out of here, Cat!" Nathan yelled. His face was blackened and his hair looked singed. I wanted to ask him if he was fucking crazy. *Didn't he know if I lost him, I would die too?*

He started dragging me away, muttering again and again, "There's nothing we can do. There's nothing we can do."

He pulled me across the street and through the parking lot. I became a robot, going into the dark place where nothing inside me lived or breathed. I was too terrified. Too scared.

Focus on something else. My feet hurt. I wanted to stop and see how damaged they were, but Nathan wouldn't let me. He kept pulling me along, unwilling to let me give up. He did the same thing after Luke died.

He made me go on.

By the time we reached the apartment stairway, the scent of smoke was filling my nostrils and burning my lungs. A breeze brought with it the smell of the fire.

And of death.

I choked back a cough and started up the stairs. Other people rushed past me on the narrow steps, trying to get to some sort of safety. Craziness was everywhere – from the burning building to the muted sounds of gunfire off in the distance. The world seemed to be going insane.

It seemed to take forever to reach the third floor landing, but when Nathan and I did, a sudden burst of energy exploded in me. I sprinted for my apartment like the fire across the street was licking at my heels.

Tate and Keely were standing in the doorway of my apartment. They both looked afraid and frantic.

"Hurry! Get in!" Keely shouted, motioning to us as another gunshot ripped through the air.

I had only a few more feet to go. I could feel the blood oozing out of the small cuts on my toes and heels. I didn't have time to assess the damage to them. Nathan snagged a handful of my shirt and pulled me the rest of the way into the apartment.

My toes sunk into the soft cushion of my apartment's carpet as soon as I hit the threshold. Nathan slammed the door closed behind me then locked it. He grabbed a small chair from the corner of my living room and dragged it back to the front door, wedging it under the door handle tightly.

"Extra security," he explained. "It stays there at all times, understand? He looked from me to Tate then to Keely.

I nodded. My chest rose and fell quickly. I felt sick and scared and hyped up with adrenaline at the same time.

"What's going on?" Keely asked wide-eyed, standing close by Nathan. "Oh, gawd! What's going on?"

No one answered her. I wasn't sure we knew what to say. Nathan stood in the middle of the room, blackened and shaken. Tate was pacing back and forth between the sofa and the dark TV, fidgeting with the edge of his shirt nervously.

I was barefoot, scared, and still wearing my clothes from last night. Beads of sweat had broken out along my hairline yet I was shaking. It started in my bones and moved outward to my fingertips. Every muscle in my body shook. Every inch of me shivered. I knew it was from shock, a product of my mind, but I couldn't control it. I knew it too well and it knew me.

I wrapped my arms around my middle to stop the trembling but just like everything else in my stupid life, there was no stopping it. My teeth chattered and the tips of my fingers turned icy. I felt all the blood rush from my head, leaving me weak and feeling empty. My eyes watered. I swiped at the tears, cursing the smoke that caused it and hating the fear that made them worse.

Nathan shot across the room, snagging the shades of the window open.

I couldn't see anything, but I could hear shouts and shrieks of terror. It was enough to make my blood go cold all over again.

He dropped the shade back in place and swung around to look at us. "Stay away from the window," he ordered, hurrying to the kitchen.

No one questioned him. Nathan had always been a born leader and now was no different. If he said jump, I would jump and not argue. Not when my life or Tate's depended on it. And right now I had a feeling they did.

Tate, Keely and I rushed to follow Nathan into the little kitchen. I reached for the light switch as soon as I walked in - an automatic response to a dark room. With just a touch of my finger, I should have light. But the ugly florescent light fixture didn't turn on. The room stayed dark, the shadows thick. It sent a chill down my spine.

Tate moved behind me, watching me try the light switch again and again.

"Ain't working, sis," he mumbled as he bit his thumbnail.

The thwack of a cabinet drawer made me jump. Nathan was opening and closing them, looking for something and growing aggravated when he couldn't find it.

He swore under his breath as he rummaged through a drawer. "You have any flashlights, Cat?" he asked, shoving the drawer closed when he didn't find anything.

I shook my head. "No. I…I don't think so."

Nathan slammed the cabinet door shut with a bang and a loud curse. It made me flinch and Keely back away. I couldn't blame her. My brother looked angry enough to spit nails and rip off heads. I wanted to stay out of his way too.

He gripped the back of one of the kitchen chairs. His knuckles turned white as he struggled to calm down. His chest and shoulders rose and fell as he drew in deep gulps of air. He hung his head and tightened his hands on the chair, making his biceps go tense.

I knew he was trying to gain control again. Good for him. I still hadn't found it. My hands shook and my knees felt like jelly. For someone that always had her shit together, I was falling apart.

It took a minute but Nathan finally raised his head. He opened his mouth to say something but screams from outside interrupted him.

"Shit!" Nathan cursed, plunging a hand through his hair with frustration. He gripped the long strands on top and glanced around the room as if it held all the answers. I wish it did, but when had I ever gotten what I wished for?

Nathan let go of his hair and grasped the back of his neck. It was a gesture he did when he was troubled. I could see him running through different scenarios in his mind, working out problems and tossing out answers. Finally he came to a decision.

"Here's what we're going to do." He dropped his hand onto the back of the chair and gripped it hard. "We're going to hole up in here and wait this out. I don't know what's going on but it will be over soon. It *has* to be over soon. The police will show up and arrest whoever's shooting. The electric company will get the power back on just like they do every single time." He took a ragged breath. "We'll be okay, I promise. We've just got to stick together and stay here."

Nathan's words calmed me like they had done before.

He was right. Help would come. We would be okay.

I just hoped it wasn't too late.

Chapter Twenty-Three

-Cash-

I limped down the middle of the road. Step. Drag. Step. Drag. On each drag I winced. On each step I prayed.

Dust swirled up around my legs, leaving a fine layer of grime on me. I looked down at it and scoffed. My jeans were already stiff with blood and sweat, what was a little dirt too?

I thought of Cat and grinned, feeling a little delirious from blood loss. *If she could see me now, she would stick up that pretty little nose of hers and walk away.* My grin suddenly disappeared. *Shit, I hope she's okay.*

I took another step then dragged my left leg. Another step then drag. The gash I got on my thigh during the wreck was giving me problems. Pain shot from it, making me grit my teeth and struggle not to puke. Finally, I couldn't go any farther. I needed to rest.

I stopped in the middle of the road, breathing hard. My shirt was stuck to my skin and my hair was soaking wet. I put all my weight on my good leg and took off my hat. Not even a breeze cooled my forehead. I wiped it then stuck the hat back on my head, at the same time glancing around.

I stood in the middle of a dusty, dirt road. There was no sign of civilization anywhere. No people. No cars. I was alone. Thick, eerie woods surrounded me on both sides. A sort of fearful stillness surrounded me. Not one branch swayed or leaf fell. There were no birds chirping or insects buzzing. It reminded me of a scene in a zombie movie. Any minute I expected one of the undead to stumble out of the woods, hungry for a little taste of me.

I was on my last leg anyway.

I stood still and slowly glanced around, taking my time and missing nothing. The silence made me nervous. Hell, everything that had happened in the past eight hours had made me nervous. Cars did not just die while traveling down the freeway. All phones did not just quit working for no apparent reason. Every business I had passed and house I had seen sat dark, without the hum of electricity. Add it all together and it just didn't make sense.

I ran a hand over my dry lips, thinking of those folks on the freeway. I had hung around a while, helping the injured, waiting for help to show up.

But it never did.

That's when I started walking. It was like something was pushing me to go home, urging me to hurry. Not one streetlight lit the way. I never passed a car or heard a siren. It was as if everyone in the world had disappeared and nobody was left but me.

I was hungry, thirsty, hurting, and still miles from home. I balanced myself on my good leg and squinted up at the sky. The sun glared back at me. *Fucking thing.* It burned like hell and set my leg on fire. The only good thing about the sun was it told me the time of day.

But I still hated the damn thing.

Glaring at it, I could tell it was midafternoon. I hadn't had a drink of water in hours. My mouth felt like cotton and my tongue was swollen. The temperature didn't help either. The weatherman had called for triple digits and I wouldn't be surprised if we were climbing there fast. I could feel my skin pulsate with the heat. I had spent enough time in the sun to know that heat stroke was a dangerous thing. Add to that the amount of water I was sweating out and the blood I had lost, and I was in trouble.

I glanced around, looking for some shade. I needed to rest and check my leg. A tree up ahead caught my eye. It was small but its branches stretched over the road. I kept my eyes open for trouble and started limping its way. Step. Drag. Step. Drag. Damn, at the rate I was going, getting home would take forever.

It took me a while but I finally reached the dry grass under the tree. I fell to the ground with a huff, poking my hands on little rocks.

The exertion it took to drag my wounded leg wore me out. I pulled my cowboy hat off and laid it on the ground beside me, hoping to catch a breeze. None came. Stillness and the heat of the day stayed instead.

I sat there until the shadows were longer and the sun was lower. The temperature hadn't dropped but I knew I had to keep going. Something was telling me to hurry home.

I looked down at the piece of fabric I had tied around my thigh. It was soaked with blood and smudged with dirt but it was the only thing holding the gash together. I tried not to think about the last time I had used the blanket. No matter how much pain I was in, Cat was still on my mind.

I swore and swiped a hand over my sweaty brow. I couldn't think about her now. I needed to keep moving.

I grabbed the ends of the fabric tied around my leg and yanked. Pain exploded in my thigh and beads of sweat popped out on my forehead. As soon as the agony passed, I pushed myself off the ground to a stand up. The world spun but I held still, waiting for it to calm down. When it did, I headed for the road.

Gravel and dirt crunched under the soles of my boots, sounding bone dry. I grimaced when I tried to put weight on my leg and it started throbbing again. I felt a trickle of blood but I refused to look down. There was nothing I could do about it anyway.

I limped to the middle of the road but drew to a stop. I heard something. *A branch breaking, maybe? Or was it a man?*

Favoring my left leg, I stood as still as a statue. My fingers hung loosely at my sides, ready to reach down and grab my knife from my boot if needed. But nothing moved. Not a leaf. Not a blade of grass. Not even a bird. I relaxed and pulled my hat brim lower.

Time to get moving.

~~~~

Dusk was settling in when I passed under the metal sign for my family's farm. I looked up at it as I limped by, watching as it swayed back and forth lazily. The sound of squeaking metal joined the noise of my footsteps shuffling on the dry gravel driveway.

A few horses grazed out near the barn and a couple of cows stood in the pasture, munching on grass. It was peaceful, but today the quiet was different.

Fear prickled along my shoulder blades as I walked toward the house. Something was missing. I glanced around, looking for trouble. That's when I realized what was wrong.

My dad's truck was missing.

"Shit," I exclaimed, picking up speed. I hurried toward the house in a running, awkward gait, pushing through the pain in my leg.

"MOM?" I called out when I got closer to the house. "DAD?"

No one answered. The house just stared back at me, looking old and sad against the setting sun.

"Mom? Dad? Hello?" I yelled as I hobbled up the porch steps and to the front door. It banged against my back as I threw it open and jiggled the door handle. It was locked and no one came to unlock it. Feeling my heart in my throat, I dug my keys out of my pocket.

Hot, stuffy air greeted me as soon as I threw the door open. I stepped inside, dragging my left leg in after me. The screen door slammed shut as I tried the light switch on the wall. Nothing happened. I tried a lamp. Again nothing.

The prickling between my shoulders blades grew. *Where the hell are my parents?*

My dad's old work boots sat near his favorite recliner, awaiting to be put back on. My mother's sewing basket sat near her chair, opened and full of knitting.

I turned away from the tiny living room and headed for the kitchen. I hadn't had a drink of water in hours. Thirst ate away at me.

I threw my cowboy hat on the table and headed for the sink. After grabbing a glass from the cabinet, I filled it with water from the tap. It felt good going down but I needed more. I filled the glass a second time and took a long drink, glancing around the kitchen at the same time.

Maybe they left a note.

I sat the glass down and limped over to the kitchen table, finding out where my parents were the only thing on my mind. Loose papers were scattered on top of the scarred table. Four wooden chairs sat innocently around it. I remembered sitting there when I was younger and fighting Keely for the last slice of Mom's apple pie.

Another time I had walked up behind her and pulled her hair, making fun of her when she first got her glasses.

I wondered if whatever was going on with the electricity and cars was happening in Austin. *God, I hope not.*

First things first. My parents. I shuffled the papers on the table, looking for something that might tell me where they went. There was nothing.

I looked around the kitchen. The counters were clean, all dishes put away. The old green refrigerator sat quiet against the wall, absent of the constant humming I had heard my entire life. I limped over to it, my attention caught on something stuck to the front. It was a note wedged between yellowed advertisements for feed and articles about the price of beef. I plucked it off. My mom's gentle, cursive letters stared back at me.
Gone to town.

My fingers tightened around the paper. "Shit."

If my mom and dad were in town, that meant they might have been affected by the crazy power outage too. And more than likely, if the vehicles there had died, their truck would be useless too. But the question was, what was causing all of it?

I pivoted on my good leg and slammed the note down on the table then hobbled across the room. I opened a cabinet door and reached into the back, grabbing the bottle of whiskey my dad kept there for medical purposes. It was half-gone but I had to start numbing the pain in my leg somehow.

I pulled the top off and took a long drink. It was just what I needed to calm my nerves and deaden the agony.

With the whiskey bottle still in my hand, I turned and stumbled from the room. I needed some answers.

I headed straight for the living room. I would try the TV first. It didn't work. I tried the battery-operated radio that my father kept by his chair. That didn't work either.

"Shit!" I limped as fast as I could down the hallway, panic growing in me. *I've got to figure out what's happening.*

I tried the lights in the bathroom then my bedroom. Nothing. Not a flicker. Not a single hum of electricity. I grew desperate and a little crazy. *What the fuck is going on?*

Suddenly, I slammed to a stop, remembering the newscaster's words that night in my truck. *'The threat is real. Americans should be concerned.'*

Was it possible? Had the United States been attacked?

I started back to the bathroom, limping slower. I had to get my head on straight. Calm down. The first thing I had to do was find out how badly I was injured.

I took another long pull from the whiskey bottle as I walked into the bathroom. I set the bottle on the counter and started digging around under the sink until I found an old, rusted flashlight in the back. When you lived miles from anyone you learned to rely on yourselves, not others. That meant being prepared.

I flipped it on. It worked, thank God.

I laid the flashlight on the counter and pulled out an old first aid kit from under the sink. The flashlight beam gave me just enough light to see the kit's contents in the growing darkness. I grabbed a fistful of supplies and sat down on the lid of the toilet, wincing when pain shot up my leg.

Gritting my teeth, I laid the supplies out then untied the strip of cloth from my leg. Agony rolled through me. I took another long drink of whiskey to help numb the pain. It helped but I knew nothing was going to take away the pain totally.

I grabbed the flashlight and shined it at the gash. It was gaping open, full of dirt and grime. Beads of sweat popped up on my forehead, thinking of what I was about to do. I pulled my knife out of the sheath on my boot and started cutting away at the leg of my jeans. They were a lost cause anyway.

With them out of the way, I could see the gash better. It was long, going from my outer hip to the middle of my thigh. It needed stitches something bad, but I didn't see that happening anytime soon.

Before I could talk myself out of it, I grabbed the bottle of rubbing alcohol my mom kept under the sink and poured some on the gash. Fire ripped through me. It burned, *shit* it fucking burned. I gritted my teeth so hard, I thought I might crack a tooth. I felt dizzy and sick and goddamn close to passing out all at the same time. I took one more drink of whiskey and then with a shaky hand, I poured the alcohol on the gash.

"Fuck!" I hissed, closing my eyes and slamming the bottle down. I gripped the edge of the counter and held on tight as waves of pain hit me.

When the agony lessened, I reached for some cotton gauze with a trembling hand. I tried cleaning the blood up as best as I could then finally gave up and tossed the gauze in the trash. The cut started bleeding again almost instantly, but there wasn't much I could do. I tore some medical tape off with my teeth and placed it across the wound, pulling the ragged edges of the cut together. I started sweating and turning paler as I fought the pain. The agony was killing me.

But I had to continue. I took a deep breath and grabbed some medical pads and taped them on top of the gash. It was a half-ass job but it would have to do. I didn't have much choice anyway.

Next, I finished off the whiskey – a very important thing to do - then I climbed to my feet. The dark bathroom spun for a minute but then it stopped. I grabbed the flashlight and left the bathroom, limping to my room.

I was nauseated and close to passing out by the time I made it to my bedroom. I dragged my leg and crossed the room to the closet. I grabbed a shirt and a pair of jeans and changed quickly, clamping my jaw against the pain the effort caused.

Once dressed, I reached into the back of my closet and pulled out a small duffle bag. I stuffed an extra set of clothes inside it then grabbed the shotgun hidden in the closet. I threw it all on the bed and limped over to my nightstand.

Inside one of the drawers, I found my revolver. It was an old .45 Colt that belonged to my granddad. The wooden handle was scarred and the barrel was rough. It was heavy in my hand, a relic from the Old West.

But now it was this cowboy's firearm.

I spun the cylinder, checking for bullets. It was loaded and ready to go. I flicked my wrist and slapped the cylinder closed then stuck the gun in the waistband of my jeans. Reaching back into the nightstand, I grabbed a box of bullets and staggered to the end of the bed. I didn't know what the hell was happening, but I was going to be prepared for anything.

I put the bullets in the duffle bag then turned my attention to the shotgun. It was a 12-gauge pump action with a wooden stock. My pride and joy. I picked it up, welcoming the heaviness in my hand. I hoped I didn't have to use it but I sure as hell wouldn't leave it.

I grabbed the flashlight and started to leave, but the bed caught my eye. I paused, indecision nagging me. My body screamed to rest. It had been over thirty-six hours since I last slept. I had lost blood and I was weak. I needed to sleep.

But there was another part of me that refused to slow down. I was a fighter and nothing would stop me from finding the ones that I loved.

With determination, I headed down the hallway, lighting the way with the flashlight. I still limped, but this time my stride was powerful. Strong. Determined to never stop.

I snatched my cowboy hat from the kitchen table and scribbled a quick note to my parents, just in case they showed up. After that, I grabbed as many bottles of water as I could fit into my duffle bag and as much food as it could carry. Next, I headed for the front door.

I was a man on a mission. One born to do what I had to do. I knew the land like the back of my hand and could be one helluva problem if I wanted to be. I dared anyone to try to mess with me.

With a duffle bag on my shoulder, a shotgun in one hand, and a revolver in my waistband, I stopped on the threshold. Twilight had descended, leaving the house dark and the land still. I could feel the fire start in me. The fire to fight. To survive.

To find my family and live.

Chapter Twenty-Four

-Cat-

Your feet okay?"
I replaced the last bandage on my heel and looked at Keely. "They're fine," I said in a clipped tone. The truth was my feet were a mess but there wasn't anything anyone could do about it. *Might as well tell a little white lie and move on.* "I won't be wearing heels anytime soon but I'll survive. I just won't look good while doing it."

The soft glow of a candle gave me just enough light to see Keely smile. I didn't want to return it with one of my own because, shit, the world was falling apart. But the real reason I didn't want to smile was because every single time I looked at her, I thought of Cash.

And that made me feel guilty.

I just couldn't bring myself to tell Keely that I knew her brother. It didn't matter anyway. It was one night. There would never be another.

"I like your apartment. It's much nicer than mine," Keely said, looking around from her position on my bed.

I frowned at her. "You live right next door, Keely. It's the same apartment."

She blushed. At least I thought she did but in the candlelight it was hard to tell.

"I...I like your furniture," she said.

"Hmm." I sighed. For the past hour we had been trying to make small talk but were failing big time. It was just a lame attempt to keep our minds off of what was happening, but it was impossible to forget.

"Hungry?" Keely asked, offering me one of the granola bars she had found in her apartment. Candlelight flickered over us, giving me just enough light to see what she held in her hand but it didn't look appetizing.

"No," I said, scrunching up my face at the cardboard-looking bar. But if I got desperate enough, I would eat it. My cabinets were bare. I wasn't home enough to keep anything in them except for a bottle of tequila and a box of cereal. My meals came from restaurants or the little hipster coffee shops around campus.

Even if I did have food, if it needed to be cooked or refrigerated we would be up shit creek. The oven and stove wouldn't work without electricity and the fridge sat dark and empty, warm and smelly.

"I'll save it for Tate then," Keely whispered, tucking the granola bar back in the messenger bag she had carried from her apartment.

I looked down at my brother. He was curled up on the bed, his back against my side. His knees were drawn up to his chest and his hand was under his cheek. I wanted to reach out and touch his shaggy brown hair, push it out of his eyes like I did when he was younger. Instead, I resisted. I didn't want to wake him. If he could escape the fear and uncertainty of what was happening for just a few hours, I would let him. God knows I wanted to.

I looked around my dark room. We had been locked up in the apartment for nine hours. I thought it was time to find out what was going on.

I climbed off the bed and headed out of my room, leaving Keely with Tate. The air was hotter in the rest of the house. I found Nathan near the corner of the big picture window in front. He was still, his attention locked outside.

"Anything?" I asked, stopping behind him.

Nathan didn't bother turning around. "Nothing. The building is still burning. People are still hanging around, trying to get their cars started."

"I haven't heard any sirens."

Nathan dropped the window shade and turned to look at me. His eyes were hard, void of emotion. "No one's showed up. Not one police officer or fireman. It's as if they don't even exist."

"Maybe you missed them," I said, pushing past him to look out the window. "They've got to be somewhere…"

"Cat, no one's coming."

I got angry. He sounded so calm but I wanted him fighting mad. If he wouldn't be that way, then I would.

"So what do we do? Just sit here in this fucking sauna of an apartment and wait? Twiddle our thumbs and gnaw on Keely's granola bars?" I snapped, hot, tired, and irritable.

"No. I go out."

"What? You can't!" I exclaimed.

"I can." He turned and headed to the kitchen. "I've already been out there a couple of times to try and start the car. I'll just go further this time," he said over his shoulder like he was talking about going for a casual walk.

"No. No," I argued, shaking my head and following him. "You're not going."

"You can't stop me, Cat."

"I know I can't but I damn will try," I said, following him into the kitchen. "What are you doing?"

Nathan looked up at me as he pulled a knife out of one of the drawers. "Weapon," he said.

God, I was beginning to hate his answers.

"A weapon?" I asked as he pushed past me on his way out of the kitchen. "Is that really necessary?"

Nathan glanced at me over his shoulder as he started toward my room.

"That's a stupid question. You were out there. You heard the gunshots. People become crazy when they don't understand what's happening or think there's no authority to stop them. It was a shit storm earlier and I have a feeling we're going to get dumped on again."

I followed close behind him as he took quick, long strides down the hallway. I had a surreal feeling that I was dreaming. Nathan was carrying a knife through my apartment to use as a weapon. Cash's sister was in my bedroom. How was I supposed to forget him when she was around? And the world had gone mad. There was no logical answer for it all.

"Do you have a backpack?" Nathan asked as we walked down the hallway.

"Yeah, in my room," I answered automatically, staring at the knife in his hand and wondering just how fucked up my life could get.

Nathan headed toward my bedroom with me right behind him. Keely jumped up from the bed when she saw us, watching Nathan as he marched into the room and went straight to my backpack on the floor. He grabbed it and upended the bag. Papers and books from last semester spilled out, adding to the mess already in my room. When the backpack was empty, Nathan stuck the knife inside then went to Keely on the bed.

"Stay here," he said in a low voice, standing very close to her.

She nodded. From my vantage point, I could see that there was something going on between them. I wondered just where Keely had spent the night after the party. Maybe Miss Innocent wasn't so innocent after all.

My eyebrows shot up when Nathan put his hand on the back of Keely's head and pulled her toward him. He kissed her forehead with tenderness then released her, running his hand down her arm and letting her go. *Whoa.* He fell fast.

I gave him a knowing look when he passed me. He returned it with a don't-you-dare-say-anything glare. I didn't, following him to the living room instead.

He stopped at the front door and slung the backpack over his shoulder. "Stay here and don't let anyone in, Cat. Got it?"

I nodded. "Yeah, but if you're not back in thirty minutes, I'm walking out this door and searching for you, Nathan."

He opened the door and turned to smirk at me. "I feel sorry for anyone that gets in your way, sis."

I tried to return his grin but couldn't. "Be careful, Nathan."

"I always am. Put the chair back under the door handle when I leave."

I watched as he disappeared down the stairs and across the parking lot. I watched him until I couldn't see him anymore.

Then I started to pray.

~~~~

Nathan came back twenty minutes later. He looked hot, frustrated, and worried. His normal tanned skin had lost all color.

"What did you see? What's happening?" I asked, bombarding him with questions as he shoved the chair back in its place under the door handle. Our fancy security system.

"Is all the power out?" Tate – who was now awake – asked.

"Who was shooting?" Keely joined in, rushing over to Nathan.

He didn't answer. Instead, he let the backpack drop to the floor by the door and walked over to the couch. His shoulders sagged heavily and there were dark circles under his eyes. He was tired. Exhausted just like the rest of us. Maybe even more.

He sat down on the couch with a sigh then scrubbed his face with both hands. He looked so distraught that I felt fear bubble up inside me.

We waited for him to say something. Anything. I could hear shouts from outside and the sound of a door slamming. It made me nervous. I couldn't stand Nathan's silence any longer. I had to know what was going on.

"Nathan, tell us," I said hoarsely.

He took a deep breath and lifted his head. I saw despair. Hopelessness. Bleakness that could only mean one thing.

"It's bad," he said. "Really bad."

"What do you mean?" Keely asked, taking a hesitant step toward him. "What did you see?"

He looked up at her with eyes full of despair.

"I saw madness but what I heard was worse. The United States was attacked. They think it was some kind of EMP bomb. The whole city is a war zone and we're in the middle of it." He took a deep breath. "We're in the middle of a war."

Chapter Twenty-Five

-Cash-

The fight to find my family turned into something else. The fight to save myself.

I thought that I would be just fine when I rode away from home. I thought the gash on my leg was nothing but a minor cut and a bandage would be enough.

I was wrong.

My body was weak. The heat was beating me down. The amount of blood I lost had drained me.

I held onto the saddle horn tightly, trying to keep myself upright. I could feel blood trickling down my leg and dripping off my boot. It splattered on the dry, dusty ground under the horse's hooves. The cut had reopened but this time it was worse. A chill ran over my body. I was burning up with fever. I don't know if it was my body's reaction to the blood loss and wound or if the cut had already become infected, but I was in trouble. If I could make it to town in one piece, it would be a miracle.

The mare snorted and tossed her head then sidestepped, smelling the blood on me.

"Easy girl," I said in a calming voice. She was all I had. Her and my guns. I had tried to start the damn farm truck before leaving but it was dead. That left me with two choices – walk or ride. I chose ride. So I saddled my dad's pride and joy. She was young and feisty. Fast. A mare with more attitude than brains. She could get me to town quicker than the other horses we owned and that's all that mattered.

The problem was I was weaker than I thought. It had taken all my energy to get the saddle on the horse and the bit in her mouth. When I tried to mount up, it caused me a helluva lot of pain, but adrenaline kept me going. I had to find my family.

And I had to find Cat also.

I didn't know if it was the loss of blood, fever, or the extreme temperatures that was messing with my mind, but I had to make sure she was okay. It was the right thing to do. Hell, the right thing and Cat didn't go together, but I would check on her for my own peace of mind anyway.

I pulled my hat down lower, trying not to think about how stupid my decision was. I was a damn fool for doing it, but I would head to her house first. It was closer and on the way to town anyway, I reasoned. I would check on her and move on. That was it.

I gave the reins some slack and poked around on my thigh. A hiss escaped me when pain flared in my leg. Warm liquid covered my hand. It was wet and sticky. My own frickin' blood.

I pulled my hand away and wiped it on my other leg. I needed help and I needed it quick. But the phones weren't working and I couldn't call for an ambulance. I had stopped at the first house I came to, hoping they had a generator or a landline phone, but they didn't. They only had fear and confusion.

~~~~

It was well past midnight when the horse's hooves finally hit the blacktop that led to Cat's home.

"Whoa," I said, pulling back on the reins. My leg

throbbed as the horse sidestepped under me. I felt cold. But that's not what held my attention.

It was the house in front of me.

It was huge and dark under the moonlight, all angles and sharp corners. Dark windows stared back at me. A barn set off to the side and I knew a pool and a fancy cabana were behind the house. It was Cat's home. The place I had kissed her the first time. The spot I had left her days ago. The house I had wanted to return to minutes after driving away.

No man in his right mind should have fallen so fast for a girl like her, but I did. Now here I was, on a damn horse in her driveway. Bleeding, weak, and wanting to see her just one more time.

I was a damned fool but I was here.

I nudged the horse up the driveway. There wasn't one car around and that didn't sit well with me. I didn't like that it was so quiet either. She had two brothers. Where were they?

When I got to the house, I dismounted and almost fell on my face when my feet hit the ground. I held onto the saddle, my only saving grace. It kept me upright as I waited for the black spots to disappear from my vision.

When they did, I limped over to a small tree and tied the horse's reins to it. I grabbed my bag and shotgun from its sheath on the saddle and unhooked its straps, letting it fall to the ground. I tried not to think about where I was standing – the same exact spot I had kissed Cat goodbye – but I couldn't help it as I went to the front door.

The porch light was off but I wasn't surprised. I hadn't seen a light or a hint of electricity since the wreck on the freeway.

I stood in front of the door and knocked, favoring my left leg and putting all my weight on my right. Nothing happened. I didn't hear the sound of someone walking on the other side or the telltale noise of a lock clicking open. I decided to try the doorbell. It was a long shot but shit, what did I have to lose? But again there was nothing.

Damn.

I laid my hand against the door and rested my forehead against it. I was so tired. The wood felt good beneath my head. Cool. Soothing. I squeezed my eyes shut and knocked again, barely staying on my feet. Again, there was nothing. Just the pain and fever in me.

"Shit," I murmured. I pushed away from the door, wondering what the hell I should do. Nobody was home, but I needed to rest and do something about my leg.

My decision was made for me when I heard a blackbird caw at the corner of the house. I started that way. It was slow going. I had to drag my leg and shuffle my feet. I grimaced with each step and gnashed my teeth together at the pain. If the damn phones worked, I would just call 911 and gladly pass out. But I didn't have that luxury.

It took some time but I finally rounded the corner of the house and drew to a stop. A deck and infinity pool took up a good portion of the backyard. The edge looked out over the pastures in the distance, now sitting dark under the stars. Moonlight gleamed off the surface of the water, glittering against the soft ripples.

I could almost picture Cat there, lounging beside the pool in a bikini. Her skin would be smooth, that flat stomach of hers itching for me to kiss. The tattoo would be dark against her hip, begging for my lips to touch it again. I wished I had known her earlier, before that tattoo. Maybe it would be my initials on her hip instead of his.

Damn. I was losing my freaking mind, thinking of a girl I couldn't have again. Only Cat would have that effect on me when I was bleeding and close to passing out.

I pulled myself up onto the deck and limped over to the sliding glass doors. I tried one then the other, shaking their handles, but they were locked.

"Goddamnit!" I swore. I was alone and bleeding badly. Sweat rolled down my body but I couldn't get warm. I had never considered breaking into someone's home before but I wasn't sure what choice I had at that moment. I needed some kind of help, even if it was only shelter.

Just then a window caught my eye, low to the deck. I staggered over to it, hoping for a miracle. I laid my shotgun near me and bent down. My hands were slippery, thanks to the blood, but I got a firm grasp on the bottom of the window frame. It gave just a little when I tried to open it. *Thank you, Jesus.* I didn't know whether I wanted to smack Cat's tight little ass next time I saw her for leaving a window unlatched or punch one of her brothers for not checking it and keeping her safer. But I was glad it was unlocked.

That simple mistake might have saved my life.

I opened the window, sweating bullets with the effort and sick to my stomach from the pain. My gun and bag went in first then me. It was a tight squeeze but I crawled inside, gritting my teeth against the pain in my leg and groaning when my thigh accidently grazed the windowsill.

When I hit the carpet inside, I almost passed out. My hat fell off and rolled away, but I didn't care. I was breathing hard and close to passing out. Somehow, I managed to shut and lock the window then pulled myself up anyway.

A dark living room greeted me. It was about the size of my whole house. The moon gave me just enough light to see the big screen TV against the wall and the furniture. I winced and grabbed my gun then slung the duffle bag on my shoulder. I limped across the room at a lumbering gait. I had no idea where I was going but I needed to take care of my leg again.

My eyes adjusted to the darkness quickly but I still stopped and dug around in the duffle bag until I found the flashlight. With its beam leading the way, I headed down a long hallway, one hand carrying my gun the other using the wall as support.

The hall led to a massive kitchen. I almost stumbled when I saw it, but the size of the kitchen and all the fancy appliances didn't matter. What did was finding some first aid.

I walked further into the room, using the counter to help me. The granite felt cold under my hand.

And wet.

I lifted my hand. It was sticky and warm.

"Shit," I whispered. I was bleeding like a stuck pig, leaving a trail everywhere. I needed to do something quick before I bled out all over Cat's floor.

I dropped my bag and set the gun down on the counter. Hurrying, I started opening cabinet doors and searching through them. I didn't find one thing that would help me.

My fever must have been getting worse because my body now shook violently. I tried not to concentrate on it and I turned on my good leg instead, starting back across the kitchen with only the flashlight. I didn't stop until I was at the stairs that led to the second floor.

As the blood soaked my thigh, I stood with my hand on the banister and shined the flashlight up the winding staircase. I knew on the second floor there would be a bathroom and first aid could usually be found in one. But I wasn't sure I could climb the stairs.

I breathed through the pain and gripped the railing harder. I didn't have a choice. I thought of my sister in Austin and my parents somewhere in town. I thought of Cat. I didn't love her but hell, I didn't want to leave this earth without seeing her one more time. That's what made me try.

I put my bad leg on the first step and pulled myself up using the banister. By the time I reached the top, I was sweating bullets. I kept one hand pressed against my thigh with the flashlight and the other against the wall, using it for support.

The first room I came to was a bathroom. I rummaged under the sink, looking for the first aid. I found a small kit, stuffed toward the back behind some hand towels. I grabbed one of the towels and pressed it against my leg. It hurt like a son-of-a-bitch but I needed to stop the bleeding or I would pass out soon.

When I had staunched the blood some, I tucked the box under my arm and limped out of the bathroom. I needed to find some thread. Cat wasn't the type of girl to sew but I would try her room anyway.

It took me a while to find it but when I did, I knew it was hers instantly. Her smell, her very presence, wrapped around me. I expected Cat to come barreling into the room with a smug smile on her face and mischief in her eyes. She didn't appear but I wished to God she would.

I pushed the thought away and hobbled into the room. I wasn't there to daydream. I was there to find a needle and thread.

I headed across the room to Cat's dresser. After setting the first aid kit on top, I pulled open a drawer and started searching it. Silk panties fell through my fingers like liquid gold. I remembered ripping one of them off her, sliding it out from under her dress.

I swallowed hard and paused, my hand buried deep in lacy underthings. I felt like a sick prick, going through her underwear drawer. I had come here to find her, not sift through her unmentionables. She wasn't my responsibility and she wasn't mine to worry about, but I was here doing just that.

My hand skimmed over a piece of paper at the bottom of the drawer. I pulled it out, stuffing down that feeling that it was wrong nosing around her personal stuff. It was a picture of her with a man. It wasn't her brother, not with the way he had his arm around her waist. I shouldn't have felt jealous but I did. Was it Luke, the man whose initials were tattooed on her hip?

Didn't matter, I thought. Cat and I were done. I had heard that much from her before all hell broke loose.

I shut the drawer and checked the next one. It held skimpy, lacy bras and little silk pajamas sets. I had almost given up, almost called it a stupid idea, when my hand closed on something plastic.

A travel-sized sewing kit.

I gripped it tightly, saying a silent thank you to Cat. I might just survive.

I grabbed the kit and first aid container then turned to head out of the room. But I was too far-gone. Riding all night and walking around on my leg was catching up to me. The fever was building. The world spun at a crazy speed. I leaned against the dresser and slid to the floor. It was getting harder to breath and focus. I knew my time was limited.

I have to do it now.

I ripped open the sewing kit and grabbed the towel that I had dropped. For the second time in less than twenty-four hours, I withdrew my knife from my boot and cut a slit in my jeans.

The bandage I had put on was soaked. I winced when I pulled it back. The moonlight streaming in through a window gave me just enough light to see the open gash on my leg. I tried not to grimace at the sight of it. The open wound wasn't a pretty sight.

"Time to get down to business," I whispered to myself.

I set the flashlight beside me and popped open the first aid kit. Some gauze, medical tape, two pain pills, ointment, tweezers, and something I sorely needed - blood clotting powder – stared back at me. I ripped open the powder and poured it all in the wound. After that, I grabbed the pills and popped them in my mouth, swallowing them dry.

Before I thought twice about it, I grabbed the needle out of the travel kit. My hands were shaking and my vision was blurry but after a few attempts I finally threaded the needle with black thread. There was no time to sterilize it. I would either die from infection or blood loss, but I wouldn't die from not trying.

The needle was tiny between my fingers. I almost dropped it a time or two. When I got a good grip on it again, I put it near the edge of the gash and paused.

Beads of perspiration broke out on my forehead. A chill went through me. I couldn't stop shaking. I grabbed the towel and placed it near the gash, catching some drops of blood.

I glanced around the dark room, looking for something to take my mind off the pain. Cat's bed caught my eye. I imagined her there, smiling and saying we were a mistake but beckoning for me to join her in bed.

The thought made me angry. I clenched my jaw. I was tired of being so damn confused about her. I would fucking resist her or die trying.

But as I sat there, the pain and fever ravaging my body, I imagined her long legs swinging out of bed. A seductive grin was on her face. I was really losing my mind now, seeing things that were not there.

I tried to blink the image away but it wouldn't disappear. I saw her strolling toward me, wearing nothing but a pair of lacy red panties.

My hands shook as she came closer. My heart pounded too hard. The fever made me hallucinate more and more. The needle stayed near the gash in my thigh as I watched Cat's tits bounce as she walked toward me.

I blinked, trying to clear the cobwebs from my mind. I knew she was an illusion. A product of pain and fever. But as she dropped to my feet and started crawling up my body, I didn't care if I was dying; I couldn't look away.

Her hair fell down over her shoulders, touching on the tips of her breasts and brushing against my jeans.

"Do you want me, Cash?" she asked in that provocative voice I dreamed about.

"No," I whispered. "You're not real."

"And if I were?"

"No," I answered hoarsely.

"Liar."

She was right. I wanted to reach out and touch her, run my finger over her nipple. But I didn't want my blood on her. I wouldn't mark her that way.

She smiled at me with that wicked way she had. God, even in my fever-induced hallucination she was beautiful and sexy.

"You need to fix your leg, Cash. People need you," she whispered.

I forgot about the pain. Forgot about the chills that shook me. "Do you need me, Cat?" I asked hoarsely around my dry mouth.

She smirked and eased back down my legs. "I don't need anyone, cowboy, but do this for me. Live."

And just like that she was gone.

It took me a second to realize I was alone. The house was still empty and quiet. I was just seeing things that were not there.

I ran a clammy hand over my face, calling myself crazy and insane. I was burning up and bleeding. It was time to do what Cat wanted.

Live.

I swallowed past the hot bile in my mouth and looked down at my thigh. Holding my breath, I did the unthinkable.

I plunged the needle into my skin.

Hellish agony ripped through me. Pain shredded my leg and ate away at my thigh. I wanted to scream. I wanted to give into the blackness creeping along my vision. Instead, I stuck the needle into the other side of the gash, gathering the edges together as quickly as I could. I was on the verge of passing out. I could feel it coming for me.

I don't know how many stitches I put in. I just knew that with the last one the world tilted. My eyelids drooped. Darkness took over.

And I lost the fight.

~~~~

For days I drifted in and out of consciousness. Fever raged in my body. My thigh burned with infection.

In one of my conscious moments, I dragged myself downstairs. I needed water like a dying man lost in a desert. My mouth felt like sand and my lips were chapped to the point of pain. I found water in the fridge. It was warm but wet, just what I needed.

I emptied the bottle, not really caring if the water ran down my chin. As soon as I had swallowed every drop of the water, I passed out again, disappearing into emptiness.

I woke up sometime later. Sunlight blinded me. It lay across my legs, lighting up the kitchen and highlighting the dried blood on my jeans. I shifted, uncomfortable. The tile floor was hard. The closed-up house was like an oven. I welcomed the discomfort. It meant my fever was gone. The chills had disappeared.

And I was going to be okay.

The stainless steel fridge was at my back. I pushed myself up into a higher sitting position, dragging my leg with me. My ripped jeans were stiff with blood and sweat. I peeled the edges back and poked around on my thigh. The gash was closed, the stitches holding strong.

"Thank God." The words were the first I had spoken in days. They came out hoarse. Raspy. No one heard them. No one came around the corner to check on me.

I was still alone.

It took a few minutes of struggling but I managed to climb to my feet. I tried to put weight on my leg. It hurt but not as much as before.

The first thing on my mind was the electricity. I checked to see if it had come back on. It hadn't. Just to be sure, I checked the phone that lay nearby. Silence answered, not the sound of a dial tone in my ears.

"Damn," I muttered. My stomach suddenly rumbled, reminding me that I hadn't ate in a while. I dragged my leg and started searching until I found a box of Fruit Loops. It wasn't my idea of a healthy meal, but in minutes I was full and my energy was replaced.

As I was drinking another bottle of water – my third in less than an hour – I wondered what the hell I should do. I was still weak and probably needed to give my thigh some more time to recover, but something was prodding me to leave. To go. To find everyone.

With my mind made up, I grabbed a grocery bag from the kitchen and filled it with the rest of the water bottles and a few cans of food that I found. I would repay Cat later if I saw her.

When I saw her.

I had left my duffle bag and shotgun in the kitchen days ago. I stuffed the grocery bag in the duffle bag then grabbed the gun. I slung the bag on my shoulder then turned to leave, but I was still wearing the ripped, bloody jeans. My bare thigh was showing underneath one leg and the other was covered in dark, dried blood. I couldn't leave looking like that. I needed to change.

I dropped my bag and gun in the living room then made my way to the stairs. It took forever but I climbed them again and limped down the long hallway. I bypassed Cat's room and found a room that must have belonged to one of her brothers. Yeah, I knew I had jeans in my bag but I needed to conserve supplies.

I found a pair of jeans hanging in her brother's closet that looked about my size. Pulling them on made me sweat and grimace but something was urging me to hurry and leave.

On my way back down the hallway, my steps slowed when near Cat's room. I stopped in the doorway, staring inside. I saw Cat everywhere, from the fluffy queen-size bed to the clothes strewn on the floor. What I didn't see was the girl that had walked away from me. The one that sometimes appeared sad and hurt, hiding pain that seemed too much for one person to handle.

I wanted to take it from her, squash it beneath my boots and shield her from everything. But I had no right to do that because she wanted nothing else to do with me.

I set my jaw tightly and pushed away from the doorframe. Downstairs, I grabbed my cowboy hat from the floor and stuck it on my head. After grabbing my bag and shotgun, I opened the back door and walked out, making sure it locked behind me.

The late July sun was hot on my back as I limped around the house, searching for my horse. I found her wandering around the yard, the reins trailing behind her. It took some sweat and tears but I managed to saddle her and mount up. A few minutes later, I was riding away.

It was time to move on. Cat was my past. Now I had to face my uncertain future.

Chapter Twenty-Six

-Cat-

I had lived through hell. I had buried my best friend and boyfriend. I had become every woman's nightmare and every man's dream. I went to bed with Jack Daniels and woke up with strangers. I had money to spend and no one to tell me I couldn't do it. I lived life to the fullest and hated every single moment of it.

But I had never had to live like this.

"Everyone know what to do?"

I watched as Nathan stuffed supplies in a backpack. A can of food. A reusable bottle filled with water. It wasn't enough for four people.

We were on our second week without power. Our fourteenth day without supplies or help. But now the waiting was over. We were going out.

"We should never let you out of our sight," Keely said, answering Nathan's question as she slung her messenger bag over her shoulder.

"And we shouldn't talk to anyone," Tate added, wrapping a hand towel around the blade of a kitchen knife.

Nathan stuffed another reused water bottle in his backpack then glanced at me. "And? What else, Cat?"

I braided my hair into one long plait and let it drop down my back. "And if we get separated, head back here. Don't stop. Don't slow down. Just get back home."

Nathan nodded then slung the backpack over his shoulder. "Then let's do this."

He opened the front door and walked out into the sunlight. I stood in the middle of my living room, watching Keely and Tate follow, but I was unable to do the same. I didn't want to leave. Something was telling me that walking out the door would be wrong. A decision we would regret.

But I had a lot of those nowadays.

"Hey? You coming?" Keely asked, stopping at the door and turning around to look at me.

I sighed. I was the one that argued we shouldn't leave. The one that had said we should continue to wait it out in my apartment. *Me* – the one that didn't play by the rules.

But one rule I wouldn't break is where my brothers went, I went. No question and with no hesitation. We were alone and we were on our own. No one was coming to help us.

No one.

I thought of my mom and dad. Were they okay? Was my dad safe in Dubai? My mother was in New York City? Were they waiting it out like us or was that part of the country and world even affected? And what about Tessa? Was she with Junior and her parents? Was she safe?

The questions bombarded me night and day. And there were no answers. I could only hope one day I would find out.

My parents and Keely were not the only ones on my mind. I also thought about Cash. I couldn't seem to help it. I dreamed about him at night. I tried not to think about him during the day. I was worried about everyone, including a cowboy that had stolen my breath away.

"Come on, Cat. We'll be okay," Keely said, motioning at me to leave.

I took a deep breath and then headed for the door. Something was telling me that she was wrong but I would go anyway.

She gave me a small, reassuring smile as I shut the front door and stepped out into blinding sunlight. A cloud floated in front of the sun, giving a moment's relief before it drifted away.

As I locked the door, Keely walked over to the top of the stairs and waited for me patiently. She was dressed in a white t-shirt and shorts, looking more like she was going out for a day in the park instead of searching for supplies and help during a war. But what did one wear for the end of the world anyway?

I bypassed her and headed down the stairs at a quick jog. Nathan and Tate were waiting for us at the bottom, watching the parking lot carefully. If trouble was here, it would find us. I could almost guarantee it.

As I rushed down the rest of the stairs, I glanced around. A few people lingered outside. Some sat on balconies, hoping for a cool breeze. Pieces of laundry hung out of some of the apartment windows, making the place look like a poor village in a third-world country instead of a housing complex near a prestigious college. Trash blew everywhere. Evidence that without proper garbage pickup, the town had become a dumping ground.

"Let's head deeper into the city. See if anything is going on or if there's any news," Nathan said, keeping a tight grip on his backpack and watching a small crowd of people lingering nearby.

"Downtown is not far from here," Keely added, shielding her eyes with her hand to look at him. "I think we should go there first." Her cheeks were already red from the heat, her pale coloring a curse under the sun.

Nathan nodded then looked at Tate. "You ready for this? It might be crazy."

Tate curled his lip up at Nathan. "I ain't a kid," he said, his voice cracking. "I'm ready for any kind of shit. I'll fight if I have to."

Nathan shifted to his other foot and glared at Tate as another cloud passed by.

"There'll be no fighting, Tate," he said. "We're just going to find out what's going on. You pull out that knife, I'll rip you apart when we get back. Understand?"

Tate kicked at a loose piece of asphalt with the toe of his boot. "We'll see," he mumbled.

Nathan ground his teeth but didn't say anything else. Sometimes arguing with Tate was a moot point. I knew firsthand.

"Let's go," he muttered, giving one more warning look at Tate.

We followed him across the parking lot. I was the last to bring up our little group. Keely was sticking to Nathan like glue and Tate was still grumbling about bossy older brothers a few steps behind her.

I couldn't help but stare at the student housing across the street as we walked by it. The building was nothing but a shell. The windows were gone. The bricks were dark with soot and blackened by fire.

We stayed close to Nathan and turned onto the main road. Thunder rumbled off in the distance. A glint reflected off of something up ahead. I shielded my eyes to see what it was, but a few minutes later I found out.

Cars were parked everywhere. On the curb. Against the curb. On the sidewalk. Against a streetlight. It was as if they had just froze where they were, paused in the middle of driving.

Some were smashed into poles while others were smashed into each other. Fenders were crushed in and doors were left open. It was a scene from a movie. An image that didn't make sense.

Keely, Tate, and I walked slower, staring at the cars as we passed them. One car had a stuffed animal in the back, sitting in the seat as if it were still waiting for its owner. Another car had bloodstains on the door.

I started shaking. All I could think about was Luke and Jenna and the blood that had coated my hands the night they had died.

But Nathan wasn't going to slow down. He charged ahead. He had already explored the streets and seen the vehicles. The sight of them was nothing new to him.

We maneuvered around cars and passed the little convenience store on the corner. The large picture windows in the front were gone, only jagged edges remaining. The shelves looked empty. The place destroyed.

It wasn't the only store that had been ransacked. The little coffee shop where I liked to get my morning latte at sat empty, the door hanging open at an odd angle. Tables and chairs were lying on their sides, some of them in pieces. Broken coffee cups were on the floor. The friendly barista who always knew how to make my drink was gone, replaced by a cash register lying on its side.

My heart started pounding harder. There was destruction everywhere. The storefronts. The cars. The few people walking around. It looked like I was on a movie set. *This is not happening. This is not real.* The words replayed in my mind until we reached the end of the street and turned the corner.

Holy shit.

People were everywhere. They lingered in empty stores. They ran down the sidewalk. They argued in the middle of the street. Hundreds of people walked up and down the main road that led to downtown Austin.

Some were crying.

Others were screaming.

Someone prayed. Another wailed for help.

It was too much and I wanted to disappear from it all.

We joined the mob of people. It was our only choice unless we turned back. We tried to stick close together as we walked down the road but there were too many people. Too many crushing bodies.

The crowd quickly closed around me, surrounding me like a predator and separating me from Tate, Nathan, and Keely. I lost sight of them. They disappeared as if they had only been a figment of my imagination.

I turned, my braid whipping across my face. I glanced around, searching for them frantically. All I could hear was the rapid beat of my heart and the sounds of shouts and crying around me. All I could see were people, people, people.

"TATE!" I screamed, swinging around.

He didn't answer. People just stared at me, pushing past me, acting like I didn't exist.

"TATE!" I screamed again at the top of my lungs, growing panicky. "KEELY! NATHAN!"

No one answered.

"Oh, fuck. Oh, fuck," I whispered, trying to hold back my hysteria.

I shot past the woman next to me, not caring when she shouted obscenities at me. I tripped over a man that had fallen. A baby cried. A mother yelled.

It was what the end of the world looked like and I was standing in the middle of it.

I shoved my way through the crowd, looking for Nathan, Keely, or Tate. I searched until the heat and the press of bodies became too much.

That's when I stopped. People pushed past me. Hitting me. Stepping on my feet. Running into my sides. No one cared. It was every man for himself.

And I was alone.

Chapter Twenty-Seven

-Cat-

My heart thumped wildly. My pulse beat rapidly. Panic gave way to terror.

Loud thunder clapped overhead and the wind picked up as I pushed and shoved, refusing to fall down when the crowd surged around me. The sound of shuffling feet on rough concrete had an ominous ring to it. Like we were being led to our death, one step at a time down a long road.

I was surrounded by hundreds of people, but I had never felt more alone. Chatter filled my ears, bombarding me with what I hoped were only rumors. *Cities were gone. The White House had burned. The government was in shambles.* I didn't want to believe any of it. I wanted to cover my ears and close my eyes until I woke up from this nightmare.

The mob of people heaved and swayed like a sea. I moved with it, trying to see over everyone's head. I looked for Keely's bright blonde hair. I searched for Tate and Nathan's tall figures. I found none of them. Just hundreds of people that all looked the same.

Tall buildings on either side of the street rose high, like giant fences keeping us in. Smoke drifted from one or two of them. Windows were missing from most and almost all were damaged in some way.

I moved with the crowd, looking up at the buildings and the dark clouds that floated by. One building held my attention more than the others. It had at least fifty floors and was made of shiny steel. On one of those floors, a small plane balanced precariously.

It looked like it had crashed through the corner, slicing through the glass and metal like butter. The nose was on one side of the building; the tail was on the other. Pieces of insulation flipped in the wind, touching the plane every few seconds then drifting into the air.

When a stiff wind suddenly hit, a deep moan emitted from the plane. My heart jumped into my throat. The plane was moving!

An awful metal screeching nose filled the air as the nose dipped more with another gust of wind. The crowd gasped and started pushing each other, screaming and shouting for everyone to move.

I shoved people out of my way and ran, glancing back over my shoulder at the plane. Panic made it hard to think or breathe. When I saw a small street jotting out from the main road, I headed toward it. I knew I should've stayed with the crowd, go where they were going because that's probably what Nathan, Keely, and Tate had done, but I didn't.

I turned on the street instead.

A few other people had the same idea. They rushed past me. I knew the street well. It was narrow and more like an alley than anything else, but it curved around and met back up with the main street. And that main street lead to the state capitol. That's where Nathan would head. I was almost sure of it.

My braid hit my back as I ran faster. My shoes grabbed at the asphalt. I could hear my breathing, loud in my ears over the sounds of shouts and screams behind me.

It was darker on the little street, causing a tinge of apprehension to run up my spine. But I knew the alleyway would open up soon. I just had to get there first.

I felt people catching up to me. I hurried, not wanting to be caught again in a crowd, but in seconds the small group overtook me. I tripped and almost fell when someone pushed past me. My foot hit the curb and I went headfirst. But a strong grip grabbed my upper arm and saved me.

"Watch it, honey."

I lifted my eyes. A man had a strong hold on me. He was short and stocky with dirty blonde hair. His grip was tight, but his smile was friendly.

"Sorry," I said, pulling my arm away from him. I started to turn and leave, but the world spun crazily around me, causing me to stumble again.

"Whoa there. You okay?" the stranger asked, grabbing me again.

I nodded, feeling stars dance in front of my eyes. "Yeah," I mumbled. "I just haven't ate yet."

"I've got food if you want some."

Something about the way he said it made my skin crawl. I lowered my hand and took a safe step back.

"No. No. I'll be okay," I said.

He smiled again, something that looked out of place in this god-forsaken world.

"You sure?" he asked. "You look a little pale. I'll be happy to give you some food. We've got to take care of our fellow man in these trying times, you know."

I opened my mouth to answer but another man appeared beside him. He was taller and bigger. His head was shaven and his deep-set eyes seemed to lack any emotion or feelings. He wore all black, from his shirt to his combat boots. But it was the sound of his voice that shook me.

"Leave her alone, Paul. Frankie won't be happy if we fuck around." He said it like I was a piece of dirt. Like I was a bug that he wanted to squish.

"Frankie ain't here now is he?" the man named Paul said, staring at me with hunger. "But this little bird is."

I backed away, realizing suddenly that the crowd on the side street had thinned out. I was left alone with two men that were bigger than me and more deadly looking than most. The time to run was now.

I turned to take off but a pair of hands grabbed my arms, stopping me. I squealed and kicked, fighting to get them off of me. I might have given men what they wanted before, but I always gave it; it was never taken from me. I wouldn't allow it to happen now.

"Hey, now. Hey, now. We're not going to hurt you," Paul said in a soothing voice as I continued to fight. He ran a hand over my hair like he was comforting a child, scaring me even more. "We just want to talk."

"I don't talk to shitbags," I snarled, trying to jerk my arm from his grip.

Paul burst out laughing. "She has a mouth on her, don't she, Hightower?"

Hightower stared at me with dark, empty eyes.

"Yeah, a real lady," he deadpanned, crossing his arms over his chest and watching the show between Paul and me with boredom.

Paul's laughter died down. "You know, Hightower, we don't got to meet Frankie for another hour. You interested?"

A chill ran down my spine. I had come across my share of douchebags and men that were a little too grabby, but this was different.

This was me alone in a world without rules.

"If either of you touch me, I'll kill you," I spit between clenched teeth. "But not before I castrate you first."

Paul's eyes got wide and his face went white but he recovered quickly. His fingers tightened on my arm and he looked over at his friend. "You hear that, Hightower? The girl just threatened us. I know you don't like people to do that." He glanced back at me and grinned. "Hightower has anger management issues. Isn't that what those doctor people told you, Hightower? You got anger issues."

Hightower grunted. "Anger combined with violent tendencies, that's what those white coat freaks said."

Paul grinned wider. "That's fancy talk for he's got a mean streak a mile long. I've seen it and that's what Frankie likes about him." He glanced back at his friend again. "Like I was saying – you interested, Hightower? It's been a while for me and shit, I know it's been awhile for you."

A few raindrops hit my nose but they were the least of my problems. I started struggling when Hightower stepped off the curb and started toward me.

"This isn't some kind of free for all! Let me go or I'll scream and bring every damn person here!" I yelled, kicking out my foot to keep Hightower away.

Paul avoided my kicks and jerked me toward him.

"Look around, little bird," he said in my ear, pulling me hard against his body. "Everybody's yelling and screaming. Ain't nobody gonna pay attention to someone else doing it too. Nobody's gonna help you." He smoothed a hand down my hair again, sending a shiver through me. "Just stand still so Hightower can check you out."

Please God. Please God. I chanted the words to myself over and over as Hightower approached me, afraid of what he would do. I squeezed my eyes shut and opened my mouth to scream, but Paul slapped a hand over my lips.

I thrashed about but he held me still. I could smell him, the scent of an unwashed male body almost making me gag. His hand over my mouth tasted like dirt and reeked even worse than his body.

I struggled to get out of Paul's grip as Hightower walked around me. I felt like an object being studied for dissection, pinned down and ready to be taken apart.

Hightower was behind me when he reached out and grabbed my braid. I started shaking uncontrollably as he ran his fingers over it.

"The thing is, I like blondes," Hightower said from behind me, dropping my braid down my back.

Paul became aggravated, relaxing his hand over my mouth.

"Well, shit, just don't look at her hair!" he whined, tucking a strand of my hair behind my ear. "You ain't gonna fuck that part of her anyway."

A sob almost escaped me but I clamped my lips shut.

"But I like to look at their hair. Gets me off when it comes away in my fingers," Hightower said, giving my hair one jerk before walking away.

Paul hurried to run his hand over my hair as if Hightower had hurt me. He spun me around as he did it again and again.

I watched as Hightower strolled back to his post on the sidewalk, his muscular body almost bulging out of his clothes. I shuddered to think what he could do to a woman. His hands were massive, probably able to break someone in half. He crossed his arms over his chest and stared down the street.

"Well, damn. Guess I'll just have to have all the fun. I ain't that particular," Paul said.

I started fighting him as he dragged me to the curb. I kicked him as hard as I could. The toe of my tennis shoes caught him in the balls. I wished I had on my heels. They could do some major damage. But heels were not my life now. Surviving was.

Paul yelped and grabbed his crotch. I saw my opening and ripped my arm from him. His fingers left marks behind but if I didn't get away, I would have more than just bruises.

I didn't get very far. Hightower reached out and grabbed me. I screamed as he dragged me back to him.

"Just because I don't want you don't mean you get to run off," he said in a deep voice.

I stared up at him, blinking against the raindrops that hit my face. He had a tattoo of a gun on his wide neck. The tip of the barrel was inked under his ear and the handle was drawn where his neck met his collarbone. I had no idea what kind of gun it was; all I knew was that if he had one, he would probably use it on me.

The gun flexed on his neck as he turned his head to look at Paul. "You okay?" he asked his friend that was still cupping his nuts.

Paul held up one finger, leaning over and putting his hands on his knees. "Give me a second," he huffed, trying to catch his breath.

"Take all the time you want, Paul. Just hurry and get your shit over with so we can meet Frankie."

Paul shook off the pain and cracked his neck as he stood up.

"Frankie can wait," he said, readjusting his balls. "Christ, the little bird has a nasty kick."

I fell back a step as Paul started for me, but Hightower held onto me like it was nothing. Strands of my hair stuck to my lips and became plastered against my tear-stained cheeks as I fought to get away.

Paul grabbed a handful of my shirt, yanking me away from Hightower and toward him. I let out a bloodcurdling scream as he grabbed my bottom and squeezed painfully. Before I could recover, he yanked me back toward a door in the building next to us.

I didn't have time to wonder where it would lead. I only knew what would happen if he got me inside.

I opened my mouth to scream again but heard a shout. "Hey!"

Nathan was running down the middle of the street. He had a knife in his hand and fury in his eyes. Tate and Keely were behind him, slowing down when they saw the men holding me.

"What do we have here?" Hightower said with interest. He was staring at Keely with sick curiosity.

"Nathan, get them out of here!" I screamed, trying to pull away from Paul.

But Paul wasn't letting me go. Lightning cracked overhead and the raindrops turned into a light downfall as Nathan raced toward us, wielding the knife in his hand.

No. No. No. These guys would take Nathan down with one punch. I had to do something.

I turned. Drawing my elbow back and curling my fingers into my palms, I swung at Paul. My fist caught his nose with a solid smack. I felt bones crunch. Pain radiated down my arm but it got me what I wanted.

Paul let go of me and grabbed his nose, howling. Blood burst from between his fingers. I didn't wait to see what Hightower would do. I took off running.

I glanced over my shoulder as I ran. Hightower was after me and Paul was still on the sidewalk bleeding. Hightower was gaining on me. My heart was thumping like a runaway train and I was scared shitless but I ran faster.

The concrete became slippery with the softly falling rain. As soon as I got near Nathan, he grabbed me and shoved me behind him. I didn't have time to wonder what he was going to do. He shifted the knife to his other hand and faced Hightower as he charged toward us.

"Come on, asshole!" Nathan scowled. "I fucking dare you."

I started to shoot around Nathan, but Keely grabbed my arm and Tate shoved me behind him.

"Oh, shit!" I hissed.

We had company.

Up ahead a group of men had turned the corner and were walking toward us. An older man led the group. He had pepper gray hair that was cut close to his head. He wore camo pants and a dark green shirt. A group of five or six men walked behind him.

And they all looked dangerous.

"Hightower, what the fuck is going on?" the old man roared, walking with authority toward where Paul stood still nursing his nose.

Hightower stopped and turned around, a safe distance from us. "Frankie."

"Get the fuck over here and stop bothering those kids," the old man roared with annoyance.

Hightower glanced over his shoulder at us. His gaze traveled over Keely before looking at Nathan.

"This ain't over."

Nathan's muscles tensed. "Don't even fucking look at her or think about her."

Hightower turned around to walk backwards and grinned at us. "Oh, I'll think about her. I'll think about her really hard." He looked at Keely one more time before turning on his heel and heading to where Frankie stood, examining Paul's nose.

Nathan started backing up, keeping his eyes on them. They were distracted and we were free. Time to leave.

"Let's go," Nathan said, grabbing Keely's arm. "Don't leave my side, Keely."

She tried to look over her shoulder but Nathan grasped her chin, forcing her eyes on him.

"I'll die before I let anyone touch you, Keely."

"Don't say that, Nathan," Keely said with fear. "No one's going to die protecting me."

Nathan grabbed her hand and laced his fingers with hers. "I will."

Tate looked at me and rolled his eyes. Normally I would do the same but Nathan sounded serious. I just hoped it never came to someone dying but I would die for my brothers in a heartbeat.

We started back down the street but I felt a tingling down my spine. I glanced over my shoulder, blinking against the rain, and that's when I saw it.

Paul's eyes on me.

He had bright red blood running down his face, mixing with the rainfall and dripping off his pointy chin. His hair was plastered down his face in stringy, wet strands and his clothes were stuck to his body from the downpour.

Frankie was in his face, yelling something I couldn't hear. Paul was listening but his eyes were on me.

In them there was a promise. A threat. A beginning that hadn't seen the end yet. I realized that I wasn't safe in this new world. Not from hunger or thirst. Not from fear or terror.

I wasn't safe from anything, including men like him.

Chapter Twenty-Eight

-Cat-

The rain was coming down in buckets by the time we turned the corner of the street. I was soaked and the inside of my tennis shoes squished with each step I took.

We headed toward the state capital. Nathan said he overheard there was a triage center set up there.

The crowd was thicker near the capitol grounds despite the storm that had rolled in. A few weeks ago I would have balked at walking around in the rain with no makeup on, but here I was, soaking wet and welcoming the rain on my face. It felt good against my skin, erasing the dirt and grime of the last few days. But the rain was forgotten when I saw what was up ahead.

Big, white tents had been set up in front of the capitol building. Hordes of people pushed and shoved, seeking whatever was offered underneath the enclosures.

"It's the local Red Cross," Nathan explained, answering my unspoken question. "We heard they're giving away food and water."

"I hope they've got something left," Tate said, walking beside me. "I'm starving. I think I can even count my ribs, I'm so skinny now."

He was right. In just a couple of weeks, we had all lost weight. Weight that we couldn't afford to lose.

As we got closer to the crowd and capitol, the louder it became. Nathan held Keely's hand and I grabbed Tate's arm. No way would I get separated again or let anyone out of my sight.

Men and women fought to get under the tents. Everyone was starving and needed food and water. We were just four of hundreds, hungry and desperate.

"Get back! Get back! We'll get to you eventually!" a woman yelled up ahead as the mob of people pushed and shoved.

I stood on my tiptoes, trying to see over the man in front of me. I caught a glimpse of the woman. She was wearing a white doctor's coat.

"This line is for emergencies only. I repeat, emergencies only. If you need food or water, go to the left," she shouted, cupping a hand around her mouth.

Nathan led us to the left, making sure we all stayed together. People pushed. People shoved. There was crying and tearful hugs. I watched it all, feeling surreal.

This can't be happening. This is America.

We found the food tent and joined the frantic crowd. Hundreds of people, most soaked from the rain, waited to get underneath.

By the time we reached the very edge of the tent, the rain stopped and the sun came out. It became blazing hot once again. I felt my hair drying and my scalp burning. My skin turned red quickly, blistering under the sun. I also felt hunger gnaw at me, knowing we were close to something to eat.

When we finally got underneath the tent, we discovered it was a hellhole. I grabbed a handful of Nathan's shirt and tightened my hand around Tate's arm as we joined the mob of people pressing forward. We needed water and food desperately. I had looked death in the eye once when Luke and Jenna were killed; I didn't want to face it again because of starvation.

It seemed to take hours to get to the front. Pushing and shoving threatened to make me fall. If I did, I wouldn't be able to get back up. I knew that. I would be trampled to death in the race to get supplies. Just one less mouth to feed.

We were able to get close enough to see plastic tables and the first aid workers who stood behind them. A few men in uniforms stood nearby. They were armed with scary looking guns and stern expressions. The American flag on their sleeves confirmed what I already knew. They were U.S. soldiers. But they were protecting nothing but empty crates of food.

"We're out of food and water, people. Out of food and water," a worker shouted. Her short gray hair was slicked back and her long fingers waved at everyone to calm down when they started yelling.

"What the hell? We're starving here!" a man in the crowd shouted with anger.

"My kids are starving!" another man bellowed.

Everyone joined in, shouting and yelling. The aid worker held up her hand, stopping everyone. "We'll get more shipments soon and—"

"Liar!" a man to my left shouted. "There's no more shipments coming! That's just a bunch of BS the government wants us to believe to keep us calm!"

The aid worker glanced nervously at one of the military soldiers. I saw the truth in her eyes. The man was right. There were no more supplies coming. We were all going to starve.

"Tell us the truth, lady! Ain't nothing coming for us!" someone shouted. "We've got a right to know!"

The woman held up her hand again and opened her mouth to argue, but a man in uniform stepped forward. He was gray-haired, older, and distinguished looking. He emanated the authority of a high-ranking official. The metals on his chest proved it.

He was flanked by two soldiers that I suddenly noticed.

Oh hell.

The blood drained from my face. I recognized one of them. He was the guy from the party. The one from the bathroom. *He's a soldier? What the hell was he doing at a frat party?*

I didn't have time to wonder any more. The crowd quieted down as the officer in charge cleared his throat and began to speak.

"Ladies and gentlemen," he said, addressing the people with respect. "We need to be civil. Supplies are coming. Help is on the way."

"Bullshit!" someone shouted.

The officer continued as if he hadn't heard. "In the meantime, share what you have with your neighbor. Take care of your fellow man. Follow the directions of military personnel and government officials. We're all in this together, people. Let's help each other. Thank you."

The crowd started talking and shouting as he turned and began to walk away. One woman yelled louder than the rest.

"Are we going to die?"

The officer stopped and turned around. Soldier boy stood at attention on his right, not moving a muscle as his superior faced the crowd.

The woman who had spoken up looked rail thin. Her hair was mousy brown and fell around her shoulders in limp strands. Her skin was leathery and her cheeks were hollow. She appeared weak but in her eyes was resiliency.

"I heard whoever did this is on our soil," she said. "That they are butchering any Americans they find. Now, I've got children, mister. I need to know. Are we safe here?"

The officer stared at the woman without emotion, without feeling. His back was rigid and his uniform crisp and clean. "You are perfectly safe here, ma'am. The government has everything under control. Thank you," he said.

Soldier boy from the party didn't move a muscle. I saw his Adam's apple go up and down but his eyes stayed focused ahead.

He knows something.

The crowd broke into chaos as the officer walked away. He disappeared somewhere behind the tent but I saw him a second later head up the hill toward the capitol building.

People spontaneously started pushing and shoving to leave. I didn't. I headed for soldier boy instead.

"What are you doing, Cat? Come on!" Nathan said, reaching for me when I went past him.

"Hold on." I kept my eyes on the soldier. He had answers and I had some questions.

Nathan, Tate, and Keely followed me, fighting the crowd going in the opposite direction. The ground was soggy and my shoes sunk into the mud but I didn't let it slow me down.

"Hey you!" I yelled at the soldier when I got close enough. "Party boy."

He turned his head and looked at me. His eyes got round when he saw me rushing toward him.

"Remember me?" I asked, pushing past the last few people that separated us.

"You know him?" Tate whispered beside me.

"Hush, Tate. Let her do her thing," Nathan muttered, him and Keely stopping on the other side of me.

I had no idea what my *thing* was but I was dirty and hungry. I would do what I had to do in order to get what I wanted.

Soldier boy looked at me with a cool expression. "Yes, ma'am. I remember you."

I cocked my head to the side, giving him my best smile. "So now it's *ma'am*. That's not what you called me the other night."

Tate and Keely shot me a look but I ignored them. I was trying to save our butts here.

Soldier boy blushed. "Sorry about that, ma'am. Too many Coors Lights."

I shrugged. "No biggie. I was drunk too."

I paid little attention to anyone else as I moved toward him. I had just been manhandled by Paul and Hightower. I had fought against them and listened as they talked trash and threatened me. The last thing I wanted to do was flirt with someone but I needed to do it. For my brothers. For Cash's sister. For me.

Soldier boy shifted and readjusted the gun hanging on his shoulder, staring straight ahead. "Ma'am, you need to move back."

I didn't. I ignored the other soldiers standing nearby and took a step closer. "I didn't know you were military."

Soldier boy stared over my shoulder. "National Guard, ma'am."

"Hmm." I looked him up and down. Time to go in for the kill. "I like men in uniform."

He blinked and the flush on his face deepened.

I took a step closer and lowered my voice. "Can you tell me what's going on, soldier. Please?"

He didn't say anything, but his eyes did glance at Nathan, Tate, and Keely behind me.

I tried again. "Is there another shipment of food coming?"

He finally looked down at me. "Ma'am, I can't answer that." But when his Adam's apple bounced up and down, I knew there was something he wasn't telling.

I was going to reach out and touch him, maybe run my fingers up his arm, but a deep voice shouted commands nearby. The soldiers next to him jumped to attention and took off jogging in a straight line formation.

Soldier boy started to follow. Hopelessness washed over me as I watched him leave. I needed his help. I didn't know what else to do.

I was in luck. At the last second he stopped and turned back around. He quickly took three wide steps and stopped right in front of me.

"I could get in a lot of trouble for this but…get out of town," he said in a hushed voice so no one could hear. "Now, while you can."

I opened my mouth then clamped it shut. Panic set in when he turned to leave. I needed more information.

I reached out and grabbed a handful of his camouflage sleeve. "Why?"

He looked around to make sure no one was listening then glanced back at me. "Because the people who did this are on the march and Austin is in their path. The last place anyone should be right now is stuck in a big city when they get here."

He turned to leave again, but I held onto his shirt tighter, refusing to let go just yet. "But we need food. Water. Supplies."

He glanced at me and shook his head. "There are no supplies coming. Only hell and war."

Chapter Twenty-Nine

-Cash-

It took me two weeks to reach town. Along the way I learned something about myself - I had a dark side. I did things during that time that I wasn't proud of. Things that would haunt me. But it was either do or die.

And I wasn't dying anytime soon.

The world had turned into damn purgatory. Hell on earth and all that shit. It changed me. Made me into a man that was tougher. Deadlier. Much more of a threat. I didn't give a damn what was right or wrong.

I just did what I had to do to survive.

It was late afternoon when I left my horse tied up outside of town and walked in, not knowing what I was about to face but hoping to find my family.

Hundred degree temperatures made the ground dry and dusty. The rainstorm that had soaked my clothes a few days ago was a thing of the past. Dust swirled around my boots, adding layers and layers of grime on my already dirty clothes.

I licked my dry, chapped lips, wishing I had a drink of water. The thirst was a bad craving I couldn't fulfill. It ravaged every part of my body, eating away at my insides and taking all that I had left to give.

I squinted up at the bright ball of fire in the sky then took stock of my surroundings. I was on the outskirts of town. It had taken me longer than I would have liked to get there. I had to stop a few times to restock my supplies. I had never stolen a thing in my life but I quickly became an expert at it. It was either steal or die of starvation. There was no other choice in a world gone mad. I had learned that fast.

The first time I stole was when I raided a little convenience store on the way to town. I wasn't proud of taking what wasn't mine but I only took what I needed. If things got back to normal, maybe I would repay the owner for the food. Until then I was determined to eat and drink at any cost. Even if I damned my own soul to hell.

I pushed back a tree branch and was careful not to step on any dead twigs as I continued toward town. I didn't want to announce my arrival if I could help it. The world had become a fucked up place. I had seen it with my own eyes.

But I had yet to see the worst of it.

I kept my eyes and ears open for any activity. I didn't know what to expect, but I was armed and ready. My pistol was tucked in my jeans and my shotgun was in my hand. I might get arrested for walking through town armed with a small arsenal but no way would I go in blind and empty-handed.

A breeze cooled me briefly as I emerged from the woods surrounding the town. A little five and dime store sat empty on my left. On my right was a deserted children's store, the interior dark despite the blinding sunlight.

I started down the middle of the road, knowing I would meet no cars. The town boasted 4,000 people. So where were they now? The street was empty. The place was quiet. The only thing that moved were the pieces of trash that blew around like they were the only inhabitants left.

I pulled my hat brim lower, protecting my eyes from the sun so I didn't have to squint. I needed to be alert and ready. Nothing hindering me.

The shotgun felt at home in my hand. I held it steady at my side. In seconds I could have it up and aimed, ready for action.

I continued down Main Street. The wind picked up, bringing with it the smell of burning wood. I was halfway down the road when I heard it. Screams and gunshots.

I ducked and ran behind a nearby building. I had no idea where the shots had come from, but I wasn't going to stand in the middle of the road like a damn target.

I plastered myself up against the brick wall, using it to shield me from anything coming my way. I was between two buildings. Still a distance from the gunshots but close enough that I knew I needed to be careful.

A loud noise broke through the sounds of screams. I held my breath and forced myself to calm down, listening. There were more screams. More pops of gunfire. But then a different sound emerged…one that sounded like a vehicle. What the fuck? I hadn't heard an engine in weeks.

I edged toward the corner of the building, careful not to make any noise. I was conscious of every breath I took and every move I made. The muzzle of my shotgun stayed pointed down as I peered around the corner. What I saw froze my blood.

A large military vehicle was rumbling down the road but it wasn't one of ours. I knew because the men walking alongside it wore foreign military uniforms and shouted commands in a different language.

I threw myself against the wall again, breathing hard. *What the fuck is going on?*

I had glimpsed guns in the soldiers' hands, pointing at the buildings they passed. They were on the hunt and I was going to be in their line of fire fast.

I needed to disappear. Before I could move, I heard shrill screams. It raised the hair on the back of my neck.

I peeked around the corner just in time to see a woman and man run into the street. They were waving their hands above their heads in a sign of surrender.

Three of the soldiers broke formation. They lifted their guns to their shoulders and with three pops, they opened fire on the couple. The man and woman fell to the pavement like rag dolls.

"Shit! Shit!" I whispered, flinging myself back against the building. I was breathing hard. Cold sweat popped up along my skin. I had just watched two people get mowed down like they were nothing.

My stomach rolled but I didn't have time to dwell on it. The sound of the rumbling vehicle was getting closer. I flexed my fingers around my shotgun and tightened my hold on it, fury growing in me. I had to disappear before the soldiers saw me.

I took a deep breath and counted to three. It was time.

I darted around the corner of the building, keeping my back against the wall. I narrowly missed being seen by the soldiers when they passed the building. I wasn't going to sit around and wait to find out where they were going.

I had to find my mom and dad.

I stayed low to the ground and ran to the next building. More trash floated around my boots thanks to an overturned garbage truck across the street. I didn't pause to wonder what the hell happened to it; I just kept running.

I followed the sounds of screams and cries. I knew

what I had to do. These soldiers were killing people. I had two guns and one thing on my mind.

I would fight.

The screams grew louder the closer I got to the town square. I ran toward it, not away. I would bring the fucking battle to the bastards if I had to. Anything to find my parents and get them out.

I stayed low to the ground and dashed between buildings. That's when I saw it. Soldiers were walking down the street, shooting everyone in their path. Men, women, children, it didn't matter. They shot them.

I slid to the ground between two closely set buildings, gravel skinning my hands and biting into my jeans.

"Shit," I whispered, running a shaky hand over my dust-coated face. Sure, I had done some terrible things the last couple of weeks in the name of surviving, but watching people gunned down wasn't one of them.

It took me a few minutes to recover but by the time I did, the rage had built in me to a dangerous level. I used the shotgun to push myself to my feet. My bad leg was throbbing like it did from time to time, but I had more important things to worry about.

I pushed away from the building and ran straight for the center of town. My heavy breathing filled my ears along with the screams and gunfire. Time slowed down but my feet never did.

Not until I saw the fence.

It was an eight-foot, chain-linked fence, topped with barbed wire and surrounding the town square. Soldiers were pushing and shoving people into the fenced-in area. Men and women were crying and sobbing, begging for their lives. Asking for their freedom.

It was a hellish scene and I was witness to it all.

The shotgun started to slip through my fingers. I wanted to yank it up and take a shot when I saw a soldier hit a woman with the butt of his gun. Another shoved an elderly woman to her knees, yelling at her in a foreign language.

It was too much, yet I couldn't look away. It hardened me. Numbed me to the danger I faced.

With my jaw set in a rigid line, I tightened my grip on my shotgun and darted to the next building. I was itching to fight and take out a few of the assholes, but first I had to figure out what my plan was. I needed to lay low and get my shit together. Come up with a plan.

I jiggled the door handle of the building next to me. It was locked. I headed back the way I had come, away from the center of town. I needed to find somewhere safe, wherever the hell that was.

I found a deserted laundromat a few blocks away. I pulled my knife from my boot and pried the back door open with the blade. The door gave with a quiet pop and I darted inside, staying low to the ground and away from the large windows in front.

It smelled moldy, with a stale, unused scent. The candy machine in the corner had been overturned but all the chocolate bars were gone. The change machine had been destroyed, leaving quarters lying on the floor. I kneeled behind a counter and gathered my thoughts, trying to sort out what I knew.

The soldiers were foreign S.O.Bs. They carried some major artillery and wasn't afraid to use it. There was no time to worry about why they were here or how they got here. There was only what I was going to do to get past them.

I stayed in the laundromat until it grew dark. It was stifling hot and almost more than I could bear but I had to bide my time. The cover of darkness was when I would make my move.

When the shadows disappeared and night fell, I left my shotgun hidden in a pile of clothes and crept out the back door. Some might call me crazy for leaving one of my guns behind, but I would come back for it later. I didn't want to be seen walking around with a loaded shotgun and I couldn't very well hide it. Plus, if I didn't look like a threat, I might survive what I was about to do.

My plan was simple, really. I was going on the other side of that fence. I needed to find my parents and I had a feeling they were behind the chain-link wall. I was also hoping to find Cat. I hope to God she wasn't one of the prisoners, but I refused to think that she had been gunned down in the middle of a street somewhere.

Clouds kept the moonlight hidden, giving me the darkness I needed to remain unseen. I kept close to the ground and ran toward the fence, using the buildings to conceal me. Twenty more feet. Ten more feet. My heartbeat went crazy as I got closer. I kept my eyes open for soldiers and my hand ready to grab my revolver if need be.

I found three men patrolling the fence line. I spotted them right away. I waited behind an abandoned car, watching as they paced one way then another. I timed them, looking for an opportunity. When I saw my opening, I took it.

The thing about that fence was it wasn't buried in the ground and it was loose in some spots. Stupid of the terrorists, perfect for me. I spotted a particularly vulnerable spot where the ground dipped just right.

I ran as fast as I could for the area, watching the men whose backs were turned. I just needed one second.

And I took it.

I hit the grass and dropped, sliding under the fence. My clothes snagged, but I didn't bother unhooking them. I was on my feet and walking away in seconds.

Behind enemy lines.

Chapter Thirty

-Cash-

I was ten years old when my dad took me hunting for the first time. We had walked through the woods quietly, making sure not to make a sound as we tracked the hog we were after. The sucker was tearing up my dad's crops, destroying our income and threatening to end our livelihood. He had to be stopped.

That night I learned to blend in with my surroundings. I became an expert at it, moving through the woods undetected or walking through fallen leaves without making a sound. I did that again in the foreign bastards concentration camp, walking casually away from the barbed-wire fence.

I kept a close eye on the soldiers as I walked away. They turned to pace the other way along the fence line. *Perfect damn timing.*

I headed toward the nearest group of people. I had to blend in. Look like I belonged there, when the only thing I wanted to do was pull out my pistol and take out a few of the foreign fucks milling around.

The group didn't pay any attention to me as I joined them. They were too scared to care. I hung around with them a minute or two then moved on to the next group, glancing at everyone. Trying to find my mom and dad. The third group I came to, I recognized two people.

One of them was Cat's friend.

I walked over to her with a calm, cool stride, despite the fury in me when I saw a soldier punch a man out cold. In the few minutes I had been behind the fence, I saw shit I would never forget.

When I got closer to the girl, I grabbed her wrist and turned her around. She was dirty and tired-looking. The man standing next to her tried to jump between us and come to her rescue, but I gave him a deadly look, ready to pull my revolver in order to get any information I could about Cat.

"Where is she?" I growled, scowling down at the girl. Niceties and politeness had no place in my world anymore.

The girl cowered and looked frightened, but then understanding dawned on her face.

"You're that cowboy aren't you? The one that started her car?"

I didn't answer. Instead, I gritted my teeth. "Cat. I need to know where's she at."

The girl's bottom lip trembled. "She went home, back to her apartment in Austin."

Relief flooded me. Cat was safe, away from this hell. That's all I needed to know.

I let go of her and turned. I got what I wanted from her. Now I needed to talk to the next person I recognized.

Jo from Cooper's Bar.

She was standing with a group of men, arguing with them in hushed tones. I skirted around the crying folks in the crowd and headed her way.

When I got closer to her, I stopped a hair's breath away.

"Where are my parents?" I asked in a whisper, listening with half an ear to a man in the group talk about the terrorists raiding the town.

Jo turned to face me. I tried not to wince. Her short gray hair was matted and dirty. Her face was black and blue, cuts and nicks everywhere. Her right eye was almost swollen shut and her left one was heading there too.

"What happened to you?" I asked, growing angry all over again.

Her eyes darted around, ignoring my question. "What you doing here, boy?" she whispered out of the corner of her mouth, watching two soldiers walk by.

They stared at us, one with a cigarette dangling between his lips. I waited until they had moved on before answering her.

"I'm looking for my parents. Have you seen them?"

Jo knew everyone in town, including my mother and father. If they were here, she would know it.

Her eyes became misty but she nodded at the 19th century courthouse and answered my question. "They're over there. In the back."

I started to leave, desperate to get to my parents, but Jo grabbed my arm, stopping me.

"There ain't nothing you can do, boy. You need to get out of here quick."

I shook her hand off and hurried toward the courthouse. I had no idea what she was talking about but I didn't have time to ask. I needed to grab my parents and get the hell out of town.

Dirty and ragged people lingered at the bottom of the courthouse steps. Foreign combatants lounged inside the open doorway, making themselves at home. They looked smug and full of self-righteous attitude, looking down at the townspeople with loathing. I wanted to do a little target practice and take a few of them out, but I avoided their eyes instead and walked by at a normal pace. My body was tense, ready to spring into action, but I stayed calm and cool. As collected as I had ever been.

As I passed under the flagpole, the sound of the flag hitting the metal pole caught my attention. I glanced up. What I saw made my blood run cold.

The U.S. flag had been replaced with a foreign flag, declaring our little town conquered and seized by the terrorist enemy. The question was what did they want with us?

With my jaw set tight and fury pounding in me, I went around the courthouse as quickly as I dared. What I saw on the other side made me stop in my tracks and feel sick.

The injured had been dumped near the back of the courthouse. Men, women, and children were everywhere. They were bleeding and wounded. Suffering and dying. I went from person to person, checking for familiar faces and hoping I wouldn't see one. But I saw two.

My mom and dad.

They might have been unrecognizable to someone else, but I would know them anywhere. My dad was sitting against the courthouse. The last two weeks had not been kind to him. His clothes were tattered and his cheeks were pale and hollow. My mother was lying on the ground beside him. Her head was in his lap as if she were taking a nap but I knew by the blood on her chest that she would never wake up.

I fell to my knees beside her, my throat closing up tight. "Mom?" My voice croaked, the tears springing up out of nowhere.

She didn't respond but my dad did.

"Son!" he gasped in his gravelly voice. He grabbed my shirtsleeve in a tight grip.

I lifted my eyes to look at him. His face was caked with dirt and blood. Tears had left streaks on his cheeks but they hadn't dried yet. He was still crying, weeping over his wife. Grieving over her death.

"What happened?" I forced out, almost strangled by my tears.

My dad shook his head in sorrow, still holding onto my shirtsleeve. "They got us, son. They got us."

The tears choked me, the grief more than I could bear.

"Mom?" I asked, unable to say the words. I reached for her hand. I needed for her to respond. To open her eyes and smile at me.

But she didn't and she never would.

"I'm sorry. She's gone, son. Gone."

I started shaking my head before he said it. Before he uttered the words I had hoped I never had to hear.

"No!" I hissed, dropping my head to hide the tears that fell down my face.

My dad lowered his hand from my arm, letting me grieve. I couldn't remember the last time I cried, but I did then until I couldn't cry anymore. I cried until my eyes were red and the tears gave way to anger.

"Tell me what happened," I ground out between clenched teeth, snapping my gaze up at my dad.

He took a deep breath, wincing as he did it. "They came out of nowhere. First the electricity cut off and the cars wouldn't run, then the soldiers came. They rounded us up like livestock and put us in here. Others they didn't bother with and just shot."

I didn't tell him that I had seen it with my own eyes. I had witnessed the evilness that walked the town streets. It was just a waste of words and right now I needed to know what happened to my mother and who I needed to kill. But my dad had other things he had to get off his chest first.

"Rumor is that they are here because of the army depot. They've got chemical weapons in there and tanks. These men – whoever they are – want it," he said around a rattling breath.

It made sense. The army depot was right outside of town. It employed many of the townspeople and held weapons and equipment essential to the military. Take the town, take the depot. The terrorists had it planned.

"What…what about Mom?" I asked, forcing the words out.

My dad coughed, a sickly, wet sound. "Your mom was trying to save a boy when she got in the line of fire. I…I couldn't stop her."

A tear fell down his face. He let it as he glanced at me. "You shouldn't be here, Cash."

"I'm here now and I'm getting you out." I reached for him, planning on pulling him to his feet, but my dad pushed my hands away.

"Get out of here, son. Save yourself and go get Keely. It's just the two of you now." Pain crossed his face with the effort of pushing me away.

I glanced over him, looking for some sign that he was hurt also.

"No," I said, shaking my head. "I'm not leaving you. I know a way out. I can get us there. Let's go."

I tried reaching for him again but there was something in his eyes that stopped me.

Sorrow.

He eased my mom off his lap, careful to place her tenderly beside him. I was almost afraid to, but I made myself glance over his lean frame. That's when I saw it, what my mother's body had been hiding.

Blood coated his shirt and one of his legs. It pooled beneath him, soaking into the earth and turning the ground a deep red.

"They got me, son."

I shook my head, tears welling up in my eyes again.

'No," I whispered, refusing to believe it. "No!"

With a sudden, powerful grip, his hand snapped out and grabbed my wrist. "You listen to me, son. I'm done for but you're still here. If there's one thing I've taught you, it's how to survive. Get out of town while you still can. Live. That's all I'm asking you to do for me. *Live.*"

On a choking sob, I grasped him and yanked him to me, hugging him fiercely. I was a grown man that was usually calm and collected. I didn't ask for much. I worked the land. I had a little money. I paid my dues. I met a girl and made love to her like a mad man, not once but twice, wishing I could forget her afterward but knowing I never would.

I was that man and more, but I was on my knees crying, asking God not to do this to me.

My dad gave my arm a gentle squeeze. He was a tough ol' cowboy that had worked hard for most of his life. He didn't put much stock in words but right then I knew what he was saying.

Goodbye.

He let me go and I touched my mother's hand one more time. I didn't want to leave. Everything in me screamed to stay. But before I could make myself stand up and walk away, my dad grasped my hand.

"Give them hell and never stop fighting."

"Never," I said, tightening my fingers on his.

~~~~

I left that makeshift concentration camp a different man. I was colder. Harder. Scars marked my soul but fire burned in my veins.

I hung around town for a while. Assessing the enemy. Learning their ways. Waiting to see their weaknesses. I moved around like a fox, sly and silent. I stole from the terrorists and took what I could, giving it to the prisoners when I had a chance.

I looked for a way to get people out but conditions worsened. When I ran into my friends, Brody and Eva, I made the hard decision to walk away from the town with them.

I would get them to a safe place and somehow find my sister.

It was the beginning of the end.

And I would fight to survive it.

Chapter Thirty-One

-Cat-

My soul had taken a beating. My heart had been ripped from my body. Life had brought me pain and heartache. But nothing had prepared me for this.

I stood under the harsh sunlight and peered off into the distance. Wavy shimmers of heat rose from the blacktop, creating mirages of liquid in the distance. The trees alongside the road stood still, not one leaf moving and not one branch swaying. It was hot. Deathly hot.

Being exposed to the elements morning, noon, and night was taking a toll on us but we didn't have a choice. We had to be under the harsh sun, baking under the unyielding yellow ball in the sky. Tate, Nathan, Keely, and I were escaping, running before the city fell further into chaos. Leaving my belongings hadn't hurt as much as I thought it would. Suddenly the designer clothes and expensive shoes didn't matter much. Surviving did.

We were on a deserted country road, trying to get home. Nathan said we had miles to go until we reached our little podunk town. I just took it one day at a time. One step at a time. One heartbeat at a time.

I readjusted the backpack higher on my shoulder and wished I had a cold drink of water. A small trickle of sweat traced its way down my back, adding to my already soaked tank top. Another drop of perspiration ran down my forehead. I didn't bother wiping it away. I was too tired anyway.

"How much further?"

I glanced at Tate. He walked beside me, looking as worn-out as I felt. His hair was matted and dirty, plastered to his head. New freckles had joined the old ones across his nose and cheeks, thanks to hours under the sun. He had seen things and done things in the past few weeks that no twelve-year old should ever have to see and do. He walked when we said walk and rested when we said rest. Without him and Nathan, I'm not sure what I would have done. They were my rocks as the world crumbled around us. My only reason for going on.

"The next town is a few miles away. Think you can make it?" Nathan asked Tate, walking on the other side of me.

"Yeah," Tate answered, squinting past me at Nathan "I ain't no baby."

"You're *not* a baby," I corrected him.

Tate peered at me with spitefulness. "Why the fuck does it matter how I say it, Cat? The world is a shithole place anyway now."

I didn't have the energy to argue with him. Plus, he was right – what did it matter anymore?

We walked a little while longer in silence, each of us in our own world of suffering. Finally Keely spoke up.

"What time do you think it is?"

I glanced over at her. Her pale blonde hair was dirty, thick strands of it falling out of the ponytail she had fastened with a string she had found on the road. Her cheeks were sunburned and her gray eyes had dark circles under them, magnified by her cracked eyeglasses. Her face was gaunt, thinner than it had been before. The hunger we all felt was more pronounced on her.

Nathan looked up at the sky, his sunburned face tilted at an angle to see against the sun. "I would say it's noon but I'm just guessing."

I wanted to laugh. He didn't know the first thing about telling time by looking at the sun. But I stayed quiet. I didn't laugh anymore. None of us did. Why should we? Our lives had changed in a blink of an eye. We went from a bunch of kids to four people struggling to make it from day to day.

The long road loamed in front of us, unending. I made my legs move, trying to ignore the muscles that ached from miles of walking. The mirage of heat waves grew.

And I swam against it.

~~~~

At dark we stopped at a small town. We couldn't go any further. Our energy was gone. Our hunger was more profound. The thirst that nagged at us night and day was more intense than it had been earlier.

We kept our eyes open for trouble as we entered the outskirts, but the town was empty. No one walked around or made a sound. It was as if the occupants were either long gone, dead, or hiding in their homes.

Despite the silence, we kept our guard up as we walked down the main road. The place consisted of only a small hardware shop, an old church, and a rundown grocery store. We headed for the grocery store first.

We kicked up leaves and trash as we crossed the parking lot. Three beat-up trucks sat near the entrance, abandoned, dusty, and forgotten.

We approached the door to the store cautiously only to find it had already been pried open. I felt my hope plummet. If the store had already been looted for food, we were shit out of luck.

Nathan went in first, followed by Tate, Keely, and me. We walked over broken glass and discarded boxes. A terrible stink filled the store. It smelled like something had died ten times over.

I gagged and covered my nose. Tate spit out the awful taste the smell created then held his sleeve over his lower face. Keely held her collar over her nose, choosing to breathe in the dirt on her shirt instead of the scent. The only one that ignored it was Nathan.

"It's coming from the refrigerated stuff," Keely said, nodding toward the back of the store. Rows of glass doors sat against the wall, hidden behind the aisles of food.

Yes, aisles of food. My eyes went wide when I saw it all. The store hadn't been looted. It was still full of groceries.

Tate shot past me to one of the first aisles, forgetting about the smell.

"Holy fuck, they have Cheetos," he exclaimed. He grabbed a bag hanging from a display and tore it open. A minute later he had devoured the cheesy chips and reached for another bag.

My stomach growled. I felt happiness for the first time in weeks. It was an amazing feeling. Before the EMP, I had everything I wanted but I was miserable. Lost in grief. Now I had nothing and a damn grocery store could make me happy. Life was screwy that way, I guessed.

I rushed down one of the aisles. Oh sweet Mother of God, they had chocolate chip cookies!

I opened the bag and grabbed two. Stuffing them in my mouth, I closed my eyes. Shit, they were good.

Keely rushed past me, her tennis shoes squeaking on the cheap tile floor.

"Where are you going?" I asked around a mouthful of cookies.

"I need a Coke desperately," she called out over her shoulder with excitement, running around the corner.

"Stay close, Keely!" Nathan yelled, going over to the cash register.

I stuffed another cookie in my mouth and watched him, wondering what the hell he was doing. Food was more important than money.

Tate was running around the store like a mad man. He rushed past me to the counter in front of Nathan and threw an armful of stuff down.

"This place is a freaking goldmine! I found candy bars, crackers, jerky, nuts, gum. We'll fucking stuff ourselves tonight," he said, his voice cracking with delight.

Nathan stopped rambling under the counter to look at all the stuff. "Did you find any rice? Beans? Canned goods? Anything besides junk food?"

Tate snorted. "Didn't look. But I did find this."

He pulled a box of condoms out from under his shirt. "Thought you might need them now that you and Keely are a thing. Wouldn't want any little Nathans running around." He shuddered dramatically and glanced at the box with a frown. "Except I couldn't find the itty bitty size. Sorry, Nate."

"You little shit. Give me that." Nathan snatched the box out of Tate's hand and scowled at him. "I swear you need your ass whipped," he muttered, stuffing the box in his backpack.

Tate broke out in a laugh as he tore open a candy bar. "You fucking put them in your bag. Epic."

Nathan blushed. "I swear, Tate…"

Leaving them to irritate each other, I tucked the package of cookies under my arm and headed to where Keely had disappeared. I was suddenly craving a Diet Coke. I hadn't had one in weeks. My mouth watered, just thinking of the bubbly drink. I daydreamed about it and wondered just how many cans I could carry in my backpack. Tate and Nathan were still arguing but I wasn't listening. A warm soda was calling my name.

I turned the corner onto an aisle marked 'Drinks' but didn't see Keely. I glanced around, but saw nothing except shelves of food.

"Keely!" I called out, wondering where she could have disappeared. I looked down the next aisle but she wasn't there either. Before I knew it, I was heading deeper into the store.

It became darker and smellier. I could still hear Nathan and Tate at the front, but I was too far away to understand what they were saying anymore. I covered my nose with my arm and moved silently. Every single part of me was on alert. My heart started pounding. I sat the package of cookies on a nearby shelf, careful not to make any noise. Something wasn't right. I could feel it.

I turned the corner…

Oh. Fuck.

Keely was standing in front of a set of swinging double doors, staring at me with terror. Her glasses were on the floor by her feet, broken, the lens cracked. Her eyes were the size of saucers and her face was pasty white.

The man that stood behind her was the size of a mountain.

It was Hightower. He had an arm locked around her neck in a chokehold and a meaty hand over her mouth. He towered above her by at least three feet and looked like a giant next to Keely's petite frame. With one snap, he could break her neck. I knew it and so did he.

Hightower stared at me with hate, his jaw grinding like giant clamps. Keely started making little mewling sounds, trying to tell me something. The muscles in Hightower's arm tightened and flexed as he squeezed her neck more, cutting off any sound from her.

Her face turned purple and her eyes bulged out in alarm, unable to breathe. She started clawing at his arm, leaving bloody marks behind.

Hightower didn't seem fazed. He leaned down and nuzzled her neck, keeping a tight chokehold on her.

I didn't know what to do. Make a run for it or attack him? Scream like a banshee or fight him off her? I could still hear Nathan and Tate. They had no idea what was going on. If I drew their attention, they were both as good as dead.

I could see the pistol tucked in the waistband of Hightower's jeans. We had no weapons except for some kitchen knives. We had no advantage. No help.

We were screwed.

I took a slow step back and heard the cocking of a gun near my ear. Keely's eyes got wider, frantically moving from me to the person who held a gun on me.

I turned my head slowly, horrified panic beating out a quick rhythm in my heart. The end of a pistol barrel met my gaze. It was pointed directly at my forehead.

The person holding it reached out and grabbed my arm, digging his fingers into me and keeping the gun trained on my head.

My blood ran cold. Terror made my world zero in on nothing but the gun and the man that held it.

Paul.

He grinned and squeezed my arm painfully. Without a word, he looked at Hightower and thrust his chin toward a set of swinging double doors. Hightower kept his chokehold on Keely and turned her around, walking her into the dark bowels of the store. Paul looked at me and motioned with the gun to follow them. *Not on his fucking life.*

He must have seen the fight building in me because he sighed dramatically. I thought I had won – maybe I had a chance – but I was wrong. I was always frickin' wrong.

Out of nowhere he grabbed my wrist and yanked it as far up my back as he could. Agonizing pain shot through my shoulder and down into my arm. I opened my mouth to scream but he buried the end of the gun against my temple and put his mouth near my ear.

"I got two bullets with your friends' name on them."

I froze.

"That's better," Paul whispered in my ear. He gave me a good shove toward the swinging doors, keeping my arm wedged up my back.

I stumbled as he pushed me along, forcing my arm higher. It was dark on the other side of the doors but my eyes adjusted quickly. I could see Hightower and Keely up ahead. They were walking toward the back. Boxes towered against the wall and in the middle of the room. It was a storeroom of some sort.

Hightower opened the back door and I was blinded by sunlight. Paul pushed me outside after Hightower and Keely. His grip on my arm never let up and the end of the pistol moved down to jab me in the ribcage.

I kicked up dust as Paul pushed me to follow Hightower and Keely. They were heading toward a little rundown white house that sat on the street behind the grocery store. The paint was chipping off of the sides and one window screen was hanging loose. The small porch was stuffed with old chairs and refrigerators and other trash. Tall weeds took up most of the yard, some reaching the top of my head. I knew if they got Keely and me in the house, we would not walk out of it. The town was deserted and we were alone.

My arm ached as Paul kept it pushed high on my back. My hand had gone numb. But my legs worked just fine. It was time to put them to good use and fight.

I swung around and brought my knee up, Paul's balls my target. He was faster and expecting it. He backhanded me with the gun, smacking me in the face.

I cried out and fell to the ground, scraping my hands and knees. My mouth was bleeding, my lip cracked. I heard Keely scream behind Hightower's hand as they watched.

I raised my head and glared at Paul. Spitting out a mouthful of blood, I snarled at him. I might be broken on the inside but I wasn't weak.

I jumped up, going on the attack. He grabbed my numb arm again. It brought him close enough that I could do some real damage. I buried my nails in his cheek and dug in deep. He howled and let go of my arm but recovered quickly.

His fist met my cheekbone. It felt like my face had met a wall. I fell back to the ground with a thud but this time I didn't get up.

"Cat!" Keely screamed.

It was the last thing I remembered.

Chapter Thirty-Two

-Cat-

My eyelids lifted then closed. Lifted then closed. I was being dragged across a dirty floor by one arm. My body was limp and my shoulder was on fire but my mind was slowly returning.

"Hurry. Barricade that door before their friends figure out they're missing and come looking," a deep voice said above me.

He dragged me to the center of the room and dumped me, leaving me in a pile. My head hit the wood floor. I lie still. Hurting. Unconsciousness playing at the corners of my mind.

My eyes drifted open to little slits when I heard heavy footsteps close by my head. I saw a pair of boots and a pair of tennis shoes, the latter struggling and kicking. I heard a cry. A slap. My brain screamed at me to get up. To run. To fight. But my body wouldn't cooperate. I hurt and my face throbbed too bad.

I closed my eyes again, just wishing the pain would just go away. The wood felt grimy and cold beneath my cheek. I wished I could just disappear in it forever.

A boot kicked my leg out of the way. I didn't respond. I was gone. I had had enough. I was giving up. Ready to die. I couldn't take it anymore. The pain. The heartache. The grief that lived with me everyday. I hated myself and I hated my life.

This was the ending I deserved.

A tear fell down my cheek then another. They fell faster as someone laid down on top of me. I heard Keely cry but there was nothing I could do.

Nothing because I was nothing.

Hands tore at my clothes, disgusting words filled my ears. Fingers pinched me and ran over parts of me that Cash had last touched. I squeezed my eyes closed, hating it all. Tears leaked from the corners of my eyes. Keely's cries wouldn't stop.

My pants were tugged down. I blocked it out. I heard a zipper and heavy breathing. My fingernails dug into the hardwood floor. He twisted my braid around his fist and tugged my head up.

"Ready, little bird."

A bloodcurdling scream ripped through the air but it wasn't mine.

It was Keely's.

I heard grunts coming from another room combined with Keely's sobs. *Oh. God.* That's when something in me suddenly snapped. Hearing her was like a bomb going off in my head. It woke me up and lit a fire inside me.

My eyes flew open. The fight came out of nowhere. I bucked my body, catching Paul off guard and throwing him off me.

"Hey!" he yelled as I scrambled back and pulled my pants up at the same time.

He came at me, crawling like a bug. I noticed he had left his gun on the floor but it was too far away for me to grab. I reached for the nearest thing instead. A dusty coffee cup.

I threw it at his head as hard as I could and scrambled backward.

He ducked and yelped when the cup grazed his head,

but he didn't stop. With his pants hanging open, he lunged at me.

I screamed and shot to my feet. He was quicker. He grabbed my ankle and yanked. I fell to the floor on my stomach, my chin hitting hard. Paul wrapped a tight hand around my braid again and crawled up my body. I kicked and screamed, trying to buck him off. Fighting with everything I had. I could still hear sobs coming from the other room.

I have to save Keely.

Paul buried his nose into the back of my neck and pushed his crotch into me. He gave my hair a good yank before reaching for my pants again.

I screamed as loud and as shrill as I could. If I couldn't fight him, I could make enough racket to drive him insane.

"Get the fuck away from her!"

I snapped my head around, my scream dying.

Nathan was standing in the doorway, looking larger than life and ready to kill. Tate was behind him, a knife in his hand and a mixture of fear and anger on his face.

"Nathan!" I shouted, pointing to the room Keely was in. "Help Keely!" *Forget about me. Forget about the sick fuck lying on me.* I wanted him to save her.

Nathan hesitated only a second but it was a second too long.

Paul jumped off me and lunged for his gun.

"NO!" I screamed, watching as he swung it up and around, pointing it at Nathan.

The shot exploded, rattling the tiny house. My hearing became muffled. I saw the bullet casing drop from the gun at the same time I heard Nathan gasp.

"No! No! No!" I shrieked, scrambling to my knees.

A red plume appeared on Nathan's chest and spread outward. He looked down at it as he dropped to his knees.

"Nathan! Oh, god! Oh god! Nathan!" I cried in alarm and terror. I started to crawl to him, but Paul swung his gun on Tate.

"Stay right there, boy," he said when Tate started to rush toward Nathan. I kneeled on the floor, my gaze swinging from one brother to the other. Tears fell from my eyes, seeing my brother on his knees bleeding.

Just then Hightower walked into the room, leisurely zipping up his fly. "What's going on?" he asked, sounding mildly interested and way too pleased.

Paul readjusted the grip he had on the pistol, tightening his sweaty hand around the handle. "These here boys found our little hidey hole," he said, jerking his chin at Tate.

"So? Finish them and let's get out of here," Hightower said, shrugging.

Paul glanced over at Hightower with exasperation. "But I ain't done with her yet," he whined, nodding toward me.

Hightower snorted. "That's your problem. I'm not going to have Frankie breathing down my neck because you can't get it up."

"Hell, Hightower, it's not that…"

I couldn't stand listening to them anymore. Nathan was bleeding out. Tate was in Paul's line of fire. And Keely…I didn't even know if she was still alive.

That left me.

I had nothing to lose. I had already lost so much. It was time to fight. Time to die. Time to stand up for my brothers' lives.

With a shriek, I bulldozed Paul from the side. He fell to the ground and the gun went flying.

Tate lunged for it like a baseball player going for the ball. Hightower shot across the room at the same time, his big body not as quick as the skinny twelve-year olds.

Tate grabbed the gun and snapped it up as I scrambled over to Nathan. The gun shook in Tate's hand and there was fear in his eyes but he looked down the barrel with precision.

"Don't move," he said, pulling back the hammer.

Nathan fell back against the wall as soon as I got to his side. I pressed two hands on his wound as Paul and Hightower froze. Tate was a dirty, scrawny kid but he knew what he was doing.

He rose to his feet, keeping the gun on the two men. "Put your hands up."

Hightower did what he said but Paul chuckled. "You're just a damn kid."

A shot rent the air. Paul screeched and jumped a foot, grabbing his ear.

"You fucking nicked my ear!" he screamed. "You fucking shot me!"

Tate shrugged, keeping the gun on him. "My bad. I was aiming for your forehead."

Hightower chuckled, keeping his hands in the air.

"Shut up!" Paul shouted, turning to glare at his friend. "Just shut the fuck up!"

Nathan moaned. He was half-reclined on the wall and floor, blood pumping from his chest. I pushed down harder, causing his life's essence to soak my hand.

I should have been frozen with memories of another time. Another man's blood on my hands. But in that moment, I became stronger. I had to be. For my brother.

A trail of blood appeared at the corner of his mouth. His lips were white but they moved. "Keely. Keely."

"Okay." I found the strength not to burst into sobs. I snapped my head around to glare at Tate. "Kill them," I hissed.

Tate's face went white. I knew it was wrong of me to put that on my little brother, but Nathan was dying and Keely was hurt or maybe even dead. Hightower and Paul had done it. These men had taken from me without remorse.

Now it was my turn to do the same.

"Kill them!" I screamed, tears streaming down my face. "Kill them, Tate!" I jumped up and grabbed the gun from him. My hand was bloody, slippery on the pistol. I couldn't see. The tears were too thick in my eyes. I shook from my head to my toes.

I took a deep breath. *I could do this.* I put my finger on the trigger, ready to pull.

"Easy," Hightower said in a calm voice. "We'll go. We'll walk out of here and you'll be free."

I motioned to the door with the gun. "You've got three seconds." They were monsters but I wasn't sure I could take a life. I had seen one too many taken from me.

"Come on," Hightower said to Paul. "We got what we came for anyway."

"You did," Paul grumbled, holding his bloody ear as he followed Hightower. At the door he glanced back at me. "But I will one day."

I kept the gun pointed at them until they disappeared through the doorway. As soon as they did, I handed the gun to Tate and dropped to my knees beside Nathan again.

"Oh, Jesus," I hissed, not sure what to do. The floor beneath him was a pool of dark red. I wasn't a doctor but I knew it was bad.

"Keely. Where's Keely?" Nathan mumbled, his eyes closing then reopening.

I grabbed a nearby blanket and put it on the gunshot wound, putting pressure on it.

"Just hold on, Nate. We need to stop your bleeding," I whispered, wiping my tears away with the back of my free hand.

Tate pushed the front door closed and shoved stuff in front of it to barricade us in and the bad guys out. I heard him head across the room toward where Hightower had dragged Keely.

Panic flooded me.

"Tate!" I shouted, glancing at him over my shoulder. "Wait. Wait. Don't go in there!"

I jumped to my feet, leaving Nathan. "Let me go. Stay with Nathan."

Tate nodded, reading my mind. I didn't know what condition Keely would be in, but I didn't want my little brother to see it.

I wiped my bloody hands on my pants and looked at the dark doorway. The first time I met Keely, I didn't want to like her. She was sweet and nice and reminded me too much of Cash. But sometime over the past few weeks, she had grown on me. In her innocence, I saw hope and happiness. I saw what I could still be. In her smile I saw friendship. Something I needed badly. I just hoped and prayed that she was still alive.

I didn't want to lose my new best friend.

~~~~

The room was shadowy. A dirty-laced curtain hung on the window. A metal bed frame had been pushed against one wall and stacks of old newspapers took up another. Filth and dust covered the floor and everything in between. I found Keely lying motionless in the middle of it all.

"Keely!" I cried out, running to her. She was laying on her side, curled up in the fetal position. Her pants were across the room and her shirt lay tattered at her feet.

I reached out to touch her but then stopped. She was covered in welts. Her arm. Her side. Her legs. Her pale blonde hair was tangled. Oh, shit. A chunk of it was gone. Hightower had talked about taking strands of hair and he had taken some of hers.

I felt sick to my stomach. I reached out with a shaky hand and pushed her hair away from her face. Her cheeks and eyes looked just as bad as the rest of her body.

"Keely, they're gone. They're gone," I repeated over and over, touching her arm gently. "They're gone."

Her eyes fluttered open. She whimpered and drew herself into a tinier ball, trying to get away from my touch.

"It's me. It's Cat," I said as gently as I could.

Hearing my name must have gotten through to her. She raised her head again and blinked at me.

"It's me, Keely."

She pushed herself to a sitting position and pulled her knees up to her chest. I laid a hand on her head when she buried her face in her knees and started crying.

When her sobs grew, I crawled closer and wrapped my arms around her skinny shoulders. I held her as she cried. When she started shaking, I grabbed an old quilt from nearby and wrapped it around her shoulders. It wasn't cold but she was naked and in shock. Warmth and security was what she needed at that moment.

She looked at me, her lopsided hair hanging in her face. She didn't need to tell me what that monster had done. It was evident.

Keely didn't say anything as I helped her to her feet. She didn't whimper when I walked her out of the room. She didn't talk when she fell down beside Nathan.

She only cried.

He touched Keely's bruised face and whispered that he loved her. Tears trailed down my cheeks as I listened. I wanted to get up and run away. Flee from the grief and sorrow that choked me. But I knew there was no hiding. It always found me anyway.

The blood poured from Nathan's wound and pooled under him. His face had lost all color and his body was going limp quickly. I didn't need to say what we all knew. The gunshot was fatal. Nathan was dying.

I had my head bent, tears dropping into my lap, when I felt Nathan's hand grab mine. I lifted my eyes, not ready yet to say goodbye.

"Let him love you, Cat," Nathan whispered.

I shook my head, unsure what he meant.

Nathan licked his pale lips. "Whoever he is, let him love you."

I sniffed loudly and ran a hand under my nose. "Don't leave me, Nathan. Don't you dare leave me."

He tried to grin but it took too much energy. He looked at Tate. "You're a good kid, Tater Tot. Take care of Keely and Cat for me."

Tate nodded and ducked his head. His shaggy hair fell over his face, hiding his tears from us.

Nathan looked back at me, his face growing paler.

"You're worth it, Cat. Remember that. We're all worthy of love."

I cried as he whispered he loved me. I sobbed when he touched Keely's face.

I wept when he closed his eyes for the last time.

~~~~

Night had fallen by the time we buried him. Tate broke into the hardware store for a shovel and he and I took turns digging a grave. We buried him in a nearby field covered with dandelions. Keely stood quietly nearby and watched.

I didn't want to leave him there. I wanted to take my brother home. But home was far away.

Tate's eyes were red-rimmed, his nose swollen from crying. He sat on the ground near Nathan's grave and cried, his body shaking with grief. I held him tight, my own tears joining his. When the sky darkened more, I urged him to his feet.

We headed across the deserted street toward the house again. Keely walked beside me, her arms wrapped around her middle. She hadn't said one word since I found her. I wanted her to yell and scream, cuss and throw a huge fit for what Hightower did to her. But instead she stayed quiet, drawing into herself more and more each minute.

The house was dreary and dark when we walked in. It held ghosts and violence that made my back stiffen. We found one candle and a half-empty box of matches. Tate lit the candle and I took it immediately. I needed to be alone.

I hurried to one of the bedrooms, running and covering my mouth to keep my cries from escaping. As soon as I got to the room, I shut the door and set the candle on an overturned box. I fell to my knees, sobbing. Terrible cries shook my body and pain ripped at my heart. I hugged my arms around myself and cried. I felt like I was dying too.

My brother was dead.

Nathan was gone.

I would never see his smirk or hear his bossy voice again. *Oh, god. Nathan's gone.*

I didn't know how long I sat there and wept, but it would never be enough time. How was I supposed to get over losing him? How would I go on?

After a while, I had no tears left. My chest ached and I felt hollow inside. The fighter in me, the one that Nathan always encouraged, rose up. I went from crying to seething mad. From one emotion to the other. I knew what Nathan would want me to be.

Strong.

I wiped the tears away with angry, jerky motions. My grief turned into purpose. I glanced around the room. I had checked it out earlier. It was a girl's – maybe a teenagers. I pushed myself to my feet, feeling shaky but determined. Sniffing, I crossed the room to the closet door. I had to shove magazines out of the way to pry it open but I finally got the cheap, wooden door ajar. I started going through the clothes hanging there. I grabbed a pair of jeans and then a t-shirt. I found a pair of military-style women's boots and pulled them out too. I wouldn't have been caught dead in the stuff weeks ago, but things were different now. We were at war. We were fighting for our lives, now without my brother.

With a quivering chin, I changed clothes quickly, lacing the boots tightly up my shins. My motions were jerky. Angry. I was mad at the world. Pissed at life in general. Overwhelmed by my loss. I didn't know whether to sit back down and cry or go on a killing spree.

Suddenly, a footstep alerted me that I wasn't alone anymore. I glanced up and wiped away another tear. Keely stood in the doorway, looking fragile and frightened in the candlelight. I jumped up and went to the closet again. I grabbed a pair of jeans and a shirt. Nathan would want me to take care of her no matter how grief-stricken I was so that's what I would do.

I walked across the room with purpose and handed the clothes to her. I didn't give her a chance to change. Instead, I grabbed the candle then her arm and pulled her out of the room.

Tate stared at my swollen, red eyes as I led Keely past him to the only bathroom the house had. It was dingy and outdated, but it probably had what I needed.

I sat Keely down on the green-colored toilet seat and put the candle on the counter. It didn't provide much light but I started rambling under the sink anyway. I found a box of tampons and some cheap, thin washcloths. Acne medicine sat beside arthritis cream. Prescription drugs sat next to a box of Band-Aids. I pulled out everything. We would take what we could carry.

"Tate, I need some water!" I shouted.

A few minutes later Tate appeared in the doorway with a big jug of water.

"Thank goodness," I muttered. I grabbed it from him and shooed him away, closing the door behind him. I wetted a washcloth and handed it to Keely. She looked at me like I was crazy.

"We're going to clean ourselves up," I told her, slamming stuff on the counter. Soap. Deodorant. Hairbrush. "We're going to walk out of here with our damn head held high. Everyone can suck it. We're survivors, Keely. Understand?"

When she didn't answer, I glanced at her. She had tears in her eyes. They dropped down her face and onto the washcloth in her hand.

I felt myself start to lose it again. My throat closed up. Tears filled my own eyes, but I blinked them away and dropped down in front of her, kneeling at her knees.

"Listen to me, Keely," I said, grabbing her hands to get her attention. "I know what that monster did and I know what you're feeling. It's not your fault. He was a pig. The lowest form of humanity. We can't let them make us afraid. They only win that way. We've got to be stronger."

Tears rolled down her cheeks and dropped off her chin. I swallowed past my own thick throat and went on.

"Nathan cared for you, Keely. He loved you. I'm going to miss him too. I'm going to miss him so damn much. But he would want for you to get up and go on," I said, my eyes watering even more saying my brother's name. "Believe me, if he was here, he would tell both of us to be strong and move on."

She shook her head violently and tried to pull her hands away but I wouldn't let her. Nathan hadn't let me give up a year ago. I wasn't going to let Keely.

"No!" I said, tightening my fingers on her hand. "You're going to clean up and fight this. For yourself. For Nathan. For Cash."

Her head snapped up. I felt something flare to life in me when I thought of her brother.

I nodded. "For Cash. Let's do this for Cash."

I didn't kid myself. We would probably never see him again. The thought of that did something to me, twisting my heart painfully. But if thinking about Cash got Keely through one more day, I would say his name a million times no matter how much it hurt me.

I let go of her hand and stood up. Wetting a washcloth for myself, I scrubbed my skin until it was red. I took off my new clothes and scrubbed every inch of my body. I scrubbed until I almost bled.

She did the same, putting on her new clothes afterward. I felt cleaner. Able to face the hell that lived outside the walls and inside me.

There was one more thing that needed to be done.

I pulled a pair of scissors out of a drawer and grabbed Keely's hand, pulling her to her feet. Her light blonde hair was lopsided, one side shorter than the other. Her eyes held a haunting look in them, one that I recognized from looking in the mirror at myself.

I grabbed the scissors and grasped a lock of Keely's hair. She gasped as I cut it off. I did it again and again until her hair was evened out. When I was done, I took a step back to look at my handiwork in the candlelight.

Her hair was shorter than before but it wasn't lopsided anymore. Her small, oval face was framed even more delicately with the new haircut.

Now it was my turn.

I fingered the edge of my braid. It was messy, coming undone. A part of the old me. I remembered Paul wrapping his hand around it and yanking my head back painfully. I remembered all the men that had wanted to run their fingers through my hair as I gave them a sinful smile.

I picked up the scissors and started sawing off the braid. Tears filled my eyes but anger cut through me with every slash.

Nathan was dead.

Keely was hurt.

Everyone I loved seemed to be taken from me.

I sawed faster, desperate to cut the braid from me. Finally it fell into the sink. I left it there along with the girl I once was.

~

Three Years Later

~

Chapter Thirty-Three

-Cash-

"This is a load of horse shit."

I stuffed the last of my supplies in my saddlebag. "Tell me how you really feel, Gavin."

Gavin scowled at me over the back of his horse. "You really want me to tell you what I think?" He rested his arms on the saddle, ignoring the horse when it shifted and pawed at the ground.

"Go ahead," I said, grinning as I checked the saddle strap on my own horse. "Let's hear it."

"Fine. I think this is a goddamn stupid decision. I think we should pack our shit up once and for all and head home." He walked around his horse, checking straps, and shaking the saddle to make sure it was on good and tight. Finally he stopped by his quarter horse's flank, resting an elbow on him and facing me. "Listen, Cash." Gavin's voice lost his edge, the one that made me want to punch him sometimes. "She's your sister. I get it. Hell, if Maddie or Ryder were missing, I would move heaven and earth to find them, but it's been three years. I just don't think we're going to find her."

I gave the stirrup a good yank, keeping my head down so my cowboy hat would shield the anger in my eyes from him. Gavin was just looking for a fight. He was a pain in my ass and a damn big thorn in my side.

But hell, the man had become my best friend.

Three years ago I walked out of the terrorist camp with a heavy heart, leaving my dying dad behind. I became a cold S.O.B., just itching to take out a few foreign fucks. Then I ran into my friends from high school, Brody and Eva. They were trying to get out of town. Trying to get somewhere safe. When they mentioned Maddie Jackson I knew I had to go.

Maddie was someone I thought I had loved back in high school. A quiet boy's infatuation. That was a long time ago. Now Maddie was like a sister. But I still had to find my real one.

"Are you listening to me?" Gavin asked, giving his own saddle a good yank to make sure it was on tight. "Are you just gonna give me a damn silent treatment?"

I put my foot in the stirrup and swung up into the saddle. Then I gave him the bird.

Gavin chuckled and mounted up too. "You just have a way with words. It makes my heart go pitter patter." He patted his chest, right over his heart.

Gavin was Ryder's brother (well, cousin technically but that was another story). Ryder was married to Maddie. He was a good guy, I guess. Most days, Ryder and I wanted to kill each other. Gavin was just a pain in my ass.

I rested my elbow on the saddle horn and faced him. "She's my sister, Gavin. You can follow me or go home. Your choice but I'm gonna find her." The rising sun was peeking over trees and through branches, blinding me as I stared at him. My horse danced beneath me, ready to go.

Gavin sighed and rubbed a hand over the black whiskers on his face. "Austin is a hellhole, you know."

I nodded. "I know."

For the past three years I had searched on and off for Keely but had been unable to get to Austin. It was ground zero for the war, it being the state capitol and all.

The news had trickled slowly to us about the EMP attack on America. It was an elaborate plan that had been in effect years beforehand. Sleeper cells had made careful arrangements, ready to jump into action when the U.S. was at its weakest. Without electricity we were vulnerable, each area of the country cut off from the other. Motions were set in place to invade when it happened. The terrorist had us right where they wanted us. But we were Americans. We knew how to fight on our own soil. We had done it before and we would do it again.

When I heard that the war was being won – that the United States was kicking some enemy ass – I had packed, only one thing on my mind.

Find Keely.

My plan had been simple. Sneak away in the middle of the night and take off for Austin. I wanted to go alone. I didn't want to be responsible for getting anyone killed and I didn't want to listen to Maddie lecture me about being careful.

So I packed my saddlebags and rounded up some food. I had waited until the middle of the night and left without making a sound. But who did I find standing in the dark waiting for me, his bags packed and his horse saddled? Gavin.

"Where're we going?" he had asked. Not a hello. Not a 'what-the-hell are you doing?' Nope. Just a 'where're are we going?' Typical Gavin.

Now here we were, on the trail of my sister who I hadn't seen in years. I glanced over at our campfire, making sure it was snuffed out. Coils of smoke rose slowly in the chilly air. Winter was setting in early. The last thing we needed for our trip.

I pulled the reins to the right, leading my horse out of the alcove of trees. We had a few miles to go until we reached the outskirts of Austin. Might as well stop sitting around and face the hell I had heard it was.

Gavin followed on his horse, humming some annoying tune. I rolled my eyes. He was just itching to draw attention to us. The man had a death wish. Maybe I did too. I had done some messed up stuff since the bomb hit. I had killed and hurt. I had stolen and taken what wasn't mine. And I had done it all in the name of survival.

I ducked my head, narrowly missing a branch as I rode under it. I thought of Austin, wondering if we had enough firepower to get in and get out. Guess we would find out.

A stiff wind blew against me. My horse's hoofs chomped quietly in the grass. I let my mind wander to a place I usually blocked out. The one where the memory of Cat still resided. I had no right to think of her, not after all these years. She was either dead or had hooked up with someone, but hell, I hoped she was still alive. To think that she may not be on this earth anymore almost knocked me off my horse. I liked to imagine her somewhere. Smiling. Teasing some poor man. Driving him crazy like she had driven me.

I shifted in the saddle, uneasy with my train of thought. No, it wasn't right to think of her. Life had changed. I had changed. I wasn't that polite cowboy anymore. The one that smiled at her and opened doors for her to walk through. I was hard around the edges. Worn raw and cut deep. Dangerous to those who didn't know me. The only thing I had left to care about was Keely.

Everyone else was just collateral damage.

~~~~

"Holy fuck."

I ignored Gavin and walked down the middle of the street, keeping a finger near my shotgun's trigger. It was quiet. Too quiet. Fallen leaves rustled as they blew down the road. Garbage was everywhere and the majority of the houses around us were nothing but piles of rumble and brick.

I glanced right and left, keeping my eyes open for trouble. More than likely, it was right around the corner, waiting to jump out. I could feel it. Taste it in the back of my mouth.

Danger.

It was my constant companion now and I couldn't shake it off.

We were still a few miles from Austin. Some old suburb north of town. The college was still a distance away and getting there might be impossible. But impossible was something I liked.

Gavin walked beside me, his pistol holstered but his crossbow in his hands. I resisted the urge to snort with disgust. The man had a thing for arrows. I made fun of him every chance I got. I would never admit it to him, but I thought he was onto something. Arrows could be made much easier than a bullet, plus bullets were getting scarce.

I preferred the five-inch blade in my boot. Or maybe the eleven-inch sheathed on my side. They both could cause some damage. Whatever we used, we still needed it despite the Americans kicking some foreign ass. Large groups of terrorists still roamed the country and militias that wanted power instead of freedom were popping up everywhere.

That's why Gavin and I were on edge. Who the fuck knew what we would have to face around a corner or a bend in the road. We were careful not to make our presence known as we walked down the street. My muscles were tense, ready to attack, if need be.

Suddenly, a door swung open to my left. I snapped my shotgun up, peering down the barrel at the house. Nothing moved but some dead leaves. It was just the wind.

"My spidey senses are telling me to get the fuck out of here, buddy," Gavin mumbled beside me, holding his crossbow in front of him.

"Yeah, well, my map says this is a short cut," I said in a low voice, not wanting to spook any people that might be lingering behind the closed doors.

"Fuck the map and fuck the short cut," Gavin grumbled out of the corner of his mouth.

This time I did roll my eyes. I lowered my gun and shot a look at him from under my hat. "You are the biggest damn whiner I know."

Gavin grinned, resting the bow on his shoulder. "But you love me."

I gritted my teeth. "I may be the only one."

Gavin scoffed as we started walking again. "That's not what that redhead said last week."

"No, she said, 'Have you put your tiny dick in me yet? I can't feel it.'"

Gavin flipped me off as he left to walk over to the curb. It was a love thing with us – the middle finger, the bird.

He walked along the edges of the overgrown grassy yards and I stayed in the street, both of us keeping our eyes open. My gut was telling me to hurry, that Keely was close. I didn't know why I was getting my hopes up. The chances of her still being in Austin were slim to none.

We got through the small neighborhood with no problem or trouble and came to a large, wooded area. It was thick with tall oak trees and a layer of dried, brown leaves on the ground. It was a big city's way of conserving nature or some shit like that – leave a few acres of trees but cut down the rest for mini-mansions. I just called the area a problem because it looked like a big, shady one. Perfect to hide in and wait for your next victim.

The leaves cushioned our steps as we started through the woods. I was glad because we would have drawn a shit storm down on us if we had announced our arrival.

Loud shouts came from somewhere deeper in the trees. *Men*. A number of them. And they didn't sound very pleased.

I raised the gun to my shoulder and Gavin did the same with his crossbow. We crouched lower and walked toward the danger, not away from it. We were crazy that way, I guessed.

Using the trees for cover, we moved silently. When we saw the men, I took one tree and Gavin took another a few feet from me. I plastered my side to the tree bark and carefully slipped my safety off. I had counted seven men. That was five too many.

I looked at Gavin and held up my hand, flashing five and two. He shook his head and held up three then pointed in their direction. I sneaked a peek. He was right. There were seven but three men were surrounded.

Scratch that – they had three kids surrounded. A tall one and two short ones. Probably teenagers by the looks of them.

They wore ball caps and heavy jackets. Two of them were scrawny. The tall one was bigger. They had their hands up in surrender, no weapons in their hands. I could tell from my vantage point that at least two of them were nervous. Hell, they should be. Seven against three weren't good odds.

I checked out the other men. They were Americans. Just some assholes bothering a bunch of kids. I knew the kind well. They picked on those less fortunate. Made a game of it. Troublemakers and outlaws roamed the countryside and took what they wanted. It had become a free-for-all the moment the EMPs had been dropped and no one was safe. Guys like these would make sure of it.

"You know the punishment for stealing out here?" one of the guys said as he walked toward the three scrawny kids standing in the center of the men.

I couldn't hear what one of kids said, but I could only guess. The leader drew back a huge fist and punched the kid in the gut. *Shit, that had to hurt.*

My hand tightened around the handle of my gun. I hated the violence that reigned everywhere. Sure, I was a part of it but that didn't mean I had to like it.

Gavin caught my eye. I knew without asking what he thought we should do.

Leave.

He pointed behind us. He wanted us to mind our own business. Backtrack and pretend we hadn't seen anything.

I glanced back at the group of men again. Hell, he was right. I had to find my sister. These kids probably had stolen something and deserved what they got. It was the way now. An eye for an eye. I was colder that way. I had to be.

I gave Gavin a short nod and eased away from the tree carefully. One mistake…one sound…and we would draw attention to ourselves. We had to move quietly but quickly. The sooner we left, the better.

We backed away, one well-placed step at a time. We were careful not to put our boot on a downed tree branch or twig. It might mean the difference between finding

Keely and finding ourselves in a heap of trouble. But sometimes the best intentions are worthless.

I took a step back and my heel snapped a small branch in two. The sound was loud in the woods.

But not as loud as the gunshot that ripped through the air. It was followed by another one then a scream.

I raised my gun and shot forward. *Fuck being cold. Fuck trouble. No one opened fire on a bunch of kids.*

Gavin was right beside me, running with his bow positioned against his shoulder. We hit the clearing in seconds, our boots breaking the branches and twigs we had tried to avoid minutes ago. What we saw almost made us freeze. Almost.

Two men were sprawled on the ground but more were on their feet. They had a nasty assortment of guns and looked to have some mean-ass attitudes. They were shouting and pointing at the kids with pistols and shotguns, screaming at them to get down.

The kids weren't listening. One held a smoking gun. Another grasped a bloody knife. *Fuck!* One of them was a woman! Her hat had come off, exposing light blonde hair. *Shit, she looks like…*

A big man stomped over to her and put a gun to her temple, yelling something about dying. That's when I lost it.

I pulled the trigger on my shotgun, taking out the man. It got everyone's attention. Guns turned in our direction but they were too late. I chambered another round and swung to the next man, all in one, smooth motion. I took #2 out then #3 as I walked forward, my jaw set tightly and my aim true.

Gavin did the same. His arrow found one man but before it had even buried in the man's chest, he dropped the crossbow and pulled out his pistol. He was fast as shit with the gun as well. Deadly quick and cold as fuck. Sometimes the asshole even scared me.

In seconds we had taken them all out. Five men. And we did it without flinching.

Legend would say two outlaws with guns on their hips did it without remorse or regret. But history would get it wrong. We were just two ordinary guys looking to right some wrongs.

I kept my head down, letting my cowboy hat shield my eyes as I surveyed what remained. The three kids still stood in the same place. Two of them watched Gavin and me with apprehension. The other one stood back behind them. Something about him made me wary. He was a dangerous motherfucker. I could tell just by the way he held himself.

Too bad. I was deadlier.

I didn't give him a second thought. I had other things to deal with. Like the blonde. I headed straight to her.

Gavin followed me. I had lowered my gun but he still had his pistol ready, waiting for one of the men to jump up. It was a waste of time. They weren't going anywhere.

My stride was quick as I headed to the blonde girl. The tall kid jumped in front of her, acting like the hero. But I was bigger and meaner and had one fuckin' goal.

"Don't come any closer," he said, holding up the little peashooter in his hand.

It didn't stop me. I grabbed his wrist and snapped it sideways, never breaking my stride. He yelped and dropped the gun. It thumped to the ground as I pushed past him.

That's when Gavin took over. He put himself between the kid and me, pointing his pistol at the boy. He didn't know what the hell I was doing but he had my back. That's what we did for each other. Brothers in arms.

The blonde took a nervous step back, ducking her head and cowering as I got closer. My heart broke.

Damn, it shattered.

The scrawny kid behind her hadn't moved. Just stood there holding that bloody knife. I didn't give him a second look. I had more important things to do.

When I got close enough, I saw her more clearly. Light colored hair rested down around her shoulders. Crystal gray eyes looked up at me through a broken pair of glasses.

"Keely?" My voice broke. Her name was only a whisper coming from my mouth. I hadn't said it in so long that it felt funny on my lips and foreign to my ears.

She blinked. Her eyes went wide, but she didn't speak. I opened my mouth to say her name again but she suddenly threw herself at me.

Her skinny arms went around my neck like a powerful vise. She rose on tiptoes and buried her nose in my jacket collar.

"Well, fuck me," Gavin whispered beside me, lowering his pistol.

I dropped my shotgun and wrapped my arms around Keely's thin body as sobs shook it. I couldn't believe it. I had found her. My sister. After all this time. I didn't believe in miracles but maybe I should start.

She cried and I held her tight, afraid to let her go. The words I wanted to say – the ones I had rehearsed in my mind a million times - wouldn't come out past my thick throat. I gave up trying and just hugged her. The fact that she was standing in front of me was all that mattered anyway.

From under my hat, I saw the scrawny fellow behind her stiffen. He kept his head down and face hidden beneath the brim of his faded ball cap. All I could see was a gently curved jaw. His body was just as thin as Keely's. Almost girly. Whoever he was, he didn't seem happy.

Too bad. He could get lost. Keely didn't need him anymore. And what the fuck was she doing with two guys anyway?

I pulled away from her and looked down into her eyes. "You okay? Are you hurt? Did they do something to you?" I asked frantically as I grabbed the sides of her face, turning her head one-way then another, looking for signs of trauma. I had to know who to hurt next.

Keely didn't say anything but shook her head 'no.' She didn't look hurt, just hungry and tired, but I still wanted to hear her say that she was okay.

"Are you sure you're okay?" I asked, grabbing her arms and giving her a good shake, desperate for her to answer me.

"Leave her alone. She doesn't talk," the tall kid barked. He tried to dart around Gavin and come to Keely's aid but Gavin held his ground, keeping the kid away from us.

I snapped my focus over to him. Something about him seemed familiar but I shook the feeling off. "What do you mean she doesn't talk?" I scowled, growing impatient. Keely could talk a person's head off; the kid had to be wrong.

He swallowed hard and looked at the scrawny guy behind Keely. I didn't know what the hell was going on but I was getting angry.

I gave Keely a good shake. "*What* is going on, Keely? Talk to me! Tell me you're okay!"

Tears filled her eyes and she shook her head 'no' frantically. I grew frustrated and scared. So damn scared that it pissed me off.

I gently pushed Keely to Gavin and then picked up my

gun. I had a feeling there was one person here who could answer all of my questions.

With my shotgun in my hand, I took a threatening step toward the small kid. I got in his personal space, the best place to intimidate the hell out of a person.

The tall kid started going bat shit crazy when I got near his friend but Gavin jerked up his pistol, keeping Keely safe behind him and the tall guy away from me.

I stared hard at the small kid in front of me. His eyes were still cast down but I had a feeling the guy wasn't in the least bit afraid of me.

Time to change that.

I towered over his thin body, itching to reach out and snap him in half.

"Why do I have the feeling that you're the cause of this?" I asked, my voice low and deadly.

The kid took a quick step back as if he was afraid I would touch him. Good. But he didn't answer me. He just kept his head bowed and that damn bloody knife in his hand.

My muscles tensed, ready to throw this little weasel down and get some answers. I resisted and tried again.

"Who are you?" I growled, sounding much calmer than I felt at the moment. "And why the hell should I not fill you with buckshot right now?"

In answer, the kid flipped the knife around in his hand, fisting it.

Gavin spun his pistol around to aim at the kid. I took a step back and snapped my gun up, pointing it straight at the boy. The tall guy started going berserk, yelling about leaving her alone. I wondered what the fuck he was talking about but didn't have time to worry. Keely grabbed my arm and started pulling, making little mewling sounds and trying to get me to lower the gun, but I was mad and willing to shed this boy's blood.

"Drop the knife and start talking," I demanded, looking down my barrel at him.

The kid held out his arm lengthwise and opened his fist, letting the knife drop. It buried in the ground with a thud, blade first. He held out his arms in a show of surrender and slowly started to raise his head.

First I saw the fine, graceful shape of his jawline. Then a delicate chin and full, curved lips. I went pale when I realized the kid wasn't a boy at all but a girl in disguise. A perfectly shaped nose appeared between high cheekbones. Her beautiful skin had a slight tan to it. Her brows lifted in audacity. But it was the green cat-shaped eyes staring back at me that made me lower my gun.

"Cat?" I asked with a hoarse whisper, unable to believe my eyes.

A dangerous smile curved her lips up.

"Hello, cowboy."

Chapter Thirty-Four

-Cat-

The two men came into the clearing with their guns blazing. They took out the group in a blink of an eye. They were cold. Calculated. Lethal. I would have known the one with the cowboy hat anywhere. He had haunted me since the night we met. Now he was in front of me.

My smile died. I licked my dry lips as he stared at me. He seemed much more dangerous than he had three years ago.

I wanted to reach out and touch him, see if he was real. But I held still, afraid if I moved he would disappear like an apparition. I was overwhelmed with happiness but also scared. The man that stood in front of me was not the man I had left standing on my front porch. This man was harder. Less forgiving and more intense.

"Take off your hat," he demanded, glaring at me.

With my heart pounding, I reached up and pulled my baseball cap off. My hair fell down around my shoulders, shorter than it had been when he knew me.

Cash took a step closer. I held my breath. My heart started pounding and my knees grew weak. I thought for sure I would faint when he reached out a hand toward me.

"Cat," he whispered, picking up a curl from my shoulder, holding it like he was trying to prove I really existed.

"Don't fucking touch her!" Tate shouted, charging toward us.

Cash's friend slapped a palm dead center against Tate's chest, stopping him. "Not so fast, kid."

Cash ignored Tate and raised his eyes to look at me. His thumb ran over the piece of my hair, caressing it. I felt time melt away. Something flickered in his eyes but then it was gone in seconds.

He dropped his hand from me and took a step back, one second looking stunned, the next looking distant and cold.

"Call your guard dog off, Cat," Cash said in a low, deadly voice, staring at Tate from under his hat. "Tell him I won't hurt you."

I recovered from the jolt of seeing him and tilted my head to the side, drawing my brows together. "You snapped his gun out of his hand with one move and pulled a gun on me. I think he has the right to be jumpy."

Cash's cool eyes traveled over my body, peeling away my clothes with just one glance.

I forced myself to remain calm. I had learned long ago not to show fear. It only invited trouble and I realized that Cash might be trouble. The EMP and war had changed people, made them harder, more willing to do what they had to do to survive. No one was immune, not even someone like Cash Marshall.

He took a slow step toward me. The sound of acorns breaking was the only noise I could hear over my rapidly beating heart.

"The only one who has the right to be jumpy is me, Cat," Cash said, lowering his voice so only I could hear. "I'm afraid my eyes are betraying me."

I smiled but there was no humor in it. "They're not," I said, taking a step closer to him until our bodies almost touched. "Sorry to disappoint you. I know I'm the last person you ever expected to see again."

"Oh, I'm not disappointed, sweetheart. Far from it. I'm just confused on what you're doing with my sister."

I shrugged, looking past him to the destruction he had left on the field. "Just raising some hell."

I expected to see Cash's lips turn up in that lopsided grin he always gave me. Instead he stayed stone cold serious.

"That's what I was afraid of," he growled low. "You and trouble just go together."

With an icy glare at me, he turned to Keely. "How did you end up with these two, Keely?" he ground out, nodding toward me then Tate. "I mean, I know you always had a soft spot for strays but shit, this one bites and the other is foaming at the mouth to attack me."

The smile slipped from my face, his words hitting too close to home. With wounded pride, I averted my gaze and watched as Keely hurried to remove the notepad from her jacket.

"What is she doing, Cash?" his black-haired friend asked, still keeping one eye on Tate.

Cash didn't answer. He kept his gaze on Keely as she wrote something on her little notepad. She thrust it at him, shaking it to get his attention.

He glanced at me then took the notepad. I let my eyes roam over him as he read. His jeans still fit his body perfectly, outlining every muscle in his legs and ass. His jacket was missing a button or two. His boots were just as worn and dirty as they had been years ago and his cowboy hat looked like it had seen its share of fights. His jaw was leaner, dusted with dark whiskers. His hair was longer, brushing the tops of his ears and jacket collar. His hands were tougher looking, one of them still holding the shotgun with deadly purpose.

I wondered how many times he had killed like he had done today. How many times he had pulled the trigger and ended a person's life without one hint of emotion. It was that new side of Cash that I was terrified of. The one I wasn't sure I should trust.

He handed the notepad back to Keely and turned his cold eyes back on me. "She says you two were neighbors in Austin. That she's been with you from the beginning."

His voice was so flat and emotionless that I wanted to ask him what happened to that cowboy I had once known. The one that smiled at my brashness and laughed at my teasing. Instead, I raised my chin even higher and looked him straight in the eye.

"That's right. We were neighbors," I said.

A tick appeared in Cash's jaw. His eyes skimmed over my lips before meeting my gaze again. "You got anything to add to that?"

I shrugged and crossed my arms over my chest. "Not really."

I refused to show how much he was affecting me. No way in hell would I let him know that my body was humming as if it was just yesterday that he had sat me on a bathroom counter and demanded that I watch in the mirror as he fucked me.

His eyes made a slow pass over my body, looking me up and down again. "Why isn't Keely talking?" he asked, still cold as hell.

I opened my mouth to reply but Keely shook her head, pleading with her eyes for me not to say anything. I wasn't sure staying quiet was the smartest thing to do; I had a feeling Cash would get his answer one way or another. But if Keely didn't want him to know, I wouldn't tell him.

I reached down and grabbed my knife from the ground, wiping the blood off in the grass. Cash stood still, waiting for me to answer. I wasn't going to give him what he wanted. Not this time.

I met his stare stubbornly as I stuffed the blade back in the sheath I kept under my jacket. "We have about five minutes before these guys' friends come looking for us. I suggest we leave," I said, walking past him. If he could be cold, so could I.

I headed for Tate, ignoring Cash's friend ogling me. I was almost to my brother when pain suddenly shot through my middle. I gasped and wrapped my arm around my waist.

"Hey? You okay?" Tate asked, rushing to me. He looked me up and down with worry. "That fucker hit you pretty hard."

I waved him off, grimacing. The punch I had taken earlier from one of the men still hurt terribly but I would survive. I always did.

"I'm fine. How many bullets do you have left?" I asked, sucking in the pain and watching as he picked his gun up from the ground. He checked the chamber and started to answer me but footsteps sounded in the tall grass behind me.

"Which man hit you?" a chilling voice asked.

I turned around. Cash stood over me, looking dangerous and ready to kill.

I shrugged. "Does it matter? They're all dead."

He lifted his head just enough that I could see his cool gray eyes under the brim of his hat. "It matters, Cat."

I kept my jaw clamped and met his arctic glare with one of my own. I didn't want to tell him which one had hit me. I could take care of myself. My bloody knife proved it. But Tate seemed to disagree.

"That one over there. The one in the blue plaid jacket. He hit her," he said, pointing to a body in the grass lying facedown. "Probably left some bruises too."

I spun around to glare at Tate. "Really, Tate? Was that necessary?"

He shrugged, stuffing the gun in his waistband. "I was standing close, Cat. The guy whacked you hard."

Without a word, Cash turned and headed straight for the prone man. I watched, a lump in my throat, as he turned the man over with the toe of his boot. I didn't know if he was dead or not but he was limp, possibly just unconscious. My knife had sliced his arm but one of the bullets might have found him.

Cash kneeled down and checked for a pulse, keeping one hand on his shotgun.

"Is he dead?" Cash's friend asked, standing near Keely.

Cash slowly stood up. Without pausing, he pointed his shotgun at the man and pulled the trigger. The sound ricocheted through the woods. Birds burst from the trees and flew away.

"He is now," Cash said without emotion.

"Holy mackerel," Tate said in an awed whisper, watching Cash cock his gun. "He's a coldblooded S.O.B."

I stood still, unable to move as Cash sauntered toward me. He was lethal. Cutthroat. More merciless than before. He hadn't blinked or paused. He just shot the man like it was nothing.

His eyes held mine, the heat in them leaving me weak and speechless. I felt like I was the only one that existed in this godawful world. Just the two of us. Cash had been the only one that could do that to me and apparently he still did. Not even Luke had that ability. Just Cash. And after all this time – after years apart – I still responded to it.

Only for him.

He stopped a foot away, paying no attention to Tate beside me. "Where's your camp?" he asked, his voice so smooth I wanted to bottle it up for the times he wasn't around so I could remember it.

I pulled my bottom lip between my teeth and let it go, calling myself crazy for still feeling something for him. "Umm...we holed up in a house near here," I whispered, hating that I sounded so weak.

"Let's go." He turned and started to walk away, not giving me a second glance. Tate looked at me, waiting for me to do something. I stayed glued in place. I wasn't sure what to do.

Cash grasped Keely's elbow as he walked past her. I didn't hear what he said to her, but she gave me a questioning look over her shoulder as he led her away.

His dark-haired friend picked a gun off of a dead man and stuffed it in the waistband of his jeans. With a glance at me, he turned and followed Cash and Keely.

"What do we do, sis?" Tate asked, as they walked away.

I sighed, hoping I wouldn't regret my decision. "We go."

Chapter Thirty-Five

-Cat-

Dust settled in and a strong storm descended by the time we left the woods. The wind had picked up and tall clouds moved in, darkening the sky. Trash blew through the streets, just left over remnants of the past.

I gathered my collar closer around my chin as a chill swept down the front of my jacket. I wished it didn't have so many holes in it, but at least I had something to protect me from the cold. I bundled deeper into it as we walked, struggling against the wind. Each step I took made the knife bounce against my leg, reassuring me that I was prepared for anything.

Ominous clouds churned above us. I blinked against fat raindrops as I stared up at them. Tornados were as common in Texas as the blistering heat. If one was about to touch down, we were in a shitload of trouble.

I fought against the raging storm, hurrying to catch up with everyone. Tate was up ahead, leading the way. Cash's friend followed, keeping his head ducked against the gusts of wind. Cash and Keely stayed together a few yards in front of me. He kept a hand on his cowboy hat to keep it from blowing away and a hand on Keely's back, talking to her. I watched as she held the notebook tightly against the wind and wrote him a note then showed it to him.

One time she suddenly stopped and threw herself into his arms. I stayed back a few feet, giving them their privacy. Keely cried against Cash's chest. I heard a few of the words he said to her. 'Dad and mom…at peace.' I knew without being told that they had lost family, just like me.

After a minute, Keely rubbed her eyes on her jacket and they continued walking. I tried not to stare at Cash's back, but it was hard not to. He was more muscular than he had been three years ago. His body was harder and lined with unleashed power. He carried the gun like it was an extension of his arm. A weapon he would use without hesitation. To hurt. To maim. To kill the man that had hurt me.

I shivered and pushed back the strands of my hair whipping into my face. A strong gust hit me, knocking me back a step as if I weighed nothing.

As if he knew I was having trouble, Cash glanced over his shoulder at me. He motioned for Keely to follow Gavin then headed back for me, keeping his head lowered against the storm.

I held my hair back as he stopped by my side.

"I've got you," he said near my ear, sliding his hand around to my waist. "I'm not going to let a storm carry you away from me."

Clouds churned above us, but inside a passion I long thought dead awoke in me.

With a hand on his hat and one around me, Cash led me on, fighting to walk against the wind and giving me the strength to go on.

We arrived at the house by the time the clouds opened up. Thunder boomed and rain fell as we walked around the big two-story house Keely, Tate, and I had been camping out in. Cash let go of me but stayed close by my side as we walked through mud and high weeds to the back door.

We had picked the house because of its location. It was on a cul-de-sac with nothing behind it but a small shed and an open field. Three other homes sat nearby, all empty and silent, each one already raided for supplies.

When we turned the corner of the house, I hurried faster, ready to get out of the rain. I was almost to the back door when Cash grabbed my arm, stopping me.

"You have a death wish? Stay behind me," he demanded with a hard voice.

I huffed and frowned at him. I had taken care of myself for years. I wasn't incapable of doing it anymore just because he was here.

He gave me another warning look then let me go and walked on ahead. I grumbled under my breath and followed him, staring crossly at his broad shoulders. Cash's friend opened the back door as Tate and Cash kept an eye out for trouble. Nothing moved but the weeds whipping to and fro by the wind and the rain that fell and hit the ground.

As soon as the door was opened, we went inside, eager to get out of the raging storm. The house was dark and cold but I felt safer with a roof over my head and walls around me. It was a false sense of security, but I would take anything I could get.

I had only made it a few steps into the house when a strong hand grabbed my arm again.

"Stay put. Let me check it out," Cash said, glancing around the shadowy kitchen we stood in.

I wanted to argue, stomp my feet and tell him I didn't need him protecting me. But if he wanted to play the hero, I guess I would let him. If it kept Keely and Tate safe, he could do whatever he pleased.

Cash let me go and moved past me, leaving his dark-haired friend to keep watch. Rain had soaked Cash's jeans and clothes, sticking them to his body. I kept my eyes glued to his back as he walked out of the kitchen, refusing to allow myself to check out how well his jeans might fit or how the wet material of his shirt clung to his sinewy muscles.

Seconds ticked by as we waited. Finally he came strolling back in, looking relaxed.

"It's safe," he said, glancing past me at his friend.

I didn't need to hear anything else. I shot past Cash, leaving a trail of water on the floor. I was drenched and wanted to change clothes.

I immediately headed upstairs and went straight to the master bedroom. It was the room I had claimed a few days ago. A dark red blanket covered the queen bed and someone else's clothes hung in the closet. They weren't my things but behind the house's solid brick walls, I could pretend the world was still the same. That there was no hunger. No heartache. No dying or killing. And I was just a girl living a normal life.

I shut the bedroom door behind me and started across the room, unbuttoning my jacket at the same time. I shrugged out of it and left it in a wet heap on the floor. I had already gone through the clothes that hung in the closet. I knew that only men's jackets and jeans took up the space, but I had to get dry. My body was shaking and my teeth were chattering.

I pulled off my shirt and started to peel my jeans down my legs when the bedroom door swung open. I squealed and spun around, expecting to find Cash but it was only Keely and she looked mad.

She slammed the door harder than necessary then stomped across the room.

"Keely, you scared the crap out of me," I said on a rush of air, turning back to the closet to grab a hoodie. It was three times my size but it would be warm and dry.

I pulled it over my head at the same time she thrust her little notebook out at me.

"What?" I asked, tugging my wet hair out of the hoodie then grabbing the notebook.

She crossed her arms over her chest and started tapping her toe. I looked down at the note.

You know my brother? Why didn't you tell me?

I felt all the blood leave my face. I wondered how long it would take for her to pick up on that.

I shoved the notebook back at her and moved past her. She followed right on my heels as I grabbed my backpack off the bed and started searching through it for an elastic hairband. Anything to avoid answering her.

She pushed her cracked glasses further up the bridge of her nose and pointed at the note impatiently. They were her fourth pair of eyeglasses. Whenever we broke into a house or convenience store the first thing she looked for were glasses. The second was paper or notepads. She hoarded both like Tate and I hoarded candy.

I stared at her as I gathered my wet hair into a ponytail and put the elastic band around it. *What should I tell her? Oh, yeah, I know your brother. I fucked him a few years ago, but it meant nothing. Or at least it was supposed to mean nothing.*

I had told her about Luke and how I had thought men and parties were the answer for my pain. She had told me about Nathan, writing it all out in her little notebook. She said that they fell for each other fast. That she missed him every day. Her and I had a bond that our new world couldn't break. One cowboy wasn't going to change that but no way in hell would I tell her that I had slept with her brother.

"Okay," I admitted. "I knew him. I didn't tell you because it didn't matter."

She wrote something quickly in the notebook then handed it to me. I almost didn't want to read it but Keely could be stubborn and persistent.

Did you date?

I chewed on my bottom lip, not sure how to answer that. Finally I gave up and handed the book back to her. "Ask him."

She scribbled again and held it up for me to see.

I did. He said to ask you.

My heart skipped a beat.

"One date, Keely, that's all it was. One date," I said. I would never admit how much that date meant to me. There were just some things I wasn't ready to face myself.

Before she could write anything else, I moved past her, heading toward the door. I was afraid to face Cash again…afraid of my own feelings at seeing him…but I was starving and the need for food won out.

I didn't get very far though. Keely tapped me on the shoulder in the hallway. I turned, looking down at the notebook she was holding up for me to see.

You knew all along and didn't tell me! You're supposed to be my friend!!!!!

I looked up at Keely, feeling terrible for what I had done.

"I'm sorry," I said, seeing the hurt on her face. "When I realized you were his sister, I freaked. I just couldn't tell you…"

She shook her head, tears in her eyes.

I wanted to explain but she brushed past me and flew down the stairs.

I closed my eyes, disgusted with myself. So many times I had been tempted to tell her but I had been afraid. She knew my story. She knew how I used to be with men. She never judged me for that, but learning her own brother was one of those men, might make her look at me differently. She might even hate me for that.

But Cash was here now. Alive. Different. Looking sexier than he had years ago. And that was saying something since he was drop dead hot before. The truth about us was going to come out. I would have to face my feelings. I realized, seeing him again, that they had never really faded. I was still that girl that was afraid to love and he was still that boy that made my heart leap. I just had to remember that I walked away from him once to protect myself.

I could do it again.

Stiffening my resolve, I followed Keely down the stairs. I found Tate and Cash's friend in the kitchen, standing around the center island.

"We left our supplies and horses right outside the neighborhood here," Cash's friend told Tate, drawing an x with his finger in the layer of dust on the island.

"I know where that's at," Tate said, studying the crudely drawn map on the counter. "It's a good hour walk away."

Keely went over to the opposite side of the kitchen and crossed her arms over her chest, avoiding me. A pang hit me as I walked to the opposite kitchen counter. I had never had many friends. I didn't want to lose her too.

"I can get to the spot in record time," Cash's friend was saying to Tate. He glanced up at me as he talked, ogling me with curiosity.

I dismissed his interest and grabbed one of the cans of food that sat on the counter. Thunder boomed outside, shaking the house and lightning lit up the kitchen as I opened the can. I could feel Cash's friend continue to stare at me as I dipped my fingers inside the metal can and pulled out a peach. I avoided his eyes even longer as I stuck the peach in my mouth and reached for another.

"I'll go with you," Tate told the black-haired man, bending down to rest his elbows on the island. "You'll need help and I know the way."

Cash's friend tore his gaze away from me to look at my little brother. "No, kid. I don't need help," he said with a smile. "I've got this."

Tate grew red. "I'm not a kid. I'm fifteen. I can shoot as straight as any man and I've killed my share before. Ask my sister."

The peach felt like a lump of dirt in my mouth. I swallowed, forcing it down my throat.

"Tate—" I started to argue. I hated when he talked about killing people.

Cash's friend interrupted. "I'm sorry. We haven't formally met. I'm Gavin." He turned to face me, leaning against the island and holding out his hand for me to shake.

I put my hand in his. "Cat," I said, shaking his hand firmly.

He tilted his head to one side, still holding my hand. "Cash never mentioned you before which surprises me. I would talk about you day and night if I were him. I damn sure wouldn't forget someone that looks like you."

I opened my mouth to respond but Cash walked into the room. His eyes ran over me, just a quick pass up and down my body.

"I never forgot her," he said in a rough voice. "Believe me I tried."

My mouth went bone dry. His cowboy hat was gone and his damp hair was slicked back. He looked gorgeous and rough and like every woman's dream. The sight of him was enough to chase away the chill in the room. The past three years hadn't changed him that much. It was just the hardness that lined his face and lived in his eyes that was new.

Gavin grinned and let my hand go, lifting an eyebrow at Cash. "So what you're saying is—"

"Not if you value your life, Gavin," Cash warned, walking past his friend to my side. His body brushed mine as he grabbed a can of food behind me. His smell wrapped around me like an old friend, someone I had missed.

"Interesting," Gavin said with a chuckle, looking from me to Cash. "Very interesting."

Cash ignored him and pulled a deadly looking knife from his belt. I watched a little wide-eyed as he started prying the can open with the knife.

"You know we have a can opener?" I said, finding my voice. I nodded at the device I had used to open my can of peaches.

"Habit," he said in way of explanation as he sheathed the knife. He opened one drawer then another until he found a fork. I watched, my mouth watering, as he stabbed a pineapple from the can and popped it into his mouth, his attention on the makeshift map on the counter and obviously ignoring me.

"The horses are long gone by now. That storm probably scared the shit out of them," he said around a mouthful of pineapple, pointing to the drawn map on the island.

Gavin shook his head. "You are such a Debbie Downer. They are still there and I'm going after them."

"By yourself?" Cash asked, leaning up against the counter near me.

I reached for another peach, watching out of the

corner of my eye as he speared another pineapple chunk too.

"Yeah," Gavin answered. His bright blue eyes flicked over to me. "Would you tell your girlfriend to use a damn fork?"

I paused with the peach against my lips. Cash looked down at me and froze. Peach juice made my fingers wet and my lips feel silky. I licked the drop of liquid off my bottom lip then popped the peach into my mouth. "Sorry. Habit," I said, repeating Cash's words.

He didn't look amused. He slammed the can of pineapples down on the counter and turned to face me.

"Who taught you to handle a knife like you did today?" he asked, forgetting about the peaches and just going for the jugular.

I shrugged, swallowing the peach whole. "I dunno. I had to learn," I answered, reaching for another peach with my fingers.

He watched me pick it up and slip it between my lips. "Okay, then what did you steal from those men?"

I shrugged again. "Some fresh meat. Some bullets," I said around the peach.

"Sheez," Gavin hissed. "Bullets? A man's lifeblood. No wonder they were gunning for you."

"They weren't *gunning* for us," I retorted. "We were just having a dispute. We had it handled."

Gavin snorted. "Yeah, looked like you did. How's your stomach by the way? Wait, don't tell me. Sore."

I gritted my teeth, fighting the urge not to throttle Cash's friend. "I'm just fine," I responded. "Just hunky-dory."

Gavin smirked. "Glad to hear that. Oh, and you're welcome by the way for saving you."

I felt my ears grow red with anger. "You saved us by killing a bunch of men!"

"We *were* in trouble, sis," Tate interjected quietly.

I glared at him, angry that he was taking their side. Was everyone against me today?

Cash took a step closer to me, gaining my attention. "This is war, Cat. I would kill again to save you," he said in a soft, but tight voice. "I would kill again to save all of you. Remember that the next time you do something reckless."

I stiffened. "Reckless? What did we do that was so reckless?"

"How many bullets did you get?" he asked, taking a step closer. "Everything the men had? That's reckless, Cat. Don't do it again."

I squirmed. He was too close. His body heat was warming me too much. As he pierced me with those gray eyes of his, I felt threatened. Tempted. Sorely in need of something from him. My hands ached to touch him. To glide along his body and touch the parts of him that made me quake. The area between my legs ached, wanting to be satisfied and ravaged. The feeling frightened me. I was supposed to be over him.

I reached for another peach, needing to do something with my hands and keep them off the very male specimen in front of me. This time I decided to be good. I used his abandoned fork and stabbed the peach as I answered him. "We only got a round or two of bullets. They're in Keely's pockets. We had to dump the others when they started chasing us."

Cash glanced over his shoulder at his sister before turning his gaze back on me. Fire and brimstone blazed in his eyes. He towered over me like the big, bad man that I was finding out he had become.

"You're a real piece of work, Cat," he said in a low whisper that only I could hear. "You put my sister at risk and you sit here and eat those damn peaches knowing full well what effect it has on a man. Time hasn't changed you one bit."

I looked down at the fork in my hand. Unexpected hurt shot through me. I suddenly lost my appetite. My throat closed up. I wasn't the same girl anymore. He didn't know anything about me. He didn't know what I had done or went through. He didn't know how it affected or changed me.

He didn't know that I would never put his sister at risk if I could help it, and that I couldn't handle losing someone else I loved. He knew nothing except what I once was. What I had done and said to him years ago.

I carefully put the can on the counter, avoiding his eyes and everyone else's. Without a word, I turned and walked out of the kitchen.

I heard Tate blow up in anger and Gavin saying that Cash was being an ass. I heard the sound of Keely's notebook as she turned a page and scribbled something. But the very last thing I heard was Cash's deep voice.

"Change of plans, Gavin. I need some air. I'm going for the horses."

~~~~

I heard a zipper and heavy breathing. My fingernails dug into the hardwood floor until blood oozed out underneath them. A tight fist twisted my braid and jerked my head up, causing pain to radiate up my neck and into my scalp.

"Ready, little bird."

I shot upright, breathing harshly. My lungs drew in

great gulps of air. Despite the chill, beads of sweat popped out along my hairline.

"It was only a dream. Only a dream," I whispered to myself, pushing strands of hair away from my face with a shaky hand.

"Nightmare?" a deep voice asked.

I jumped and twisted around. Moonlight spilled in through the window but it wasn't enough to light up the room. I could only see the outline of Cash. He was just a shadow lounging in a chair, his feet spread wide, his hands resting on the arms.

"How long have you been there?" I asked, whispering loudly as my chest rose and fell.

"Long enough."

I faced the window again and drew the blanket up around my shoulders. "You always had a way with words, Cash."

"And you always had a way with men, Cat. Gavin won't stop asking questions about you."

I rolled my eyes and drew my knees up to my chest, hugging them. "I think you have it wrong. He was by Keely's side the whole time you were gone."

Cash didn't say anything. I wondered if he had even heard me. When he left to get his horses, I had fallen asleep in the living room. I didn't mean to. Sleep was something I didn't do much of thanks to the nightmares that wouldn't leave me alone.

I rested my chin on my knees and stared out the rain-splattered window. The rain had let up. Now it was just a soft patter on the windowpanes.

I could feel Cash watching me. Studying me.

"Come here, Cat."

My body purred, just hearing him say my name, but I couldn't give into it. "I don't think that's a good idea, cowboy."

"I don't know. Might be the best damn idea I've had all year."

I blushed. *Me.* Three years ago I would have been in his lap in a split second. Now I turned beet red like a schoolgirl and stayed in place.

"Cash, I'm not the same…" I whispered, shaking my head.

"I just want to talk," he said, stopping me.

I turned around slowly, chewing on my bottom lip. It was a terrible habit I had picked up to deal with situations I couldn't control.

And Cash had always been one situation I couldn't get a handle on.

I climbed to my feet and padded across the room, keeping the blanket around my shoulders. The temperature had dropped during the night and we were low on blankets. I still missed the warmth of hot air as it blasted me from a vent, but missing was all I could do. There was still no electricity this far south. We had heard that parts of the north were getting power back but as for us, we were still in the dark.

Cash watched me approach. His eyes never left me, even when I sat down on the couch by his chair. The leather was cold against my thin jeans. I snuggled deeper under the blanket, not quite ready to meet his gaze. We were essentially alone, everyone upstairs sleeping. I wondered if Cash was on watch or just here watching me. Knowing we were alone in the dark made sitting here with him intimate. I felt stripped bare, everything laid out for him to see. And that scared me.

"Tell me where you've been," Cash said in a low voice, just a whisper in the dark.

I lifted my eyes. Gray ones met my gaze.

"We've been in Austin," I said simply.

Cash didn't move. He was like a statue in the chair, his hands gripping the arms with relaxed fingers.

"Austin? We heard it was a hellhole. How did two girls and a kid survive?"

I shrugged, causing one corner of the blanket to fall off my shoulder. Cash watched as I pulled it back up, his eyes lingering on the hollow in my neck.

"I don't know. We just survived," I answered, picking at a loose thread in the blanket. "We tried to make it home a few times over the years but always ran into trouble."

Cash's eyes moved over my face, touching on my lips before returning to my gaze. "What are you doing out here in the suburbs?"

I sighed and dropped the thread, feeling like a witness on the stand. "We got tired of having to fight for every little scrap of food we could find and we got tried of fighting the crazy people in the city. We decided to take our chances elsewhere."

Cash didn't move one muscle. "So why won't Keely talk? Did something happen to her?"

I dropped my eyes and found a new thread to pull at, anything to keep from looking at him.

He leaned forward, bringing him closer to me. Much closer. "Tell me, Cat."

It took me a second to answer. "I can't," I whispered, keeping my eyes downcast.

His hand shot out and grabbed my wrist. I snapped my gaze up to his with anger. "Don't touch me, Cash."

He tightened his fingers on me. "Tell me or I'll touch you a hell of a lot more," he warned.

Fire burned where his fingers touched me. It traveled along my body, igniting the old me I thought was dead.

"Then I'll keep my mouth shut," I said with a smart-ass smile, meeting his cold eyes with my own. "You know, since time hasn't changed me."

Cash grinned but it held no humor. "You always had a smart mouth, princess."

I returned his smile with a sarcastic one of my own. "You know it, cowboy."

His jaw clenched and his eyes flared.

"Fuck," he hissed. "I've missed you."

I didn't even have time to blink before he yanked me off the couch and lifted me into his lap. I landed against him with a huff, my hands automatically going to his chest.

"What the hell do you think you're doing?" I asked in a loud whisper, pushing away from him and trying to crawl off his body.

His hand slapped down on my leg, keeping me in his lap. "Getting my answer."

His hand plunged under my hair and his lips met mine with desperation. They bruised mine. Took mine. Ravished me with hunger.

He said he missed me and god, I missed him too. That one night with him had replayed in my mind again and again. We might have been a mistake but it was a mistake worth repeating.

His fingers tightened in my hair as he kissed me hard. We suddenly couldn't get enough of each other. We became wild, two animals that only wanted one thing. He pushed my hoodie up, leaving my mouth only long enough to pull it over my head. His lips were back on mine in seconds, throwing the hoodie down to the floor.

"I've dreamed of you every night," he whispered around a kiss. "Tell me I'm not dreaming anymore."

I ran my hand down his chest to the top of his jeans. "Well, cowboy, sometimes dreams really do come true."

He groaned when I ripped his zipper down.

Before I could reach inside, he dragged his mouth from mine. His voice was harsh, needy, sexy and demanding.

"Stand up," he growled, running a hand up over my ribcage to cup my naked breast.

I crawled off him quickly and stood up between his bent knees.

He unzipped my jeans and shoved them and my panties down swiftly, no gentleness in his touch. As soon as they were gone, his mouth went to my hip.

I hissed. Hot, wet lips tasted my skin. His fingers slid across my abdomen and down between my legs.

I held my breath, praying he would touch me, but he pulled me back down on top of him instead. His hand went under my hair, holding my nape tightly as he kissed me like a starving man.

"God, I want you," he mumbled, nipping at my bottom lip. "I wanted you the moment I saw you again. It's what you do to me. Drive me fucking crazy."

"I missed you too, Cash." The words were easier to say than I thought they would be. I ran a hand over his hardness, hidden under his boxer shorts. "Now show me how crazy I drive you."

An animalistic growl escaped him as he pushed my hand out of the way impatiently and shoved his boxers down. His cock jutted out, big and powerful. It brushed up against my hand, sending tingles through me.

With a hurried grasp, he clutched my hip and urged me up onto my knees. I held onto his shoulders tightly as he grasped his cock at the base and positioned it at my opening. The fingers of his other hand gripped my hip firmly.

"You really want this, sweetheart?"

"Fuck, yes," I moaned.

With one thrust, he plunged up into me. I cried out and threw my head back, feeling torn in half and filled completely. There was nothing between us but hardness sliding against wetness. He was so big and wide that I trembled and whimpered with the size of him in me. I seized a handful of his shirt and rocked against him as he withdrew then thrust back into me.

"God, sweetheart, you feel amazing," he groaned, tightening his fingers on my hips and moving me up and down. He wasn't gentle or slow. It was hard and quick. Desperate and greedy.

We didn't make love. We fucked with need and a raw craving. It was down and dirty. He moved in and out of me like a piston. His hand tangled in my hair, grabbing a fistful of the strands, and dragging my lips back to his. The gentle cowboy he had once been was no more. The badass he had become controlled everything, including taking what he wanted from me.

His thrusts were fast and rough. His hardness drove me insane. He hit me at my deepest point only to slide back out and do it all over again.

"Did you miss me?" he asked against my mouth, pumping deep into me. "Or did you miss my cock in you?"

I trembled as he pulled out then thrust back, stretching me. "Both."

He growled and moved faster. I was at his mercy, taken and controlled.

His lips left mine to travel to my ear. "You're soaking wet," he whispered, "Is that what I do to you?"

"Always," I said, breathing hard.

"Hmm. I like that word on your lips."

His cock filled me full until I cried out. He held my face tightly between his two large hands and kissed me deeply as he dove in and out of my pussy. I wiggled and squirmed, crying against his mouth as the orgasm shattered me. Oh, god. I was dying.

His body coiled tight and a hiss escaped him as he plunged up into me one more time. I felt him come a second before he withdrew and shot his seed on my stomach. His semen hit my belly button, shooting warmth on me.

His breath was ragged as he caught my mouth in a kiss again. His cock hit my stomach, pulsating against me and smearing his come on me until the last drop left him.

"Sorry," he whispered against my lips. "No condoms." His fingers left deep indents in my skin as he held me still.

I kissed the corner of his mouth. "It's okay. But you should know - you were the last one," I said, the words slipping past my lips before I could stop them.

Cash went still at my words. "Three years—"

"And no one," I whispered, pulling back to look at him.

He glanced away and ran a hand over his scruffy chin. "Hell, Cat. You don't know what that means to me."

I looked at him between the strands of hair falling in my face. "Then tell me."

He shook his head, refusing to, so I filled in the blanks.

"You did something to me, Cash, and I haven't recovered. I didn't want anyone else after that night with you." *Oh, damn. Did I just admit that?*

His eyes snapped back to mine. His hand shot to the back of my head and pulled me down close.

"You did something to me too, Catarina. You *ruined* me. I've never been the same."

He kissed me again, gentle this time. His lips worshiped and I offered everything to them. He didn't stop until he noticed I was cold.

"Shit," he muttered. "You're freezing."

He tucked himself back in his boxers quickly and zipped up his jeans. Putting a hand on my bare thigh to keep me in his lap, he glanced around the dark living room. On the cluttered coffee table beside the chair, there was a crushed box of tissues, something Tate had proudly found in one of the bathrooms.

Cash grabbed it and pulled out a few tissues. He wiped my stomach clean then dropped the tissues on the floor and grabbed my hoodie. His hands drifted over my breasts and ribcage as he pulled it over my head.

"God, you're so beautiful. I almost forgot how much," he said quietly in the night.

I blushed. Three years was a long time since he told me I was beautiful. I wanted to hear it again and again. The clothes I once wore, the makeup and outrageous amount of money I had once spent on my hair never really mattered. Cash thought I was beautiful just the way I was. My heart had cracked a little open the first night we were together; now it burst wide.

He helped me pull my jeans back on then tugged me back to his lap. I rested my head against the crook of his shoulder as he gathered the blanket around us, cocooning us together. His lips went to my head, the strands of my

343

hair tangling in the whiskers of his five-o'clock shadow on his jaw.

We sat that way for a while, just the two of us in a strange house during a strange time. Last time we were together I was afraid, so afraid of feeling something for him. But seeing him again just proved that despite time and distance, the feeling wouldn't go away no matter how much I fought it.

I flattened my hand right above his heart. I could feel it beating. Thump. Thump. Thump. Strong. Powerful. Alive. For the first time in a long time, I felt safe. Watched over. My eyes started to drift closed, my body tired from being ravaged, when Cash ran a hand over my hair, smoothing it down.

"You cut it."

Bad memories washed over me, chasing the sleep away like they always did.

"I had to," I whispered, keeping my head on his chest. "For Keely."

"Tell me what happened," his voice rumbled under my ear, back to sounding cold and dangerous.

"There were two of them. I ran into them in the city. They cornered me in an alley but Nathan saved me."

Cash's body went stiff and his hand tightened on my waist but he didn't say anything. Through my lashes, I could see his whiskered jaw clenched in fury.

I let my eyes drop back down and continued, knowing I needed to tell him. "They found us again later. We were raiding a store when they dragged Keely and me away. They barricaded us in a house and…" I raised my head, looking into his eyes. Fear rushed through me when anger and hatred stared back at me.

"What did they do, Cat?" Cash asked in a harsh voice.

I started shaking my head, tears in my eyes. "I fought but one of them – Paul - knocked me out. The next thing I know, I woke up and Keely is screaming and…and Paul is pulling my clothes off and—"

Cash ran a hand through his hair in rage. "I'll kill him."

"He didn't get very far. Nathan and Tate stopped him. But then he shot Nathan…" my voice drifted off, reliving the nightmare. "And it was too late for Keely."

Cash refused to look at me. He let go of my waist to rub both hands over his face. "Shit, Cat. Shit. I'm sorry. I'm so damn sorry. I should have been there protecting you and Keely."

I sat up on his lap. The tears running down my face were nothing compared to the hurt and guilt I felt.

"I'm the one who's sorry, Cash. I tried to stop them. I tried to protect Keely, but…" I swiped the tears on my cheeks away with the back of my hand. "Paul was stronger. I just couldn't get to her in time."

"It's not your fault, Cat."

I shook my head. "Yes, it was. She refused to speak after that. I think the trauma was more than she could handle."

His gray eyes, so cold and clear, looked at me. "And now you have nightmares about it?"

I nodded. "I relive it all the time. Most nights I can't sleep. I see him and feel his hands. I hear Keely screaming and I can't get to her."

He ran a hand down my side but his jaw was set firmly.

"You're both safe now. That's all that matters. No one will ever hurt you or Keely again. I promise."

"You can't promise that, Cash," I whispered. "Things happen."

He smirked but it was a dangerous smile. "Oh I can promise it, sweetheart. No one will touch you. No one will threaten you. I'll make sure of it."

I rested my head against his shoulder again but I could feel the rigid muscles under it. I could sense his anger and the fury he contained.

"You've changed," I mumbled against his shirt, feeling sleep hover around my consciousness. "You're colder. More dangerous."

His voice was deadly. "You have no idea, sweetheart."

Chapter Thirty-Six

-Cash-

I didn't sleep much. I held Cat and thought over everything. Keely. The men that had hurt her and Cat. Cat's brother, Nathan, dying to protect them. And Cat.

Always Cat.

I thought about her in my lap, riding me. I thought about her in the woods, ready to protect my sister and her little brother. I thought of that last phone call with her right before the EMP, the words *mistake* and *broken* still burned in my mind still. I thought of it all and knew this time I wouldn't walk away from her again.

Morning came too early. I eased out from under Cat and stood up. She whimpered in her sleep and curled deeper under the blanket. I brushed a lock of her hair out of her face then left the living room quietly.

By the time I made it to the kitchen, my knuckles were white, curled into fists. I was beyond angry. I wanted to kill. Destroy. Goddamn hurt someone for what happened to Cat and Keely. But one thing at a time. First I had to face the light of day.

And Gavin.

He smirked at me as I walked into the room.

"Rough night, Romeo?" he asked.

"Fuck off," I grumbled, grabbing a bottle of water from the kitchen counter. I glared at him and unscrewed the plastic top then chugged the lukewarm liquid down.

Gavin blinked, his smile disappearing. "What the hell happened? You never tell me to fuck off. That's Ryder's job."

I emptied the water bottle and slammed it on the counter. "Yeah, well I'm taking over for Ryder. Fuck off, Gavin."

Gavin opened his mouth to argue but Keely walked in. Another wave of anger hit me, knowing what she had endured.

"Give us a moment, Gavin," I ordered, barely holding it together. I couldn't think of what that monster did to my baby sister. I might go insane with rage.

"What's going on—" Gavin began, never able to do what was asked. Damn him.

I cut him off, snapping my gaze over to him. "Get out!" I snarled, pointing to the door. "Now!"

Gavin took his time standing up, looking ready to ring my neck. No one raised their voice to Gavin. Well, no one but Ryder. But I just did and I would do it again if I had to.

He walked slowly past Keely, still staring at me. His arm brushed hers, his body close to her small one. I knew it was intentional and I was about to kill him for it.

When he was even with me, he stopped. His voice dropped down to a whisper.

"You find out why she's not talking?" he asked. I could feel the tension rolling off him like heat waves. He had become very protective of my sister in a short period of time. I wasn't stupid. I saw it. Damn, I recognized the feeling. I had felt the same way toward Cat as soon as I met her.

"Yeah," I answered in a low voice, for his ears only. "I found out what happened."

Gavin rolled his shoulders. I recognized the action. He was ready to fight.

"Who do I have to kill?" he seethed.

I gritted my teeth. "Two motherfuckers. But keeping the girls safe is our number one priority now. Nothing else matters."

Gavin looked over his shoulder at Keely. "Yeah. I agree." His body relaxed. He gave her a short nod and then turned and strolled from the room.

I took a deep breath as he left, needing strength. Keely looked at me questionably as I walked around the kitchen island toward her. She started chewing on her bottom lip then rushed to pull out her pad of paper. It hurt to see her do that, to know why she wouldn't talk.

When I got close enough, I pulled the paper gently from her grasp.

"Cat told me what happened."

Tears welled in her eyes. She reached out and grabbed the pad back from me then pulled her pencil from her pocket. I watched her write something, one lone tear slipping down her cheek.

I trusted her. She wasn't supposed to tell you.

I read the note and nodded. "I know, but I got it out of her. I have my ways."

She frowned and started writing again in her little notebook. A second later, she held it up for me to read.

Don't look at me like that. I'm not broken. I'm just kind of bruised.

She always had a sense of humor and I was happy to see she still did. At least that fuckhead hadn't taken that away from her.

"I know you're not broken, Keely. I'm just pissed that it happened. I should have been there." Frustrated, I rubbed a hand over my face and muttered, "I should have been there for you both."

She shook her head frantically and started writing again.

No, you could have been killed like Nathan.

I inhaled deeply, hating the pain behind her written words.

"I'm sorry, Keely," I whispered. "I'm so damn sorry."

She wrote something, a tear falling on her hand.

I was in love with him.

That hurt to read like nothing else. I pulled her toward me, smashing the notebook between us when I wrapped my arms around her.

"No one will ever hurt you or Cat again. I swear," I said against the top of her head as her tears soaked through my shirt.

After a second, she pulled away and started writing on her pad. I waited patiently until she held it up for me to read.

Cat? What is she to you? I want to know.

I blew out a breath and ran a hand through my hair, peering at Keely sheepishly. "Truth?"

Keely rolled her eyes then nodded.

I took a deep breath. "I don't know but I'm afraid she just might be everything."

~~~~

The tall grass brushed against my jeans later on as I walked toward the shed. I had left Gavin's horse and mine tied up there before going inside last night. It was a miracle I had found them in the first place. The storm yesterday had been a big one.

I glanced up at the sky. Dark clouds still lingered. They matched my mood. Ominous, threatening, and churning with anger. I was still fucking mad even after Keely and Cat telling me they were okay.

Promise Me Once

My hands clenched and unclenched when I thought of the two assholes that had touched them. I wanted to kill. I wanted to maim. I wanted to punch a hole in the brick of the house until I bled and the pain disappeared. But I kept it all inside. I would need it later for when I met up with the two fuckers. I knew I would. It was only a matter of time.

As I walked up, my eyes flicked over the tall kid standing next to one of the horses, rubbing its ear. Cat's little brother. The one I had made the promise to on our first date that I wouldn't hurt her.

"She bites," I said in way of a greeting, nodding at the horse.

Tate looked up at me, surprised. I walked to the other horse and bent down to check her hoof. She had been limping last night.

"You dated my sister at one time. I remember you now," he said, standing with one hip cocked.

I looked up at him, noticing the gun in his waistband. "Guilty. You took care of her too. Thanks for that."

He huffed but didn't say anything.

"You good with that thing?" I asked, nodding at the gun.

He stuck his chin up with pride, so much like his sister that I wanted to grin.

"Yeah. I survived this long, didn't I?" he scowled, looking peeved that I had to ask.

"Guess so." I let the horse's hoof go and stood up, dusting the dirt off my hands. "Sorry to hear about your brother."

His Adam's apple bobbed up and down. "Cat tell you that I couldn't pull the trigger on the man that did it?" he asked, trying and failing to hide his shame.

351

I studied the toe of my boot, the brim of my hat hiding my face from him. "She didn't." I looked up at him, squinting against the sun as a cloud passed by it. "But to kill a man eats away at your soul. I should know. Best that you didn't do it."

Tate scoffed and kicked at a dead weed. "I was a little chicken shit back then, but I've changed. If I see him again, he'll bite my bullet."

I grabbed the crown of my hat and readjusted it on my head, needing to do something with my hands before I punched something. "Get in line, Tate. If I see him, my dark side is going to come out to play."

Tate crossed his arms over his chest and looked me up and down, eyeing the knife I kept on my hip. "You like my sister don't you?"

I grinned. "Yeah, guess I do."

Tate stuck his chin up. "If you like her so much, why didn't you look for her all these years? She sure could have used you along the way."

The grin slipped from my face. I felt guilt hit me from all sides. "I did," I admitted. "But you gotta understand that she didn't want anything to do with me...but I still looked for her."

He nodded but stared at me hard. "I get it. But just know - if you hurt her, I won't hesitate to kill you."

"Well, I'd deserve it. But you're gonna need that anger for what we're about to do."

He looked at me suspiciously. "And what's that?"

Calmly, I walked up to him until I was a step away. "We're going home, Tate, but it's going to be hell getting there."

~~~~

"This is a bad idea. A fucking bad idea," Gavin grumbled, tightening the strap on his saddle.

I slipped my shotgun into its scabbard. "I found Keely. That's what I came for. But we'd be crazy not to check out that town. It's on the way home. We can trade for supplies and get some news."

"Get killed is more like it," Gavin muttered, glaring at me as he stuffed a stuffed frog in his saddlebag. Something he had found for Ryder and Maddie's daughter, Emma.

I ignored him and glanced over at Cat. She stood next to Keely, watching me and chewing on her bottom lip. She never did that before but I guessed her nerves were rattled. Can't say that I blamed her. Last night had shaken me to the core.

"If I get killed saving your ass, tell Maddie I love her," Gavin said, interrupting my thoughts. He tied the leather string on his saddlebag then paused, cocking his head to the side and thinking. "Better yet, tell Maddie I love her like a sister. I don't want Ryder messing up that pretty boy face of yours."

I grinned. "Tell him yourself. I'm not suicidal."

Gavin grinned too. We were in our element, about to face unknown danger. It got our blood pumping and our spirits up. Made us feel alive in this hellhole of a world we lived in.

"Okay, ladies. Who's riding with me?" Gavin asked, clapping his hands together and turning to look at Cat and Keely.

Keely wrote something in her little book.

"'I'm riding with my brother,'" Gavin read, squinting to read the note she held up. He looked over at me and smiled. "That note just made my day. I get the little cat."

I bristled as he motioned to Cat. "Come on, Kitty Cat. You're up."

I kept my mouth shut as Cat walked over to him. I didn't know what would be worse – watching Cat ride with him or my sister. But when Gavin put his hands around Cat's waist to help her into the saddle, I knew that she might ride with him but I was the only one that was going to touch her.

I shoved my horse's reins at Tate and stalked toward them. They both looked at me, Cat with astonishment in her green eyes and Gavin with laughter in his.

"I've got this," I muttered, giving Gavin a malicious look.

"I bet you do," he quipped, holding up his hands and taking a step back from Cat.

I wanted to tell him what he could go do to himself, but I resisted. Cat was looking at me with a come-get-me look. I wanted to grab her and lock us in that big master bedroom upstairs. Show her what this cowboy was capable of doing with a little time and a heck of a lot of energy on his hands.

She turned to me as I put my feet on either side of her, ready to help her up.

"Be careful," she whispered in my ear as I leaned toward her. "I'm a little sore."

I blushed like a schoolboy. Lust shot through me. Not caring if we had an audience, I buried my hand in her hair and put my mouth against her ear.

"I want you sore every single day, sweetheart. Sore and wanting more."

This time it was her turn to blush. I quirked my mouth up in a half grin and lifted her into the saddle. She grabbed the saddle horn and looked down at me with need. I gave her leg a squeeze, letting her know I felt the same – *God, did I feel the same.* But I had a more urgent need at the moment I had to take care of.

I had to get her home.

~~~~

By dusk we were tired, hungry, and cold. The wind had picked up and the temperature had dropped. It was slow going, with one of us walking and the rest of us riding, but we made it to the outskirts of the town, Hilltop, by nightfall.

"Such a goddamn stupid idea," Gavin muttered as we kneeled behind a clump of thorny bushes, checking out the town.

Hilltop wasn't a big city. From what we could see, it looked like every small town in Texas. A few turn-of-the-century buildings took center stage. The road leading into the little community was littered with abandoned cars and trash. Black plastic bags of garbage sat among old tarps and turned over shopping carts. Dusty vehicles made a maze out of the street. A few had smashed in fronts and crushed sides. Others had their hoods up, some with wires dangling out. My gaze shot to one car as a black crow burst out of its engine, squalling as it flew away.

"Like I said, bad idea," Gavin said, keeping his crossbow ready. We had left Tate and the girls hidden a few yards back behind a clump of trees. Gavin and I had crept closer to check out the town. Hilltop had a reputation. It was a militia stronghold and was rumored to have medical supplies, running water, electricity, and a shitload of supplies.

We had first heard about it a while back. When the EMP hit, lawlessness reigned. In answer to the lack of police or military force, militias formed everywhere. Most defended our country from terrorists and tried to keep people civil. Others decided to make themselves rulers and carve out their own little strongholds.

I wasn't sure where Hilltop fell, but I was curious about it. I had a feeling it was a goldmine and I couldn't live with myself if I past it without trying to get something useful.

"They built a damn wall, Cash. That means *'stay the fuck away,'*" Gavin whispered beside me, nodding at the metal shipping containers that had been shoved together, blocking the road and any outsiders from entering the town limits.

"But there's a door. That says *'knock and come in,'*" I said, nodding at the patched metal door in the center.

Gavin snorted. "Your sense of humor is screwed up."

"Comes from spending too much time with you," I muttered, moving away from the bushes.

Gavin gave the wall one more look then followed me. We headed toward the clump of oak trees we had left the girls behind with Tate and the horses. Gavin gave a short whistle as we approached but our boots slashing through the tall, thick grass was announcement enough.

"What did you find?" Cat asked as soon as we appeared.

"A wall," Gavin answered curtly, bypassing Keely to go to his horse.

I went straight to Cat. "You still have that knife?" I asked, studying her bright green eyes in the growing darkness.

She nodded, her pink nose and chattering teeth letting me know that even with my coat on, she was freezing.

"Stay close to me but don't be afraid to use it if you have to," I told her, feeling uneasy that I was about to put her in danger.

"Where will you be?" she asked, her eyes full of fear.

I gave her a reassuring smile. "Right beside you, sweetheart, don't worry."

The tension left her body. I was happy she trusted me. I damn well liked to know it.

I turned to Tate. His long, shaggy hair was hanging in his eyes as he looked at me.

"You stay on your sister's tail. I'm not sure what we're going find in there, but I want her covered by both of us," I instructed, knowing the kid would watch over Cat like a hawk.

"Yes, sir." Tate nodded and rested his hand on the gun butt sticking out of the front waistband of his jeans.

I turned my attention to my sister. She was wearing Gavin's jacket and looked as cold as Cat. Her pale skin was even whiter and her light-colored blonde hair was sticking out from under her hat in soft waves.

"Gavin, stick to her like glue," I said, nodding at Keely. "She moves, you move."

"Understood, but you didn't have to say it. I've got her," he said, for once stone-cold serious.

I nodded then turned to my horse.

Time to see what was behind those walls.

Chapter Thirty-Seven

-Cat-

When I was younger, my mother once told me that she hated small towns. She didn't understand their simple ways or the incessant need of the inhabitants to know everyone's business. The bane of her existence was having to visit my dad's ranch the few times he insisted she did during their short marriage. I didn't like to think that I took after my mother but she had instilled in me an inherent dislike of nosy people and cute little hometowns. As we walked toward Hilltop, I felt it now like never before.

The large metal wall surrounding the town stood feet above my head. I stared up at it with a combination of awe and fear as Gavin knocked on the makeshift door. No one answered so he tried the handle. It gave with no problem and squeaked loudly when he pushed it open.

On the outside of the wall, trash and debris littered the ground. On the inside, it was spotless. The streets were clear, not one blade of grass out of place or one piece of paper floating around. The buildings were in one piece, not destroyed or burned to the ground. No one greeted us but once inside a very tall, older gentleman and two younger ones headed our way.

The older one smiled and gave a short wave as he walked toward us. He was gangly with long arms and an equally long torso. His face was scraggy and his neck skinny. He reminded me of a giant, but hopefully he was a gentle one.

The younger men walking beside him held rifles and didn't look too excited to see us. They were shorter and had the element of distrust about them. The first thought that popped into my head when I saw them was that they were modern day gunslingers. Not the kind that saved the day. No, these were the bad kind. The ones that tried to kill the good guys.

Cash eased me behind him with a hand to my waist, leading his horse at the same time. I wasn't going to argue. He could protect me. I didn't feel safe in this perfect, little town or under the scrutiny of the men heading our way.

I glanced over my shoulder, making sure Tate and Keely were staying close. They were, Gavin staying by Keely and Tate watching the men carefully.

"Hello folks!" the older man called out to us, holding up his hand in greeting. He started down the sidewalk at a brisk pace, his long, bony legs moving stiffly.

Cash positioned himself in front of me, almost blocking my view of the man. I glanced around and saw a few people peeking out of store windows and hiding behind cracked doors, but other than the three men on the street, the place felt empty. An eerie ghost town.

The older man was breathing hard by the time he reached us. His white hair was flapping in the wind and his cheeks were red from the cold despite the turned-up collar of his black jacket.

He went straight to Cash and held out a knotty, bony hand. "My name's David. I'm the reverend here. Welcome to Hilltop."

Cash took his hand and shook it, tipping his hat in greeting. "Hello."

The older man's faded blue eyes skimmed over Cash then glanced at the rest of us.

"Y'all look like you've traveled a mighty fine way. May I ask your names?" he asked with a wide, friendly smile, his eyes dancing with excitement.

Cash didn't answer but Gavin stepped forward. "My name's Gavin and this is Cash, Keely, Tate, and Cat."

David's smile grew wider as he looked at each of us. "Welcome! Welcome! Welcome!" he said, rolling forward on his toes then back on his heels. "Hallelujah! We love visitors here!"

The other two men standing guard on either side of him cradled their guns and remained silent. Neither of them smiled or showed the slightest bit of welcome. I didn't think they were as happy as David to have guests, but at least they weren't shooting us.

Yet.

David seemed to suddenly realize they were there, which seemed ludicrous considering the firepower they held.

"Oh, forgive my manners! This is Timothy and Zack. Boys, put those guns away," he said, waving at the rifles. "These kids aren't trouble."

Timothy and Zack didn't move but David didn't say anything else. He turned back to us with a huge grin and happiness dancing in his eyes. I jumped when he suddenly clapped his hands together.

"Dear Lord! You must be hungry and cold! Come! Come! We have a hotel," he said, turning and motioning for us to follow him.

A thrill of excitement went though me. *They have a hotel?* Thoughts of fluffy white towels and soft, clean sheets filled my mind. I knew it was silly to hope for them but a girl could dream, couldn't she?

Cash didn't move, despite the invitation. "We don't

have any money to pay for rooms," he said, deflating my dream.

"No need to pay, son," David said, holding his hands at his sides, palms out. "You look like you need a rest. Consider it help."

Cash stared hard at him, assessing David's trustworthiness. "Nothing's free," he said in a calculated voice.

David smiled gently. "True. But it's just help, son. That's all."

Cash studied David one more second then gave a short nod. I could almost hear the collective sigh coming from all of us.

David smiled at Cash once more then turned. "Follow me, friends!"

Gavin led his horse past us, following David as he started across the street. Keely and Tate followed, both glancing around with uneasiness. We had learned not to trust anyone and even though David looked like someone's grandfather, the two men beside him looked like killers.

Cash had a calm expression on his face but his shoulders were set in a rigid line. He was on guard and ready to jump into action at the drop of a hat or pull of a trigger.

He angled his head, hiding his face from the strangers under his hat. "Stay close to me," he whispered to me, his breath washing over me. "Something doesn't feel right."

I nodded. I wanted a hotel room worse than anyone, but I wasn't desperate enough to ignore the bad feeling that wouldn't leave me.

The horse's hooves clomped on the concrete as we headed across the street to follow everyone. David turned to look at us, smiling widely. His eyes glanced over us and the horses, touching briefly on the gun scabbards on the saddles.

"Forgive me!" he exclaimed, suddenly spinning around. "Zack - takes those horses to the stable." He pointed at the horses, authority in his voice but a smile on his face.

The man named Zack headed for us, his face solemn, the rifle in his hand looking big and deadly. Cash gripped the reins a little tighter when Zack held out his hand for them.

David smiled warmly. "Not to worry, my friend. They will be fine. More than fine. Zack will take good care of them. He'll make sure they are well fed and when you're ready to leave, they will be refreshed and waiting for you. Right, Zack?"

The man is too happy, I thought, frowning at him. *Who the fuck has that much to smile about? Has he looked around him lately?*

Zack didn't comment or smile at David's words. He just held his hand out for the reins, a look of arrogance on his face as he stared at Cash.

Cash wasn't going to make it easy. He dropped the reins on the ground, leaving them there for Zack to pick up. I knew that no way in hell would Cash hand them to the man.

He continued to stare at Zack as he unstrapped the two bags on the saddle horn and handed them to me. Next he unleashed the saddle and let it slid off the horse.

Zack glared stonily at Cash and picked up the reins. With a warning look that spoke of retribution, he led Cash's horse over to get Gavin's.

I could tell Cash wasn't too happy. That tic appeared in his jaw again, right below his unshaven cheek. He worked his jaw a couple of times then picked up the saddle without a word and started walking again.

With the horses going in the opposite direction and us going in the other, David led us to a large brick building. A rusted water tower sat on top with the words *Hilltop Hotel* proudly displayed in faded green letters.

The other henchman, Timothy, followed a few steps behind us. I felt like we were being walked to the gallows. It wasn't too hard to imagine. We had a reverend leading the way and a guard watching us. I just wondered how long before they put a rope around our necks and pulled the lever.

I frowned as David skipped excitedly up onto the curb, a hop to his step and a wide grin on his face.

"They must not get visitors here often," I muttered out of the side of my mouth to Cash. "Who gets that excited anymore?"

Cash's voice was low and husky, for my ears only. "I might have when I saw you, Cat."

I lifted my eyes up to his, surprised. He always could shock the hell out of me.

"And did you want to skip when you saw me?" I asked, feeling warm suddenly.

His eyes smoldered as he looked down at me. "Not skip, but I damn sure wanted to kiss you."

"Why didn't you?"

Cash shifted the saddle in his arms and glanced at the door we were about to walk into.

"Because I'm scared to death of you, Cat."

"Why?" I asked, tilting my head to the side. "Am I that much of a badass?"

He didn't laugh. With a burning look in his eyes, he put a hand to the small of my back and leaned down, putting his mouth close to my ear.

"You have the ability to knock me to my knees, Cat. You always have and you always will. That's why you scare me, sweetheart."

I gazed up at him, stunned, but he straightened as if he had never said anything. With slight pressure on my back, he urged me to follow the others as they walked into the hotel.

My hands shook and my body pulsated with awareness. I could feel Cash behind me, sense his heat as he stayed close to me. I wanted him again. In a bathroom. On a chair. I just wanted him and that big cock of his in me.

I tried to concentrate on our surroundings as we walked into the hotel. It was hard with Cash so close beside me, his hand still on my back, but somehow I managed. The hotel was dark, shadows dancing everywhere inside. We crowded into the entranceway, unsure what we were about to face.

"Now, where is Ms. Mary?" David muttered to himself. He reached toward the wall and flipped a switch. The small chandelier hanging above us flared to life.

I gasped, so unused to electricity that I couldn't stop myself. David laughed, a deep, booming sound, when he saw our astonished looks.

"We rigged up a system years ago," he explained. "We have electricity, heaters, fans—"

"And friendliness," a round, pudgy woman said as she turned the corner into the entranceway. "What have we here, Reverend David?"

"Ms. Mary these are our new friends. Gavin, Cash, Cat, Keely, and Tate," David said, pointing to each of us. "They will need rooms tonight."

I was surprised his memory was so impeccable and he

remembered our names. I didn't know if that was a good thing or bad one.

Mary beamed at us. She wore a flowery shirt and polyester pants. Her body was thick around the middle, making me think they had plenty of food in Hilltop, unlike where I had been.

I felt uncomfortable as she looked us up and down. The difference between her immaculate appearance and our disheveled one was apparent. She clucked her tongue a few times in disapproval at Tate's scruffy appearance and fluttered nervously around Keely, making comments about her tangled hair and the smudge of dirt on her face. When it came to me, Mary stopped right in front of me, assessing me slowly.

"You're one beautiful girl. What's your name?" she asked, eyeing me up and down with a twinkle in her eye.

"Cat," I said. I didn't like women judging me. Their reaction to me wasn't always nice. In the past, I would pretend it didn't bother me, but the truth was it always did. I never measured up according to my mom and grandmother. I didn't expect I would to this woman either.

She reached out and touched my hair. "You have such pretty hair. Anyone ever tell you that?"

"A time or two," I said, sticking my chin up with boldness.

She chuckled. "I bet the men love you. You got spunk."

Cash went stiff beside me.

Mary seemed to notice. She turned her smiling eyes on him, dropping her hand from me. "So that's the way it is. You two married?" she asked, looking from one of us to the other.

"No, ma'am," Cash said, not at all embarrassed by her question. "But I might have a problem if another man loved her."

My jaw dropped open. Mary laughed loud and shrill. "I like you," she said to Cash around a snorting laugh. "I like you a lot."

Tate looked ready to kill Cash for saying what he did and Keely looked at her brother with surprise. Gavin just smiled that shit-eating grin that I had discovered was his signature smile.

Mary gave my arm a pat. "Well, I'm glad you're here, deary. I've got enough room for all of you, despite who loves whom. Come with me."

She started to turn, explaining how the hotel was laid out, when David interrupted.

"I'm going to head home," he announced, smiling broadly. "Miss Mary will take good care of y'all. God bless you and I'll see you tomorrow."

With a nod and a quick smile, he moved past us and out the door, motioning for his gun-toting friend, Timothy, to follow.

Mary watched him go, a small frown causing deep creases to appear between her eyebrows. When she looked back at us, the frown was gone.

"Okay kids, follow me." She turned and started shuffling toward a dark stairway, her pink slippers flapping on the scarred hardwood floor.

We followed her upstairs to a long hallway. Cheap artwork covered the walls. Between them were closed doors, each numbered in brass figures.

"Okay. Here's one room," Mary said, heading for the first door. Cold air rushed over us as she opened it. Tate didn't seem to care. He went inside, trying the light switch

366

and almost smiling when a single light bulb came on in the center of the room.

"I'll take this one," he declared, dropping his backpack on the floor.

"Lovely. Next!" Mary led us to a room decorated in browns and blues. Gavin claimed it for himself, dumping his saddle inside the door.

"I want her across the hall from me," he said, nodding at Keely. His bright blue eyes blazed as they stared at her.

Keely blinked at him, her owl-like glasses accenting the delicate lashes around her eyes. Her mouth formed a small O and her fair skin grew pink.

"You got a problem with that?" Gavin asked, turning his attention to Cash.

Cash shook his head, his light-colored eyes shadowed by the brim of his hat. "Nope. Do I need to have one?"

Gavin glanced at Keely. "I'll let you know."

Cash's eyes went from friendly to dangerous. The tension was almost palpable between the two of them, full of warning and threats.

Keely pulled out her notebook and scribbled something in it, looking furious.

"'Do I have a say?'" I read when she held it up. "'I may not have a voice but I have an opinion.'"

Mary chuckled. "The blonde has some spunk too. Better watch it, big boy," she said, winking at Gavin. "I bet she would eat you alive."

"That's what I'm afraid of," Gavin murmured, leaning against the doorframe.

I grabbed Cash's hand and pulled him away before he attacked his friend. The two of us followed Mary further down the hallway, leaving Keely and Gavin to duke it out and Tate to wallow in his new bedroom.

Mary led us to a room decorated in warm mauve colors. It was warm and inviting and felt like home instantly. I went straight to the bed, almost running across the room. My fingers ran over the satin cover, loving the way it felt against my skin. I wanted to crawl underneath it and sleep for twenty-four hours straight. Maybe never leave this room with its heat and lights.

Mary talked about the history of the hotel as she puttered around the room. Cash didn't seem to care. He kept his gaze on me as he stood in the middle of the threshold, the saddle resting on his hip. With the light of the hallway behind him, he was only a silhouette. His tall frame was relaxed but I knew it was a lie. The gun in his holster and the rigid set of his shoulders told otherwise.

I wasn't sure how much longer I could survive under his scrutiny. We stared at each other, the air almost bursting with our desire. Mary was forgotten, what she said was ignored. I wanted only one thing and he was standing near me.

Cash never removed his gaze from me as he sauntered into the room. God, the way he moved had the ability to make me drool. He dropped the saddle on the floor and stared at me with a challenge in his eyes. My heart started pounding, his message received loud and clear.

He was staying with me tonight.

Mary interrupted, shuffling over to me and blocking my view of Cash. She fussed over me like a mother hen, looking me up and down then clicking her tongue in disapproval.

"No. No. No. This will never do," she said, pinching Cash's dusty jacket that I wore between her fingers. "SARAH!"

I jumped as she shouted, wondering who exactly Sarah was and if I should be worried. But a minute later a red-faced girl rushed past Cash and into the room. She was homey and young with mousy brown hair and washed out pasty skin. A thick book was under her arm and reading glasses were perched on the end of her long nose.

"Yes, ma'am?" she asked.

Mary looked at her with a stern expression. "Our new visitor needs some clean clothes. Check our supplies and find something for her."

Sarah looked me over quickly. "Yes, ma'am." She bobbed her head once then turned to rush out of the room, but not before I saw her stare at Cash with curiosity.

He paid no attention to her, keeping his eyes on me. Mary went on chatting, not noticing the sexual vibes being exchanged between Cash and me.

"I'll just fire up the stove and reheat dinner. In the meantime, the bath is down the hall," she said, rushing around the room to fluff pillows and smooth out wrinkles on the bedspread.

All the air was sucked out of my lungs, the tingles I got as Cash stared at me forgotten. Mary had just said the magical word.

"Bath?" I asked with a squeak.

Mary smiled a gentle, understanding smile. "Yes, with hot water and soap and everything else, my dear. Enjoy." With a motherly pat on my arm and a wink at Cash, she left, shutting the door behind her.

I looked at Cash with excitement. "A bath," I said in wonder as he walked past me. "Can you believe it? I haven't had a *real* bath in ages."

He went over to the window and peeked out between the wooden blinds. "I don't know. It seems too perfect."

I wanted to throw one of the bed's satin pillows at him. He was ruining my good mood, damn him.

He dropped the blind and turned back to look at me. His eyes traveled down my body, taking their time. I grew warm, craving something other than a bath that was guaranteed to get me just as wet.

There was fire in his eyes. He blinked and it was gone like it had never existed.

"Stay here, Cat. I'm going to go check things out," he said, removing his cowboy hat and tossing it on the bed.

"In case you haven't noticed, I can take care of myself," I grumbled, throwing my chin up in defiance. "You don't have to tell me what to do."

He swung up his gaze to glare at me. Fire and anger and dangerous emotions played out in his eyes. I backed up when he started strolling toward me, slow but purposeful. I felt hunted. Pursued. Cornered for him to have if he wanted. His hair was disheveled and his eyes were stormy as he looked down at me.

"I know you can take care of yourself, Cat, but I'm here now. Let me do it."

"Why do you want to?" I asked breathlessly, wanting to see just how far I could push him. "Why you?"

"Well, your guess is as good as mine," he said, his eyes burning on me. "Let's just say I'm a sucker for a dark-haired Beauty Queen with a sweet mouth and smartass attitude."

I harrumphed, putting my hands on my hips. My eyes slid over him and to the saddle on the floor. "I don't remember you asking if you could stay with me."

The corner of his mouth lifted in a grin. "I didn't ask, but you don't have to worry. We're only going to sleep, Cat. That's all. I just want to make sure you're safe."

My heart pounded. "And who's going to protect me from you?"

His smile grew. "Sweetheart, I'm the one who needs protecting. There's nothing I wouldn't say or do for you. That will either get me killed or make me fall in love." He leaned down, putting his mouth right by my ear. "And right now I don't want to die. Loving you sounds a whole heck of a lot better."

Without another word, he turned and walked out of the bedroom, leaving me alone to recover from his words and stare at the notorious cowboy hat he had left sitting on the bed.

Chapter Thirty-Eight

-Cat-

I was in heaven.

The hot water run over my body. It had been so long since I stood under a steady flow of water that it didn't feel real. None of it did. The town. Cash. His words to me. It all seemed surreal. I was waiting for the bubble to burst. It always did, it seemed.

Putting my hand against the tile wall, I leaned forward. Hot water drenched my hair and ran down my face. I closed my eyes, letting the drops hit my sensitive skin. I could almost feel Cash against me, sliding into me. I wished he were with me now, sharing the shower and whispering more words in my ear like he had said earlier. *I don't want to die. Loving you sounds better.*

Anguish suddenly choked me when I thought about his words. I reached down and touched the tattoo on my hip, the one that reminded me that someone had died because they loved me. Luke. Jenna. Nathan. I was the cause of each of their deaths. I didn't want Cash to be added to that list. If he died, I died too. I couldn't let that happen. There was only one way to avoid it.

I pushed wet strands of hair out of my eyes, my mind racing over what I should do. I couldn't fight the carnal attraction for Cash. That was a given, something I couldn't fight. It consumed me. Drove my addiction for more. I couldn't control the feelings I had for him. They enticed me. Dared me to take down the wall around my heart and let myself love him. I couldn't control any of it, but I could control how he saw me.

I would become that girl again - the one that teased and fucked and didn't feel one thing. I would do it to protect him this time, not to protect me.

I shut off the water and hurried to dry my body. Dropping the towel, I grabbed the thin dress that Sarah had found for me. My panties were a lost cause so I wadded them in a little ball and dumped them in the trash, wishing I still owned some of the pretty lacy ones that I had once oohed and awed over long ago.

I pulled the dress over my head and let it cascade down my body. It was a cream-colored shift dress, a little too big for me but it was clean and that's all that mattered. It fell over my naked breasts and slid down around my hips, the hem ending at my knees.

The mirror above the rusted sink was foggy but I could see enough of me. I pulled my fingers through my wet hair and pushed a curl behind my ear. My skin was squeaky clean and my lips were full and nude, badly in need of some lip-gloss. Since that was a thing of the past, I had to make do. I pulled my teeth over my bottom lip, trying to put some color back into them.

Satisfied I didn't look too bad, I left the bathroom on bare feet and padded down the hallway. The last thing I wanted to do was put back on the dirty boots I had found a few weeks ago.

A strong aroma of cooking assaulted me as soon as I reached the top of the stairs. It made my mouth water and my stomach grumble with hunger.

I took a deep breath, dragging the smell into my lungs. Muted voices drifted up from the dining room along with the clink of silverware. I followed the sounds and delicious smell, unable to resist one moment longer.

Hazy yellow light danced and flickered over the small dining room as I entered it. The single bulb over the room cast a faint glow on the three people sitting around the table. My eyes went instantly to Cash, seeking him naturally. It was a reaction, an action as normal to me as breathing.

He sat between Gavin and Keely, eating. He put a spoonful of something in his mouth and I felt my insides clench, remembering his lips on me. I almost missed a step as he smiled at something Tate said. The curve of his mouth made him go from a good-looking cowboy to a drop-dead gorgeous sex symbol. I couldn't resist either. But I could play it cool and try to ignore both.

I walked across the room with more grace than I felt. Gavin looked up at me and grinned.

"Well, well, well. Kitty Cat is here. Meow."

"Ha. Ha. Very funny. Don't think I've heard that before," I said with a roll of my eyes. "You are sooooo clever."

Cash chuckled, glancing up from his bowl to look at me.

I kept my gaze off him and pulled an empty chair back, giving Gavin a don't-fuck-with-a-hungry-girl look as I sat down.

Gavin's smile grew wider. "Oh-oh. Cat's got claws. I bet if she had a tail she would be flicking it right now."

I cut my eyes over to him under my lashes. "Maybe I would. Want to chase it, Gavin?"

All the blood left his face. The smile died on his lips. I chanced a look at Cash. He was staring at me, a storm brewing in his eyes. He looked like he either wanted to jump across the table and strangle me or demand I explain what the hell I was doing. Good. I needed him confused. Maybe then he'd see that he was better off without me. It might save his life one day.

Gavin cleared his throat and shifted in his seat. He crossed his arms across the table and glanced at Cash.

"Control your pussycat, Cash."

Cash's teeth gnashed together like they wanted to rip into someone's carotid artery.

"Obviously, I don't control her," he ground out, glaring at me. "Nobody does."

Tate and Keely looked from him to me with amusement, taking bites of their food and watching the showdown.

My freshly scrubbed pink skin burned brighter as Cash continued to stare at me. Thick tension flowed between us. He was pissed and I suddenly doubted myself. I couldn't sit across the table from him without feeling something. How was I supposed to convince him not to?

The silence became suffocating, the heat between my legs irritating. I shifted in my seat, wishing I had on some underwear. Being naked under my dress and sitting so close to him was killing me. Knowing something was still happening between us after all these years was threatening me.

Mary bustled into the dining room right then. She was like a whirlwind of gray hair and wrinkles, saving my day.

"You're here! I thought I heard you," she exclaimed, seeing me. "Oh, you look beautiful. Just beautiful." She wobbled over to the table on arthritis-ridden knees and sat a steaming bowl in front of me. "Here's some stew, honey. It'll warm you right up real quick and put some meat on your bones."

"Thank you," I said, picking up my spoon. The smell that waffled up from the bowl was heavenly. My stomach growled again. I forgot about Cash. Forgot about sitting here with no panties or bra on in front of him and what he was doing to me. All I cared about was eating.

I dug in as Gavin turned his charm on Mary.

"The food is delicious. Will you marry me, Ms. Mary?"

Mary blushed and laughed, waving away his compliment. A twinkle sparkled in her eyes. "Well, Reverend David does love to perform marriages."

Gavin smiled, his dark looks adding to his flirty personality. "Well, ma'am, I'll keep that in mind," he said, glancing over at Keely on the other side of Cash.

Cash cleared his throat and sat forward, blocking Gavin's view of his sister.

"So is Reverend David the leader of Hilltop?" he asked Mary, resting his arms on the table and looking at her with interest.

Mary shook her head. "Oh, no," she said, picking up Tate's empty bowl and wobbling around the table to get Cash's. "The Reverend just looks over the town when our leader is gone."

Gavin went taut. Cash didn't move. I could almost see the wheels turning in their minds.

"So when will your leader be back?" Gavin asked, seriousness turning his teasing nature into something dark and dangerous.

Mary didn't seem to notice. She fluttered around the table. "Oh, he'll be back in a day or two. Him and his men go out scouting for supplies every few days. That's how we get most of the stuff we have here. Like your dresses," she said, nodding at Keely and me.

Keely's face went white and the bite of stew in my mouth suddenly didn't taste so good. I knew better than anyone that supplies were stolen, found, or traded. I just hoped that I was wearing someone's traded dress, not one stolen from its owner.

Cash's gaze skimmed over me, traveling over the sheer dress I wore. "So how many men does your leader have out searching for see-through dresses and other supplies?" he asked Mary, the sarcasm not lost on me.

My face blazed. My heart hammered against my ribcage. I glowered at him.

Mary paused, reaching for Keely's bowl. "Well, I don't know." A frown creased the place between her eyebrows as she thought about it. "It doesn't matter. They're harmless," she said with a shaky voice, clearly lying.

I stuck a bite in my mouth and chewed slowly, watching her. There was a certain firmness around her mouth that made me think that she was scared. Were we in danger? Something was telling me the answer was 'yes.'

Mary fluttered to the kitchen with nervousness. It left all of us silent, wondering what the hell we had walked into.

I started to lose my appetite, worry leaving a sour taste in my mouth. I laid my spoon in the bowl and wiped my lips with a napkin. When I looked up, Cash was staring at me. He appeared cool and distant, but when his eyes dropped to the low collar of my dress I wanted to reach across the table and yank him to me.

Instead I looked away.

My face burned and my body screamed. I pushed my hair back and kept my eyes down, fighting the urge that ran through me.

Tate and Keely got up to leave after a few moments, Tate talking nonstop about sleeping in a warm room for a change. Gavin followed them at a leisure pace, telling Tate to keep his gun close and to sleep lightly. That left Cash and me at the table, right across from each other.

I raised my eyes, finally getting the guts to face my addiction. He was staring at me in the yellow glow of the lone bulb, something unreadable behind his gaze. My body purred and pulsated. My insides ached. I couldn't take it anymore.

I shot up out of the chair and headed across the dining room. I had to get out of there before I burst into flames.

My foot hit the first stair. My hair flew around my shoulder. I grasped the railing but a strong hand grasped my wrist, stopping me.

I turned, my heart beating fast.

Cash was staring up at me, his eyes level with my breasts.

"What the hell was that, Cat?" he hissed, anger in his tone.

I knew what he was referring to but I forced an innocent smile on my face anyway. "What are you talking about, Cash?"

He ground his teeth together. "What are you doing?"

I lifted a brow. "Uh, I'm going to bed."

Cash stepped up beside me on the stairs, towering over me and invading my personal space.

"You know that's not what I'm talking about," he clipped out, simmering with anger. "Spill it. What the hell are you doing?"

I gave in and let my eyes run over his smooth, cleanly shaven jaw and chin. He smelled faintly of soap, something that made me want to lean forward and take a big whiff. Instead, I forced my eyes to meet his again.

"I have no idea what you're talking about," I said sweetly. Too sweetly. "Just tell me."

He grasped my wrist tighter, his thumb running over the delicate bone. "You want me to spell it out? Fine. You come downstairs wearing that dress with nothing under it. Then you sit across from me and talk to Gavin the way you did, inviting him to chase your tail. I'm not a jealous man, Cat, but you've got some nerve."

I smiled, giving him my best innocent grin. "You forgot who you're dealing with, Cash. Me. The girl that fucked you in a public restroom on the first date." The words hurt to say but I had to remind him why he shouldn't love me. Why he should keep himself safe. I was just a floozy. Someone passed around. Nobody like Cash should want me. It was better for him that way. It might save his life one day.

But he had other ideas.

He shoved his hand under my wet hair and pushed me back against the wall, knocking the air out of me.

"You want to play that card, princess? Well then, why don't you hike up that dress and we'll have a repeat? I'll remind you again where I belong."

I jutted my chin up, meeting his fiery eyes with my own. "You already showed me last night."

His lips lifted in a cocky smile. "Sweetheart, I plan on showing you a thousand times more."

He seized my mouth, thrusting his tongue inside. His hand ran down my body, over my bottom then around to my leg. Suddenly, he grasped a handful of my dress, gathering the material in his fist and pulling it up. Just when I thought he would finish what we had started and thrust the dress up to my waist, he pulled his lips from mine.

"Let's get one thing straight, Cat. We're together. You're mine and I'm yours. No one can chase your ass anymore but me. I don't know what you're so afraid of but get over it." He gave me another hard kiss, sealing his words with his mouth.

I moaned, grasping his shirt. Wanting more. Desperate to have it all. But he tore his lips from mine.

"Now, go to bed," he ordered in a quiet voice inches from my mouth. "And that's not a request."

"Come with me."

I could see the struggle in his eyes but he shook his head. "I want to. God, do I want to. But I'm going to go check out the town and you're going to bed where I know you're safe. Understand?"

I looked down at his lips. "When did you start giving orders so well?" I asked in a whisper.

Cash leaned over and put his mouth by my ear. "When I met someone to care about."

With that, he dropped his hands from me and left me standing on the stairs alone.

Chapter Thirty-Nine

-Cat-

*M*y fingernails dug into the hardwood floor, drawing blood. I heard Keely's screams but I couldn't get to her. He had a strong grip on me. His fist was wrapped around my braid, pulling until tears leaked from my eyes.

"Ready, little bird."

I cried out and shot up, breathing hard.

Someone turned over beside me in bed. It was Cash. I couldn't see him. It had to be in the middle of the night. The room was dark. Too dark. Perfect for nightmares.

He sat up. "Shit, baby, it's okay," he said, reaching for me.

I threw myself at him. The dream had been so real. Too real.

His arms went around me. His strength became mine. I couldn't remember him crawling into bed with me. I had been so tired. But it didn't matter now. He was here and I needed him.

"It's okay," he muttered against my hair, cradling the back of my head. "It was just a bad dream."

I shook my head. "No, he was here. I could feel him…touching me."

Cash's body stiffened. His biceps tightened around me. "There's no one here, Cat. Only me."

He held me a second. A minute. An hour. I don't know. He just held me. But I couldn't stop shaking.

"He was touching me…"

"Cat, look at me." He pulled away to see my face.

I didn't want to. I didn't want him to see the tears running down my face or the fright that I couldn't seem to shake. But this was Cash. He could make me do things.

He put a finger under my chin and tilted my face up. "Look at me."

I lifted my eyes, expecting to see concern, but instead I saw a calmness that steadied me.

"I'm the only one touching you," he said, running his finger from my chin down to my collarbone. "Just me."

I clutched his shirt. *Just Cash. Just him.* It's what I needed. What I had to have.

I uncurled my legs and straddled his lap, my movements slow and erotic. I knew what I wanted and it was right underneath me.

Cash dropped his hands down to my waist, watching me with wariness as I reached for his zipper. Damn, the man was still fully dressed.

"What are you doing?" he asked as my fingers fumbled to unhook the buckle.

"Touch me more," I begged in a throaty voice, popping the buckle loose and sliding it from its belt loops, letting it drop to the floor. "I need this."

Cash spread his fingers over my ribcage. "Do you need me or will any man do?" he asked bluntly, his voice rough.

I wove my fingers through his hair and pulled his head toward me. "Just you. Only you."

He moaned and captured my mouth, slanting his lips across mine. His hands stayed on my ribcage. Such a safe place, not at all what I wanted them to do.

I sucked and lapped at his lips like a woman starved. My hips rolled against his of their own accord, desperate and dying for him. I needed my fix. My hit of sex. I needed Cash in me.

I could feel him, long and thick under me. My breasts became sensitive as they rubbed the thin material of my dress and against his shirt. They ached to have his hands on them. Have his lips wrapped around them. Have his teeth bite at them.

The thought made me go insane. I grabbed a handful of his hair and yanked his head back. "Touch me," I demanded, rocking my hips against his. "Now."

His eyes blazed. "Here's the Cat I used to know. A princess that always got her way."

I smiled seductively. "What does that make you? My prince or my slave?" I asked, reaching down between us to run my hand over his hardness.

"It makes me your king, sweetheart."

He grabbed the back of my head and dragged my mouth back to his. His tongue dove past my lips, filling my mouth with him. He yanked my head back roughly and dropped his mouth to my neck, nipping and sucking my skin.

I hissed and closed my eyes, getting lost in the feeling. My appetite for him exploded. I unzipped his jeans with a forceful tug and yanked them open. He groaned against my neck and thrust his cock up into my hand as I wrapped my fingers around him. Impatient, I raised myself up. There was nothing holding me back. I was ready to sink down on him.

But he wrapped an arm around my waist and flipped me down onto my back. In seconds he had his jeans off and was between my legs. His mouth went to the curve of my throat and his hand went to my breast.

I sucked in a breath as his thumb and forefinger pinched my nipple and rolled it through the thin material of my dress. It was erotic in the best kind of way.

Cash lowered his head and took the other nipple in his mouth, giving it just as much attention. He drew it into his mouth, sucking on it through the dress. His tongue and teeth played and teased until I thought I would go crazy.

He reached down and grabbed a handful of my dress. Bunching it in his fist, he shoved it up around my waist.

"Spread your legs. Show me what's mine," he ordered, running his hand down my thigh.

As soon as I did, his fingers were in me.

I gasped and arched, thrusting my nipple back into his mouth. He took it greedily while he fucked me with his fingers.

I came quickly, but he didn't stop. He continued to drive me crazy. His fingers spread me open. Slid over me. Plunged inside and filled me full.

He did it again and again until I came apart. The orgasm uncoiled in me like an animal awakening. I shattered and screamed.

He shot up my body quickly, covering my mouth with his. Cries erupted from me but his fingers never slowed down. I whimpered and squirmed, needing him to stop before I burst into a million tiny pieces.

His fingers kept at it – sliding over my clit then into my pussy - even as he left my mouth and moved down my body. He pushed my dress higher, exposing more of me. When he came to my hip, I froze. The tattoo still marked me.

Cash withdrew his fingers. His lips turned gentle on my skin. His hands traveled up to grasp my hips and hold me still when I tried to roll away. I couldn't deal with the memories tonight.

"Not this time, sweetheart," he whispered against my

skin. "Tell me what happened." He traced the letters on my hips, leaving a trail of heat behind.

I squeezed my eyes shut. I just wanted to have sex, not face the terrifying images that bombarded me.

Cash bit at the skin over my hipbone. "Talk."

I twisted away but didn't get very far. He yanked me back under him.

"Talk or I don't touch," he growled.

Well, when he put it that way…

"I killed him," I said in a whisper, wishing he would just forget about the tattoo and go down on me. "I killed my boyfriend."

Cash froze. I felt his eyes on my face but I couldn't look at him. I was too embarrassed that with just one touch – one kiss - he could break me and make me talk. No one had ever had that kind of control over me.

Not even Luke.

"What happened?" Cash asked again in a clipped tone, demanding an answer.

I shivered, suddenly cold. "It was a car accident. I was acting stupid and he was too busy worrying about me. The car flipped. We hit a tree. I'm surprised you didn't hear about it. Everyone in town knew about the wreck."

"Not me," Cash said, his voice becoming softer. "I didn't give a damn about rumors and gossip."

"It wasn't gossip…I killed him and my best friend, Jenna."

Cash was quiet a moment. I quivered when he ran a thumb over the dark ink on my skin. "No, you didn't, Cat. I know you. You didn't kill anyone."

An awful ache started in my chest and rose up to choke me. "Yes, I did, Cash. Luke loved me and he died because of it. I wanted to die too." I gulped. I wanted him to know everything. Every gritty, awful detail of my life.

"And you don't know me. You think you do, but you don't."

Cash moved his hand from the tattoo down to my thigh, his fingers hot on my skin.

"I know your heart. I know how you would die to protect Keely and Tate." He moved his fingers to my opening again, sliding over me. "I know your body. I know what you like and how to make you cry and come." He removed his fingers and glided them over my hipbone. "Tell me what I don't know, sweetheart, because I want to know everything else."

I took a deep breath and delved right in, trying to ignore the power he had over my body. "I've been terrified of love since Luke died," I said. "I had to prove to myself that I couldn't feel anything anymore. That's when I turned to men. They were distractions from the pain and grief. You were supposed to be just another one of those distractions."

Cash didn't move or speak.

I found the nerve to look at him. He was staring at me, still halfway down my body.

"And was I?" he asked, his voice deadly quiet. "Just another man? Another distraction?"

"Yes. Too much of one. I started to feel things for you. It scared me so I bailed. We never should have slept together. I wasn't ready for someone like you. It was a mistake." I took a shaky breath. "That's why I called you that night. To tell you that I was broken. That we were a mistake. But the truth is I made a lot of mistakes, usually bad ones, but you were one of the good ones."

He didn't say anything. I expected him to climb off me and rush out of the room. I had just said we were a mistake. That I had used him as a distraction. He should hate me. Call me a bitch. Deem me unworthy.

Instead he moved up my body and settled between my legs. He grasped my head with both hands and made me look at him.

"Is this still a mistake?" he asked.

I shook my head slowly, mesmerized by the fire in his eyes. "No. But you still scare me and so does love."

He flinched with each word. Pain filled his eyes. He hung his head, wounded.

I felt frantic and guilty and ready to slit my own wrists. I had hurt people but I didn't want to hurt him anymore.

I touched his jaw, wanting him to look up at me. He did. Fierceness was in his eyes.

"Let's pretend, Cat."

I blinked, confused, then the memory of him saying the same exact words to me on our date came back.

"I'm already yours," I said, remembering that is what we had pretended before. His words from that night still burned in my mind.

Cash shook his head. "I know but let's pretend something different this time. Let's pretend that I love you. That I'll always love you. If we pretend this once, will you not be afraid?"

My heart pounded. "Just once?" I asked, repeating the same words I had asked him that night long ago.

"Just once," he said, lowering his mouth down to my neck. "I'll take away the pain any time you want. I'll make you forget and I'll be a distraction if you need it. I'll do anything and be anything for you, but I don't want to scare you so I'll just say I'm pretending."

I nodded. "Okay. Pretend."

Cash grasped the underside of my knee, lifting my leg up. "I love you, Catarina."

And with those simple four words, he thrust into me.

I cried out and immediately wrapped my legs around him, taking him deeper.

"God, I love you," he whispered.

Planting his hands on either side of my head, he started moving in and out of me, taking his time. Savoring the feel of me. Letting my slick, wet walls hug his thickness.

His eyes stayed on mine, traveling down to my breasts. I grasped both of them in my hands, needing to be touched. It made him crazy. He started moving faster and faster. Deeper and deeper. *Oh, fuuuck.* When he hit the deepest point possible, I let go of my breasts and cried out, clenching the sheet under me.

"Tell me you love me," he demanded, slowing down to a torturous pace. Killing me. Fucking me. Making love to me. "Let me hear that sweet mouth lie."

I couldn't. The blood was rushing through my body too fast. My skin was too sensitive to concentrate on anything else. His legs rubbed against the inside of my thighs as he thrust and withdrew. My pussy was wet and stretched like never before.

But I couldn't lie.

He growled and held still, keeping only the head of his cock in me. "Say it, Cat."

Frustrated, I wiggled under him, wanting all of him to slide into me. But he stayed motionless, looming over my body.

"Damn you," he hissed.

He thrust into me hard. I cried out, arching my body. It offered my breasts right to his lips. He leaned down and sucked my nipple into his mouth, biting it hard. It sent me spirally. I convulsed around him, tightening on his cock so hard he swore.

His ribs and hips pumped faster, reaching for his own climax. I pulled his head down, putting my lips against his ear. "Come for me, cowboy."

He growled and thrust deep. I felt a rush of warmth before he grabbed himself and pulled out. His cock pulsated against me, spurting his seed on my vagina. He rubbed his essence on me then thrust back inside, going as deep as he could go. Lowering his head, he kissed me.

I knew at that moment that things had changed.

He might be pretending.

But I was in love.

Chapter Forty

-Cat-

I had known anguish. I had lived it. Breathed it. Walked down its dark path and let it consume me. It had made me make a deal with the devil when Luke died. I wouldn't love and he wouldn't take someone from me. But I had broken that promise. I loved Cash. Now the devil might take him from me.

Keely and I walked down the sidewalk, checking out the town. Leaves blew in our path and crunched under the little flat shoes Sarah had found for me. It was cold. I gathered my ratty jacket closer around my shoulders, snuggling in it deeper. The sun was out, shining brightly, but the warmth was only an illusion.

Tate lingered behind us, kicking brown leaves out of his way. He wasn't happy to be tagging along with Keely and me. He wanted to go with Cash and Gavin. They were trying to trade for supplies out near one of the outposts in town. Word was that the leader was back and had lots of new goods. Cash wanted whatever he could get before trouble came looking for us. Something was telling us it would and we needed to get out of town quickly.

Despite the danger that loomed over us, I was feeling on cloud nine. Last night was an awakening for me. I loved Cash. I might have from the start. Don't get me wrong. I didn't believe in love at first sight. It was a stupid, made up idea romantics came up with to explain lust without guilt. But I never had guilt. I had been with men and not felt one thing.

Not until Cash.

It only took the end of the world to show me that I was worthy of love. It took me changing and him finding me again to do it.

I was so afraid before. So determined to keep my distance from everyone. From feeling anything. I was afraid to fall. Afraid I wouldn't be able to get back up again. But I couldn't deny it any longer.

I loved Cash.

My heart thumped hard. Little breaths of frost escaped between my lips.

Yes. I love him.

Excited shouts came from down the street, interrupting my happiness. Men and women suddenly rushed by. A large crowd was gathering in the middle of the street. They were clean, happy, and seemed oblivious to what was going on outside the metal walls. In just the short amount of time we had been here we realized life was different in Hilltop. There was no grief. No hunger. No deadly diseases that had killed hundreds. It was as if we had walked into a different time and era. A different world.

But this utopia felt wrong in some way. We couldn't put our finger on it. Cash was on edge and Gavin was itching to leave. Something was about to happen. We had learned to listen to our gut feelings and right now they were screaming loud and clear.

Go.

"What do you think is going on?" Tate asked, watching as people ran by with excitement, yelling with joy.

"I don't know," I said, feeling my skin prickle in warning.

Keely grasped my arm and pointed to the growing crowd. A large group of men were walking down the middle of the street. They looked ragged and tired. Most wore a hodgepodge assortment of clothes, most smudged with dirt and grime. Each had a gun, some with more than one. The townspeople greeted them as if they were heroes. Men smacked them on the back with warm, excited welcomes. Women hugged a few with tears in their eyes. Children danced around their legs as they walked down the street, talking rapidly.

These people seemed happy to see the men. So why did I feel a chill run down my spine?

As the crowd came closer, Keely's hand on me tightened. She let out a high-pitched mewing cry.

I gaped at her. She hadn't spoken or made any sort of noise in ages. I swung back to look at the crowd, wondering what the hell had frightened her so bad. I didn't see anything, just a bunch of military-looking men being welcomed home with excitement.

Keely started backing away, dragging me along with her and squeezing my arm so much it hurt. Her colorless lips moved wordlessly. She was pale, shaking. Scaring the shit out of me.

"What's wrong?" Tate asked, following as Keely tugged me back along the sidewalk.

"I don't know," I whispered. She was freaking me out.

Little whimpering sounds escaped her. She drew in a sob and tears filled her eyes. My shoes scraped along the leaves and cement, creating a soft sound, as I hurried to follow her. When I felt eyes on me, I looked over my shoulder at the crowd again.

That's when I recognized him. Frankie. The man who had appeared in the alleyway in Austin. The leader who Paul and Hightower answered to years ago. Time had been easy on him. He was older but more distinguished looking. He was heavier than he had been but power still radiated from him as he walked down the street. I knew suddenly who Hilltop's leader was – a man that led rapists and murderers.

By this time Keely was frantic, her nails burying in my arm through my coat. She pulled me faster, glancing over her shoulder every few seconds. Tate jogged to keep up with us, looking confused on what the hell was happening but following us anyway.

The crowd was heading toward the town square, right across the street from the hotel. Frankie and his men walked with authority. Power. They owned this town. I could almost see it in the way people looked at them with worship, brainwashed by some sick fucks.

We hurried down the sidewalk, trying to outrun them. I couldn't stop staring at the group of men. They looked like soldiers returning home from war. Violence was in their eyes and malice seemed to bleed from them. Frankie was in front, walking with purpose and ignoring the exclamations of the townspeople as they welcomed him home. His eyes stayed straight ahead and his finger stayed near the trigger of his gun.

I watched as he spoke to someone beside him. The man listened then ran off, breaking away from the group. Another man appeared by Frankie's side.

A man that haunted my dreams and terrified my thoughts. A man I should have killed long ago.

Paul.

I slammed to a stop, dragging Keely with me. I started trembling, not from the cold but from terror. Pure, bloodcurdling terror. This is the man who had killed Nathan. That had taken my brother from me. The man that had almost had me. That almost took what I didn't want anyone to have but Cash. I knew what he was capable of and what he would do if he saw me.

Behind Paul was Hightower, walking along and cleaning his fingers with a long-bladed knife. From his pocket hung a line of…chunks of hair.

Bile rose in my throat. I felt sick to my stomach. Keely started shaking her head frantically, backing away. I grabbed her.

"They'll see us if we run," I said, keeping my head turned away so they wouldn't see my face.

Tate glanced at the men. "It doesn't matter. I'm going to kill them this time!" he roared, realizing who it was.

I reached out with my other hand and snatched a hold of his jacket before he could dash across the street and do something stupid.

He tried to yank away but I held on tight. I couldn't let my other brother die. Not for me. Not for Keely. Not for anyone. I held both him and Keely. One from fighting, the other from escaping.

"Tate, go get Cash and Gavin," I instructed with a stern voice despite the terror I felt. The world had just dropped away. My nightmare was here.

Tate glared down at me and opened his mouth to argue but I stopped him.

"Go now!" I ordered.

He nodded and shot off, heading toward where Cash and Gavin were supposed to be.

I looked back at Keely. She was crying and drawing in on herself. I could see it. She was shutting down even more. I wouldn't allow it to happen again.

"Come on." I grabbed her arm and pulled her along, walking at a brisk but nonthreatening pace. We had to appear like we were just minding our own business.

We made it to the hotel without being seen. Mary was walking out of the kitchen as we bust in, wiping her hands on a faded towel.

"Hello, girls! Are you hungry?" she asked in her over-the-top friendly voice.

"No," I snapped, pushing past her and dragging Keely with me.

Mary looked at me open-mouthed. "What's wrong, darlings?" she called out as we rushed up the stairs.

I didn't bother answering. We had better things to do. *Like get out of this freaky, fucked up town.*

Keely and I ran to the second floor and down the hallway. I went straight to the bedroom Cash and I had shared last night. I hit the door with the palm of my hand, slamming it open. Letting go of Keely, I kicked the door closed behind us and rushed over to the rumbled bed. I gave the wrinkled sheets that I had clasped in passion just a quick glance then dropped down to my knees and shoved the bed skirt up. Two rifles stared back at me, lying innocently under the bed where Cash had hidden them.

I grabbed both and stood up, letting the bed skirt fall back. Keely watched me, sobbing quietly, as I checked both barrels to make sure they were loaded. They were. Setting them on the bed, I rushed over to the small wooden chair where Sarah had neatly folded my washed clothes.

It was time to return to the real me.

With my back to Keely, I unbuttoned the jacket and let it fall to the floor. A cold draft ran over me. The lightweight dress I wore was no match for the chilling temperature. I lifted it over my head and let it drift down to the floor in a silky puddle at my feet. Giving it no more thought, I picked up my jeans and pulled them on with jerky motions.

This was me. Jeans, a white shirt, and black boots. I wasn't hiding behind dresses and cute little shoes anymore.

I sat down and shoved my feet into my boots, glancing up at Keely. "Go change," I said in a stern voice, hoping to break through her fear.

She looked at me with tear-filled eyes but her mind was still down on that street, seeing the man that hurt her. I understood. I was barely holding it together myself, but we had to keep our heads on straight.

I laced up my boots and shot to my feet. I headed to her in two quick strides.

"We've got to leave, Keely. Go!" I said, grabbing both of her arms and giving her a hard shove toward the door.

My words finally got through to her. Or maybe it was my fingers biting into her skin. Whichever it was, she flung open the door and ran from the room.

I turned and went back to the chair. My jaw was set but my heart was pounding and my hands were shaking.

If Paul and Hightower saw us, what they would do wouldn't be pretty. Cash, Gavin, and Tate would be right there too, putting themselves in danger for Keely and me. I didn't want that on me. Never again. No one was going to die or get injured because they cared about me. That's why we had to leave.

I put on my jacket and started buttoning it up with shaky, cold fingers. *We could do this. We could get out of this town alive, in one piece. All we have to do is keep our wits about us and sneak out without being seen.*

Panic filled me as I pushed the last button through the hole. *What about Cash? What will he do when he found out who was here?*

I broke out in a cold sweat. Tears flooded my eyes. I had taken so much from men. Money. Sex. Attention. I had used them, thinking they would all save me from myself. But now I wanted to save the one man that I wanted to give everything to.

"Cat."

I turned around.

Cash was standing in the doorway. His eyes were hard under his cowboy hat. The crystal gray of his irises was smoky and penetrating as they looked at me. His body was tense, ready to fight and kill. His fingers were relaxed at his sides, long and powerful against his jeans. Capable of hurting. Skilled at eliciting need and desire.

He sauntered into the room, heading straight for me. A few tears escaped past my lashes and dropped down my cheeks. I brushed them away, angry that I was crying at a time like this. I needed to be strong. Be ready to run.

Cash stopped right in front of me.

"Is it them?" he asked bluntly.

I didn't answer but the tears must have betrayed me. He swore softly and I saw his fist clench at his side.

He took a step closer and put his hand under my nape. His fingers were firm on my neck as he pulled me to him and put his warm lips against my forehead.

"Forgive me, Cat," he whispered. "There's something I have to do. I have no choice."

Before I could ask what exactly he meant, he let me go. Without a word or a look, he moved past me, back to being cold and indifferent.

And godawful calm.

A growing sense of fear filled me. I realized what he planned to do. *Damn him. He's going to play the freaking hero. The damn knight-in-shining-armor.*

I watched with a mixture of anger and panic as he grabbed both of the guns from the bed and headed back to me.

"Keep it on you," he said, holding out one of the guns to me, the tenderness gone. He was unemotional. His tone held too much finality and was way too composed. It made me mad.

"Don't you dare, Cash," I said, the tears in my eyes welling up more. "Don't you fuckin' dare do it."

His jaw hardened but a flicker of something passed over his eyes. Tenderness? Regret? Love? Whatever it was, it was gone in a flash.

He reached out and grabbed my hand. With forcefulness, he curved my fingers around the gun, making me to take it.

"Don't fight me on this, Cat. Gavin went for the horses and Tate's taking you and Keely to meet him," he said with so much composure that I wanted to scream. "I want you to ride fast and hard away from here. Don't stop until you're a safe distance away."

"No!" I said, balling my hands into fists.

Cash looked at me with impatience. "Yes. Do what I say, Cat. Go."

That's when I got rip-roaring pissed off. He was standing in front of me in his damn hat and boots with a gun in his hand and another in his belt. I knew he had at least two deadly knives on him. I had watched – satiated, sore, and oh so satisfied - from the bed this morning as he dressed and hid them under his clothes. He might be a human arsenal but he was mine. I wasn't going to let him walk into a bloodbath. And that's what it would be against all those men on the street. A suicidal bloodbath.

I took an angry step toward him. My body brushed against his, seeking what it always wanted. I could feel his heat, his power, around me. It gave me the courage I needed to do what I should have already done.

With my heart thumping wildly and fury plus fear racing through me, I glared at him.

"Why should I take orders from you?" I asked, trying hard to keep the desperation out of my voice.

Cash gazed down at me with rage. "Because I'm the man who pretends to love you."

My mouth went dry. My lips parted to draw in a swift intake of air.

Cash didn't seem to notice the effect it had on me. His voice was still harsh. "They used my sister, Cat. They hurt *you*. Do you know what that does to me, knowing that someone touched you?" He shook his head. "No, I'm not going to leave without making them pay. Don't ask me to."

He took a step back as if he was done talking, but I wasn't having any of it. I reached out and grabbed his jacket, yanking him back to me.

"Don't do it," I demanded, tightening my fingers in his jacket.

The corner of his mouth lifted in a lopsided grin but it held no humor, only danger.

"Sweetheart, I'll do whatever I please."

I pulled him down until his lips were level with mine. "Then stop pretending."

His nostrils flared. The rage disappeared from his eyes. He took a step closer but didn't touch me, just stared down at me under the brim of his cowboy hat.

"I'll stop pretending when you tell me you're not scared of feeling something for me anymore," he said in a taut voice, sounding angry. "Hell, I'll even turn my back on those men to hear you say it."

I looked down at his mouth, only a hair's breath from mine. "I'm not scared, cowboy."

He slid his hand around to my bottom. His fingers spread over my waist and the curve of my backside. He pulled me toward him and ducked his head, his mouth going to the shell of my ear.

"Then say it," he whispered, his warm breath washing over the delicate skin of my ear. "Just once let me hear it."

I shivered and gulped, knowing what he wanted to hear. "I love you, Cash."

"I love you too, Beauty Queen."

His lips captured mine. Everything I had denied myself filled me again. Love. Hope. Dreams. Feelings. I felt them all flood me, giving me life. Giving me Cash.

Too soon, he slid his mouth from mine, letting his hands linger on me. "Let's go home, Cat. Together."

He grabbed my hand and pulled me out the door.

With the knowledge that we loved each other, we walked out of the hotel.

And into hell.

Read the rest of Cash and Cat's story in
Promise Me Forever.

ACKNOWLEDGMENTS

I would like to thank author Kele Moon. Not only is she an awesome writer but she's also a wonderful friend. Thank you, Kele, for the shoulder to cry on when my characters would not behave and the words of encouragement when I believed my writing was terrible. Thanks for taking the time to read my stuff, no matter how busy you were. And thanks for the numerous texts discussing serious issues such as another word for penis. You've made me laugh and you've made me go on in this crazy, wonderful world of writing.

Author Tiffany Snow also deserves a big thanks from me. She is wonderful and amazing and I want to be her when I grow up.

I want to say thank you to Emily Smith-Kidman for all that she has done. She was patient when I refused to divulge any Cash information and went above and beyond for me in so many ways. I'm thankful I met her during the early days of *Promise Me Darkness* and I value her friendship greatly. Thank you, Emily, for all the teasers and posts and support you have given me! The book gods were smiling down at me when they introduced me to you.

For Bev and Iris and Jennifer on my street team. You girls amaze me every day! Thank you for all that you do!

For Christy Conque – I have enjoyed our conversations and am truly happy that we met. You are a wonderful supporter of my books and a great person. Thank you for everything!

For Jess Jduadne who always assist me at signings. You volunteered for the job and I'm so happy you did. Everything always runs smoother because of you. Thank you!

For Krista Webster, my friend across the pond. Thank you for traveling to Kensington to visit with me and thank you so much for the offer of a real London dinner. I can't wait for my next trip to the U.K. and a chance to see you again! (Oh, and thank you for Daryl. I love him.)

To my husband – Thanks for being the slayer of geckos and the master of hotel room faucets. Thanks for keeping me company while I traveled, finding a Starbucks for me in foreign cities, and making me do things I didn't think I could do. Thanks for all the late nights, reading over my manuscripts and correcting the gun and/or male perspective lingo. Thanks for listening to me cry when all you wanted to do was sleep and acting interested in my excitement over a scene when all you wanted to do was watch the Discovery Channel. You didn't have to help me with this journey but thank God you did. I would have been lost and a little bit confused without you.

Last but never least, I would like to thank the readers, especially the ones that waited patiently for Cash's story. You are such loyal fans that I cannot begin to express how much you mean to me. I've been at book signings, in restaurants, at church, shopping, and even at a funeral, when readers approached me and ask, "When are we getting the next book?" You know who you are and I will never forget those moments. Thank you.

ABOUT THE AUTHOR

Paige Weaver lives in Texas with her husband and two children. Her love for books became a love for writing at a young age. She wrote her first book as a teenager and continued writing throughout the years. Encouraged by her husband, she finally decided to self-publish. Her debut novel, *Promise Me Darkness*, was released in April 2013 and quickly became a *New York Times* and *USA Today* bestseller. When she is not writing, you can find her reading or chasing her kids around.

Find out about future books and connect with her on:

Website: authorpaigeweaver.com
Twitter: @AuthorPWeaver
Instagram: AuthorPaigeWeaver
Facebook: AuthorPaigeWeaver

~~~~

BOOKS BY PAIGE

Promise Me Darkness
New York Times and *USA Today* bestseller

Promise Me Light
USA Today bestseller

Promise Me Forever
The epic conclusion of Cat and Cash's story

Sweet Destruction
A stand-alone novel

Made in United States
North Haven, CT
24 February 2022

16467925R00245